THE UNIVERSAL KILLER

by

R. L. NAPOLITANO

1 3 5 7 9 10 8 6 4 2

ALSO BY THE AUTHOR:

THE TWINS

GIRVAN

LEOPOLD CHRIST

THE SONS OF ABRAHAM

THE DISAPPOINTMENT OF ANNIE BROOKS

For Alexander Lattanzio.
While he deals with a life-altering situation, he continues to support my efforts. And for that I am eternally grateful.

ISBN 979-8-9908044-0-1

Cover design Christina Gedick

1

I decide to paint the tree brown, with thin vertical lines of gray on the trunk for effect. When I'm finished, I cast a critical eye at my work. Satisfied that it is as I remembered, I clean the brush of the gray and begin a second coat of black on the cape, careful not to mess up the red on the underside of the billowing garment. I am working from a memory of more than twenty-five years ago, but I feel quite confident that I am re-creating colors exactly as they were. My powers of recollection are quite amazing, especially about things that interest me greatly. And this interests me.

The lush sounds of the Mantovani Orchestra, another fond remembrance of that long ago time, softly fill the space where I sit working. The volume is kept low, as I remember it being when I first heard those marvelous instrumentals, played now on my turntable that is hooked up to speakers that cost several thousand dollars. When I had first heard this recording, with ears not quite as sophisticated as they are now, it was on a Philco phonograph player. And while it may have been an LP that the record jacket promised would surround the listener with amazing stereo effects, music only came from the right speaker of that Philco cabinet. The balance knob had to be turned all the way to the right because of the static that came from a damaged left speaker. But at the time, I didn't mind. It sounded fine to my ears. Like I said; Unsophisticated.

I knew very little about music back then, back when I was ten years old. I am embarrassed to admit, I hardly know much more now, all these years later. I don't often listen to music in the car. I don't have a large record or Cd collection. Unlike so many others who can, I can't name one famous guitar player who isn't named John Lennon or Paul McCartney, or one country/western singer who isn't named Willie Nelson. I do have five Mantovani long playing albums, however, and a music system worth several thousand dollars on which to play them. And even then, the only time they are being played is when I am sitting at this wooden workbench in my basement, doing what I love to do. The music, and the work, take me back to the best time of my life. A magical time. A time when I was happiest. A time when everything made perfect sense. A time I had wished would never end, in a room much smaller than this one. And yet, so much of my best memories come from that small space.

My Grandfather's house was on a quiet city street in a neighborhood where the two and three story houses were usually only separated by the width of a driveway, and maybe another three feet of grass and gravel. His two story house had a four foot high galvanized chain link fence across the front of the property, with a three foot wide gate in the center that opened up to a walkway. The cracked cement walkway was ten feet long and three feet wide, with a patch of grass on either side. It led to five wooden steps that were painted dark red, and those steps brought all visitors up to a small porch and the front door to the house. On this porch, by the side of the entrance, was a wicker chair with thick cushions that my Grandfather would sit in and calmly watch the world passing by, as he occasionally puffed away on a cigarette. He did this most days after he retired from the railroad, much to my Grandmother's consternation. She felt, now that he was retired, they should be doing some traveling. But Grandfather, who refused to fly, and had absolutely no desire to ever set foot on a train again, told his wife that he would gladly travel anywhere she wanted to go, as long as it was no further than a half hour bus ride from their home. Or a two hour drive in their car, the big Oldsmobile 98 that he washed in the driveway once a week, whether it was needed or not.

There were only four things that could get my Grandfather out of that chair before supper; rain, snow, a trip to the bathroom, or me. And sometimes I'd find him sitting there when it was raining. Usually, those times, it was a particularly hot day and a cooling shower was just what the doctor had ordered. At least that was what Grandfather had said.

On days when I could, I'd come running down the street, push open that creaking gate and bound up the steps to stand in front of him. "Hey, Grandpa," I'd say, "what are you doing?" And he'd say something like, "Well, I'm contemplating just exactly what advice I'm going to give that actor fella who's president should he ever knock on my door." Or he might say, real serious, "I hear millions of people go to bed every night hungry. I'm thinking up ways that we can end that." Then he would say, "Why? You have something you want me to do that's more important than that?" And I would tell him I most certainly did. I'd grab his big calloused hand, with the thick fingers, and he'd pretend I was pulling him up out of that chair, and into the house we would go.

Grandma would call out a hello from the living room, where she was watching her afternoon soap operas, as we walked down the long hallway to the kitchen. There was a door at the end of that spacious kitchen, beside the table where meals were served, that opened up to a small room. For years, that room was used for storage. I had been told that that room, before it was used for storage, was also the bedroom for my Uncle Sal back in the day, when he was young and before he joined the army and moved out of the house. There is a door at the end of that room that opens up to the back porch. But the room was no longer being used for storage. When my Grandfather retired, he did that when I was eight, he made the room into something he said he always wanted to have, but never could find the time to fix up the way he wanted. But, after he retired, he had the time and he did the work. And then, when he was finished with the renovations, he proclaimed that space his study.

It was nothing fancy. Not at all. Not like those big studies you see in those English manors in the movies, all dark wood and spacious. It was eight feet by ten feet, and that might be giving it more space than it actually was. The walls were just painted plaster. But back then, I never felt like it was a small, plain room. I always felt it was a perfect sized room. When I was ten, that room was big enough to be my entire universe. Well, the only part of the universe that really mattered. At least for a few years. After Grandfather died, I never stepped into that room again. Except once.

Beside the door that led back into the kitchen, stood a five shelf bookcase that Grandfather had filled with books of various sizes and thicknesses. Above the bookcase, he had hung a dozen framed pictures. All of them were of family, with my third grade picture right there in the middle of them all. There was one really big painting on the sidewall of a cowboy on a horse, maybe a Pony Express rider by the look of it, and the horse was in full gallop on a flat ground of patchy grass and low slung brush. It was a landscape without a hint of a mountain or river anywhere in sight. In the distance could be seen cacti, so I always thought that that rider was making haste across the

Arizona Territory, carrying in his saddle bags the most important correspondence from one wild town to the next. Maybe carrying wanted posters from one Marshall to another. Beneath that painting was the Philco, a stack of records on the floor leaning against one side of the cabinet. There was a brown vinyl high-backed chair in one corner and beside it a small round end table that held a lamp, a glass ashtray, and whatever book Grandpa was reading at the time. Opposite the chair, and near the outside door, was a coat rack, the clothes that he would wear when he worked in his small garden hanging off the hooks.

The most important thing in Grandpa's study, at least to me, was the narrow work bench tucked along a sidewall, opposite the Philco, that doubled as his desk. Above that workbench was a shelf that ran the entire length of the wall, and on that shelf were posed the results of the labors that he and I had accomplished together. On the workbench would be our current project, just waiting for us to finish.

Even to this day, I can remember the line-up on that shelf, that memory etched into my brain like grooves in a new radial tire. In fact, what I'm working on now, in my own space, on my own workbench, was the first piece on the farthest left facing that wall. It was the first model Grandpa and I had ever worked on. Dracula.

Oh, what a horrific sight he was, I have to tell you, dressed in that black evening dress suit, shirt as white as a bar of Ivory soap, arms raised up drawing you towards him with the irresistible power of his hypnotic eyes. Bringing you under his spell. That look on his face of pure evil. Eyes that could penetrate to your very soul. Red blood on his lips and chin from his feeding frenzy. It was all enough to frighten any ten year old.

Standing on a base of uneven ground, the Count towering over a stunted, pitiful tree stump, his long cape billowing out from the wind. A bat, with wings outstretched, clung to a leafless limb.

Dracula may have appeared to be a normal man, but we know better. He was a vampire. A blood-thirsty, blood-sucking vampire. The greatest, most fearsome, most powerful of all vampires. Even now, no longer a child, I can still feel how fearful any human would be encountering such a monster.

When I finish painting Dracula, the tree, the ground, the entire eight and a half inch tall scene, I will place it on my own shelf that I have built above my workbench. Below the shelf is the television that I watch when I watch my collection of monster movies, which I enjoy doing, and while watching the movie I can glance up and see my collection of models. So far, I have completed King Kong and The Mummy. Dracula will be done soon.

My wonderful Grandfather and I would watch the movies together, back then, back when I was nine and ten, and when I watch those movies now, I can feel his presence beside me. It is such a comforting feeling.

We had a set routine for our creations, and it never varied. First, Grandfather would take a book from his bookcase and bring it to the chair by the outside door. I would sit on a pillow on the floor beside him. He would then tell me the title of the book, open it and begin to read. I would listen to every word. I would only interrupt him if I didn't know the meaning of a particular word and he would tell me what the word meant. Other than that, I sat enthralled by the words he read, picturing each scene vividly in my mind. Quasimodo pulling on the rope to ring the bells. The Frankenstein Monster opening his eyes for the first time. Dracula rising from his dirt filled casket. The mask being ripped from the Phantom's face. All of it. Poor Esmeralda, the gypsy girl. Poor Elizabeth, the bride. Poor Christine, so innocent, so trusting. All of them touched my pure, young heart and lit my over-active imagination. And yet, even then, as now, my greatest concern was for the monsters. How I pitied them.

It may have taken weeks before Grandfather finished his reading of the book, so much depended on my availability. It isn't like we could do it every day. I had school. Chores. Homework. But I would run to my grandparents house, four streets over from mine, every chance I could and find my Grandfather sitting in his cushioned chair, on his front porch, and ask what he was doing.

After the book was read, we would then go to the living room and he would insert a VHS tape into his new video player, and close all the curtains, and we would sit and watch the movie of the book we had just finished. Grandpa would sit in the recliner and press the play button on the remote. While we watched, Grandma would place a bowl of popcorn on the coffee table. Sometimes, I would sit in the chair with him and sometimes I would sit on the floor in front of the television, my knees drawn up and my arms hugging them. I would sit like that, instead of with him in the recliner, so that when I flinched from some scary thing that happened in the movie, Grandpa would not know that I had been frightened. But when things got really intense, I would retreat to his chair, desperate for the safety I would find there. We watched these movies in glorious black and white, with actors whose real names were Bela, or Boris, or Lon.

Then, the next time I visited, the movie now watched, Grandpa and I would go back to the study and, from a shelf in the bookcase, he would take a small rectangular box. In that box, with a cover that depicted a vivid scene from whatever book and movie we were done with, were the pieces of the model. You can not imagine the anticipation that shook me as I sat beside him at the work bench waiting for him to take off the cellophane wrapping and lift off the cover. What would all those gray, or white, pieces inside look like? How many pieces would there be? Twenty-five? Thirty? The arms. The legs. The torso. The head. The base. How would it all go together to make the monster come to life? I couldn't wait for him to lift that cover off.

Once the cover did come off, Grandpa would lay the box on the wooden work bench and sit quietly while I peered inside. I could picture in my mind how all those parts would be glued together. Where the feet would stand on the landscape. Where the bats or rats could be placed. Where a snake might slither. How sinister the entire scene would be when it was built and painted. The anticipation to get it done was, at times, overwhelming to my young mind. But Grandpa had always cautioned patience. So, with great care, I would reach into the box and gently take out each long, round, plastic piece that had the parts we would need to glue together attached to them. Thin, fragile plastic pieces that sometimes had to be snipped to release the parts that were important. One by one, I would take those out of the box and lay them on the work area in front of us.

When that was done, Grandfather pushed the bottom part of the box off to the side and then propped the cover up so we could see what we were about to build. Then, very carefully, taking the greatest of care, he allowed me to begin twisting the parts we would need from the plastic rod that held them. Two or three turns were usually enough to free the part. Sometimes, the plastic was thicker, and I would get nervous if the part didn't come free after a half dozen turns. Grandfather would then gently lay his big hand over mine and smile at me. He would then hand me an Exacto knife, and with the greatest of care I would slice through the tether, my small fingers tightly holding the thin shaft of the knife. Once all of the parts were free, we discarded the plastic poles and gazed down on the parts neatly lined up on the workbench. Now, it was time to build. Almost.

Grandfather always insisted we first discuss the procedure we would use before gluing any parts together. Each model was different. Sometimes, we began with the building of the base. Sometimes, it was the monster. Legs, then arms. But nothing was glued together until we had a plan. Then he would open a drawer in the workbench and take out the tube of glue.

If you have never built a model, you can't imagine the effect that had on me. The anticipation when he opened the drawer and the thrill when he laid that thin four inch long tube on the bench in front of me, it was electric. Like when Heather Wilson kissed me under the bleachers when we were twelve years old, while everyone in the stands were cheering a touchdown being scored. Electric. He would unscrew the cap, then take a sewing needle and poke it into the nozzle, either breaking through the seal if the tube was new, or through dried glue if it had been used before. And then the unmistakable odor of the glue would permeate the air we were breathing. If you have never smelled the odor of model glue, you don't know what you are missing. Nothing on God's green earth is as intoxicating.

Then, while I was selecting two pieces from the display on the bench that were to be glued together, Grandfather would be selecting a record to be put on the turntable inside the Philco console. After a few seconds of scratchy sounds hissed from the lone speaker, the magical sounds of the Mantovani Orchestra washed over us and filled that small space, and Grandfather would sit down again and ask if I was ready. I would nod, my hands shaking slightly in anticipation of the task at hand. He would smile at me and say, "Well, then, let's begin."

We would take our time, only working on several pieces each session. We talked about each piece. What it meant to the overall scene. The bend of the leg. The angle of the arms. The turn of the head. Where to place the rats. The snakes. Was it an honest depiction of the pages read and the movie watched? If we agreed that it was, then we would proceed. Honestly, as much as I was impatient to finish our work, I knew, that by dragging out the process it gave us more time together. I'm sure that is why my Grandfather, also, was in no rush to hurry through anything that we were doing. Because the reality was, there were only a few monster kits that we had to work on. Eight all together. That was all. So, no rush.

Each piece receives four coats of paint, just the way Grandpa taught me to do it. There is a set way that things must be done, Grandfather had said, and short-cuts had no place in the maintenance of railroad cars or in model building. If you rushed either, disaster might follow.

When Grandfather and I worked on our monsters, there was always a snack time. Feeling a little hungry now while I wait for the paint to dry, I leave the workbench and climb the cellar stairs, passing through the door into the kitchen. Taking two paper plates from a pile, I lay two slices of white bread on each. Each slice then receives a layer of grape jelly and a layer of peanut butter. The smooth kind. Not the chunky. They are then joined together and sliced in half from corner to corner, not side to side. A handful of potato chips and three Oreo cookies occupy space on each plate. An eight ounce container of whole milk, the kind kids get at school lunch, occupies a final space, and the plates are full. I carry both plates down the stairs. I lay one plate on the bench beside the drying Dracula, pleased at how menacing he looks all painted up. I turn and take several steps and lay the other plate down on the cold cement floor, pushing it forward along the cement with my foot. First eight inches. Then another eight. Finally, six more.

"What do you think, Mina?" I ask. "Is there too much blood on the old boy's chin?"

Dull eyes stare up at me from the woman whose bare, bruised back presses against the cement wall as she sits on the stained twin sized mattress. Her legs are drawn up, pitifully trying to shield the damaged right hand, the heavy gauze bandage around it blood soaked. She's been this way for two days now. Silent. Not eating. Not moving. Probably in shock. More than likely resigned now to her fate. She doesn't answer my question. I didn't expect her to. She never really participated in the process. Never got into the spirit of what we were accomplishing together. Actually, so far, none of them have. Well, I'll just have to keep trying.

2

You got a package, Miller," old Sergeant Bates announced as he entered Homicide. With a latex-gloved hand, he laid a six inch cubed cardboard box in the center of Detective Erik Miller's cluttered desk. Miller looked at the box as if it might unleash the Bubonic Plague if opened up. Or maybe something just as bad. All activity in the room ceased and a quiet settled over the space. The other detectives migrated over to Miller's desk, stood silently, and waited.

Written across the top of the box, in neat bold print from a black magic marker:

DETECTIVE ERIK MILLER
POLICE DEPARTMENT
MANCHESTER, N.H.
VERY IMPORTANT

A smiley face, with a winking eye, was drawn neatly after the word IMPORTANT.

"Where did it come from this time?" asked Miller.

"Mercier brought it in," replied Bates. "It was on the hood of his squad car. Someone put it there while he was breaking up a disturbance at Victory Park. He never saw the guy. Or woman."

Miller looked up at him, eyebrows raised.

"He's not a rook. Wore gloves. Saw your name and knew what

it was about. Brought it right here."

Detective Miller drew in a long breath and looked up at the faces who stood patiently waiting for him to open the box. This was the third such box to arrive at the station in the last three months, and the second addressed to Miller. They all knew nothing good was going to be inside it.

Wearing a pair of latex gloves, Miller used a brass letter opener and easily sliced through the clear packing tape, then lifted the flaps. Inside was a small, black, plastic jewelry box, the kind that would hold a pair of cufflinks. Miller looked at it for a second knowing cufflinks would not be inside, then lifted it out and laid it on his desk, thankful it was not the size of a necklace box. He looked back into the cardboard box. Like the other two boxes, there was a folded piece of unlined white paper on the bottom. He lifted that out and set it beside the jewelry box. His desk was now rimmed with officers and detectives quietly watching. In the stale air in the over crowded room, Miller caught the faint smell of body odor and the vibration of nervous anticipation.

Holding the base of the jewelry box with his left hand, he swiveled the top up to reveal a human thumb resting on a blue felt covered cardboard insert. A woman's thumb by the look of it, severed from the hand just above the lower knuckle, the nail painted a dark green. Wrapped around the thumb was a thin gold chain with a tiny gold cross attached. One young officer reacted to the sight of the thumb, turning his head. All the others, veterans of much worse carnage, stood passively. No one could have been sure what was going to be in there, but none were surprised. If anything, they were surprised that that was all it was. They had been expecting an escalation in the mutilations. They had been warned to expect it.

The first such box that had found its way into Homicide, had held a woman's cotton panties, white in color, with a woman's ring lying upon them. The ring had an eighteen carat thin gold band with a solitaire diamond stone. The waistband of the panties had been slightly frayed. A folded note written on plain white copy paper had been placed below them, with a warning that a body could be expected in the next few days and they should be on the look-out for it. Included was a four line riddle that made no sense at the time, and not much more sense even after the discovery of the promised body.

The ring and the panties had both belonged to a woman named Maryanne Darrow, whose body was found on the freezing cold morning of January 26th, three days after the package had arrived. She had been found hanging by her wrists from a tree along the trail that followed the curve of the river that led to the old mill buildings. She was discovered in the early morning glare by two women getting in their morning run. Ms. Darrow's fiance, Arthur Houle, who had first notified the police two weeks earlier that his girlfriend was missing, and had confirmed that the ring in the box was indeed the engagement ring he had given to her only a few months before, identified the body later that same day. With the discovery that the missing woman was now more than just missing, Arthur Houle briefly became the prime suspect in her death. But his alibi was airtight. He was at a conference in Phoenix when she first went missing from her job at the DMV, fifty people would swear to that. Also, he was staying at his mother's house in Athol, Massachusetts, the night the body was left hanging. The mother, and two older brothers, had stayed up most of that night with him, comforting him as best they could as he lived through the nightmare of his missing fiance. They would swear in court to that. They would also swear in court that Maryanne was the love of his life. She meant everything to him. The distress he exhibited while identifying the body was, at least to Detective Miller, either quite genuine or worthy of a Daniel Day Lewis type Oscar winning performance. The fiance was not the killer, of that Miller was positive.

It was sometime during the early morning hours of the 26th that Maryanne Darrow had been strung up to a tree, ropes tied to her wrists and then to a low hanging limb, her arms outstretched, her toes barely scratching at the thin layer of snow that covered the grass below them. She was dead, however, before she was left there, with death coming from a neck that had been viciously snapped. The coroner's report determined death was six hours before she was discovered by the women at 6:45 that cold morning. Even before the coroner's report verified it, it was thought by Miller, the first detective on the scene, that the victim was dead before being left there. Her wrists showed no sign of any struggle. The thin layer of snow beneath her toes had been swept of footprints and the toes had made no further impressions, like they would have had she struggled. So why, became the question, was she posed like that. And why was she in a dress that was fashionable almost a century before? Was the killer sending some kind of message with his choice of style? The fabric? Did the frilly collar on the dress mean something? Did the large buttons provide a clue? And if they did, then what was the statement the killer was making.

That first box, when received at the police station, did not bear Erik Miller's name. It was addressed to no one. It was opened by the Sergeant on the Desk and then brought to the detectives when the Sergeant saw what was inside. The second box, the one Miller received on March 5th, did have his name on the box. At the time, Miller found that to be quite interesting. He was the lead investigator on the Darrow murder, but had not spoken about the crime with the press or television, leaving that to his Chief. But a newspaper reporter had spotted him at the crime scene down by the river, and had reported in the next day's morning paper that it appeared Detective Erik Miller, honored for his capture of the killer in the gruesome murders of Justice Lawrence Freed and his wife, Francine, several years before, was working the case. So, Miller had surmised, the killer read the Union Leader. So did a hundred thousand others. It appeared the killer was emphatically signaling that he wanted Miller to continue on the investigation when the second body showed up.

The second box, with his name on it, meant there would soon be another victim. There was a note inside, just like there had been in the first box, and it told them there would be another body in the next few days. Included on the folded sheet of unlined white paper was another rhyme, just like there had been in the first note. While the first rhyme had made no sense when first read - there was yet to be a body - it made no more sense after Maryanne Darrow's body was found. The second rhyme, again at the time, made little sense, also.

On the overcast morning of March 7th, the lifeless body of Helena Johnson was found lying on a sculptured bench in front of the Currier Museum. She was discovered by three students walking on their way to Central High School. At first, the boys thought it was just a homeless bum sleeping on the bench and they went up onto the grounds for a little mischief. One of the boys punched 9-1-1 into his cell when he recognized the face as that of a teacher at his school.

When Detective Erik Miller arrived, he found Helena stretched out on the bench, lying on her back, legs together, fingers laced and resting on her chest. Her entire body had been tightly wrapped in a large piece of tan colored linen. As with the murder of Maryanne Darrow, forensics found not one shred of evidence at the scene.

The second murder caused quite a stir in the community. One of the boys had taken pictures with his cell phone and had posted them on social media. Also, in the heavily residential area around the Museum, more than a hundred people stood on the three streets that surrounded the entrance to the Museum and watched with great interest as the police worked the crime scene. The killing led the six and eleven o'clock news, as well as the following mornings front page of the Union Leader. Long shots of Detective Miller standing over the body were prominent in both.

With the drama of the third box now over, the other detectives went back to their desks. Only Chief Hendricks remained. He stood staring down at the thumb and the note.

"Get that down to the lab," said Hendricks, "and then come to my office. Bring the note. We need to talk."

When Miller entered the Chief's office, Hendricks indicated he should sit. Then he held out his hand for the note. Only he and Miller knew what had been written on the second note, the two of them deciding to keep that information only between them. Hendricks quickly read the new note, then looked over at his detective.

"This make any sense to you?"

Miller shook his head.

"Anyone reading this would think the guy was bat shit crazy," said Hendricks.

"Yes, they would," agreed Miller.

"But he's not."

"No, he is not," Miller agreed again. "The killer is telling us something in this stuff - I don't know what yet - but we'll figure it out. Just a matter of time."

"Time isn't something we have a lot of," Hendricks said. "The mayor's called me several times in the last few weeks asking about the investigation. The Johnson family wants answers. The Museum wants answers. The school wants answers. Mayor is taking heat from all sides and deflecting it my way. So, what have we got?"

"Very little new. If there is a link between the two women, I haven't found it yet. Darrow was young enough to have been a student in Johnson's class almost ten years ago, but she went to high school in Lawrence. Moved up here four years ago when her parents retired to Florida. They were vacationing in South America when Maryanne went missing. When we finally tracked them down, they had no idea their daughter had been missing. I spoke with them. It seems they communicated infrequently with their only child. I got the feeling, once the nest was empty, they were happy that it was so they could live life the way they wanted to. Free spirits would probably be the kindest way to describe them. They were unaware that their only daughter was engaged.

"We've even checked students that Johnson had over the years, the ones still living in the area, and that's a lot of people, and not one can be tied to Darrow. Or to her fiance. No common threads yet. But we're still working on it. Something might come up."

"What about Ms. Johnson?" asked Hendricks. "The father owns two restaurants on Elm Street and another four around the state. Knows a lot of people. Always been active politically."

"We checked. The family has money. Businesses are solid. As you know, we expected a ransom note up until the time part of her ear showed up on my desk. Up til then there was no reason to believe the two were linked. Ms. Johnson led a quiet life. Lived with her parents in the big house in Bedford. Helped with the care of her mother, who isn't exactly an invalid but does seem to have some emotional problems. Traveled a bit during the summers. Europe. Middle East. Her mother came from Israel and there is family in Tel Aviv. She dated someone a few years ago for about a year, a woman, very low key, but they went their separate ways. According to friends, it was amicable. The father didn't know about it, but the mother did. Everything was checked out by our guys. Then the box came and we realized she was going to be victim number two. That was when she became my problem."

Hendricks held the note up. "In a few days, it looks like we'll have victim number three. You're going to need help."

Anticipating that Miller was about to say he preferred to work alone, Hendricks said, "Save it. I'm giving you Day. Now, you have any idea who the victim might be?"

"We're looking into missing persons in the last two months. But those are just the ones reported. If we get lucky, the print off the thumb will be in the data base. I don't anticipate any luck. But you never know."

Miller shifted in his chair. "Day's a little green behind the ears. How about Connors?"

"Connors goes on medical leave in a week," replied Hendricks. "His back is acting up again. And forget Blanchette. He's talking like he's packing it up. Day will be fine. She may be new, but she's sharp. And working with someone like you will be a good experience for her. But, if you really don't want to work with her, I could give you Allen."

Miller reached over and took the note from his Chief's hand.

"Detective Day will be just fine," he said.

"I thought she might," said Hendricks. "Now get out of here. I need to call the Mayor back."

Sitting at his desk, Miller held the note from the killer and read it over and over again, trying not to let the taunts get to him, trying to make sense of the rhyme.

HELLO DETECTIVE ERIK MILLER, it began, printed neatly in uppercase letters with a thin black magic marker. I HOPE YOU ENJOY MY GIFT. GREEN NAILS? CAN YOU BELIEVE IT? THIS YOUNGER GENERATION. HOW WILL THEY EVER SURVIVE? NOT THAT MINA HAS TO WORRY ABOUT THAT NOW. KEEP AN EYE OUT FOR HER, ERIK. SHE'LL BE HARD TO MISS. I MUST SAY, SHE'S BEEN RATHER A DISAPPOINTMENT. WELL, I'LL JUST HAVE TO

HOPE FOR BETTER LUCK NEXT TIME. BY THE WAY, I'M GLAD YOU'RE ON THE CASE AND WE'LL HAVE THIS CHANCE TO CHAT. TALK SOON.

Thinking back to the list of names he was reading each morning, there was no one on the missing persons list with the name of Mina. If the name was a clue, Miller didn't yet know what that might be. And he wondered what exactly did 'rather a disappointment' mean? He then read the rhyme a dozen times. It was also in uppercase print with the same black marker.

THE COLD OF THE EARTH WE SHALL FEEL ONE DAY
WITH NO HOPE OF ESCAPE. BUT FOR HIS KISS.
BE HE SAVIOR OR WARDEN, I DARE NOT SAY,
WHEN BLOODY PROMISE PROVES TOO TEMPTING TO RESIST.

'The cold of the earth' could mean a cemetery, thought Miller. He would request the cities cemeteries receive nightly patrols until the body showed up.

Just who the hell is 'He' suppose to be, wondered Miller. God? The Devil? The killer? Three rhymes so far, and none that made any sense. Not yet. But they would. Eventually, they would. Miller was sure of it.

3

Detective Erik Miller walked into Homicide the following morning at seven, an hour before his shift officially began. Detective Kristen Day was sitting in the chair beside his desk sipping coffee from a Styrofoam cup. Another container of coffee was in the middle of the desk beside a small white paper bag. Inside the bag was a blueberry muffin.

"Best muffins in the city," she said as Miller sat down. "Maybe in the entire state."

"We start at eight," said Miller, lifting the top off the cup.

"Yet, here you are," said Day, and tipped her cup towards him before taking another sip.

"Couldn't sleep. Expected the phone to ring."

Detective Day wore a light gray pants suit over a white blouse that was buttoned to the neck. She had on sensible, comfortable looking black rubber soled shoes. Her long dark brown hair was severely pulled back into a ponytail. She used very little make-up on a face that possessed strong features. High cheekbones, rounded chin, eyes deep set and brown. A pouty lower lip that seemed out of place. A nose that had been broken several times by elbows during her playing days, yet it seemed to belong. She had the body of someone who could play small forward in college basketball, which she had done fifteen years before, with wide shoulders tapering down to narrow hips and long legs. At an aggressive six foot two, she had averaged sixteen and a half points and five rebounds per game in the two years she had been a starter, before the new coaching staff took over. The body carried only ten more pounds than it had when she played, and the rumor mill promised it was finely toned. She hit the weights several times a week, and ran at a brisk pace every night through the sparsely populated roads of her neighborhood in nearby Goffstown. It was known she had martial arts training in two disciplines and had handled herself well on the streets during her years as a patrol cop in Goffstown, and in her four years working Vice in Manchester. She was single, and her reputation around the building was she didn't flirt and she was verbally cutting to anyone who tried flirting with her, leaving absolutely no doubt that she was totally uninterested in any station house romance. It was not known if she had ever been married or if she was currently in a relationship. All of that was not in her file. What was in her file was impressive. Graduated near the top of her class. Marksman with pistol and rifle. Exemplary record in over seven years in Goffstown, before the four year stint in Vice, where she handled herself quite well. She tested as physically fit as any cop in the city. Maybe the state. Miller could see she would be an asset in the investigation. Still....

"It's well known you prefer to work alone," said Day deciding to get the unpleasantness out of the way early. "And I get it. But I'm hoping you can get past that with this case. It looks like you have something here that doesn't come along often and I can gain valuable experience."

"You're a twelve year veteran," said Miller, taking a bite from the muffin. "You have plenty of experience."

"Yeah. But not like this. A few years in Vice, which I wasn't crazy about, but Homicide is where the action is. It's where I always wanted to be.

"What took you so long to get here? There's a couple mentions of excessive force, but no disciplinary action. Can't imagine that held you back."

Day leveled a hard look at him as an answer.

"How many women you see in this room besides me, Detective Miller? Exactly. Glass ceilings and all that bullshit, but I should have been here four years ago."

"Well, you're here now. Take it from me, there will be days you wish you weren't."

"And as far as the excessive force nonsense," said Day, "total bullshit. A man sees a woman officer and thinks he can intimidate her. I don't intimidate easy. There were never any charges brought. How many tough guys want to go to court and admit a woman kicked the shit out of them?" Day shrugged.

Miller finished the muffin just as Detective Mark Allen burst into the room like Emmett Smith into the Giants secondary. He stopped when he saw Day.

"I heard the rumor that the Golden Boy of the MPD was given a babysitting assignment, but I didn't believe it. I see now it's true."

Kristen Day smiled up at Allen, all five feet eight inches of him, and said, "You have to get past the rejection, Marky. I told you, I don't date people I work with. It had nothing to do with your height. Or lack of it."

Allen reddened a bit and was about to say something in response, when Miller said, "It's too early in the morning for your bullshit, Mark. Go drink your coffee and try to look busy."

"You're the one who needs to get busy, Miller. Soon to be three dead bodies and you're chatting up the new girl. I think Hendricks might be losing patience with you."

Mark Allen chuckled to himself as he walked to his desk, sat down and opened up a newspaper.

"He hit on you?" asked Miller.

"Second week I was here," responded Day. "Pretty much half the building has. Not nearly as much as when I first started on the force, fresh meat and twenty-nine back then, but enough to make it aggravating. Even some of the married ones." She looked at him. "I don't date people I work with."

"My New Year's resolution was to give up women," said Miller with a wave of his hand. "That was three years ago. Haven't broken it yet."

"Sounds a little harsh," said Day.

"Yeah, maybe," Miller said. "Life can be a little harsh sometimes. All I care about is, I'll watch your back, and not to see your ass sway, and you better watch mine. Do that, and we'll get along just fine."

He drained the coffee and looked at her. "I do prefer working alone, Detective Day, that's true. But when this next body shows up, there's going to be more work than one person can do. I'm glad to have the help. How much do you know about this case?"

"Not much beyond what I've read in the newspapers and stuff I've heard around here."

"Hendricks and I have been playing this one close to the vest. Each box we've received has had a note and a riddle in it. We don't want what is written to get out to the public."

"Makes sense."

"I talked with some guys yesterday in New York and L.A. after the package arrived. Guys who have been through similar investigations. Been there at the beginnings of a serial spree, which is what I think we have here. Then another two at the F.B.I. who were suggested to me. They all said the same thing. It's a process. You look for something, the one thing that links the victims together. Sometimes that one thing is easy to spot. They're all hookers. Or they all have blonde hair and are about the same height. Maybe they're all bartenders and they are paying for the one bartender who refused to serve the guy one night and that set him off. Whatever. There is always a link. Something that triggers the guy to pick them as a victim."

"Always?" asked Day.

Miller shrugged. "So they said. You would think that would make it easier to catch them. But it doesn't. It seems, when there is a reason for the killing, in the killer's mind anyway, the killer is more methodical, more intelligent and more disciplined. The random killer is sloppier. Leaves clues that are easier to follow. He just wasn't prepared for the killing. Hadn't planned it out. And the ones of passion? Well, you'll find those are the easiest to solve."

"Like the Justice Freed killer?"

"Not exactly, but yeah. Don Carlisle was careful, but he left an imprint of a sneaker in the dirt outside the window where he entered. Even then, it took luck to get him. I think he never thought the police would ever think of looking at him, the connection between the two so long ago. Obviously, we spent our time running down everyone who Freed had sent to jail or who had gotten a harsh settlement in his courtroom. There was no shortage of suspects there. Carlisle didn't fit into any of those scenarios. He had never been in trouble with the law. Never been in a courtroom. But we got lucky. I got a feeling about something I had heard about Judge Freed - I like to call those feelings I get when they come 'a moment of clarity' when everything clicks, - and it took the investigation into another realm. That was when Carlisle entered our radar screen. After that, it was simply putting the pieces together.

"Anyways, the people I talked with yesterday told me to expect a shorter time between killings, to expect more written clues as the killer becomes more confident, and more taunting, and to be prepared for the possibility that our little box may eventually contain something bigger than a finger or a thumb."

"I've studied a few serial killer cases," said Kristen Day. "That seems to be how they progress."

"Here's the fun part," said Miller, without smiling. "When the third murder hits the newspapers, we can expect several people to confess to the murders. The third one brings the crazies out. I'm guessing none of them will be able to tell us what is written on the killer's notes. But that might just be my pessimistic side speaking. Who knows. Maybe the real killer will confess."

Miller unlocked the middle drawer of the desk and took a thick folder from it. He handed it to Detective Day.

"Take this over to your desk and read it. Spend time on the notes and poems. See if any of it makes sense to you."

Day stood. "What are you going to do?"

"The note yesterday mentioned the name Mina. There is no Mina on our missing persons list. I'll call around a fifty mile radius and see if anyone has a Mina on their list. Then I'll call the people who have missing wives, daughters, girlfriends and see if any of the missing were nicknamed Mina. I'll do that all day or until the call comes in that a body has been found. Looks like a heavy coffee day."

The morning passed with Miller on the phone and Kristen Day at her desk reading over the folder that contained photos and reports on Maryanne Darrow and Helena Johnson. A little after noon, Day sat down beside Miller's desk again.

"The last rhyme you got makes me think we could be finding a body in a cemetery," said Day. "Not unusual to have a body in a cemetery, I know, except this one will be above the ground."

"Yeah. I thought that, too," said Miller. "I have asked that each shift patrol the cemeteries each hour through the night for the next few nights." He leaned back in his chair and rubbed his eyes. "You get any sense as to who '*he*' is in that poem? God? Devil?"

"Not God," said Day. "Maybe the Devil. '*Savior or warden*'. Interesting. The victims are being held for a while, so, perhaps warden is apropos. *'But for his kiss'*. Maybe the killer sees themselves as a Savior who could save the victim if they choose. Or, when the victim has to die, for whatever crime the killer believes them guilty of, then their soul must go to hell and then the Devil becomes their warden. *'Bloody promise impossible to resist'*. Even more interesting. Obvious sexual overtones there. Sick. Kinky. Maybe a jilted lover from her past."

Day shrugged her shoulders. "Who knows. In looking over Maryanne Darrow's file, and reading the rhyme that came in with her panties, I got the feeling of sexual tension in those words, also. Were any of her old relationships ever considered?"

"The ones we know about didn't pan out," Miller said. "She had several relationships before getting engaged. Nothing too serious with any of them and none that had lasted more than a few months. There didn't seem to be any hard feelings about any of the break-ups."

Miller suddenly frowned.

"What?" asked Day.

"There may have been a period a few years back, in her late teens early twenties, when she may have been a little wild," said Miller. "She, and a girlfriend she hung with going back to her high school years in Lawrence, may have been partying hard. We know that her late teens were chaotic to say the least. We're still investigating that, but drugs maybe played a role. What we do know is, the last few years she was clean, worked steady, and was engaged to a solid guy."

It was Days turn to frown. "Well, not as unusual as you may think, especially at that age. When you work Vice, you begin to wonder if any teenage girl is innocent."

Miller shrugged. "Maryanne may have swung both ways. It was alluded to, but we didn't find any female lovers. It does appear she was promiscuous, however, and until her engagement played a crowded field."

Day flashed a knowing smile. "Brief encounters that end amicably after a short fling tend to be no big deal. Both parties happy to move on. But longer relationships are something else, especially to someone who isn't used to that sort of thing. Someone who may have been searching for something more. Desperate for something more, and believe they have found it. '*This world is full of monsters who yearn',* the very first line in that first poem. The emotion there is strong. I think her death was one of passion."

Day gazed across the room. "The second line, *'A terrible lesson did Miss Darrow learn*'. That one is interesting."

"How so, beyond the fact she died for whatever it was she did?"

"It gives the impression that she was not a random victim. That she provoked the killer in some way.

Miller leaned forward again and nodded his head a few times. "Yeah," he said. "Didn't look at it like that. You get a sense from any of the other lines?"

"I'm thinking of some things," Day answered. "Nothing I want to share yet. I want to kick it around a little more. Things may become clearer when the next victim is found."

"Keep at it."

As Day walked back to her desk, Miller thought back to the other two rhymes that had been received. Looking at them from a jilted boyfriend angle he saw possibilities, except for a couple of things. One, all old boyfriends of Maryanne Darrow had been looked at closely. At least the ones they knew about. There was nothing there. But a one or two night stand with someone? Someone who wanted more? That could be anyone. And second, there was no indication anywhere that Helena Johnson had ever had a relationship with a man. Friends of hers were quite adamant that Helena was a Lesbian and always had been. She was a woman in her forties who still lived with her parents, and from all indications had led the life of a nun for the past three years. If she had had a lover recently, none of her friends had known about it. Still, that first rhyme, found in the box with the panties and ring, seen in this light, was interesting. Miller didn't need any notes to remember it.

THIS WORLD IS FULL OF MONSTERS WHO YEARN.
A TERRIBLE LESSON DID MISS DARROW LEARN,
THAT IT'S A JUNGLE OUT THERE, TO SAY THE LEAST,
AS IT IS FOR ALL WHO ENCOUNTER THE BEAST.

A jilted lover, believing they had found the woman of their dreams, only to be rebuffed after a short time. Could that be the thread, despite what friends had said of Helena Johnson? They would know more when the next victim was found and identified.

By the end of the work day there was still no report of a body being found. That came early the next morning.

4

Detective Erik Miller drove between the two stone pillars that held the arch of the main gate to Mount Calvary Cemetery at 6:20 in the chill of an April fifth morning, twenty minutes after receiving a call while he was shaving and two days after receiving a box that contained a severed thumb. Two Manchester police cruisers and an ambulance were already parked along the narrow paved road that wove throughout the rows of headstones about a hundred and fifty feet into the gently rolling landscape of the beautiful grounds. Detective Kristen Day pulled up to the scene as Miller slowly exited his car. He waited for her to walk over to him. Four officers and two EMT's stood off to the side waiting for the detectives to do what they do. Miller recognized one of the officers, Joe Mitchell, and waved him over.

"Who found her?"

"Landry," responded Mitchell, indicating a young officer who was leaning against the fender of a squad car. He was tall and lanky and dabbing at his forehead with a handkerchief, despite the chill of the morning.

"New guy?"

"Six months. First body he's found. Shook him a little bit." Officer Mitchell looked up at the dead body of a woman who was draped over a cement cross on top of a crypt. "Would have shaken me, too. And I've seen bad."

"Yeah," said Miller. "Ask him to come over."

While Mitchell went to get Officer Landry, Miller said, "Detective Day, Vice don't look so bad now, does it?"

"Thumb's missing on her left hand," said Kristen Day, ignoring the question. "Your eyes good enough to see that?"

"Your file didn't mention you were a comedienne, Day. Yeah, I can see that. She's our girl."

Officer Landry came and stood beside them. He was at least three inches taller than Day and slim as a sapling. His eyes, in an ashen face, danced between the two detectives.

"What time did you find her, Officer Landry?" asked Miller.

"Five before O six hundred," replied Landry in a voice that was struggling to remain calm and professional. "I exited the squad car and began to approach the crypt, but it was obvious she was dead. I got no closer than fifteen feet from the front of it."

"You called it right in?"

"Yeah."

"Did you see anything, hear anything?"

"Nothing."

"Do you normally patrol through here during your shift?"

"No. Not unless I notice lights or something. There have been a few nights where there were kids parked in here making out, but no vandalism or stuff like that. But I was told to do an hourly drive through by the Sergeant for the next few nights, so that's what I was doing."

"So you would have driven through around five o'clock, also?"

"That's right. Four forty-five to be exact."

"Do you think you would have noticed her up there at that time?"

"If she was there, I didn't. I don't know. It was still dark and I was looking for cars or someone at ground level. I could have missed her. Probably would have. While I was driving through, there was a stop over on 293 for a speeder, and I was going to head there as back-up. I may have been distracted. But, like I said, I was looking at ground level."

"Okay," said Miller. "Head back to the station. Fill out your report. You'll be okay."

"What do you think?" asked Day after Landry slowly walked back to his cruiser.

"She could have been up there all night, or left there between 4:45 and 5:45. I'm thinking she was there before that. Risky to be out here after five. Sky is lightening this time of year. Dog walkers. Joggers." He looked at her. "You ready?"

"After you," said Day.

They did a slow walk around the cement crypt. The crypt was eight foot square and stood five feet high. A three foot tall gray cement cross stuck up over the entrance to the crypt. The ground around the tomb was flat, hard and covered with patchy grass. The detectives searched the entire area and found nothing. Then they moved to the front of the structure and looked up at the women's body, her thighs at Day's eye level. She had been posed behind the cross in a kneeling position, with her arms draped over the horizontal part of the 't' of the cross for balance. Her forehead rested against the vertical top of the 't'. She was clothed in a flimsy, pale white nightgown that extended to her ankles. Her arms were bare and bruised, but not as bruised as her face. She had been severely beaten.

"How did he get her up there?" wondered Miller. "There would have been an indentation of a ladder in the ground if he used one. Did you notice anything?"

Day shook her head. "It's only five feet off the ground. She could have been placed on the top, then the killer hoisted up there to finish the job."

"And then he would have carefully lowered himself to keep

from leaving an indentation in the ground had he jumped down."

"Sure," agreed Day.

Detective Miller stood looking up at the dead woman. "Can't tell how heavy she is under that nightgown, but she has to be at least one twenty. A hundred and twenty pounds of dead weight is a lot. A human body isn't like lifting a steel bar with weights on the end. It's not an easily managed load. We had thought he was pretty fit just by the way Darrow was strung up, but this is a whole other level of power. This guy is strong. He could easily overpower his victims."

Miller signaled the photographer over. "Jack, take a lot of pictures. Front, back, sides. We'll get you a ladder."

"Got one in the van," said the man with the camera.

"Go ahead. Don't touch a damn thing and don't step on the roof."

Jack Morgan frowned and gave Miller a look as if to say, 'this ain't my first rodeo', then went to get the ladder.

"There's a Dunkin' down the street," said Day. "Want me to get us some coffees?"

"Sure. I'll talk to Mitchell. We'll seal the area up. Find out when the ME will be here. Get a few more guys to keep the thrill seekers away. They'll be showing up soon. Grab me a couple of honey dips, too."

"Don't start without me," said Day as she walked to her Jeep.

"Wouldn't think of it," replied Miller as he began walking towards Officer Mitchell.

THE PHOTOGRAPHER WAS just finishing the last batch of photographs when Day stepped from her car carrying two coffees and a bag.

"Looks like our boy used some kind of brush or broom on the top of the crypt," said Miller as he took the cup handed to him. "Plenty of dirt up there, but it's been disturbed. He was prepared.

There will be no footprints, or anything else for that matter. But we'll check. Maybe a partial if he was rushed."

"You'll have these later today," said the man with the camera as he stepped off the last rung.

"Leave the ladder there, Jack," said Miller. "I'll make sure it's returned to you."

The photographer nodded and went to his van.

Miller finished off one of the doughnuts and then, as he set the coffee down on the roof of the car, said, "Let's go." He climbed up the ladder first, Day following.

"What's he trying to tell us, posing the body like this?" asked a kneeling Miller as he lifted the flimsy nightgown to check the left ankle. "Bruises. She was manacled, just like Helena Johnson."

"There are puncture wounds on her neck," Day said, standing on the opposite side of the body.

"Teeth marks?" asked Miller excitedly, standing quickly and coming over to look.

"No," said Day. "Done by something sharp. Two of them, spaced about two inches apart."

Miller looked at the punctures and then his eyes drifted up to the woman's face. Her right eye was almost completely shut from swelling and the cheek was bruised a deep purple.

"He beat her face worse than Darrow and Johnson," said Miller.

"An escalation of anger?" asked Day.

"Maybe," replied Miller. "It happens. Usually, the method of death stays the same, but the damage to the victims becomes greater. We have three deaths and none of them are the same, but the damage is still heavy. There is a lot of anger here. With the other two, there was significant trauma to the body, rather than the face. We'll have to see what damage was done to her body."

Detective Kristen Day gently pulled the head of the victim

back so they could see the entire face.

"Shit," said Miller. "Joe," he yelled down to Officer Joe Mitchell who was wrapping tape around a large section of the site, "tell Jack to get back up here with his camera."

The photographer had not yet left and heard through his open van window what Miller shouted. He grabbed the camera and walked back over to the crypt.

"What have you got?" he asked Miller

"Did you pull her head away from the cross?"

"Didn't touch her."

"I'm going to need more shots of her face. More specifically, her forehead."

Day and Miller stood off to the side while Jack re-positioned the ladder so he could get full frontal shots of the victim's head.

"Beating her wasn't enough?" said Miller. "He had to burn her?"

"It means something," said Day.

"Yeah. It means he's a sick son-of-a-bitch."

"No, it means something. We just have to figure out what that is. The rhyme, the note, the pose, the setting, the nightgown, they all mean something."

"Yeah, I know. But this guy is starting to piss me off."

"Don't let the killer get to you, Erik. Stay focused. We follow the clues. Add them all up. The killer is talking to us. It's a language we don't understand yet, but we're going to learn it. We'll figure out what it all means."

"Sure. But in the meantime, if it's okay with you, Detective Day, I'm going to be pissed off."

Day smiled reassuringly.

'She has a nice smile,' Detective Erik Miller thought to himself, 'but this job has a habit of making smiles disappear.'

Miller looked toward the west entrance from the street. A small group of people had begun gathering near it, held in check by a uniform. They had their cell phones out and were taking videos, no doubt using the zoom feature. The WMUR van was just pulling up. He saw a Union Leader reporter that he knew standing beside the uniform. So it was already going viral. He looked at Detective Day and nodded toward the crowd.

"Something for the masses to enjoy with their morning coffee," he spat out. "Something else to piss me off."

THEY WERE SITTING at Detective Kristin Days' desk two hours after noon looking at the photographs that the photographer had brought in fifteen minutes earlier. As asked, he had taken a lot of shots. Earlier, they had stopped in to see the ME who had already worked on the dead woman's body. By ten they had the woman's name and had notified next of kin. They were at the morgue when the dead woman's parents had identified the body. After, sitting on a bench in the lobby of the building, the two detectives spoke briefly with the parents.

The mother, Mrs. Katherine Seward, a heavy set woman of fifty, dabbed a tissue at her eyes and sat quietly on the bench, a sob escaping from her every so often.

"I held out hope my Maddie would be found alive," she whispered. "That she would come back to us. But I think, deep down inside, that I knew she would not. I don't know why, Detective Miller, I really don't, but it just seems that God takes the good ones from this world much too early and leaves the bad here to make our lives miserable. Why is that?"

"I don't know, Mrs. Seward," said Miller. "I truly don't." He looked at Mr. Seward. With the saddest eyes imaginable, the father, now looking much older than his fifty-four years, stared unseeing across the space. He had not uttered one sound since a cry of anguish had escaped him at the sight of his only daughter's face when the sheet was pulled back.

"Why would someone do that to my beautiful daughter?" asked

Mrs. Seward, slightly shaking her head. "Madeleine's a nurse. She helps people when they are in pain. She helps save lives." A sob wracked her body. "She was so full of life. How can a human being do that to another human being? My God, how she must have suffered."

She looked up at the two detectives, Miller meeting her teary eyes, his face an unreadable mask as he fought to contain his rage. Kristen Day stood passively beside Miller, allowing him to deal with the parent's grief.

Mrs. Seward looked at her husband. She placed her hand on his. He made no sign that he noticed the touch. She then looked at the two Detectives again.

"Will you find the person who did this to our daughter?" she asked. "Will you find this monster?"

Detective Day flinched at the vehemence the mother put into the word monster. It was the only expression of the anger that the woman was obviously feeling.

"We'll find him," said Miller with finality, certainly sounding more convincing than he felt. "We won't bother you today, Mr. and Mrs. Seward, but we will need to speak with you soon. You understand?"

"Of course," said Mrs. Seward. "We want him caught, Detectives. Whatever we can do. Right, John?" She looked at her husband. He sat staring into oblivion, making no indication he had heard her.

Twenty-six year old Madeleine Ann Seward had gone missing ten days before after a night out with friends. The last anyone had seen her alive was when she said goodnight to two of her girlfriends after a night of dinner and clubbing in downtown Portsmouth, not twenty minutes from her apartment in Exeter. That was on a Saturday night.

When she didn't show up Monday morning for her shift in the Emergency Room of the hospital where she worked, there had been immediate concern. Madeleine never missed a shift. Repeated calls to her cell had gone unanswered. One of the night nurses, a friend of Madeleine, drove to her apartment. There was no answer to the knock on her door. Her car was not in the buildings parking lot. The night nurse made calls to known friends. No one had heard from Madeleine on Sunday. When Madeleine Seward failed to show up for work on Tuesday, the same friend called a friend of hers who was a cop in Portsmouth. He called her back within the hour. Madeleine's car was in a metered parking lot not far from Market Street. Beneath the windshield wiper was a ticket. It was dated on the Sunday at 10:45 A.M. Within an hour, a missing person notice went out.

"A bad case of luck that she was posed on the crypt between police patrols," said Detective Erik Miller, putting the last of the photographs on top of the others.

"Do you think the killer drove in, wrestled the body up there, and then drove out?" asked Detective Day.

"If he didn't, then that means he carried the body, all one hundred and thirty-two pounds of her, almost two hundred feet. If he walked in from the back or the side, it is considerably longer. Also, he was carrying some type of sweeper to erase the footprints."

"Certainly not out of the question," said Day. "Safer than driving a vehicle into the cemetery."

"Again, if he carried her, this guy has strength beyond the norm. What bothers me is that, if he didn't drive in, then he expected there to be patrols in an area that isn't regularly patrolled."

"What are you saying?" asked Day. "You think the killer expected patrols?"

"No. I'm saying bad luck. We could have used a break and we didn't get it. We took a stab at the poem and we got it right. The meaning of cold earth. We went with the theory that it may mean a cemetery and we took precautions based on our theory. It would have been nice to catch a break."

"It's been my experience," said Day, as she slowly went through the photographs again, "that luck rarely enters into an investigation."

"After you've been here a few years, Detective Day, you may reconsider. It's rare, but every once and a while...."

He watched her as she studied each photograph.

"That's a lot of facial damage," he said, keeping his tone low. "Less on the body this time, but the face still suffered. I still don't understand why the burn on her forehead. What the hell is that all about? Why take a clothes iron, heat it up and place it against the skin of a woman who is already dead? Why take a metal object and create two holes in the side of the neck, in a person who is no longer living? Why pose the body draped over a cross? What does that mean? Does it mean anything? She was a nurse. Does the damage have anything to do with her profession? What the hell could it possibly be? Why did Johnson, a teacher of mathematics, get wrapped up in linen and get left on a bench? If there is a method to this madness, a reason for this abuse, I don't see what it is. Do you?"

Day squared off the photos and put them into the file and placed the file in her middle drawer.

"There's something about this that is gnawing at my mind," she said. "You know how you get that feeling that there is something going on and you should know what it is, but it just isn't coming to you? Well, that's how I feel now. It'll come to me. I just think every thing the killer is doing to these women is being done for a reason. It may seem like mindless rage, but I don't think so. With serials, there is a common theme. As far fetched and remote as that may seem to us, to them there is a continuity. Maybe what you see as rage, is just the abuse that was needed in that situation. But beyond the anger, there is the posing of the bodies and, I think, that is the real importance. The posing. The clothes. And now the punctures."

"Like he's depicting a scene he wants us to see?" Miller asked, his brows knitted.

"Maybe," said Kristen Day. "Probably. There are easier ways to dispose of a body. Each way these women were posed in death has presented a degree of danger to the killer. Those minutes out there in plain sight where the activity could draw attention, even under the cover of darkness. Why take that chance if it isn't being done for a reason beyond just a thrill?"

Miller frowned, then rose and stretched.

"Okay," he said. "If you figure out what it all means, I'd love to know. I just want to catch this son-of-a-bitch. In the meantime, I'll talk with the people I interviewed in Johnson's homicide and see if there is a connection with Seward. You take Maryanne's. Then we'll both go and speak with Seward's friends and workers."

Detective Kristen Day stood and said, "You okay? You look worried."

"There were six weeks between Maryanne Darrow and Helena Johnson. Four weeks between Helena and Madeleine. Yeah. I'm worried."

Just then, Chief Hendricks stepped from his office and waved them to come in.

"Close the door," he said to Day as he took his seat behind the desk. They stood in front of his desk.

"Rough morning," he stated. "You two okay?"

They both nodded.

He drummed his fingers on his desk as he looked up at them.

"That was good work deciphering that note and putting the cemeteries under patrol," Hendricks said. "Just bad luck we didn't get him."

Day looked over at Miller who did not return the look. She

noticed he wasn't smiling, but she had the feeling he wanted to.

"Third body," said Hendricks. "Anything feeling like a pattern or an idea about what is going on?"

"It's early," said Miller. "I know it doesn't feel like it, but in these things we are early into the process. All we can do is wait for a break. But I'd say we're looking for a guy twenty-six to thirty-six years old. Over six foot. Six-three, six-four. Maybe bigger. Strong. In shape. Probably works out. I'd say clean shaven. Maybe a shaved head, too. Definitely a loner. Can't keep prisoners in a place where others live. Anger issues. Big time anger issues. Methodical. Careful. Nothing under the fingernails of any victim, but I have to believe at least one of them would have struggled. Not a fiber, not a strand of hair, not a print. Clever. Being prepared to sweep off the top of that crypt speaks volumes. How many people would have thought of that? And I think he expected the police to patrol the cemeteries, and it didn't worry him. So he's bold. Eventually, that may be his downfall. He may feel the need to take more chances, the adrenaline rush difficult for him to pass up. The high comes from the killing and the posing and the taunting, but the chances he could get caught in the setting of the scene may be the icing on top for him. Often, it's something that seems insignificant that gives them away. The key, for us, is to notice that one insignificant thing and see it for what it really means."

Hendricks looked at Day. "What about you, Day? Any thoughts?"

Kristen Day shook her head. "This is only my second day on this, Chief. Anything I might add wouldn't be worth the air it would take to say it. Ask me in a few days, and I'll have plenty to say. But, I've seen nothing yet in the files or at the scene this morning to dispute what Detective Miller just said. Right now, I'm following his lead."

Hendricks nodded. "Okay, what's next?"

"Interviewing everyone we talked to before, and then talking with people who knew Seward. And then seeing what social media has to say about Seward. It was no help with the other two, but you never know."

"I heard from the Mayor again," said Hendricks. "She is beyond concerned. Said anything we need, any overtime we have to use, we have Carte Blanche. Just find the son-of-a-bitch. Although she was a little more colorful with her words."

He waved them out of his office and his parting words were, "Find him."

I LOVE THE Internet. No, really, I do. It makes my life so much easier. Type something, anything, and boom, in a few seconds, the screen fills up with information that you can use. I love it. So, I type in a name. Just a name. A random name. Of course, to me, it isn't just a random name. I am looking for a person who has that name, but there is some criteria that has to be met when the list pops up. And you may be surprised to know, especially if you have never done it, but almost any name you type in will give you a lot of people who have that name. That's where the criteria comes in. Immediately, all people who are an unreasonable distance from me are eliminated. Then age becomes a factor if there are still multiple choices available. The nearest age to the character that I am trying to match is desirable. But even then, after observing someone who is a good match age wise, they may not appeal to me, and then I try someone else on the list, if there are others on the list. If not, well, beggars can't be choosers, can they?

Let me give you an example of what I have to go through, because it isn't always easy and sometimes I just have to settle. The main female character in the 1932 movie *The Mummy* is a woman named Helen Grosvenor played by actress Zita Johann. I know, you never heard of Zita, but take it from me, at the time, she was well known. Did several movies in the thirties and starred on Broadway. Something else you may not have known, Hollywood was always looking for new talent back in the early days of movie making and the studio heads loved finding that talent in legitimate theater. Made them look high brow, or so they thought. Anyway, how many women under the age of thirty with either of those names do you think live in New Hampshire? Exactly. So, I had to settle. When I have to settle, maybe I need to put two names together. Maybe a mix between the character and the actress. Maybe I might really have to settle, like I did with Helena, and just go with the first name. Of course with Helena, it was personal. I wasn't settling. Just settling a debt.

I won't say I got lucky with Maryanne Darrow. The character that Fay Wray famously played in *KING KONG* is Anne Darrow. But, you see, I knew this Maryanne Darrow. Oh, yes, I knew the bitch. She's the reason for all of this. Well, maybe not the entire reason, there are other circumstances that enter into what I hope to accomplish, but it all started because of Maryanne.

I hadn't seen her in a few years, four years one month and four days to be exact. I had no idea she was back in town. Once I did know, well, I just couldn't let it go. I tried. Really, I did. But it gnawed at me. What she had done. It gnawed at me. Festered. Kept me awake. Muddled up all my other thoughts. And the anger, anger I had managed to suppress most of the time, bubbled to the surface like Mt. Saint Helen's. Who the hell could blame me after what Maryanne had done?

Anyway, sitting here at the computer, I type in the name I need for my next helper and fourteen names pop up. Two are within a hundred miles of me. One is not very far at all. I'll check her out in the next week or so, see if she is a good match, get a feel for her daily routine. And, if she is a good match, then figure out the best way to snatch her. If she doesn't work out, then I'll check the other one. If she isn't a good match, then we'll start name combinations. Eventually, it will all work out.

Glancing from the screen, I look at the front page of the newspaper that is lying on my workbench. The photo above the fold and under the bold headline shows Detective Erik Miller standing on top of the crypt beside Mina. Well, not really Mina. Couldn't find one of them. Had to settle for a Madeleine. There he stands, the Golden Boy, lead investigator, searching for clues, and completely lost. He has no idea what is going on. How many clues do I have to leave before he gets it? He better pick up on them soon. His reputation is taking a beating. I couldn't be happier. If it hadn't been for him, Maryanne never would done what she did.

5

They were on the one oh one heading east towards Exeter. Detective Miller was driving and Detective Day was sipping coffee from a Styrofoam cup. It was two days after finding Madeleine Seward's body on top of a crypt.

"You look like you didn't sleep," said Day, looking over at her new partner. She noticed he had done a poor job of shaving. She also noticed he needed a haircut and that there seemed to be more gray hairs in the full head of black than had been there four months before when she had first entered the Detective Room.

"I slept," replied Miller, checking the speedometer and keeping the car at seventy. "Just took a while to fall off. Caught the news at eleven and then tossed and turned. Last time I looked, it was two thirty. What about you?"

"I got my four hours," said Day.

"Four hours? That normal?"

"Oh, yeah. Goes back to my college days. We had a six A.M. basketball practice before classes. I carried a full load of studies and I was there to learn, so I took my classes seriously. Practice again in the afternoon or games at night. Study until one in the morning and then do it all over again the next day. I got used to four hours of sleep and I still go with it."

She took another sip. "You know, not to change the subject,

but I like that suit you're wearing. That shade of brown shows off your eyes. But instead of a white shirt, you might try a yellow one. Yellow, like a daffodil. And a tie with some dark blue in it." She turned to look out the side window, and smiled.

"What are you, the fashion police?" asked Miller. "I won't criticize what you're wearing and you keep your opinions about my clothes to yourself. How's that?"

"What's wrong with what I'm wearing?" said Day. "I like this color."

"You wear the same style pants outfit every day," said Miller. "Only the color changes."

"I look professional. And they're comfortable. You have any idea how difficult it is to find clothes in my size? You're what? Five eleven? You can buy stuff off a rack. I don't have that luxury."

"I don't buy off the rack," Miller stated.

His right hand on the wheel steered the car, while his left fingers lightly tapped the wheel to a melody only he recognized.

"What is it with women? My ex used to tell me that another shirt would look better with what I was wearing than the one I picked out. I mean, is this like something all women are taught by their mothers to say to all guys? Is this supposed to be a subtle little reminder that men need women, because if men can't do a simple little thing like picking out the correct shirt, well, just imagine how many other things we will need help with during the course of the day. It's a Goddamn miracle we can wipe our own ass."

"You were married?" asked Day, again changing the subject.

Miller looked at her and frowned. This was not a problem he had with male partners. And certainly not when he worked alone, which was why he preferred it that way. He wasn't big on small talk.

"It's a twenty-five minute drive," he said. "So, you want to do bios. Sure. Why not. Let's get it out of the way. Yes, I was married. Divorced eight years ago. After five years of marriage, she told me she couldn't be married to a cop. It was too unsettling. Couldn't handle the hours, the mood swings, the lack of conversation. She's on her third husband now. Guess what? All of them cops. Loves the uniform, I guess. Or maybe she's just getting used to us. Third one is going into year five. Hopefully, she's happy."

"Any kids?" asked Day.

"No. What about you?"

"No. Never married. Never even close. I don't think marriage is for me."

"Did you grow up around here?" asked Miller.

"No. Daddy relocated up here for his job when I was thirteen."

"Tough age to move. Leaving friends. New schools."

"I didn't mind. My older brother did. He was going to be a junior. Last thing he wanted was to leave all his friends. But I didn't have a lot of friends. Actually, it worked out for me. I was always the tallest girl in my age group, gawky and thin, but that summer we moved my co-ordination caught up with my height and when I tried out for the basketball team in ninth grade, I made it. I'm not sure that opportunity would have been there for me if we hadn't moved."

"What did your father do for work?"

"He was a pharmacist. When CVS started putting in stores up here, he jumped at the chance to get out of the city. My mother was livid. Leaving friends and family. She never let a chance go by to berate her husband for dragging her off into the boonies, as she liked to call Goffstown. It was a lousy fifty miles, but she made it sound like we had moved a continent away. Christ, that woman could whine."

"They still in Goffstown?"

"No. They're both dead. Father was shot fifteen years ago in a robbery by a zonked out druggie. Mother totaled her car one night on black ice and was in a coma for three weeks before she finally died."

"I'm sorry. Where's your brother?"

"He lives in Texas. I visited him eight or nine years ago. He's doing okay. He loves it down there."

She finished off the coffee and placed the cup in a holder.

"What about you? You a local guy?"

"Grew up in Manchester. Went to Memorial."

"Play any sports?"

"Not for the school. No. Played with guys I grew up with. I was good enough that I could have played football and baseball in high school, but I hated the idea of practices and coaches. Then I joined the army after graduating, because I had no idea what I wanted to do at the time, and I learned the importance of coaches and practicing and discipline."

They cruised through Candia into Raymond. He looked over at her. "Now that we have the bullshit out of the way, tell me what you think about the crime scene. I have my thoughts, but want to hear yours."

"Well, it's fairly obvious what the killer wanted us to see and it makes the rhyme crystal clear."

"And that is?"

"Vampires. Only thing it could be. The punctures on Madeleine's neck, spaced like they were made by fangs. The use of the cemetery like she was raised from the coffin. But the real teller is the burn on her forehead."

"And why is that?" asked Miller.

"You don't know?"

He shook his head. "I'm not big into vampires."

"If something holy, like a cross or holy water, touches the skin of a vampire, it will burn them. In the movies, vampires always hiss at and turn away from a cross. And they only come out at night. Direct sunlight can kill them. Didn't you ever watch vampire movies or even *True Blood* when it was on television a few years ago?"

"I'm not big on horror movies," said Miller. "I saw a few when I was a kid, but found them foolish. Freddie, Jason, Michael Myers. Not my kind of entertainment. I like Westerns and War movies. And I don't watch a lot of television other than History Channel, sports and the News. But I agree. The guy wanted us to see a tie-in to vampires. How does that relate to the first two killings? Where is he going with this? Any ideas on that?"

"As a matter-of-fact, I do," said Day. "It will sound a little crazy, but hear me out. We agree Madeleine was made to appear as if she had been made a vampire and then died. Let's take the rhyme. *It is the cold of the earth we shall feel one day with no hope to escape, but for his kiss. Be he savior or warden, I dare not say, when his bloody promise proves impossible to resist.*
We die and a cold grave awaits us. But if a vampire mingles his blood with yours, you can live forever as a child of the night. Yes, the master is your savior. But he is also your warden, because you can not escape him. You belong to him. Or her. The bloody promise is the bite. And we all know vampires are impossible to resist when they hypnotize us with their eyes. The most famous vampire, of course, being Dracula."

"Okay. So this nut job is acting out some scene from a movie or something?"

"Maybe," replied Kristen Day. "I think most definitely."

Miller looked over at her.

"And I think that because of the other murders," said Day meeting his gaze.

"I don't follow."

"The first victim. Maryanne Darrow. She's found on the path along the river, left dangling from a tree limb with ropes tied around her wrists. She's wearing a dress that has been out of style for seventy years. But it's the buttons that give it all away."

"The buttons?"

"Well, the buttons, the pose, the victim's name. And, of course, the rhyme."

"I'm listening," said Miller.

"*This world is full of monsters who yearn. A terrible lesson did Miss Darrow learn, That it's a jungle out there to say the least, as it is for all who encounter the beast.*
Everything adds up to King Kong."

"King Kong? Are you serious?"

"Oh, yeah," said Day. "When Kong rampages through the jungle towards the native village, the first thing he sees when he breaks through the vegetation is a woman on a raised platform, her wrists bound and she's spread-eagled. It's love at first sight. The beast takes her and goes off to his cave high in the mountains. The dress the woman is wearing is similar to the one on Maryanne."

"You've seen the movie?"

"The Internet shows you everything."

"But what made you think of King Kong?" asked Miller as he passed through Epping.

"The victim's name, Erik. Ann Darrow is the character's name. She was played by an actress named Fay Wray."

"So he's choosing his victims based on their names?"

"I think so."

"Wait a minute," said Miller. "His taunt to me in the last note said *Mina* was a disappointment. But we have a Madeleine Seward who is dead."

"Yes. But when you Google the 1931 movie *Dracula,* the cast of characters shows that actress Helen Chandler played Mina. Mina Seward. Madeleine Seward, Mina Seward. Close enough."

"Christ. What about Helena Johnson?"

"That one took a little longer to figure out," said Day. "When I typed in that name, nothing showed up that would help us. But then I looked at that rhyme again and it gave me an idea. Remember: *Death need not be eternal. It was no obstacle to me.* Someone has died, probably dead for a long time, and then lives again. Then: *Words spoken in the dead of night released my bonds and set me free.* A spell of some kind or a curse that is broken by certain words. Words that break the spell or curse. The next line tells us that, right? *Now ancient incantations.* But it's the next lines that give it all away. *My Queen and I must obey. And now for all eternity together we shall stay.*

"And just what is that giving away?"

"If you take the premise that a man returns from the grave, and then wants to bring his love back also, and that they must have lived in ancient times, perhaps in ancient Egypt, you might be looking at the plot of *The Mummy."*

"The Mummy?" said Miller, taking his eyes off the road to stare at her

Day shrugged. "If we buy into *King Kong* and *Dracula*, then buying into *The Mummy* is not a stretch. The body was found outside of a museum. Posed like it was ready for eternity. Wrapped in a linen cloth. All of this, taken independently, adds up to nothing. But put it all together and we have a solid working premise. You do see that, right?"

"What about the name? There is a tie-in with Darrow, a tie-in with Seward. What's the tie-in with *The Mummy?"*

"I haven't found that yet," replied Day. "The actress in the original Mummy from 1932 was a woman named Zita Johann. She played the character Helen Grosvenor. You would think it would have been the other way around. Anyways, we have a Helen and a Helena. Thin, I grant you. On the other hand, there aren't many Zita Johann's running around in New Hampshire. None that popped up on Google. But there have been a lot of remakes and sequels and I haven't had the time to check out all of the casts for those movies."

Detective Erik Miller put on his right blinker and took the first exit for Exeter. "So we have a maniac killing women just so he can pose them in scenes from some old horror movies. And he's choosing his victims because of their names. Is that what you're telling me?"

"I think it's obvious," said Detective Kristen Day.

"How the hell do you catch a guy like that? There will be no similarities among the victims. They won't know each other. Chances are none of the women will know the killer. Speaking with friends of the victims will yield no results."

"Probably not," said Day, shifting in her seat, "but we have to do it. And hope the killer screws up."

Miller drove into the apartment complex where Madeleine Seward had lived and pulled to a stop in front of her building. He looked over at Day.

"Good work, Detective."

"Thank you, Detective Miller." Day stepped from the car thinking that maybe now she would be taken more seriously, because up until now she had felt like she hadn't been by the men she worked with.

MADELEINE SEWARD'S SECOND floor apartment showed a woman who was not particularly neat in her housekeeping, nor lavish in her wardrobe or furnishings. It was a one bedroom apartment with a sleep sofa in the living room. Two uncomfortable looking chairs flanked the sofa and a fifty-inch flat-panel television hung off one wall across from sliders that opened to a small balcony. There was a full size bed, hastily made, in the beige carpeted bedroom. Occupying the center of a six drawer dresser was a twenty piece collection of small ceramic mice in all manner of cute poses. Lined neatly across the back of the dresser was a row of paperback books, all of them romance novels, most by a very popular author who made a fortune writing them. The front covers of each depicted a virile, young, muscular, long-haired man hugging a beautiful woman to their hairless massive chest. In the kitchen, appliances were in the new fashion of stainless. Under one kitchen cabinet were two unopened cans of cat food and a half-full bag of kitty litter, but there was no litter box or cat in the apartment. Several photographs hung on the wall behind a small dining table showing Madeleine posing with people her age and laughing. Only one was a shot of Madeleine alone. In it, she was wearing a big floppy hat on her head and was smiling radiantly into the lens. Miller noted she had been an attractive brunette, with big brown eyes and a dazzling smile.

The calendar that hung beside the refrigerator had notes written on several dates. *Portsmouth at six* was neatly printed on the Saturday that she had disappeared. Several notes were written in cursive on dates that were coming up, including an optometrist appointment for the following Monday at four. Presumably, the optometrist would be there. Madeleine would not. She wouldn't be making her father's birthday party on May fourteenth, either.

After leaving the apartment, Miller and Day drove to the hospital where Madeleine Seward had worked as a nurse in the ER. They spoke with several of her co-workers, who told the detectives that Madeleine was a terrific nurse, caring and professional. She had worked there for four years and had never missed a scheduled shift. She was friendly with the staff, occasionally joined co-workers for drinks after work on Fridays and had dated two doctors that they knew of, none seriously. None had ever heard anyone address her as Mina.

After a quick lunch at a Wendy's, Miller and Day drove to a condominium complex in Portsmouth. They went there to speak with a woman named Ashley Price. Ashley was one of the women who had been with Madeleine on the night she disappeared. As the detectives stepped from their vehicle, a blue Corolla came into the parking area and pulled up in front of number 122. A woman of medium height, slim, with light brown curly hair, came out of the car and walked towards the door of the condo.

"Looks like we're right on time," said Miller.

As they began walking towards the building, the woman turned when she heard them coming. She waited.

"Mrs. Price?" asked Miller

"Yes."

"I'm Detective Miller. This is Detective Day. Thank you for seeing us."

"I'm sorry," said Ashley Price. "Did I keep you waiting long? Traffic was bad today. An accident, I think."

"No, no," said Day. "We've just arrived."

"I was afraid I was going to be late for my daughter. Her school bus should be here any minute."

As if being cued, a school bus pulled into the complex. The doors opened and fifteen kids under the age of ten bounded noisily off, back packs hunching all of them over. One tiny seven year old girl walked towards them. She looked at the two strangers who stood next to her mother.

"How was school, Honey?" asked Ashley, smiling at her daughter.

"Okay," answered the girl shyly, eyeing the two strangers.

"These are two police detectives, Christina. They need to ask Mommy some questions, okay?" said Ashley as she opened the front door. "Could you please go on up to your room while we talk and after we're done I'll get you a snack. Okay?"

The detectives were ushered into the kitchen while the little girl went up the stairs.

"Would you like a cup of tea?" asked Ashley Price. "I need a cup of tea."

Both detectives declined as they took seats at the kitchen table.

"Cute kid," said Miller. "How old is she?"

"Christina is seven," said Ashley as she put a cup of water in the microwave. "She's my everything."

"Is there a Mr. Price?" asked Day.

"Occasionally," replied Ashley, "when he's not out looking for himself." She frowned and shrugged, as if she had come to terms with the arrangement, even though she didn't understand it. "Someday he'll find himself. Hopefully, before his daughter gets much older."

The buzzer on the microwave went off and she carried the cup to the table, sat and looked at the two detectives.

"I still haven't fully processed what has happened," she said. "I probably won't until the funeral. I still can't believe it. I was shocked when Madeleine disappeared, and, of course, you worry that something bad had happened to her and that it won't be a good ending, but you never are ready for the finality of it, are you? I mean, it doesn't feel real. You know what I mean? Today, at work, I had to go to the ladies room because I knew I was about to break down crying. I'm a receptionist in a doctor's office. How would that have looked to our patients?"

"You were with her the night she disappeared," said Miller. "Did she seem agitated at all? Maybe worried about something? Apprehensive?"

"No. She was Maddie. She was in a good mood. We had dinner. A few drinks. Fun conversation. There were three guys at another table that hit on us, but we paid them no attention. Laughed it off."

"Did they seem bothered by that?" asked Day.

"No, I don't think so. It was nothing really. They left before us."

"You were good friends?" asked Day.

"Since grade school, yeah. She was a bridesmaid in my wedding party. We were tight. Of course marriage and a baby tends to slow down one's social life, but we tried to get together at least once a month. Usually, Patty would join us.

"Patty?"

"Patricia O'Malley. Another childhood friend of ours. She lives in Rye. She married well, so when she divorced it was a sweet settlement. She was always the smart one."

"Do you know if Madeleine was dating anyone, or had seen anyone new recently?" asked Miller.

"I don't think recently. A few months ago she had been dating a doctor, but she broke it off after a few dates. She said he was a boring snob. Before him, there was another doctor. Maybe two years now. But she broke that off, too."

"Any reason?" asked Day

Ashley shrugged. "She didn't really say, but I got the idea that he was a little off. Maybe a little too kinky for Maddie, and that would be saying a lot, because Maddie could be adventurous in bed if she had had a drink or two. She was game for most anything, or at least she said she was. Maddie liked to have fun."

"Did she mention his name?" asked Miller.

"Yeah. He didn't work in her hospitable. He was in one of the Manchester hospitals. She was introduced to him at a party. What was his name? Tom, I think it was. Yes, I remember now. It was really strange and I got a kick out of it. We laughed about it. Thomas. His name was Tom Thomas."

"Thomas Thomas?" asked Day.

Ashley Price giggled. "Yeah. Can you believe it? Who would do that to a kid? Probably born to a couple of drug crazed hippies. The poor guy. No wonder he's a little odd. I'd be too if I had to deal with that every day of my life."

"You ever hear anyone call Ms. Seward, Mina?" asked Miller.

Ashley shook her head. "Never. Why would they? She was Maddie. I saw the picture of her in the paper. They're saying she is the third victim of some psycho killer. Is that right?"

"We're investigating. Too early to make that call," lied Miller. "But there are similarities. Could you give us a phone number for Mrs. O'Malley? We'd like to talk with her."

"Sure," said Ashley, reaching for a pad of paper on the counter and writing down a phone number.

"I can't believe she's gone," she said as she slid the paper across the table. "Why would someone kill her? Why would they do that? When did the world get so crazy?"

PATRICIA O'MALLEY HAD been home, but she yielded nothing new beyond what Ashley Price had told them.

"We need to have access to the names of all missing persons within a hundred and fifty mile radius," said Erik Miller, once again behind the wheel and heading back to Manchester. "If someone is reported missing, we need to know their name. Then we Google it and see if something pops up that mentions a character in a movie. A horror or monster movie."

"I agree," said Day.

"Then we'll know which monster we're dealing with, if, in fact, your theory is correct, and maybe have a clue where the victim will be left."

Day nodded. "We may have to do variations of names. Maybe a mix of character and actress, or similar names, like Maryanne Darrow instead of Anne Darrow, but I agree it will help us."

"Any idea how many monsters there might be that this nut job could use?"

"Well, let's see," said Day. "We've already had King Kong, Mummy and Dracula. Of course there was *Frankenstein*, *The Wolf Man*, those are the obvious ones. There was *Godzilla*."

"Godzilla?"

"Didn't you watch television when you were a kid?" asked Day.

"I was out playing," replied Miller. "I spent the least amount of time that I could at home."

"Godzilla and all the spin-offs from him. Like *Mothra."*

Day looked out the side window. "You know," she said, "King Kong and Godzilla were actual monsters."

"What?"

"I don't mean they were real. I mean they were monsters. Big. Massive. Scary. Obvious monsters. Not men. Dracula was a man. Granted he was an evil man, but still a man. But, if we take the first line from the first rhyme, *This world is full of monsters who yearn,* then Dracula and the Mummy are being lumped in with real monsters. Which means that Frankenstein, The Wolf Man, and others, might also be regarded as monsters. Not evil men. Hollywood regarded them as monsters, also. So the term monster isn't just some colossal beast. For our killer, I think, it means those old movie monsters."

She turned from the window. "Oh, I just thought of one more. The Hunchback. I'll have to Google that."

Miller looked at her. "Try not to sound so excited. Even if we know the victim's names. Even if we have a clue as to how they might die, unless this guy screws up and leaves a clue that leads us to him, we are searching in the dark."

"What if we get proactive?" asked Day.

"Proactive?"

"We determine who the victim's might be in the future because of their names, and put them under surveillance."

"We can run that past Hendricks, but the manpower to do that isn't there. When we get back, let's find out which hospital Dr. Thomas Thomas is at and go see him tomorrow. Tonight, I'll be Googling some movie names. Seems I've got some catching up to do."

ELIZABETH, IS THAT you? I wonder as I watch a young woman walking along the cement walkway towards the parking lot. She walks straight to a white Nissan Sentra and opens the door. Lucky me, it is her. The time is five thirty-five P.M.. I follow her out of the lot, where she takes a right onto the busy street. I stay two cars behind her, just in case she might notice my vehicle, because I'll need to do this four or five times before I learn her schedule. Maybe more. Ten minutes later, she pulls into an Applebee's and parks at the end of the lot. She locks the car and hurries inside. I back into a space in the far corner of the lot and settle in, popping open a bag of chips. After two hours, it is obvious she wasn't there to have dinner. It's ten thirty before she walks through the doors and hurries to her car. There are only six cars still parked in the back of the lot. She seems oblivious to her surroundings, completely unaware of the danger that darkness and solitude present. Lost in her own little, inconsequential world. *You really need to be more aware of your surroundings, Lizzy. It'll be the death of you.*

She drives back the way she came, parking once again in the lot, much too far away from the lights that throw insufficient lighting in the area. But at this time of the evening there are few spaces available. She walks back along the cement walkway and enters her dorm.

"Good night, Elizabeth Clarke," I whisper out loud. "Sleep tight. Don't let the bed bugs bite. See you soon."

I'm only fifteen minutes from home. On the drive, I find I am quite excited. Elizabeth is perfect. The best one yet. I hope she gets into the spirit of what we will soon be doing. That will make our time together so much better. Another few weeks, Lizzy. *Stay safe my darling girl.*

6

The nurse at the desk paged Dr. Thomas, asking that he come to the reception desk. Miller and Day stood calmly waiting, while all around them orderly chaos reigned. As it is in all hospitals, there was constant movement among the staff, and to those uninitiated to such energy it appeared chaotic. But when witnessed over time one sees that there is order to it all, an almost choreographed magnificence.

A tall man in scrubs approached the desk. He had wide shoulders and a thick head of black hair. He was clean shaven. He walked with a confident stride, as if he owned the place.

"You paged me, Cynthia?"

"Yes, Doctor," replied the receptionist, and she nodded at the two detectives.

Doctor Thomas turned to them and Miller held out his identification.

"Doctor Thomas, I'm Detective Miller and this is Detective Day. We have a few questions we'd like to ask you."

Thomas, at six foot-five, knitted his brow and looked down at the two of them.

"What's this about?" he asked.

"Is there somewhere we could talk?" asked Miller.

Doctor Thomas looked first at Miller, and then shifted his

gaze to Day, where it lingered for a few seconds too long, then turned and said, "This way."

He brought them to an empty break room and indicated they could sit. He poured himself a cup of coffee. Both detectives remained standing.

"I'm on a tight schedule this morning," said Thomas, sipping at the coffee, his face registering that he wasn't pleased with its taste. Or maybe he wasn't pleased with their intrusion into his routine. "What can I help you with?"

"We'd like to ask you about Madeleine Seward, Doctor," said Miller. "I believe you knew her."

"Madeleine Seward," said Thomas, again knitting his brow, slowly stirring in another packet of sugar into the coffee. "We dated a few times. Maybe two or three years ago. Why? What's this about?" He was answering Miller, but looking at Kristen Day.

"Ms. Seward was murdered several days ago," said Miller.

"That's terrible," said Thomas, his eyes shifting to Miller.

"Anything you can tell us?" asked Miller.

"About her murder?" replied the doctor. "How would I know anything about that, Detective?"

"About Ms. Seward," said Miller. "People she knew at the time. Places she may have favored. Was your break-up amicable?"

"Break-up implies we had a commitment," said Thomas. "We dated a few times. That's all. It was no more than just a little fun." He looked at Day when he said that.

"So you haven't seen her recently? Maybe ran into her at a social get-together?"

"Like I said, it's been a few years since we last saw each other." He looked at his watch. "Unless there is something else, I really am quite busy. Wish I could have been more helpful."

"Did you read about the murder in the newspaper?" asked

Day. "See it on television?"

Once again, Thomas' eyes shifted to Kristen. Miller looked at her, also. He didn't appreciate being interrupted in his questioning. *What the hell?,* he thought to himself when he saw that Day had unbuttoned the top three buttons of her white blouse, exposing more than a hint of cleavage of full breasts.

"I'm afraid I only read the Times and the Journal. Born and raised in New York. Local stuff holds no appeal."

"Do you live in Manchester, Doctor?" asked Miller, taking control of the questioning again.

"Amherst. With my wife and baby daughter."

"You're a cardiologist, is that right, Doctor?" asked Miller.

"Yes. Graduated Harvard Medical. Been here five years. Why all the questions, Detective? What could you possibly expect me to tell you about a woman I haven't seen in over two years?"

"We're just contacting people who knew Ms. Seward. Touching all the bases. Hoping something comes up that leads us to the killer."

"Who told you about me?"

"A friend of hers," said Miller. "How long have you been married, Doctor?"

Doctor Thomas drank down the rest of his coffee and frowned at Miller. "Almost two years, Detective. I was single when I dated Madeleine. Any other questions? I have patients to see."

"Did you play sports in college, Doctor Thomas?" asked Kristen as she slid down into one of the plastic chairs.

Thomas smiled. "Two years. Football. Tight-end. Stopped playing when I decided to be a heart surgeon. Couldn't take the chance I'd damage these hands, Detective Day, once I realized what they were capable of. How about you? You look athletic. You play?"

"Basketball. All four years."

"Bench player?" Thomas asked with a smile.

"All Conference Freshman year."

"Not surprised."

"Doctor Thomas," said Kristen Day, "do you know a woman named Maryanne Darrow?"

He looked at her, his eyes taking a slow journey along the landscape. It was several seconds before he answered. "I don't think so, Detective Day. Should I?"

"She was murdered a few months ago," replied Day.

"Maryanne Darrow was the first victim," said Miller. "Madeleine Seward is the third. We believe they were killed by the same person."

"You have a serial killer on your hands, Detectives?" asked Thomas.

When Thomas received no response, he said, "I see. I wish I could help you, but I don't see how."

Miller reached into his suit coat pocket and took out a three by five color photograph of a smiling Maryanne Darrow.

"Does this woman look familiar, Doctor?" Miller asked, handing the photo to Thomas.

"Pretty girl," said Thomas. "No. I'd probably remember her. Who is she?"

"Maryanne Darrow. How about this woman?" Miller handed him a three by five of a smiling Helena Johnson.

Doctor Thomas looked at the picture for several seconds.

"She looks familiar, but I don't recall where I might have seen her," said Thomas.

"Maybe you dated her at one time?" asked Day. "She's about your age."

"I don't think so. What's her name?"

"Her name was Helena Johnson," replied Miller. "Victim number two."

"I have seen her. Talked with her. She's Bradley Johnson's daughter, isn't she? I did a by-pass on him. Must be ten years ago. Pity. She seemed nice. School teacher as I recall."

Thomas looked at his watch again. "I really have to get to my rounds, Detectives. Anything else?"

"No, not right now, Doctor," said Miller. "Thank you for your time."

Thomas laid his cup on the counter, nodded at Miller, smiled down at Day, then walked out of the room.

"What the hell was that all about?" asked Miller, as Day stood and buttoned up her blouse.

"The man has a very high opinion of himself," said Day. "Of his importance. He would have dismissed us after your third question. In his world, he's a heart surgeon. He saves lives. In his mind, he's one rung below Jesus Christ. But if you really push him on that, he'll confess he actually believes he's a rung above. He makes twenty times our pay. Who the hell are we to question him? I just figured it would be good to keep him interested."

"By unbuttoning your blouse? That's not professional."

"Screw professional. All I care about are results. Work Vice for four years and you'll see that always being professional won't get you anywhere. You do what you need to do to get the scum off the streets. Break some heads in a back alley and no one gives a shit. Just get the job done. Can't rough up the good doctor to make him talk, though. But there are other ways. I employed one.

"The man's a pig," Day continued with a smirk. "God's gift to women. I saw it right away. A man like that wouldn't want to disappoint me if he thought I was coming on to him. He'd stay and talk, which he did. Size up the situation. See if it looked promising."

"Even though he's married?"

Day shrugged.

"I doubt that matters to the good doctor," she said. "I think he sees a woman my size and he sees that as a challenge. But I'm guessing he likes women who are petite. He can be really physical with them. I'll bet his wife is under five-four."

"Madeleine was five-four," said Miller.

"Yes, she was. As was Maryanne Darrow. Helen was five-two."

"What do you think? Could he be our guy?" asked Miller as they walked out of the hospitable towards their car.

"I don't know," replied Day. "He knew Madeleine. Knew Helen. I'm willing to bet he hit the night scene often before his marriage. Probably still does. May have had a one-nighter with Maryanne a few years ago. We know she was a bit wild before her engagement. But that doesn't make him a murderer. What would be the reason? Maybe he had a dalliance with each of them and got worried the wife would find out? Divorce his ass. That might do it."

Miller stopped walking and looked at his partner. "A dalliance?"

Day shrugged.

"Johnson didn't date guys, remember?" said Miller as he began walking again.

"The man saved her father's life," said Day with another shrug. "He comes on to her. Maybe an exception was made. A sense of gratitude. She may have felt an obligation to allow the pig to feast at the trough once or twice."

Miller stopped at the car door and looked over at Day on the other side of the car.

"Feast at the trough? Jesus Christ. You worked Vice too long."

"Four years too long," agreed Day as she got into the car. "But I don't see the Doctor being the murderer just because I would like him to be."

"I agree. I don't think he's our guy. But someone tossed Madeleine Seward up onto that crypt," said Miller. "Someone big. Someone strong. We need to get a picture of the good doctor and show that around to friends of Maryanne."

Driving out of the hospital parking lot, Miller said, "I spent some time on the computer last night, checking out what we talked about yesterday. Checking names. Looking at the cast of movies made about monsters. I made some notes. Let's get some lunch and we'll go over them."

"Sure," said Kristen Day. "I did the same thing. We can compare notes. But no fast food today. Let's go to a diner. You really have to eat better, Miller. You're getting a little soft in the gut."

"Yeah, well, I don't have to unbutton my shirt just to get noticed."

"Usually, neither do I," said Day. "But a girl has to do what a girl has to do."

She looked out the window.

"Both my parents used to say, 'Use the gifts God gave you, Kristen'. Father meant use my basketball skills. My dear departed mother meant my more obvious gifts. And she wasn't subtle about it, either."

MILLER HAD WOLFED down his burger. He was nibbling at the fries on his plate as he glanced over the notes he had made the night before. Day was slowly working at a chicken Caesar Salad, commenting twice about how much she was enjoying the dressing.

"So, if you are correct about this being about monsters," said Miller, "then we have had King Kong, Mummy and Dracula. It is then reasonable to assume Frankenstein and the Wolf Man might be monsters that we should be looking at. I'm sure there are others. Freddie Kruger, Michael Myers, Jason Vorhees might be in that mix, too.

"What I've done is, I've listed the main names of the women

characters that are in the movie and the real names of the actresses who played them. Of course, there are multiple problems with all of that."

"Such as?" asked Day, already knowing what the answer would be.

"There are multiple sequels for each *Nightmare on Elm Street*, *Halloween* and *Friday the Thirteenth*. That is a lot of cast members and victims. There have been multiple Frankenstein movies over the years. Multiple Dracula and Wolf Man, too. Plus sons and daughters of. It is potentially a lot of names."

"Sure," said Day. "But we get all the names. Get the variations between character and actress and we check the missing persons as they come in."

"But that doesn't help us to keep them from being taken," said Miller.

"No, it doesn't. I'm afraid that would be impossible. It will literally be hundreds of names. But, once we have a name, and we know which movie the killer is using - and we will have a better understanding of the rhyme - we may be able to figure out where the body will be posed and we can be there when it happens."

"Same thing I was thinking," said Miller. "But we still end up with a dead woman."

"Yes, we do. But maybe it will be the last one. I don't see what else we can do."

Day pushed a piece of chicken around on her plate, coating it with the dressing. "You know, I don't think the murderer knows the victims."

Miller nodded. "Yeah. I was thinking about that last night. There is no way he would happen to know multiple women who would have the names he would need. I think it is incredibly co-incidental that our Doctor Thomas knows two of the victims."

"Maybe three," reminded Day.

"Extremely doubtful, but we'll look into that tomorrow. What I really don't understand is, why are the killings tied to monster movies? What could they possibly have that would trigger someone to such rage?"

Day looked at him and frowned.

"Yeah, I know," said Erik Miller, "I know. I'm trying to make sense of an insane mind. But really, what would be the trigger? Did he watch these scary movies as a kid? Did they frighten him so badly that he had nightmares? Did he worry they might be hiding in his closet? Under his bed? Scared him so badly that he now seeks his revenge? Maybe the killings are his attempt to purge the monster from his mind? But I don't think so. But maybe, just maybe, this is an attempt to show that he is even more powerful than the monsters that scared him, because when they killed they died at the end of the movie, but when he kills he survives. So far."

"I don't buy that," said Day. "Wanting to be considered the greatest monster of all time?"

"Then, maybe, the greatest serial killer of all time. Run the body count up, but do it as a game. Have a goal, and use his love of the movies to do it."

"I don't know. It's a crazy reason. But I've checked some of these serial killers and it may not be as crazy as some of the reasons for their murders. But scenes from movies?"

"Then why is he doing it?" Miller asked. "What motivates him to create scenes from the movies? Why can't he just kill any woman and pose her? Why do they have to have a name in common with the movie?"

"That's the first question we will ask when we catch the killer," said Kristen Day, finishing the last of the salad.

"If we catch the guy," said Miller. "You know, often these guys are never caught. Sometimes the killings just stop and the killer is never found. Maybe they die. Maybe they move away, leave the scene of the crimes. Go somewhere else. Go into hibernation. And then years later, in another state, similar deaths start stacking up."

Looking out the window of the diner, Miller said, "Do you have any idea how frustrating that will be if that happens? To have bodies and no answers. To have victims and no justice. I don't know if I could handle that."

"Don't do that, Erik. Don't think like that. You know how many times I was on a bus heading to an arena to play a team that I knew we couldn't beat? Lots of times. But if you allow a defeatist attitude to creep into your thoughts, then you are already beaten. We'll get the killer, Erik. Maybe not with the death of Madeleine, and maybe not with the next death either, but eventually we will. I just know it."

"Yeah? How do you know it?"

Kristen Day smiled. "Same way I knew to unbutton my blouse. Women's intuition."

Miller rolled his eyes and smiled. "Just warn me the next time you're going to do something like that, so I'm prepared."

"And deny me the fun of seeing that look on your face? Not a chance."

"What look?"

Detective Kristen Day smiled, picked up the check and slid from the booth. "Lunch is on me. And you know exactly what look I'm talking about. I notice everything, Detective Miller. Everything."

THE FOLLOWING DAY, Miller and Day showed a picture of Doctor Thomas Thomas that they had taken off the hospitals website to people they had talked to during the investigation of Maryanne Darrow's murder, either in person or by email. No one remembered ever seeing the good doctor. Neither Detective was surprised. They also attended the burial of Madeleine Seward at a cemetery in Portsmouth, standing a little away from the twenty people who stood by the grave listening to the prayers of the priest. Almost all of the mourners were women. Mrs. Seward sobbed softly. Mr. Seward stood stoically, the thousand yard stare the same as he had exhibited on the bench at the ME's. When the service was over, and only the parents remained at the grave site, Mrs. Seward approached the Detectives.

"Do you have news, Detective Miller?" she asked. "Have you found this monster?"

"Not yet, Mrs. Seward," Erik Miller said. "But we are looking into everything." He showed her the photograph of Doctor Thomas. "Did you ever meet this man?"

The grieving mother stared at the photo for several long seconds. "Do you think this could be the man who killed my baby?"

"No, Mrs. Seward, we do not," said Miller. "Do you recognize him?"

She shook her head. "No. I've never seen him before. Did he know Madeleine?"

"They dated briefly," said Miller. "Not long enough to become serious. But, like I said, we are checking everything."

Mrs. Seward nodded, then reached a slightly trembling hand out and touched Miller's arm.

"You will keep us informed?" she asked. "You won't forget us? Won't get too busy? Won't let my daughter's murder become something you work on occasionally when another murder takes your time?" She looked at Kristen, tears that she had been fighting finally escaping from red eyes. "You're all we have left. Please, don't forget us. Don't forget Madeleine."

MY SOON TO be partner works at Applebee's two nights during the week and on weekends. Two other nights during the week, Tuesday and Thursday, Elizabeth Clarke walks across campus from her dorm to the Performing Arts Center, where she rehearses with a group of her peers scenes from *The Taming of the Shrew.* She doesn't have the lead role, just part of the ensemble, but she is very energetic in her performance, every movement slightly exaggerated as she flits about from spot to designated spot. I watch her from a bench about fifty yards away from where the troupe `romps about in a small clearing next to the building. It appears the group will be performing the show as a Shakespeare in the Park, weather permitting. I have noticed posters around the campus that herald the play will be performed the third weekend in April, evening performances on Friday and Saturday with matinees on Saturday and Sunday. It's April in New England so it could be a pleasant, slightly chilly evening, or there could be a snow storm. Who knows. Certainly not the weathermen on television. They're a clueless bunch.

My Lizzy appears to be a delightful young woman. She smiles and laughs often while interacting with the rest of the cast. She is slightly overweight, just slightly, with short, chubby legs and she is a little top heavy, which I like, but certainly not obese. Perfect for my Elizabeth. Her hair is brown and shoulder length. She moves with the grace of an athlete. Probably played field hockey in high school. I really like this girl.

Sitting there, I decide to allow Lizzy to participate in the play, even though I'm getting anxious to get on with my own production - in my production lovely Elizabeth Clarke will have THE starring role - of the creation of Frankenstein, but I don't want to deny her the opportunity to perform in front of a live audience. I will attend the Saturday night performance and watch as she has the time of her young life. I can't wait. It will be unfortunate that the dear girl will miss the Sunday matinee, but some things can't be helped.

As I watch the rehearsal, I get the impression that she is flirting with a young man who often occupies similar spots with her as they move around the area in their acting. There is a lot of movement in this particular Shakespeare play, and a lot of interaction between the characters in a madcap way, but I think Lizzy has a thing for this guy. I can tell these things. Also, I can tell he doesn't seem to feel the same way about her. I think he has his eye on the lead, and I don't mean Kate. He seems to be quite taken with the tall, muscular guy playing Petruchio.

While eyeing Lizzy now from my hiding place in the dark of a clump of trees, I am enjoying watching her young body, with those chubby legs and delightfully bouncing breasts, bounding so energetically around the lit area, laughing and engaging with her playmates. I can't help but feel that I have finally found someone who will enjoy working with me. Who will get into the process. Who will realize, like all those who love the stage, that the show must go on. First, she will need to get over the shock of being selected, no doubt, but once that passes, I'm hoping she sees the opportunity I will be giving her. Top billing, my lovely Lizzy. I'm going to make you famous. I promise.

7

"You can't be serious," Police Chief Hendricks said as he leaned far back in his chair behind a cluttered desk. "You want to run that by me again."

"I know, Chief, I know," said Detective Erik Miller. "It's a lot to get your head around. But we both feel this is what's happening."

Hendricks looked at Detective Kristen Day. She nodded.

"Crime scenes based on old monster movies and victims with names from the women who starred in those movies?" said Hendricks. "That's what you're telling me? We have a psycho out there who's a movie fan. Jesus Christ."

Hendricks ran a hand back and forth over his balding head. "I've heard all kinds of crazy shit in my thirty-two years on the job, and this may not be the craziest, but it's certainly in the top three."

He took a long drink from his coffee cup and leveled a gaze at his two detectives.

He said, "Look, we have one victim strung up from a tree. Another left in the front court of a museum and a third left in a cemetery, okay? Bodies get left in places. That's how we find them. Maybe there is a reason they end up in a certain place, maybe it's just random. Could this just be random?"

"They're posed," stated Miller. "Posed a certain way. Now, if

Maryanne Darrow had been left in a cemetery, and if Helena Johnson had been strung up to a tree, and if Madeleine Seward had been left on a bench, then there would be holes in what we are suggesting, but that isn't the way this is going down. We have a serial, and he's using old movies to choose his victims."

"The rhymes that are sent point to the same conclusion," said Day.

Hendricks looked at her and frowned. "Okay. It's two weeks since Seward was found. What's next? What are you doing?"

"We've gone back to everyone who we talked with before. There is nothing that we can find that ties any of the three together," Said Miller.

"Except Doctor Thomas," interrupted Day.

"Yeah," said Miller. "Except the doctor."

"Who's this doctor?" asked Hendricks.

Miller told him about the conversation they had with Thomas and that he knew two of the victims.

"Knows two out of three?" said Hendricks. "We need to be paying him more attention."

"We won't forget him," Miller said, "but I don't think he's our guy."

"So, where do you go from here? What's next?"

"We are having all missing persons names being sent to us from a one hundred and fifty mile radius," Day said. "If our theory is correct, we should be able to go through those names and pick out the one who is the next victim to be found. If there is a next victim."

"Using the names of the actresses who were in these old movies?" asked Hendricks.

"It could be the actress, the name of the character, or maybe a combination of the two," said Miller.

"We believe we have the names of all the characters and actresses from the monster slash horror movies. We just have to apply them to the names of the missing," said Day.

"And," said Miller, "when we have that name, we will know she is not just missing but that she has been abducted. We can begin looking into where she may have been taken and we'll have a name before we have a body or a box with a clue in it. We may know the last thing she did, and the last place she was, a day or two after the abduction, not a week to ten days later. It may be easier to find someone who may have noticed something, even if they didn't know what it was they were seeing. Maybe a surveillance camera picked something up. Somebody remembered a car in the area. A large man who seemed out of place."

"Any idea how many movies we're talking about?" asked Hendricks.

"A lot," replied Day. "Dozens and dozens of them."

"Which means a lot of names," said Hendricks in frustration. "Dear, Jesus."

"When we do get a name," said Miller, "we will know which movie he is using and maybe we can figure out where he may try to pose the body. We will have more time to prepare than we have had after receiving the rhyme."

Hendricks shook his head, again in frustration. "Okay. In the meantime, what?"

"We keep digging into the past of the three victims. I believe it is an exercise in futility, only because the odds that the killer knew three women with the names that he would need for his psycho game would be a billion to one. Still, you never know."

"You need more manpower?" asked the Chief.

"Not until we get a name," said Miller.

"Keep me posted," said Chief Hendricks as he waved them from the office. "And I want to know as soon as a name pops up, if a name does pop up."

When the two detectives got to the door, Hendricks brought

them up short.

"Hey, good work you two. And keep an eye on that doctor. My money is on him."

THEY SAT AT Day's desk.

"I think we can eliminate Jason, Michael and Freddie," Miller said.

"Why do you say that?" asked Day.

"Just a feeling."

"You agree we're looking for someone who is probably in their late twenties or thirties, right? Don't you think those three killers would be the obvious choice for the killer to emulate? Isn't it a little strange that we're dealing with crime scenes from sixty to eighty years ago?"

"Again," said Miller, "I haven't watched horror movies. I just have a feeling, based on what we have so far, that we need to be looking at films from the thirties to the late fifties. Again, just a feeling. I know we can't eliminate the names we have from the newer films, but I am going to be surprised if one of those names pop up."

He crumpled up a piece of yellow lined paper and sent it on a long arc from the chair he was sitting in to a waste basket twelve feet away. It hit the top of the metal receptacle and bounced away. He looked at Day, who had watched the balled up papers' flight.

"You probably would have sunk it," he said.

"With my eyes closed," she replied. "I think we need to watch some movies."

"*Moneyball* is playing in Hooksett. Brad Pitt. Baseball. Get our mind off this mess. How about tonight?"

She looked at him. "What's wrong?"

He balled up another piece of paper and sent that one flying. This one found the middle of the basket.

"I'm frustrated," he said. "Frustrated and angry. This waiting around for the next victim, this feeling of being powerless, inadequate, is driving me nuts. I can't stand it."

"I know what you're saying," said Day.

"I work a homicide," said Miller, "I follow the clues. I piece it all together. They take me to the killer. Someone who knew the victim. Had a reason to kill. But this? This is random. There are no clues that lead to the killer and unless he fucks up there won't be. So I run around like a blind man in a room crowded with too much furniture, banging my knees and shins, bruising up my body, and all for nothing. And that really pisses me off."

He reached over and lifted another piece of paper and balled that up. But he didn't toss it, just kept squishing it in his right hand.

"You don't like feeling like you're not in control," stated Day.

"Of course not," said Miller in response. "Because I'm not. No one likes that feeling."

"I imagine it's difficult for a man to admit he isn't in control of a situation," said Kristen Day. "That powerless feeling. But most women have that all the time. We may bluster. We may display all the confidence in the world. But it is never, ever, lost on us, that we may only control a situation until it comes to push and shove, and then we are no longer in control."

She leaned forward in her chair.

"A man can walk down any street and never think about a situation arising that would put him in jeopardy. He can sit in a bar and quickly assess things he would need to say or do, or not say and do, that keep him in control of his well being. Women don't have that. Just walking to her car can put a woman in a situation she can't control. If Madeleine Seward were still alive, she would tell you the same thing."

Miller stared at her for several seconds, then placed the balled up paper on her desk.

"But not you," he said.

She raised her eyebrows. "I'm not the average woman. But that doesn't mean there haven't been times when I thought things may go south and I would be over matched."

"You know what's really worrying me?" he asked rhetorically, not wanting to pursue what his partner had just shared. "The damn broom. He thought to bring a broom with him so he could sweep the dirt from the top of the crypt. That worries me. This guy isn't going to make a mistake. Without a mistake, how do we catch him?"

In one quick motion, Miller snatched the ball of paper and sent it arcing across the space toward the basket. It fell soundlessly into the receptacle.

"You mentioned movies?" he said as he pumped a fist in the air several times.

Day shook her head and smiled. "I think we should rent the monster movies and watch them. Maybe we catch something that will help."

"Good idea."

"They are going to be in black and white if we watch the old ones. Can you handle that?"

Miller frowned. "I have an old TV. It shows everything in black and white."

Day shook her head again. "Some of them have newer versions. They are in color. Maybe we watch both. There is a video store on my way home. I'll go in tonight and see what they have. How does that sound?"

"Sure. You want to watch them together?"

"No. I think it's better if we watch them by ourselves. I'll probably put a movie on at midnight, while I'm in bed, curled up with a bowl of popcorn and a Sprite."

Miller stood. "I'm going to speak with Mr. and Mrs. Johnson about our good Doctor Thomas. Want to come?"

"No," said Day with a shake of her head. "I'll work the missing persons list and expand it a bit further. We'll talk after lunch."

Several hours later, Miller entered the Detective Room and saw Day sitting at her desk, just as she had been when he had left.

"Anything?" he asked.

She shook her head.

"Isn't it strange," she said, looking up at him, "that it is a good thing that none of the names of the missing are names that mean anything to us, yet we need one of those names to mean something so we can move on, even if it means they may die."

"It's sick," said Miller as he sat next to her desk. "The bastard is playing a sick game and he's dragged us into it."

"Anything new from the Johnson's?"

"No. Doctor Thomas saved his life. As far as they are concerned, Thomas is a god."

Day looked up from a report she was reading and saw Erik Miller staring at her.

"What?" she asked.

"Has he called you?"

"Who?"

"You know who?"

"Thomas Thomas?"

Miller raised his eyebrows.

"I would have told you if he had," she said.

"But he will?"

"I don't know," she said and looked back at the report. "Maybe." She looked back up. "You'll be the first one to know."

"You know what he said to me?"

"Who? Doctor Thomas?"

"No. Johnson."

Day gave a slight shake of her head.

"Please, don't forget my Princess. You have another victim,

Detective Miller. Maybe you'll have more. But please don't forget Helena. I beg you. Same thing Mrs. Seward said to us. Same thing Maryanne Darrow's fiance says in his weekly calls. Don't forget. Like I ever will."

There was nothing she could say to that.

"Can we talk about what I've been doing since you were gone?" is what she did say.

"Let me get a coffee first."

When Miller returned to her desk, Day placed several sheets of yellow lined paper in front of him that showed a list of names. And one that showed a list of movies.

"I called the video store," she said as he sat. "By the way, not sure if you have noticed, but video stores are going out of business. There aren't many left. Remember when it seemed every corner had one? Anyway, I ran down a bunch of titles to the guy who answered the phone to see what they carried, and they had quite a few. It's only two o'clock now. I thought I'd run over there and rent several and we can start watching them tonight. You okay with that?"

"Sure. You go ahead. There is someone I've been trying to track down since the Darrow murder. A woman I talked with after Maryanne Darrow was murdered told me that Maryanne was very friendly with someone named Megan Roache. Said they were best buds down in Lawrence and may have come up here together a few years ago. We do know that for a while, Maryanne was living on the streets. Presumably, this Megan woman was with her at the time. It looks like, for a time, they both may have been staying at a shelter over on Pine Street, but that was four or five years ago so, obviously, it's all sketchy now. Maybe, Megan did what Maryanne was able to do, and that was to get off the streets. But I want to check out a few more shelters. I have spoken with people Maryanne knew in Lawrence and there is more to find there, too. There are pieces missing and

I'm hoping this Megan can fill in the missing parts."

They walked out together and returned almost at the same time, Detective Kristen Day carrying a white plastic bag that held six DVD's and one VHS tape.

"Any luck finding your girl?" she asked as she sat down beside Miller's desk.

"No," he answered. "She's back on the street, though. No one at the shelters knows where she is. She's done this before. She'd be gone for months at a time, then pop back up. But at least we know she is still a homeless and in the area. What's in the bag?"

Day pulled the seven movies out and laid them on the desk.

"Wasn't sure if you have a DVD player or not, so I grabbed a VHS movie, too."

"I don't live in a cave, Detective Day. I have a microwave and internet service. And a full service bathroom actually in my apartment."

Ignoring his sarcasm, she said, "Well, I have both, so I can watch the tape. Pick out the ones you want."

Miller was looking them over as Detective Mark Allen passed by on his way out.

"You kids having a movie night?" he asked. "Planning a sleep-over? Big bowl of popcorn and a few beers? Must be nice to have nothing to do while waiting for the next body to show up."

"Up yours," said Miller as Allen kept walking.

At the door, Allen gave a loud laugh and a middle finger salute as he pushed through. Neither Miller or Day noticed.

"I'll take these three," said Miller as he selected *The Wolf Man* with Lon Chaney, *Frankenstein* with Boris Karloff, and *The Hunchback of Notre Dame* with Charles Laughton, leaving Day to watch *Halloween, Nightmare on Elm Street* and the first *Friday the 13th.*

He looked at Day. "You know how crazy this is?"

"You have a better idea?"

"Yeah. I need a drink. Care to join me?"

"I'll take a rain check," said Day. "Get some rest."

She put her movies in the bag and left for the day.

DETECTIVE ERIK MILLER stayed at his desk until a little past five, looking over the names of those who had been reported missing in the last two weeks. It was a diverse group. Two married women in their thirties who probably had decided they had had enough of the life they had been living and were off to find something different. Two old men, both suffering from the early stages of dementia. Three teenage boys, two of whom had a history of leaving their homes for weeks at a time. Three teenage girls, all missing for the first time, all from cities in western Massachusetts, all from broken homes, hopefully all to return back home when they realized the streets were nowhere to be. Four more women over eighteen and younger than twenty-two, all with histories of drug abuse, all probably being reported missing by their families for the last time. Whatever life path they had now decided on, it was a road that led them to people who would not contact the police were they to go missing again. None of the names on the list of the missing matched any name that interested Miller. He glanced at the clock on the wall, stood, lifted his suit coat off the back of the chair and headed for the door.

When he entered the bar he took a quick look around. There were only a dozen people in the place, most sitting at the bar watching a taped MMA fight on two of the flat panels on the wall. Two men, both police officers that Miller knew, were playing pool on one of the two tables on the side. They both looked up when he entered and nodded a hello. Miller nodded back. Looking left, Miller saw Matt Blanchette sitting alone at a table playing a game of solitaire. Miller looked back towards the bar, caught the young bartenders eye and held up two fingers, then went and sat down across from Blanchette.

"You have time for a game?" asked Miller.

"Time for one," replied Blanchette as he began scooping up the rows.

Eve, the young, black, busty, blonde bartender, put two beers on the table.

"How's it goin' today, Erik?" she asked, her brow furrowed. "You're lookin' a little tired. Don't he look tired, Matt?"

"How old are you, Eve?" asked Miller.

"Why you always askin' me that?" said Eve, a hand going to her hip. "You know how old I am."

"Remind me again."

"I'm twenty-two, Erik. Why you keep askin' me?"

"And how old were you when I busted you?"

"Why you bringin' that up for?"

"How old?"

"Jesus Christ, Erik."

"How old?"

"Fifteen. You know I was fifteen."

"Fifteen," said Miller, looking at Blanchette who was smiling and shaking his head. "I was twice as old as you at the time and you were begging me not to bring you in. Not to tell your parents. Not to send you to Juvenile Court. 'It's just a little weed, Officer Miller, sir,' you said. 'I'm not hurting no one, Officer Miller, sir,' you kept saying. Officer Miller, sir, this and Officer Miller, sir, that. When, in our relationship, did I go from being Officer Miller, sir, to Erik? And this man," Miller said, pointing at Blanchette, "is a highly decorated veteran in the Manchester Police Department and old enough to be your father. This is Detective Blanchette. Not Matt."

Eve stared down at him, not breaking eye contact, and then took another step closer to his seat. Then, with both hands, she reached down for his neck and loosened his tie and undid the top button of his shirt. She gently brushed his stubbly chin as she lifted her hands away. She smiled tenderly at him.

"You aren't getting enough sleep, Erik," she said, then narrowed her eyes. "You'll get this guy. You know you'll get this guy."

Miller gave her a half smile. "What do you know? You're just a bratty kid."

"I know my Erik," said Eve. "He always gets his man."

As she turned, Miller said, "Eve."

Turning back, Miller was holding up the beer bottle.

"Another one of these when Matt leaves," Miller said.

"Yes, sir, Detective Miller, sir," said Eve and added a smart salute before going back behind the bar.

"She's a hoot," said Blanchette.

"A hoot?"

"That's what us old timers say about people who make us smile."

"Old timers? You're only ten years older than me."

Blanchette did a quick scan of Miller's face as he shuffled the cards.

"Eve's right. You do look tired. You got yourself a bad one with this serial. Don't let it get to you."

Miller looked at him.

"I know, easier said than done," said Blanchette. "I've had a few that have kept me up at night, but never had a serial. Don't envy you."

"Then deal the cards so I can think of something else for a half hour," said Miller.

"How come only one game?" asked Miller as six cards were dealt to him.

"Carol is trying a new recipe tonight," said Blanchette. "Meatloaf. Without the meat."

"Is that possible?"

"Apparently it is now. She thinks I need to eat healthier. She thinks we should go vegan."

"Vegan?"

"Yeah. And you think you have problems."

Miller selected two cards from his hand and slid them across the table for half of the dealer's crib.

"Rumor has it you're thinking of retiring," said Miller.

"I'm only forty-seven," said Blanchette as he played an ace for thirty-one for two. "But, yeah. I'm thinking about it. Twenty-five years on the force. There's a security job I can have with a firm my nephew works for. Easy work. I'm seriously considering. Carol is pestering me every day to take it. I'll decide soon."

They played the hand out, Blanchette pegging for twenty-four between his hand and the crib, Miller having only seven. As Miller dealt the next hand, Blanchette asked, "How's it going with Day?"

Miller shrugged. "Not bad. Only been a few weeks. But she's sharp."

"But?" said Blanchette.

"Well, you know," said Miller. "You've worked alone and you've worked with a partner. Hell, you worked with me my first couple of months in the bullpen. It's different working with someone, that's all."

"Yes, it is," said Blanchette. "But I never had to work with a woman."

"Yeah, it's different. I'll give you that. But not as bad as I thought it might be. She's an asset. And she wants to learn. She wants the experience."

"She's good looking," said Blanchette, pegging another go.

Miller looked up from his cards and frowned.

"And I hear she's single."

Again Miller frowned. "And she's my partner. Just another cop. And I'm going to keep it that way." Miller smiled. "That way I don't have to worry about somebody cooking me a meatless meatloaf."

Detective Matt Blanchette won the cribbage game, Miller getting sixteen on his final hand to keep from being skunked. As Blanchette left the bar, Eve brought another bottle of beer to the table.

"He won again," she said. It wasn't a question.

"How have you got time to tend bar and watch our game?"

"Matt always wins," she said with a wicked smile. "I don't have to watch."

"I should have sent you to Juvie seven years ago."

"No one said you had to put in a good word for me when I applied for this job last year, Erik. You have no one to blame but yourself for me being here. Now you have to see me when you come in. Lucky you."

He looked up at her. Her dark eyes were clear. There was a healthy glow to her face. She had shed a few pounds of baby fat over the past year. Legs and arms were toning up from the work. She had the perfect disposition for the job.

"You sign up for fall classes?"

"Two nights a week up in Concord."

"Transportation going to be a problem?"

"Got it covered."

"Everything else good?" he asked

"Never better."

"No problems?"

"Not since you took care of the last one?"

Early on, a customer had been coming on to her a little too hard, despite her constant no's. Erik had found out and had a serious talk with the guy. Explained that no meant no. After their talk, the young man understood things better.

"You'll let me know if there is."

"My guardian angel," she said with a smile.

"Just a cop doing his job."

"Nah," she said. "You can tell yourself that if you want, but we're friends. Best one I have."

She smiled down at him. "By the way, my name now is Eve L."

"Sure, if that's what you want," said Miller. "But I'm fairly certain most companies might think twice before hiring someone who wants to be called Evil. Unless you're selling motorcycles."

"Not Evil, Erik. Eve L," she said, separately pronouncing each syllable.

"Eve L," he said mimicking her. "What the hell is that?"

"My Rapper name," she replied. "Catchy, don't you think?"

"Why do you need a Rapper name?"

"I started doing some Rapping on karaoke nights in some of the clubs. People say I got talent."

Miller shook his head. "Yeah, well, don't give up the day job, and get that diploma just in case the music business doesn't work out."

She smiled again. "You have to come and see me perform some night. I want you to come."

He frowned up at her. "Sure. Love to. I'm a big fan of Rap. Everyone knows that."

She graced him with a toothy smile that beamed and a quick wink of an eye before leaving him alone.

He nursed the beer and gave his attention to a soccer game that was on one of the flat panels. One of the cops who had been playing pool walked out of the bar, the other cop came over to Miller.

"Mind if I sit?"

"Haven't seen you in a while, Cam," said Miller as he used his foot to push a chair away from the table.

"Nights for the last three months," said Cam Boyce.

"That's right," said Miller with a nod. "You were working that

Asian thing. That was good work. You boys in Vice did a hell of a job. How many women was it?"

"Fourteen," said Boyce, "that we know of. Maybe more. Probably more. We're still working it, still gathering shit. Working with Lawrence Vice. A dozen arrests so far and probably another dozen before we're through, although the mastermind got away. Back to Vietnam before we could pull him in."

Cam Boyce took a sip from the beer bottle he had carried over. "Speaking of guys getting away, you have yourself a brutal one."

Miller nodded. He had come into the bar to get away from his case for a few hours, but others weren't going to let that happen.

"You have anything?"

"Nothing," said Miller.

Boyce nodded and looked away. He could tell by the tone of the word that Erik Miller did not want to discuss it.

Boyce looked back at the Detective and smiled. "Word is you're working with Kristen Day."

"She's working with me," said Miller, wishing he could drink his beer in peace and watch the game.

"I worked with her a couple of times while she was with us," said Boyce, noticing that Miller's eyes had strayed back to the television. "You need to watch yourself."

Miller's eyes snapped from the television to the Vice cop. "What does that mean?"

Boyce held up one hand in front of him. "I'm just saying. Kristen has a bit of a temper. It's not there all the time, but I've seen her go off. She doesn't take any shit from the scumbags on the street. There were a couple of times when we were making a bust and the scumbags were either drunk or high on something, and they gave us a rash of shit. Cool heads could have easily diffused the situation. Would have let the bums have their say, let it all play out, and then come along with no trouble. But

Kristen wasn't having any of that. They got loud, she got louder. They huffed and puffed and she got physical. There were just times when she wasn't going to put up with any shit. All of a sudden, I find myself in a fight and calling for back-up. Things can get hairy pretty quick dealing with the scum I deal with. Well, you know. You walked the beat enough years."

"How did she handle herself when it got physical?" asked Miller.

"The girl can handle herself," said Boyce. "She knows that Oriental shit. I've seen her beat the crap out of guys bigger than her. I'm just saying, there wasn't any need for it to come to that. I talked to her about it, but she just waved me off. Said we were the good guys and we didn't have to take no crap from any whore or pimp."

Boyce emptied his bottle and placed it on the table.

"There was this guy, a couple years back, he's doing ten to fifteen in Concord now, a real dirtbag, who ran some girls. Fourteen or sixty, he didn't care. He housed them up here, over on Concord Street, but he would have them do the business in a motel down in Salem. He'd drive them down and wait and then drive them back. He was a sadistic son-of-a-bitch. If the girls gave him any grief, he'd burn them with a cigarette. Back of the arm, back of the leg. They try to escape the life, they'd get a brutal beating.

"So, a couple of years ago we bust in on him at the house where he kept the girls. Daytime. Girls are sleeping. Most zonked out on one thing or another. The guy is sitting there with one of his homies playing a video game. We got him, he knows it, he's giving no resistance. We cuff him and his buddy. Kristen stays in the living room while me and two other cops check the bedrooms. All of a sudden there's a commotion in the living room. I run out there and she's beating the shit out of the guy. She said he tried to kick her."

Boyce shrugged. "Not just the guys, either. One little honey gave us a lot of shit in an area near the stadium. She was servicing some guy beside a dumpster. The guy runs away when he spots us coming, but she's so zonked she falls flat on her face when she tried running. We stand her up and she goes on a tirade. Day takes about ten seconds of that and slaps her around until the bitch finally figures out she better shut-up. Like I say, your girl can have a short fuse."

Boyce lifted the bottle, realized that it was empty and put it back down.

"I also saw her show remarkable tenderness to some of the girls at times. Especially the younger ones. She'd take them off to the side and sit with them, you know, heads bent and talking low so none of us guys could hear. She'd talk, the girls would nod. Sometimes, the younger ones might be crying. It was like she was their mother, you know. Then she'd let the girl walk away and Kristen would give me a look that said, 'let her go. She's going to be alright.'" Boyce shrugged. "Mike Tyson one day, Mother Teresa the next. Go figure. Probably had to do with her time of the month, know what I mean?"

Boyce stood. "Gotta run. Listen, good luck with your case. I hope you catch the bastard."

Miller drained his beer after Boyce left, put a twenty on the table, nodded at Eve and walked into a chilly dusk. There was a constant flow of traffic on Union Street, but very little pedestrian activity.

He knew his new partner had an edge to her. He knew about her being called on the carpet for what others deemed unnecessary force. So far, he had seen no sign of it. Homicide was not like Vice. Homicide was a lot of asking questions. Conversations. More cerebral than Vice. Less dangerous. But there were times when things could get hairy.

'Screw that,' thought Miller, thinking about what Cam Boyce

had said. 'We're not out here hosting Tupperware parties. It's a violent world, getting more violent every year. And more crazy every year. Good to know I have a partner who isn't going to freeze up if things get tight. When we catch this son-of-a-bitch, I just might turn my head if Kristen decides she wants to vent a little. Serve the bastard right. I wouldn't mind a shot at him myself.'

THERE HE IS now, the great man himself, finally exiting the bar. He was in there for an hour and forty-five minutes. I know because I've been sitting out here, waiting in my car, since he went in. I wonder, like me, did he sit alone? Or was he with someone? A friend, perhaps? A colleague? Did he have a conversation with someone, or just sit by himself and brood over his beer? Maybe he played a game of pool. Watched some game or other on the flat-screens? I'd like to think he sat by himself and only thought about me and the things I'm trying to accomplish, all the while spinning that beer bottle round and round in frustration. I'm thinking the beer probably didn't taste all that good either. Poor Detective Miller.

I can imagine him, sitting alone, oblivious to everything around him, so lost is he in the sacrifice of three women. He's lost. Can't piece it all together. Can't make rhyme or reason for it. He must feel like he's out in the middle of a huge lake in a row boat without oars. He can't even see the land. Night time is coming, and he knows it, and he is powerless to stop it. Yes, he is powerless. How does that feel, Detective Erik Miller? It's not a pleasant thought, is it, Detective, this feeling of weakness? Poor baby.

I watch as Miller takes a slow look around the street before getting into his car. It's a cop thing, looking around, scoping out the territory, noticing if something is not quite right. You just never know when a police officer might be needed, the super hero coming to the rescue. Especially if you're the decorated one. The Golden Boy. Yeah, it would be good to have one of them around if you find yourself in trouble. Wouldn't it?

I think I'll drop him a note soon. Ask him how things are going. Let him know I'm thinking about him and that it's almost time for me to be choosing another helper. I'll do it before I enlist Miss Elizabeth Clark into service. That doesn't give me a lot of time, though. The show is this coming weekend, so, yeah, there is not a lot of time.

In this note, I could advise him to go back to the beginning. Back to Maryanne Darrow, my first accomplice. Dig deeper, Miller. Dig deeper. Like all great quests, something happens that triggers the journey and sets the path. Maryanne was my trigger. What has happened since, and what will continue to happen, well that is the stuff that legends are made of.

My hand, resting lightly on the steering wheel, is trembling slightly. Just the slightest quiver. This always happens when I have decided it is time to secure my next accomplice. The anticipation builds. By Saturday night I will be razor sharp, all five senses so keen it will feel almost sexual. In truth, even better. What a rush! God, I can't wait.

I imagine Miller is driving home now. I'm going to drive home, too. I have to get the cellar ready for my next guest. Tomorrow, I'll do some food shopping. Peanut butter, grape jelly, Wonder bread, eight ounce cartoons of milk, Oreo's. Bag of chips. Not a big shopping. Just the important things.

The delicious Ms. Clark and I will be spending some time together, so there must be plenty of nourishment to keep us going. There is a book to read, a movie to watch and a model to build. A lot of work to accomplish, and only six days to do it all. I'm on a tight schedule.

But we won't rush. We'll take our time. Make sure we cover everything and understand everything before we begin to build. I think, of all the projects, this one is the most important. This is the one that started it all. This is the one tortured soul who was the most misunderstood. What happened to him was terrible. I remember, as a child, grieving for him when my grandfather read me his story. I remember crying, tears running uncontrollably from my eyes, while watching his agony at the end of the movie in that horrific fire. I still cry every time I watch it, the fire now holding even more meaning to me because of what happened on that horrible day.

I wonder, will Lizzy see what I see when we view the old black and white film? Will she understand his misery? Will she pity the poor brute, as I do? Perhaps. As an actress, she may understand his emotions better than others would. I'm hoping she will. I have great hopes for my darling Lizzy. My greatest hope is she doesn't disappoint. It will be better for her if she doesn't disappoint me with her effort. I'm really getting tired of being disappointed.

8

Detective Kristen Day was sitting at her desk when Miller entered the bullpen on Friday morning. She looked up, lifted a hand slightly as a 'good morning' greeting and then went back to what she was reading. Miller sat at his desk and lifted the lid off of the coffee cup he had carried in with him, then picked up a folder that was lying there and opened it, making like he was reading the contents, but he was not. His mind was on the folded piece of paper that was in his suit coat pocket, a little note left for him sometime the evening before. He found it that morning under the windshield wiper of his car, in the parking area of the apartment complex off of Wellington Road where he has lived since his divorce. It was typewritten and unsigned, but he knew who had left it there. Another short, taunting correspondence from a psychotic killer who was making it all very personal.

There would be no fingerprints on the white paper, Miller knew, so no need to dust it. There were no smudged letters or exotic bond weight that would eventually lead to the identity of the sender, like the bullshit that crime novels like to cleverly enter into their story. There had been no barking dog that had awakened Miller during the evening, sending him to his bedroom window where he thought he noticed a dark, hulking figure moving quickly through the lot. None of that. Just a neatly folded eight and a half by eleven inch sheet of unlined paper with eighteen lines of neat print and not one word misspelled.

"How was your night?" asked Detective Kristen Day as she eased her tall body onto the chair beside Miller's desk, crossing long legs at the ankles. She was dressed in her standard pants suit that gave no hint of the body beneath it. This particular one was black and covered a lavender blouse. Her shoulder length brown hair was pinned back behind ears that had a simple diamond stud in each lobe. Fingernails that were usually polished bright red were now dull black. She wore no rings, an inexpensive watch on her left wrist.

"Nothing out of the ordinary," replied Miller, making no mention of the taunting note.

"Did you get a chance to watch a movie?" asked Day.

Miller nodded. "The Hunchback. It was good. Laughton was terrific. I had never seen him as a young man. He was really quite good. Athletic. What about you?"

"*Nightmare on Elm Street,*" said Day. "I've never watched the slasher movies and I wasn't particularly impressed. I do think now that I agree with you. I don't think the killer will mimic anything from these newer movies. These guys aren't monsters. They're psychos. I'll watch *Halloween* tonight, but I think it will be a waste of time."

She turned in the chair to face him better. "If we can eliminate those movies, then we can eliminate a lot of names. Most of our list becomes unnecessary. That would help. I checked the missing list again this morning. Nothing yet."

Mark Allen came through the doors, grinned at them as he passed by on his way to his desk, but made no comment. They ignored him.

"It's almost a month since Madeleine Seward," said Day. "What do you think?"

"About what?"

"I don't know. I'm getting this feeling that something is going to happen soon. I mean, real soon. It hit me this morning on the ride in. This feeling just came over me, you know."

Erik Miller stared at her for several seconds, then reached into the inner pocket of his suit coat and pulled out the taunting note, handing it to her.

She looked at the paper for a second then took it from him.

"What's this?" she asked.

"Left for me on my windshield," Miller said. "Go on. Read it."

Unfolding the paper she read the first line, looked up at him and then continued reading.

How's it hanging, Erik? I hope you don't mind me calling you Erik? I feel like I know you now. Frankly, Erik, I would have thought that by now a decorated Detective like yourself would know me a little better, too. I'm not sure that you do. By the bye and bye, I watched you at work in the cemetery. Cute little booties on your feet, looking for any tiny bit of evidence that could help in your investigation. Didn't find anything, did you? Maybe next time. Speaking of next time, Erik, get ready. I've selected my next partner. She'll be with me soon. I get goose bumps just thinking about it. You too? You seem a little lost, Detective Erik, so let me help you if I can. You know how great journeys begin with a single incident? Columbus. Lewis and Clark. Phileas Fogg. My journey is no different. All you need to do to stop me from completing my journey, is to figure out what led me to take the first step. Go back to the beginning. In other words, Detective Miller, be a better detective and detect. Try to live up to your reputation. Several women are depending on you being better. Try not to let them down. We'll talk soon.

Day refolded the paper and handed it back to her partner. Miller put it in the middle drawer of the desk.

"On your car?"

Miller nodded. "If he saw me at the cemetery, then he saw you, too. Be aware of everything. There's nothing that says he won't target us."

"Did we have photos taken of the people who were watching us from the road?" asked Day. "I don't remember if Jack took any."

"He didn't. I saw the report on the news. If they took shots of the people, they didn't end up on the six o'clock news. I think I need to call WMUR and ask." Miller shook his head. "He was there watching us. Should have thought of that. These guys, these serial killers, they often show up at the scene to watch. They get off on it. Sons-of-bitches."

Miller drank from the cup, made a face and threw the cup into a waste basket.

"From now on, we get pictures of the crowd," he said, his voice hard. "Multiple shots. While we're going over the scene, I'll have an undercover cop walking around, looking for a big guy, someone showing just a little too much interest. He wants to play games, I'll play fucking games."

Day looked at him, said nothing, letting him vent. She could see the anger in his eyes. Understood it. When she worked Vice, she often ran into guys who were smug, played it cool, knew they'd be back on the street before lunch time if she arrested them. She wanted nothing more than to wipe that smug look off of their face. To do whatever it took to wipe it off. Taunting was a sure-fire way to piss a cop off.

Frowning, Erik Miller looked over at his partner. "He's going to take another woman soon. Maybe already has. Any ideas?"

Kristen shook her head. "Powerless until it happens," she said. "But we'll be ready when it happens, Erik. We'll be on it fast and hard. We'll have a fighting chance."

"You really believe that? I don't know. We need a break and he needs to make a mistake. The odds on either one happening are long. Very long."

He took a deep breath. "Let me have that list of names we have that we got from the old movies."

"What are you going to do?"

"I'm going to put each name into the computer and see if anyone in a seventy-five mile radius pops up with the same name."

"I've done that," said Day. "You will have a boat load of names."

"You've done it?"

"Sure. Multiple hits on each name and hundreds when they are all added together. What did you think, Erik? Did you think there might be twenty names and we'd just call those women and tell them that they should use extra caution right now because they may be a target for a serial killer? It's hundreds and we can't go around spreading panic like that, especially on what right now is simply a theory."

"The note suggests that the first killing was not just a random thing," said Miller leaning forward to rest elbows on the desk. "That the killing of Maryanne Darrow was not done because of her name, but because the killer knew her. And then, because of her name, the killer, in his pathetic, psychotic brain, suddenly decides, 'wouldn't it be fun to slay other women and have fun posing them in scenes from old movies, like I did with Maryanne? And to really add further brilliance to the spree, let's see if names can be similar. Wow, what fun!' He's riding me for something I missed in that first killing. Something in the past of Maryanne Darrow. Something that she did that set this psycho off."

Reaching into the bottom drawer, Miller took out a thick folder and placed it on the desk. "You and I are going to go over everything in here. I want to talk with everyone I spoke with before. I want more names. I want to know everything about Maryanne from the time she was born until the day she died.

Somewhere in her past is our killer. He's there. We have to find him."

He leaned back in the chair. "I need to find Megan Roache."

"Did the fiance know Megan?"

"No. But he knew nothing about Maryanne before meeting her two years ago. He said anytime he asked her about her life before meeting him, she was vague. Always said she just wanted to forget the past and concentrate on the future."

"And no photo of Megan?" asked Day.

"No. The description I got was white, about five-two. Thin. Very thin. Mousy brown hair. Tattoo on her left arm. Looked like it may have been a penguin. Very active eyes, like she was unable to focus on anything. The eyes of a woman who has spent too many nights on the streets, was how they were described to me. In other words, Megan looks like a hundred other homeless women out there."

Miller looked at Day and said, "But I don't have to tell you about that look. How often did you seen it, four years in Vice? You ever run across someone who looks like Megan?"

"Every night," replied Kristen Day. "They all look like Megan Roache, or did at one time. The thing about the Megan Roache's of the world, they're on the street one night and then staying on someone's couch the next night and hitching a ride to Haverhill the night after that because they heard so and so had made a score and was having a party. She could be up in Portland right now sleeping in a tent, or lying on the bottom of the Merrimack and sleeping for eternity."

"Speaking of Vice," said Miller, "not to change the subject, but I ran into an old partner of yours. Cam Boyce."

Day smiled. "Cam was all right. A bit of a goody-two-shoes, but he was okay. Knew his way around the streets. How's he doing?"

"He just got off that Asian thing."

"Yeah, I saw that. That was good work. You make a bust like that, it feels good."

"You miss it?"

Day shook her head. "Nah. You work Vice, you feel like you need to shower three times a day. Besides, we have a serial on our hands. How many Manchester cops have been able to say that over the years?"

"Mr. HOULE, THIS is Detective Miller."

Miller, sitting at his desk, leaned his chair as far back as it would go, looked into the Chief's office, and saw Mark Allen sitting in front of the Chief's desk looking like he wished he were somewhere else. Chief Hendricks was being just a little bit animated, which was like saying Old Faithful was just a little bit of a burp every ninety minutes or so.

"Yes, Detective," said Arthur Houle. "Is there news? Have you caught Maryanne's killer? Please tell me you did."

"I'm afraid not. But I do need your help."

"Of course. How?"

"I need to know more about Maryanne. More about her life before you met her. Before you became engaged."

"I've told you all I know, I'm afraid. Maryanne was very private about her life before I met her. Like I told you before, every time I tried to get her to discuss her life, she refused. She would instantly shut down. Become angry, even. So I just stopped asking. I know she wasn't close with her parents. I never met any of her old friends from childhood. Anyone I met that she knew was always someone she worked with.

"Once, I asked one of them if Maryanne had ever discussed her childhood with her. You know, like women will do sometimes. Talking about things from high school or girlfriends who may have gotten into some trouble. She told me Maryanne never talked about anything before being hired there. It was like she had no life before twenty-three years of age. Is this something you think might be important?"

"I don't know, Mr. Houle. I'm grasping at straws here. I'm thinking Maryanne may not have been a random victim. That she knew the killer. She knew him from a time before meeting you. Someone from her past. Can you think of one name that maybe you recalled the past few months that Maryanne may have mentioned? Anyone. Even in the most innocent way."

"No, I'm afraid not. I've gone over our time together a million times and nothing new has come to me. I wish I could be more helpful, Detective."

"Well, it was a long shot," said Miller. "I appreciate your time."

Miller hung up the phone just as Allen stood up and took a step towards the office door. He looked out into the bullpen and saw Miller looking at him, looked away and then closed the door.

"Better you than me, asshole," Miller whispered aloud.

"You say something?" asked Kristen Day as she walked into the room.

"Where have you been?"

"Went over to Vice and asked around about your girl, Megan. Came up empty."

Miller shrugged. "So what's new. I just spoke with the fiance. Nothing new from him. I think I need to go back to Lawrence and ask around her old neighborhood. I just need some more names. Want to come?"

"No. While I didn't get anything for you from Vice, I did pick up something that might help me in an open investigation I was on before joining your little party. I'm going to look into that."

Miller grabbed his suit coat from the back of the chair.

"Any wild plans for the weekend?" he asked.

"Of course," replied Day. "Drinks with friends tomorrow night and an intimate rendezvous on Sunday with my Maytag. Long overdue. You?"

"I think a few more of our rented movies, a six pack and a pepperoni pizza. See you Monday."

THE PARKING LOT is full and quiet just before midnight and the rain has stopped. A sliver of a moon is playing hide and seek with clouds that speed across a wind blown nighttime sky. Stars are visible whenever there is an opening in those clouds. Because of the earlier rain, the performance of *The Taming of the Shrew* was performed inside the theater. Unfortunate. I wasn't about to go in tonight to watch it. Don't need to take the chance of being discussed when the police begin questioning people when lovely Lizzy comes up missing. Tomorrow night, Saturday night, promises to be clear, so, hopefully, I'll get to watch an outside performance from a safe place in the trees.

Sitting in my car in the outer spaces of the lot waiting for Ms. Clarke to return to her dorm, I am feeling very agitated. The anticipation of our union is, at times, almost overwhelming. From the moment I first decide who my partner will be, it starts. The anticipation. Anticipation then becomes desire as I formulate my plan, and desire becomes need as the moment nears. And, dear Jesus but it's true, the need consumes me. I'm fidgeting now. Sitting in my car, in the dark of night, my senses tuned to a pitch that is beyond sensual, I can't keep my hands from moving and parts of my body are twitching. Brushing one sleeve of my jacket, my fingers detect a slight static release and it feels like an electric current has stung me. Through a slight opening of the car window, I smell the musty damp earth of the dirt on the edge of the lot, rotting vegetation from the previous year and the promise of rebirth for the coming season. My eyes notice every muted glint of reflected moonlight off the puddles on the ground. I hear the scurrying of tiny feet through the deadened leaves, vermin searching for an evening meal in the safety of the dark. I am so aware of everything around me that I feel like I am no longer in my body, that I am floating above the parking lot and witnessing everything in the finest detail from above. Up there, I am calm. Down here, I am a mess.

And yet, interestingly enough, tomorrow evening, the night when Lizzy and I finally meet, I will be quite calm. You would think that would not be so. That the act of taking another against their will would be one of extreme anxiety. For me, it is not.

I notice two people now walking up the path that leads to the far end of the parking lot, coming from the direction of the Performing Arts building. I can tell by the way the shorter of the two is moving that she is my Lizzy. The other figure is thinner and taller and as they weave through the lines of parked cars and nearer to an overhead light, I can see it is another woman. I don't recognize her as another cast member. Perhaps she attended the performance or, maybe, she works behind the scenes. As they continue onto another walkway that leads from the parking lot to the dorms, they stop at a fork in the walkway and stand talking. The tall girl says something that I can't hear and Elizabeth laughs. Elizabeth Clarke has a wonderful laugh. Really quite genuine. I shudder involuntarily when the tall girl reaches out, and with her index finger pushes a few strands of lovely Elizabeth's hair away from those smiling lips. She says something else that I can't hear that receives a nod from Elizabeth, then turns and walks in the direction away from Ms. Clarke's dorm building. Lizzy stands there for a few seconds watching the girl walk away, then turns toward her building. I watch her short, bare legs climb the inclined path until she is out of sight.

I wasn't anticipating her walking back to her dorm with someone. Probably, I should have. If she does it tomorrow night, that will be a problem.

I slam the dash with an open palm. Stupid! I should have

foreseen it. Of course she wouldn't be alone after the performance. It's a big cast. Lots of students. Of course they would walk to their dorms together. Jesus Christ, how could I not have expected that?

There is nothing to do now but be here tomorrow night and see what happens. If she is not alone, then I will have to go to Plan B. Not that I have a Plan B yet, but I will. Probably grab her at the restaurant next week after her shift. I slam the dash again. That's three more days. I can't wait three more days. I can't. I need her. I need her now.

THE PLAY WAS a delight. For the most part. The actress playing Katharina chewed up the scenery a few too many times, and I thought the kid playing Petruchio was so full of himself that I just wanted to slap him. But the rest of the cast were so energetic that they saved the play. The energy may have come from skimpy costumes and chilly temps.

I had worried that the performance would be moved indoors because of the chill in the air, but by five o'clock the wind had died down to nothing and the sky cleared entirely. Surrounded by enough electrical lights, and under a canopy of a billion stars in a moonless sky, *The Taming of the Shrew* went off without a hitch as I watched from my spot in the woods. I must say, from where I stood, I watched my Elizabeth Clarke give a flawless performance. She looked beautiful, those short, lovely, strong legs propelling her effortlessly across the landscape time and again. Her voice was strong and her smile could melt a cold heart. I have chosen well.

I had left my place in the trees just as the play ended, following a darken path through the trees to my car at the end of the lot, where I now sit patiently waiting for Lizzy to appear. If she is alone, she will be with me this evening. If she is not, then I will take her after her shift on Monday night. I have settled it in my mind, her fate now rests with the gods. But I have a plan for where she must be discovered and Monday will make for a tight schedule. A very tight schedule.

It's almost midnight when I hear voices walking up the path. They are loud and excited. Three people walk into my view, two girls and a guy. It's Lizzy, with the tall girl she walked with last night and a kid I recognize from the play. Shit.

They stop behind a car that is about twenty from mine and I can hear their conversation in the still and quiet of the night.

"Why don't you come with us?" the tall girl says as the guy opens the car door and gets behind the wheel. "It'll be fun."

"I'm really beat, Heather," says Lizzy. "I hardly slept last night I was so wound up from the performance. We have the matinee tomorrow and I picked up a shift at Applebee's tomorrow night. I better get some sleep."

"We'll only stay an hour. Come on."

Don't you do it, Lizzy. I have other plans for you tonight.

"No, really, you and Ryan go ahead. Have a good time. I need to get some sleep."

Good girl.

"Okay," said Heather, "but you're missing out. Colby's going to be there."

"Goodnight!" said Elizabeth with a laugh. "Go have fun."

Heather reaches out and gives Lizzy a quick hug then gets into the car. The kid quickly puts the car in gear and races for the exit. And then the night is still once more. Elizabeth watches the car until the red lights fade from view. I quietly step from my car as she turns for the walkway to her dorm.

"I saw your performance," I say when she is about twenty feet from me. She turns quickly, obviously startled that she is not alone.

"Excuse me," she says, looking for me in the darkness. She spots me and takes a quick step backwards.

"I said I saw the show tonight," I say, taking a few steps slowly towards her. "I have to tell you, I thought your performance was terrific."

The smile is hesitant, the eyes wary. "Thank you," she says. "It's just a small part, but I enjoy doing it."

"I couldn't help but think," I say, another two slow steps closer, "that you should have been playing the lead instead of the cow who played Kate. She constantly over-acted."

My Lizzy smiles again. Her shoulders relax just a bit. I'm ten feet from her.

"Jennifer always plays the lead," says my beautiful girl. "At least that's what I've heard. This is my first production."

"She must have a thing going with the Director," I say, smiling, too. Eight feet.

"No," says Lizzy, her eyebrows arching, "that's how Brad got to play Petruchio."

We both laugh. My God, but she is a delight.

"I was wondering," I say, stopping five feet from her, "if I could get your autograph on the playbill."

"My autograph?" my Elizabeth Clarke says, and even in the dark I swear I can see her blush.

"Yes," I say, holding the playbill out to her and smiling. "I think you have an amazing talent and I wouldn't be surprised if someday you're in some play on Broadway. I'll be able to show my friends that I saw you when."

She smiles again. "Oh, I don't think that's ever going to happen. I'm planning on being a nurse not an actress."

"Elizabeth," I say, the wise older adult now, "you never know what God has in store for you. What path He keeps you from going down, only to show you another." I place the playbill on the trunk of a car we stand beside. "It would mean a lot to me."

"Okay," she says shyly, taking the pen that I offer. "Why not?"

As she turns to sign her name, I take the syringe from my coat pocket and stick her with it at the base of her delicious neck, plunging the special concoction of Propofol that I have modified just a bit into her blood stream.

She turns quickly and cries, "Hey, what are you doing?" as the pen falls from her hand. She takes a step backwards and opens her mouth as if to scream, but a second later she is off to dreamland. She falls back against the trunk of the car and I easily catch her before she smashes onto the ground.

Looking around, I see that we still have the parking lot all to ourselves. I pick up the playbill and the pen, then easily lift my new collaborator into a cradling embrace and carry her to my car, gently laying the young woman across my backseat where she will sleep until reaching my house. Just as I get into my vehicle, a car pulls into the lot and parks in the space recently vacated by Heather and Ryan. Two girls get out and weave across the lot to the walkway that leads to Elizabeth's dorm. After they enter the building, I start my car and drive away.

9

Monday morning and Miller was sitting at his desk when Kristen Day entered the Detective's room.

"You look like you've been here a while," said Day.

"About an hour. I may have picked up something on Maryanne Darrow."

"Over the weekend?"

"I was down in Lawrence on Saturday. Did a little digging. Found someone I hadn't talked to before. From them, I got a name of someone in Lowell. Found them. Found out some things about Maryanne and Megan that we didn't know before."

"Such as?"

"When Maryanne attended Lawrence High she hung out with a girl named Megan."

"That's all in the file," said Day as she sat on the edge of the desk sipping coffee from a Styrofoam cup.

"Don't interrupt," said Miller with a frown. "Maryanne managed to graduate Lawrence High School, just barely. But Megan Roache did not. In fact, I just got off the phone with an office secretary at the high school. She told me no girl named Megan Roache attended Lawrence High in the years Maryanne would have been there. Or ever, for that matter."

"Did she attend Central Catholic?"

Miller frowned.

"Sorry," said Day.

"The guy I spoke with in Lawrence only knew the girls as Maryanne and Megan. He had been to a few parties that the girls had attended. He knew Megan worked in a local food market, had seen her there, and that she drove a six year old Corolla. He also knew, or had heard, that the girls used that Corolla two or three nights a week and on weekends to drive the ten miles to Lowell where they hung out with a tough crowd. We already knew this. We also knew that that crowd was heavy into drugs and minor theft. Two of the guys who hung with them are doing a little time in Walpole. An unsavory group.

"The guy in Lawrence gave me a name of a guy in Lowell. A name I didn't have before. I spoke with the guy in Lowell Saturday night in a dive in Lowell. He said he remembered the girls. That they liked to party. Party hard. Some weekends, the guys that they hung out with would make a deal with a local biker group. Megan and Maryanne would be traded for a score. Drugs for sex. Again according to this guy, the girls had no problem with the arrangement. No problem at all. In fact, he said, he thinks it was Maryanne who first proposed the swap. That the guys they hung with wouldn't have had the imagination to come up with the idea themselves."

"And you believe this guy?"

Miller shrugged. "Who knows. Maybe he was the one who hustled the girls and he's just covering his ass. Doesn't matter now. What does matter, according to him, five years ago Maryanne and Megan vanish from Lowell. One night they're hanging out and the next they are gone, never to return. Eventually, word comes down that the two are in Manchester and living a new life. Although it may well be living the same life just in a different city. So it looks like Maryanne was here sometime in two thousand five or six. And then something changes. She changes. Cleans herself up. She begins working in two thousand seven and meets Arthur Houle in two thousand nine. Completely turns her life around in three years."

"And Megan?"

Miller shrugged again. "Megan doesn't. Not that we know of. But that's not all."

Kristen raised her eyebrows after waiting several seconds for her partner to say something.

"You going to tell me?"

"I said to the guy in Lowell, 'What can you tell me about Maryanne Darrow and Megan Roache?'"

"And?"

"He said, 'I never knew their last names. But I don't think Roache is the skinny one's last name. The guys used to call her Megan the Roach. Every time the pretty one was around, and you thought you might be alone with her, the skinny one would pop up. You know, like you open a kitchen drawer and a roach scurries out. The skinny bitch was just like that.'"

"So what is Megan's last name?" asked Day.

"I don't know. When I get a chance, I'm going to go to the high school and see if someone there might know. She may have gone to school with Maryanne. And now we need to look into the guys she partied with in Lowell to see if anyone down there may have been angry when the girls stopped hanging out. Maybe they stole money and headed north. Stole money from the wrong guy. Or maybe they hooked up with the wrong people when they got up here. She had two years to mess up before finally getting her footing. We need to find out who Megan is and where she is. She could be in danger. Even if she's not, she'll be able to fill in the blanks."

Kristen stood. "But how does all of that lead to a serial killer? It might lead to Maryanne being murdered, but why does the killer then go on to kill two more women who had nothing to do with each other?"

"That we know of." Miller leaned back in the chair. "You know, long shot I admit, but if Maryanne came up here and was still partying in late two thousand five, willing to turn some tricks for drugs, our Doctor Thomas Thomas may have been a willing partner in those transactions. The good doctor may have been good for some Oxy for services rendered. Not that far-fetched. Maybe Maryanne, an expensive wedding in her near future, a dad refusing to foot the bill, comes to the good doctor four years later and threatens to tell the Medical Board about his drugs for sex bartering."

It was Day's turn to frown. "Aren't you the one who said he's not the killer?"

"Yeah, well, what do I know? The good doctor knew Helena Johnson. Dated Madeleine Seward. Could have swapped drugs for sex."

Just then Chief Hendricks opened the door to his office and pointed at the two detectives.

"Miller, Day, got a minute?"

"What's new in the case?" Hendricks asked as they sat down in front of him.

Miller told him what he learned over the weekend, and showed him the letter the killer left on his windshield.

"Cheeky bastard, ain't he," Hendricks said. "What do you think?"

"I think," said Miller, "that we'll have another victim very soon."

"Until then, I need you two to work on other things. There was just a shooting on Hayward, a triple decker. Two injured, one dead. We got the shooter. Miller you head over there now. Day, I need you to pick up on a case Detective Allen has been working. See what you can dig up."

"Do I have to work with him?" Day asked, leaving no doubt she found that idea unpalatable.

"Detective Allen is on a two week vacation," said Hendricks, not elaborating. "We pick up the slack." He handed her a file. "Off you go. Keep me informed on the other thing. Mr. Johnson is still a weekly call into the Mayor, and every time I hear about it." He waved them from the office.

Miller scooped up his suit coat and headed out. Day quickly scanned the file and left to take a first hand look at the murder scene, a motel room that was still sealed off ten days after the body had been discovered by the cleaning woman. Neither Detective checked the missing persons report before leaving. College student, Miss Elizabeth Clarke, was just being added to it.

DAY WAS SEATED at Miller's desk when he came through the doors four hours later. He took one look at her and knew something was up.

"What?" he asked, standing in front of her.

She handed him a print out with a short list of names of people who were missing. Elizabeth Clarke's name topped the list. He recognized it immediately.

"One of ours," he stated. "Elizabeth Clarke. Which movie?"

"*Frankenstein.*"

"That's one of the ones I watched," said Miller. "Elizabeth was the daughter. The one Doctor Frankenstein was in love with and was going to marry. Where does the Clarke come in?"

"Actress who played her in the original was Mae Clarke. She was popular back in the thirties. I looked up her bio."

"So, *Frankenstein*. Have you seen it?"

"I have."

"What do we know about our Elizabeth Clarke?"

"Nothing yet," said Day. "I just saw this. Let me make some calls."

Day went back to her desk and picked up the phone. Miller

knocked lightly on Hendricks closed door and entered.

"Well?" asked Hendricks.

"Drug deal gone bad. Nineteen year old knocks on the apartment door and when it opens he hands the guy three hundred dollars. Door closes. Kid waits patiently until his patience runs out. Knocks again. He's ignored. Puts a beefy shoulder to the door and enters. Three people sitting at a kitchen table, two guys and a woman. Guy who answered the door pops up and starts yelling at the guy to get the hell out. Waves a long bread knife around like he's a Ronin warrior. Kid pulls a pistol from his waistband and shoots as the guy is lunging at him. Bullet right in the heart. Guys dead before he hits the dirty, cracked linoleum. The other two back away from the table. Kid sees his three hundred sitting in a neat pile in the middle of the table. He goes to get it and the other guy makes a move. Kid panics and unloads the pistol. One bullet catches the guy in the side, another bullet takes the woman down with a leg shot. Four other bullets enter and exit the wall behind them into the next apartment. Luckily, no one was home."

"Okay. Write it up."

Hendricks picked up his pen and started writing and then looked up when Miller was still sitting in front of him.

"What?"

"A woman has gone missing. Has a name that is on our list. Just came in."

Hendricks leaned back. "From a movie?"

"*Frankenstein.* Day's getting information now."

"You know, I had my doubts about this wild idea you two had, but it looks like you nailed it. Okay. This takes priority over everything else. I'll get someone to pick up Hayward Street. Go do what you gotta do."

Miller stood.

"Keep me up to date," said Hendricks pointing the pen at his detective. "Whatever you need, you got it."

Back in the bullpen, Miller stood beside Day's desk waiting for her to get off the phone.

"Well?" he asked when she hung up.

"Twenty year old student at the college. Studying to be a nurse. Failed to show up Sunday afternoon for a play she was part of at the college. Failed to show up for a shift that night at the restaurant that she works at. Failed to show up for an early class this morning. School officials were notified and they called the parents who live in Virginia. Parents were very concerned. Elizabeth is not someone who fails to show up places she is supposed to be. It was agreed that the police should be called. Two officers have already been out to the college and are on their way back here. They know to see us as soon as they arrive."

"So she goes missing Sunday morning or, more likely, Saturday night. What did you say she was doing? A play?"

"Shakespeare. An on campus thing. She was there for the Saturday night performance, but didn't show up on Sunday."

Miller sat his almost six foot frame heavily in the chair next to Day's desk.

"As soon as we talk to the officers we need to get out there. See if there are surveillance cameras for the dorms, parking areas, walkways. See if she walked back to the dorm or went out with friends after the performance. What do you think? Maybe the show was over around ten, ten-thirty. Early for a young woman on a Saturday night. Maybe she drove somewhere. Met up with someone. Went out with her boyfriend if she has one."

Miller took in a deep breath, while Day just watched him as his mind worked. He looked at her.

"You know, when you first brought up this name thing from old movies, I was skeptical. But now.... We are on this at the very beginning. An advantage we didn't have before. And if this is anything like the other murders, we have six days, give or take a day, in which to react to what we know about the victim. Plus, we know the movie and can take an educated guess on how he'll pose her and where he might leave her."

Miller smiled, surprising Kristen Day.

"What are you smiling about?"

"For the first time we'll be reacting to what he did, not to what he's done. That gives us hope. We haven't had hope before."

When he saw her puzzled look, he continued.

"Up until now, we've had nothing to go on until we had a body. Now, we have a fighting chance. Slim, I grant you that, but a chance to save Elizabeth Clarke. Which is more than we had with Maryanne, or Helena, or Madeleine. You played ball, Kristen. We're in the game with this one. The buzzer hasn't gone off, like with the others. We might get our asses kicked, but we are in the game. And I intend to fight like hell to win. Even if the odds are long."

They both looked up as two officers in uniform walked through the doors. The detectives stood and met them halfway across the room and led them to an interview room where they learned everything that the officers knew about the disappearance of Elizabeth Clarke, a twenty year old college student studying to be a nurse.

THE DORM ROOM was eighteen feet long and twelve feet wide. A single bed, made and neat, ran along one wall. A mini fridge, desk with a lap top and several books on top, and a stuffed chair were lined up along the opposite wall. One third floor window looked down onto a thin setting of deciduous trees not yet leafed, sparse lawn, and a walkway that led to another three story dorm a hundred feet away. Under the window was a three drawer dresser. Detective Kristen Day was methodically searching through each drawer, finding nothing more than bras, panties, blouses, shorts and jeans. No diary, no drugs, no sketchbook of drawings in black and white. Detective Erik Miller was going through the drawers of the desk with the same care and having the same result.

"Elizabeth is certainly neater and more organized than I was in college," stated Day as she closed the bottom drawer. "My room always looked like a bomb had gone off in it." She turned. "Find anything?"

He shook his head.

"Are you the police?" came a soft voice from the open entrance door, left open with the hope someone would ask that question.

"We are," said Day, looking at the young woman who stood in the doorway hugging a book to her chest. "Do you know Elizabeth?"

"We're good friends," said the woman. "Is she really missing? Doesn't anyone know where she is?"

"What's your name?" asked Day.

"Heather James."

"Can we ask you some questions, Heather?" asked Day.

Heather nodded. "Okay."

"Why don't you come in the room," said Miller, "and close the door so we have some privacy."

Closing the door behind her, Heather James hugged her book even tighter.

"Did you see Elizabeth at all on Saturday?" asked Miller.

"We were together at the play Saturday night," Heather said, looking from one Detective to the other. "*Taming of the Shrew.* It was performed here on campus. Liz had a part in the production. I worked the set. Just helping out. My boyfriend, Ryan, had a part in the play, too."

"Did you see what Elizabeth may have done after the performance?" asked Miller. "Did she go somewhere? Did she leave with someone?"

"She walked with Ryan and me up to the parking lot near our dorm," said Heather.

"What time was that?" asked Miller.

"Eleven thirty. Maybe a little earlier."

Miller gave a slight nod for her to continue. Taking a breath, Heather did.

"Ryan and I were going to a small get together of the actors at a house off campus. I tried to get Liz to come along with us, but she said she was tired. She just wanted to get some sleep. And then, the next day, she doesn't show up for the final performance. I ran up here before the show to see if she was alright, but she wasn't here. Her car was in the lot, but she wasn't around. I thought maybe she had some kind of an emergency. I tried her cell for the rest of the day, but it was never answered. Just went to voice mail."

Elizabeth Clarke's cell phone had been found an hour earlier laying beside the road that led to the campus, but the detectives did not share that information with Heather.

"Did you notice anyone hanging around after the performance," asked Miller, "that maybe looked out of place? See anyone on your walk to the parking lot? Anyone in the parking lot?"

Shaking her head, Heather said, "No one. Parents hung around for a while after the performance, but by the time we left the Performance building, it was quiet. Liz waved to us as Ryan pulled out of the lot and I waved back." Heather's eyes teared up. "I wish she had come with us."

"Does Elizabeth have a boyfriend?" asked Day. "Another girlfriend she may have visited Sunday morning? Maybe the pressure of the show, or college life, got to her and she needed to get away for a bit?"

"That's not her," stated Heather, a quick wipe of her eyes with the back of her hand. "She actually likes being here. She likes school. Loved being in the play. She has so much energy. Something must have happened to her for her not to have been here Sunday."

"No boyfriend?" persisted Day.

"No. She dated occasionally, but between studies and her job, there wasn't a lot of time for boys. But she would date if someone asked her out. She isn't shy."

Detective Day handed Heather a business card. "If you hear anything, or think of anything, I need you to call me, Heather. Okay? No matter what it may be. Okay?"

After Heather left, Day opened the door again as the two of them stood in the middle of the room slowly looking around one last time.

"He has her," whispered Miller harshly. "Probably snagged her in the parking lot as soon as Heather drove away. Was sitting in his car waiting for her to walk back to her dorm. He must have been scouting out her movements on the nights of rehearsals. The Friday night performance, he would have been waiting in the lot, waiting for her, watching to see how she got back to her dorm, knowing she'd be coming that way. Maybe he panicked when he saw Heather and Ryan with her Saturday night. Wasn't expecting anyone to be with her. His plans suddenly screwed. That would have pissed him off. And then the relief when they drive off and she is all by herself. In the dark. All alone. He must have felt like the gods were giving him their blessing. Take her now. She's waiting for you."

Miller's hands clenched into fists. Day noticed.

"Let's talk to the drama coach and get a list of the cast," said Day. "We need to talk to a lot of people and there's nothing more to find here. Come on. The clock is ticking."

By the end of the day, they knew no more than they had after talking with Heather James. No one remembered seeing any large man hanging around the Performance Center during the production, and while several men in the audience during the performances were larger than average, most were known to someone in the cast or had been accompanied by others.

Day one in the investigation of missing college student Elizabeth Ann Clarke was rapidly coming to an end. The investigators had hoped to find someone who may have seen something that would help, but, other than Heather and Ryan, no one else had. Still, they had reason for hope.

Elizabeth Ann Clarke, shackled by an ankle to the cement wall in a damp cellar, was bereft of hope. She knelt on a twin sized mattress that lay on the floor, her back slumped against the cold of a bare wall, an untouched plate of toasted white bread and an empty plastic bottle of water beside her. She was alone again. Alone and afraid and wondering when her abductor would return. She was hoarse from screaming and craved more water. She was confused. Why was the novel F*rankenstein* being read to her? Why had she been slapped hard several times when she tried asking questions during the reading? Questions of why she was here. Why was she shackled. What did it all mean? She was frightened beyond rationality. But most of all, she feared she was going to die. Here, in a cold basement. And she didn't know why.

10

The air is damp. It always is after it rains. Sometimes, I might open the bulkhead and let in the air if it is dry out, but it wouldn't be a good idea to do that now. I do live at the end of a short country road, my nearest neighbor more than three hundred feet away, but sound can carry with the right conditions, so I keep the bulkhead closed when I have company staying overnight. Or longer.

Sitting on my swivel stool at the workbench, I bite into my peanut butter and jelly sandwich and close my eyes, savoring the freshness of the bread I had purchased after work. When I open my eyes, I frown down at Lizzy.

"You aren't eating. You have to eat, my darling. You have to keep up your strength."

She refuses to look up at me, her eyes focused on the bare cement wall instead. The anger those eyes have held for the past three days is now gone. Those eyes now show only fear. In another day, if experience is any teacher, those light blue eyes will dull into acceptance.

"Let's talk about what we just watched," I say, not allowing her mood, or the air, to dampen my spirits.

Of all the movies, *Frankenstein* is the most interesting when compared to the novel. I have always wondered if dear old Mary

Shelley had rolled over in her grave when the movie came out eighty years after her death.

"What were the major differences between the book and the movie?" I ask, my tone conversational, as if we were sitting in a late-night diner discussing a movie we had just seen at the local cineplex. "God knows there were plenty of them."

My young companion makes no reply. She kneels on the edge of the mattress, at the end of her tether, only several feet from me, and ignores the question. I don't want to slap her pretty face again to gain a response. Her face has already suffered enough damage in my attempts to calm her down, and I don't like that I had bruised Mina's face so badly when she was here. Mina's pictures in the newspaper made me look like I'm some kind of crazed animal. So, instead, because I am not a monster, despite what others may think of me, I slap the back of her head in an effort to impress upon her the need to converse with me. This is very important. How can we move on to the next step if we don't analyze what we know? The blow sends her toppling sideways and she lets out a painful scream.

"Are you with me now, Lizzy? I asked you a question. Notice anything different between the book and the movie?"

Years ago, my Grandfather and I had spent a great deal of time discussing this particular topic, mainly because there is so much to talk about.

My partner is looking up at me now, her fearful eyes teary.

"I don't know," she cries. "I don't know. Why are you doing this to me? What do you want?"

"I want to talk about the movie we just watched. I want to talk about the differences between it and the book I read to you. I want to have a meaningful conversation about these things before we take the next step. It's important, Elizabeth. It's very important."

Smiling down at her, hoping to lessen her anxiety and fear, I bend down and open her milk container.

"Drink some milk, Sweetie. Have some of your sandwich. Have an Oreo. You'll feel better. I don't want to hit you, Lizzy. I don't want to be angry. I just want us to have a conversation about what we are doing here in our time together."

Look, sometimes, I know, I have anger issues. I don't deny it. Lots of people do. I've had them ever since I was a kid. I was kind of geeky and tall and gangly when I was young and the other kids made fun of me. You know how mean kids can be. 'Look, here comes Frankenstein's kid'. I wasn't that homely, but, like I said, kids can be cruel. And I got angry and defensive about that. And the scars on my arms and back from the fire didn't help. But I got past all that when I matured. Still, sometimes the blood boils a bit when people don't respond the way I want. But I'm working on it. The anger. Really, I am. You know, deep breaths. Count to ten. Sometimes, I forget.

"What are we doing?" sobs Lizzy, as she moves a little further away from me, out of quick striking distance. "I don't understand. You said we are creating something. What? How? Why am I chained to a wall in your basement? I don't even know you. You're going to kill me, aren't you? I don't even know you and you're going to kill me. Why? I don't want to die."

I smile again in an attempt to calm her fears a little. "I know. I can understand your confusion. We really haven't started creating yet, but we will tomorrow. You'll see. And I'll want your input. You'll see. You can be a big help. We will create this together. The book. The movie. Those are just the necessary previews to what we are going to build. I can hardly wait.

"You know what I find to be the most distressing difference between the book and the movie?" I ask, figuring I will get the ball rolling. "Well, the most obvious difference are the names. In the book, it is Victor Frankenstein and his friend Henry Clerval. Remember? While in the movie, it is Henry Frankenstein and his friend Victor. How could the screenwriter screw that up? Crazy, huh, Lizzy? I asked my Grandfather that very same question. He told me the movie was based on a play from the 1920's that was based on the book and maybe that was how it happened. So, was it the playwright who got it wrong or the screenwriter? I don't know. It's pretty frustrating though, don't you think? I mean, all movies differ somewhat from the books, but *Frankenstein* is the worst."

I take another heavenly bite from my sandwich. "Do you remember, in the book, the Monster actually saves a little girl from drowning, but then, in the movie, he throws a little girl, Maria was her name, into the water and she drowns. Remember? He kills her. Why did they have him do that? I can remember how upset I was when that happened the first time I watched the movie with my Grandfather. My ten year old mind knew, even then, that that was wrong. Not that he did it, but that the writer and the director had him do it. With that stunt, they made him more of a monster than even Dr. Frankenstein had. In my mind at the time, and even now, the Monster was a hero. What they did was an injustice.

"Yes, I know, I can see it in your eyes, Lizzy, that the Monster did kill a little boy in the book. But we know why he did it. He was angry with Dr. Frankenstein. And he never meant to. Well, not until the kid freaked out, anyways. Can you think of anything else that was different?"

Lizzy looks up at me, her eyes then darting from corner to corner as if looking for somewhere her lovely, chubby legs could crawl to. Somewhere to hide. To cower. She shakes her head slightly.

I sigh. "A conversation, my darling girl, is a discussion between two or more people. I am trying to have a conversation."

"I don't know," she whispers through a swollen lower lip. "I don't remember much about the book."

I can believe that. The bitch had screamed and cried through most of my reading. 'Where am I? Who are you? Why am I here? What do you want? When can I go home?' All the W's in that whiny little voice that is so unlike the strong, teasing voice she used in *Taming of the Shrew.* So pathetic. Just like the others. I thought she'd be different. Professional. She's an actress for God's sake. I am not a violent person, usually. I don't enjoy hitting women. I get no pleasure from it. But how else can you get a hysterical person to calm down and listen? Just once, JUST ONCE, I would like to have someone just sit and listen and make comments and get into the spirit of what we can accomplish as a team. Is that asking too much? Is it?

"Well, Lizzy," I force myself to speak calmly, more calmly than I am feeling, "in the book, Mary Shelley has the Monster learn how to speak by having him hide in a hovel observing a family and learning words from listening to them speak, while in the movie, Boris Karloff does little more than grunt and scream. I will tell you, in *Bride of Frankenstein,* an old blind man who lives in a cabin teaches him a few words, like bread, good, bad. In the book, however, the Monster has the vocabulary of a college professor of language at Cambridge, that he learns in just a year or so by eavesdropping on the simple dialogue of the simple family in the simple house he is hiding beside. A little hard to believe, don't you think, but I suppose more entertaining than a bunch of grunts and groans.

"Did you notice, Lizzy, that Shelley made us feel quite sympathetic to her monstrous creation. Yes, he killed. Yes, he destroyed. But only because mankind scorned him. Recoiled at his hideousness. Refused to see him as a human being. He was seen only as a monster by the populace, because of his appearance. In his cold, dead heart that had been resuscitated, all he really wanted was to be accepted. To be loved. To be good.

To live freely among others. Society would not allow that, however. They created the Monster. Right? But in the movie, Karloff goes off in a mad rampage of murder and mayhem. There is no sympathy from the audience. I'm sorry. It's terrible what was done to the Monster in that movie. Don't you agree, Lizzy?"

Elizabeth Clarke looks up at me, her eyes darting again. I slide off my stool and take a step towards her.

"I said, don't you agree!" I probably said it louder than I should have, because she slides back another foot and her right arm comes up to shield her face.

"I guess," she stammers, her voice weak. "I don't know. Maybe."

I take another step towards her.

"Yes," she quickly says. "Yes. I agree." She begins to sob again. "Yes. Yes. Please, don't hit me again. Yes, I agree."

I sit back down on the stool.

"Of course you do, Sweetie. Yeah. Anyone can see that. Of all the monsters, at least to my way of thinking, Frankenstein may be the most sympathetic. Don't you think, Lizzy? I mean, the Hunchback runs a pretty close second. Think about it. King Kong made the fatal mistake of falling for a dame. A scrawny little blonde with pale skin. Quite different from the other women the tribe had placed outside the gate for him. He fell in a big way, if you get my drift."

I chuckle at that, even though it really was quite tragic, the humor lost on my partner.

"The sad part is, they just should have left him alone. He was minding his own business until they came to his island. Kong would take his occasional sacrifice back to his cave for a little fun. That's all. Really, a small price for the tribe to pay for his protection against the terrors that inhabited that jungle. Kong didn't deserve to die. Creatures that just want to be left alone, should not be bothered. Believe me, I understand them. And what about people who don't get what they deserve? Why does that happen? Then people wonder why there is so much anger in the world."

I take a deep breath and count to five, feeling myself getting a little worked up. It certainly wasn't Lizzy who had screwed me over. She shouldn't have to pay for the sins of others. She would, of course, unfortunately, but there was no need to get angry at her about it.

"It's tough to have a lot of sympathy for Godzilla, though," I say, smiling at her and continuing our conversation. "I'll give you that. The whole radioactive thing. I get it, but he damned near burned all of Tokyo down. And the Japanese were innocent. Those poor people had done nothing wrong. It should have been New York or San Francisco that was destroyed. It was the good old USA who had the nuclear weapons. Right? Did the nuclear testing. Dropped those damn bombs. I mean, am I right or not?

"But, for the most part, the ones we deem monsters were made that way by someone or something else. They have all gotten a bum rap. Except one, of course, but we won't talk about him, that pompous ass, living in his subterranean fortress. It's not right. Not right at all. It's people who create the monster, either through deeds or ambition. And it is people who then hunt the monster down and kill it. That's not right. A little human decency might have prevented their deaths and the deaths of those they killed. You agree with that, Lizzy?"

Elizabeth Clarke is looking up at me, and even through the fear in her eyes I can see she has no idea what I am talking about. Well, I will continue trying to make her understand as we build the model, but I can see she is a hopeless partner. And I had had such hope for her.

Maybe the next woman will be better.

I can only hope.

Picking up the paper plates, I walk up the cellar steps and shut off the lights when I reach the top.

"Please, don't shut off the lights!" Elizabeth cries from down below.

"You weren't helpful today, my darling," I say, "so no lights. Maybe tomorrow night you will participate more."

Her cries of 'Please!' become muted behind the heavy door as it closes. Tossing the plates into the waste basket, I then open the fridge for a nice cold glass of milk that I will have with my Oreo's. Closing the door, I glance at the article I clipped from the Sunday newspaper two weeks ago that is held in place by a cute little magnet shaped like a unicorn. The article reminds me that I only have four more nights to finish up this particular project. No time to dawdle. Fortunately, the Frankenstein model is the easiest to build. The big guy standing on a grave, huge arms outstretched, towering over a headstone. Easy to build, easy to paint.

The article, dated April 18th, heralds the happy union of Doctor Danielle Rose Gallagher to Dr. Richard Preston Hartigan in a double ring ceremony performed by a Justice of the Peace, surrounded by two hundred of their closest friends. The happy couple would be leaving on a three week tour of Europe immediately following the reception, before returning back to their Manchester home to resume their practices.

I wasn't invited to their wedding. But I still have a gift to give them. I wish I could see their faces when they receive it.

FRIDAY MORNING, FIVE days since the reported disappearance of Elizabeth Clarke. Detective Erik Miller was working the phones, speaking with people he had interviewed before in the murder of the other three women. So far, no one he has spoken with knows Elizabeth Clarke. Kristen Day was with the parents of Ms. Clarke at a breakfast diner near the hotel they have been staying at since flying in to Manchester Tuesday morning. This is the fourth time one, or both, of the Detectives have conferred with the parents, Jason and Melanie Clarke. Miller was alone in the Detective Room, the other detectives all out on investigations of their own. Captain Hendricks sat in his office on the phone, behind a closed door. Miller looked up as the doors into the bullpen were pushed open and Sergeant Bates entered carrying a six inch cubed cardboard box. Miller took a deep breath and swallowed down rising bile.

Bates stopped in front of Miller's desk, holding the box away from him like he feared something might leap from inside it. Something lethal. The Detective hung up the phone, leaned against the back of his chair and nodded toward the open area on his desk. The Sergeant gently laid the box down and then took two steps back.

"It was on Rodgers' hood when he came out of Dunkin'. Never saw who put it there. Saw your name and knew what it was."

"He look inside?"

"Had no desire to. Came right here with it."

Miller stared at the box, making no attempt to open it. The deliverer stood waiting patiently. Miller went to Hendrick's door, knocked once and opened it. Hendricks looked up and frowned.

"I'll have to call you back," he said into the phone and replaced the receiver. "Tell me it's a small one."

Miller didn't answer as he walked back to his desk, Hendricks following. Just then, Detective Matt Blanchette came through the doors, saw the three men standing by the desk, joined them and said nothing when he saw what they were looking at.

Detective Erik Miller did not sit. He took a razor knife from his middle drawer, bent over and sliced through the packing tape, lifted the flaps. Some white tissue paper filled the top of the box. Lifting it, he uncovered a lone finger lying on more tissue paper, the nail a dark red. The finger wore a band of gold with a tiny jewel attached, the stone appearing to be a diamond less than a quarter carat. Miller gently lifted the tissue paper with the finger out of the box and laid it beside the box. The other three men, veterans of decades on the force, stood stoically.

Beneath the tissue paper was a folded piece of unlined white copy paper. Miller unfolded it and read what was typed on it, then handed it to Hendricks for him to read, which he did before handing it back.

"Tell me you and Day have an idea where this poor girl might end up," said the Captain.

Miller shrugged. "We do. Frankenstein supposedly died in a fire in a windmill kind of building. No windmills around here, but we have a few ideas."

"Well, let's get them all covered. Where's Day now?'

"With the parents."

"Call her. Get them all down here. See if the ring is Elizabeth's."

Hendricks went back to his office and the Sergeant back to his post. Blanchette said, "Want me to run that to forensics?"

"Please," said Miller, placing everything back in the box except the note. That, he folded up and put in his shirt pocket.

"Taunting you again?" asked Blanchette.

"With great enjoyment." replied Miller. He picked up his cell phone and dialed his partner while Blanchette went out the doors.

"Kristen," he said when she answered her cell, "you still with the Clarke's? Bring them here. We just got a package."

MELANIE CLARKE WAS visibly shaken. While she could not verify that the finger was Elizabeth's, she did verify that the dark red nail polish was a favorite of her daughters. The ring, however, she had never seen and doubted it was Elizabeth's. So, while sipping water from a plastic bottle, Melanie Clarke held out hope that the finger belonged to the daughter of another woman.

Jason Clarke paced the interview room like a tiger in a cage. He was a man of action, and since Monday when the call had come in that his baby girl was missing, the days of inactivity had taken their toll. The finger had sent him over the edge. He peppered Erik and Kristen with questions about the investigation. He inquired about the deaths of three other women and why the killer had not been caught. He demanded to know what the finger meant. Did it mean his daughter would be victim number four? What were the police doing to find his little girl? Twice he had walked to the door. When his wife had asked where he was going, he had stopped and stood looking into space. 'I don't know,' was his reply both times. 'I have to do something. We have to do something.' Then he would turn from the door and continue his pacing.

Detective Erik Miller eventually convinced the Clarke's that they should go back to their hotel. That he and Detective Day had a theory that they were working on and that every minute was vital. They would keep them posted, but they needed to get moving. An officer was called in to bring the parents back to their hotel.

It was nearing noon when Erik and Kristen had the room to themselves. During the week, they had narrowed down a short list of where the body might be brought when it was time for the killer to pose it. Now, when faced with that eventuality, they both recognized the futility of the attempt. In the movie, the monster supposedly dies in the ruinous fire in a windmill, only to be miraculously resurrected in *Bride of Frankenstein,* somehow having survived the blaze. Manchester has no windmills. It was Detective Miller who thought they should consider hospital morgues and the city morgue as possible sites.

In the book and movie, the creation of the monster began there and in graveyards. They both agreed that cemeteries would probably not be used, even though Doctor Frankenstein and his aide had dug up the dead. The killer was more imaginative than that, they reasoned, and having used a cemetery in the murder of Madeleine Seward, they thought it doubtful one would be used again. But various research labs in the city, especially those doing work in the renovated brick mills that ran along the Merrimack River, might be possible sites. A blazing inferno in one of them? A body discovered in the ashes? Who knew what madness the killer could conjure up. They would need to be staked out. The old mills, that had at one time employed thousands in the creation of fabric and stretched for a mile on both sides of the river, was the obvious place in which to pose the body, but it was not the only place where it might happen.

And now they had what appeared to be a wedding ring on a finger in a box. Could the body be left in a church, to be discovered as the church filled for a wedding? How many more police would be needed to cover every church in the city?

Miller looked up from the list that he had been reading aloud from with each site receiving a nod from his partner. "Here's the reality: We are trying to rationalize an irrational mind. It's impossible. We have no idea where the son-of-a-bitch will pose Elizabeth, do we?"

Kristen shrugged. "We're doing everything we can, Erik. You know that."

"You want to tell the Clarke's that when their daughter shows up dead? I'm sorry, Mr. and Mrs. Clarke, we did everything we could."

She looked at him. The anger seemed to radiate off him in waves, like heat off a wood stove, as he once again looked over the list of sites.

"You going to let me see the note?" she asked.

Without looking up, he reached into his shirt pocket, took out the folded paper and handed it to her. This time the note was written in lower case. She read it aloud.

I am born again! Although I made no such plea.
My cursed fate reversed, so still I remain,
Yet my Father shuns me, I, his great shame,
The rabble cower and scream out my name
In terror. Yet all I desire, a chance to be free.

"Obviously, if we hadn't known *Frankenstein* before, we would have known now," said Day.

"A lot of good it's done us," replied Miller, still looking at the list.

Kristen read the rest of the note to herself.

Erik, Erik, Erik. Tsk, tsk. You flounder around like a child in a Fun House with the lights off.

I left you a note on what you should do. I know you got it. Have you done what I said? The answer is right there in front of you. Yet you are blind. And another woman dies. I know I repeat myself, but my partner, a lovely young woman who I believed held such promise, has proven to be a disappointment. As they all have. But I am persistent, if nothing else, and will soon select another to help me in my endeavor. I am filled with hope that she will perform better. Soon Erik, I will take her soon. And there is nothing you can do to stop me!

Elizabeth, yes that is the name of my current associate, will soon be enjoying the eternal sleep on a bed of roses, Erik.

I give you yet another clue, confident that your deductive powers are vastly overrated. Though I take no pleasure in her death, my young thespian must play her part in helping me to avenge. I think I may have loved this one, given a different situation, Erik, as I did the first, so know that I am suffering, too. Do you find satisfaction in my misery?

When Day folded the note back up, Miller said, "We need to

find Megan the Roach."

THEY WORKED THE weekend, Erik putting in twenty hours each day, coordinating police presence in the expanse of the mills that they had determined might be used to pose the body and torched, plus an officer at every flower shop in the city because of the "*bed of roses*" clue in the received note. There would be a car covering every church all night long. Late on Saturday night, while the two sat in Miller's car peering down on an empty parking area in front of one of the renovated mill buildings, Detective Erik Miller broke the long silence that they had fallen into.

"Why the hell doesn't Manchester have a windmill?"

Detective Kristen Day actually chuckled.

"Think how easy this would be if there was a damn windmill," continued Miller.

He fell silent again. From the far end of the enormous brick building built over a century before, car lights entered the empty parking area. The vehicle progressed slowly across the expanse of tar. As it neared the dimmest part of the space, it slowed. Miller became more erect in the driver's seat. Day noticed his right hand tightly gripping the steering wheel. The car drove very close to the brick building and stopped. The lights were extinguished and the car sat idling for several seconds. Suddenly, the driver's side door opened and the interior light shone on a man stepping from the vehicle. He closed the door and stood beside the car, slowly looking around the poorly lit empty lot.

"Shit!" Miller swore when the man began urinating. Day said nothing. This was no time for levity.

When the man was done relieving himself, he re-entered the car and drove quickly away.

Miller's fingers relaxed on the wheel and began a soft,

rhythmic tapping.

"It looks like Matt's going to retire. Go to work with his nephew."

"I've heard the rumors," Kristen replied. "You think he'll miss this?"

"Miss this?" Miller said with a slight shake of his head. "No one in their right mind would miss this."

"You'd miss it," said Kristen Day.

"Yeah," said Miller, a quick glance at his partner, then back to the lot. "What the hell does that say about me?"

IT HAD BEEN a first-class honeymoon all the way and was ending the way it had begun, as the limo drove up to the door of the large Victorian house on the far north end of Elm Street late on Sunday afternoon. Doctor Danielle Gallagher-Hartigan drained what was left of the champagne in her glass and smiled at her husband of three weeks.

"Europe was fantastic," she said, "but I'm happy to be home. Happy to be sleeping in our own bed tonight."

"I couldn't agree more," said Doctor Richard Hartigan. "Why don't you go air the place out and I'll help the driver with the luggage."

"You don't want to carry me over the threshold?" she asked and then smiled. "I start my diet tomorrow, baby. I promise. We both do. Doctor's orders."

With the luggage in the front foyer, Hartigan handed the driver a generous cash tip and closed the door behind him. He stood watching the limo drive away and took in a deep breath. 'And so it begins', he thought to himself.

Suddenly, he heard his wife scream from the rooms upstairs. "Dani," he called out in alarm as he raced up the stairs two at a time.

"Dani!"

11

Brushing past two of Manchester's finest, Detective Kristen Day entered the large bedroom on the second floor of the stately Victorian styled home. Detective Erik Miller was already there. He stood beside the queen-sized bed looking down at the body of Elizabeth Clarke, wondering how anyone looking so peaceful and pretty could be causing him so much pain.

"Does this make sense to you?" he asked without looking up.

Day quickly took in the scene. Elizabeth Clarke lay peacefully stretched out on the bed atop an expensive looking spread. She was dressed in an off-white wedding gown that almost reached her ankles, almost covering the bruised right ankle. A veil of the same color was on her head, the lace pulled back so her face was visible. White shoes with a three inch heel completed the ensemble. Her hands, minus the ring finger of her left hand, were folded on her lap and they held a beautiful bouquet of red roses. Surrounding the body, rose petals of red were scattered, and appeared to be under her as well.

"Frankenstein did go into Elizabeth's bedroom," said Day, "on her wedding day in *Bride of Frankenstein* while the Doctor and others were searching the house for him. The Doctor had locked her in her room to keep her safe, thinking the monster was in the big house. But Karloff came in through the window and surprised her. Her screams brought the others running."

"Maybe if I had watched that movie I might have seen this coming," said Miller. "Or something like it." He slowly shook his head. "I thought it would be a lab. Or a church. I didn't see this coming. You see now why I say it might be futile trying to anticipate the direction this crazy bastard is going to go? The possibilities might not be endless, but they are many. Now we're into sequels. Does it mean something, or is he just getting sloppy. Maybe he's just getting bored. Taking the easy way. Maybe, he's not as smart as we think he is."

"I disagree, Erik. This looks like something that required a great deal of planning. Elizabeth posed in a wedding dress, lying in a bed, may be the perfect scene."

He looked at her.

"Look," she said as she walked to the other side of the bed. "Madeleine Seward was left in a cemetery. The cross on the crypt used as the prop. She could just as easily been left in any of the Funeral Homes we have in this city. Placed in a coffin to be discovered when someone entered in the morning. You've watched the movie. There are several scenes that show the vampires rising from coffins. Dracula was in Mina Seward's bedroom. Madeleine could have been posed in a bedroom that looks much like this. Only she would have been in a nightgown instead of a wedding gown. Possibilities are many.

"It's the same here. Elizabeth could have been posed in any number of places, she ended up here. We do the best we can, Erik. It's all we can do. But don't underestimate the killer. Think of the planning that had to go into this."

"They're doctors," Miller said, his eyes moving from his partner to Elizabeth and back to Kristen again.

"Who?"

"The couple who live here. Just back from a European honeymoon. They were gone three weeks."

He kept looking at her, waiting for a response.

"Anyone else we know who's a doctor?" he finally asked when none came.

Just then the police photographer, Jack Morgan, arrived.

Miller nodded at him then stepped away from where he was standing and, as Day came back around the four poster allowing the photographer more room to work, Miller pointed down at the bedspread that was plush and the color of canary yellow, the red of the petals scattered atop it vibrant in contrast.

"A bed of roses," Miller said, shaking his head, "just like his note said. In a fucking house on Elm St. Asshole has a weird sense of humor."

"Ready to talk to the doctors?" asked Day.

"Why should we bother? They won't know Elizabeth. They'll have no idea how she got here. They'll have no idea they are now part of something that is mind blowing."

"Are you ready?" she asked again, refusing to be drawn into a negative argument. She knew it was just his frustration.

Miller took a deep breath. "As Bill so elegantly stated in one of his plays, lead on, MacDuff." He quickly regretted saying it, realizing that the murdered girl had only a week before played a character in *Taming of the Shrew.*

"Shakespeare actually wrote *Lay on, MacDuff*, in *Hamlet,*" said Day, stopping at the doorway, "but that means something entirely different and not something for today. *Lead on, Macduff,* was the misquote by Haggard in *King Solomon's Mines*."

When Miller frowned, Kristen said, "Just sayin'. I took a course on Shakespeare my last semester senior year. That whole 'lay on, lead on' thing was a pet peeve of the professor."

"Can we go downstairs now?" said Miller, in no mood for a lesson on Shakespeare and pissed at himself for his weak attempt at levity.

Kristen stepped aside and swept her left hand in front of her. "Lead on yourself, MacGrouch."

The doctors were quietly sitting in their living room. The room was large, furnished in a way that mixed Early American and Scandinavian designs together that Kristen found to be quite ridiculous. It was as if the two occupants of the house had their own idea of how to furnish the room, couldn't agree, and this was the compromise. Three large windows faced Elm Street. The heavy brown drapes were pulled closed, shielding those inside from dozens of curious eyes that had gathered outside, across the wide street, their interest drawn by the police cars parked in front of the Victorian home.

Doctor Richard Hartigan was sitting in an uncomfortable looking high backed padded chair beside a cold fireplace with a mantle of white marble, his legs crossed and a half gone bottle of beer balanced precariously on the thick, rolled arm of the chair. Doctor Danielle Gallagher-Hartigan sat in the center of one of the two matching loveseats that faced each other in the center of the room. In front of her, within easy reach, an empty glass rested on a ceramic coaster atop the smoked glass top of a low slung mahogany and chrome coffee table that separated the two loveseats. Two melting ice cubes shared the bottom of the glass with several drops of amber liquid. She looked up at the two detectives as they entered the room and folded her arms across her chest. She appeared to be in her early to mid thirties, perhaps ten years younger than her husband. Her hair was cut short and dyed blonde. Miller thought she looked remarkably calm for someone who only an hour earlier had found a body in her bed dressed in a wedding gown. Her wedding gown.

"It's a hell of a thing," she said, "to come home from a magical three weeks in Europe to find a dead body in one's bed, I have to tell you. Any idea why she was in my bed?"

"We do," said Miller.

"Care to share?" asked Richard Hartigan.

"It's an ongoing investigation, so I can't divulge much."

"Are we in any danger?" asked Hartigan, refusing to be put off.

"No," replied Miller

"So this isn't some kind of a warning to us from a deranged former patient? Some kind of extortion threat?"

Miller looked at Day and she gave an imperceptible shrug.

"We have had a series of murders in the city the last four months," said Miller, deciding to try and put the two doctors at ease. "I'm sure you've read about them and seen the news on TV."

"We have," said Danielle Gallagher-Hartigan. "Is this young woman another victim of the serial killer?"

Miller looked at Day again, but she showed no reaction to what the woman had said.

"Detectives," said Hartigan, "if this woman is connected to those other deaths, then this makes victim number four, doesn't it? At least as far as the public knows. Perhaps there are more. I'm fairly certain that is the definition of serial killer. The only question is, why is she posed in our bed dressed up as a bride? I think, maybe, you two know why. Again, care to share?"

"I'm afraid we can't," said Day.

"Well, I think that is rather unacceptable, considering the situation." He stood. "I think I need something a little stronger. Can I get either of you something to drink," he asked. "Something cold? Coffee?"

"Nothing," said Miller. Kristen shook her head.

Hartigan crossed the room to a glass table that held an array of liquor bottles. He selected bourbon and poured two fingers into a glass. He held it up to see if his wife wanted more, but she shook her head. Returning to his seat, he said, "Obviously, our friends and neighbors will have a lot of questions. This isn't the sort of neighborhood where police cars are parked in front of homes."

Miller said, "We understand. We can't stop you from talking about this, but it won't help the investigation if certain details become public."

"Like the murder victim was found in my bed?" said Danielle.

"Yes," said Miller.

"Dressed in my wedding gown?"

Miller nodded.

"Does it all mean something?"

"It does," said Miller, "and that is all I can say about it. Do you have an alarm system? Cameras? Anyone who may have been watching the house for you while you were gone? Might Ms. Clarke have been a patient of either of you?"

"Ms. Clarke?" said Hartigan.

"Elizabeth Clarke," said Kristen Day, speaking for the first time.

"So you know her name already," said Hartigan, "which must mean you knew she might be a victim. Am I right? Had she been reported missing?" He lifted his glass, but took no liquid. A slight smile creased a face that wore three days growth. "My God, the killer is corresponding with you, isn't he? Taunting you, perhaps? 'I have this girl now. I'm going to kill her.' The sick bastard."

Miller gave the doctors his best poker face.

"Fine," said Hartigan with a frown. "I'm a big reader of mysteries. Love them. To answer your question, no. Neither of us know her. We have no alarm system, didn't think I needed one in this part of town, but I'll soon remedy that. And yes, we did have someone who kept an eye on the place. My brother, who lives in Windham, came by once a week. I called him after we discovered the body. He was here Friday. Walked through the house and stocked up the fridge with fresh milk, eggs, a few veggies."

"What time would that have been?" asked Day.

"Late afternoon. Five, five-thirty he said."

"Who discovered the body?" asked Miller.

"I did," replied Doctor Gallagher-Hartigan. "As soon as we arrived home, I went up to the bedroom to get into something more comfortable. After the initial shock, I checked to see if there were any vitals, even though I knew there would be none, while Richard called 9-1-1."

"You didn't disturb anything?"

"No. Nothing. We came back down here and waited for the police."

Just then Forensics came through the front door into the foyer.

"Bedroom upstairs on the right," said Day.

Danielle Gallagher-Hartigan leaned over and picked up the glass, looked into it and then placed it down again. "I could see her face had been abused. That she had been hit multiple times. Maybe over a period of several days. Make-up had been applied to conceal some of the damage, but the puffiness was obvious." She looked up at Detective Day. "Have the other women been beaten, also? It's not enough that he kills them, he has to beat them, too? What kind of a monster is walking our streets, Detective?"

Jack Morgan came down the steps and Miller went to speak with him.

"You two really don't have much on this killer, do you," stated Richard Hartigan to Kristen. "Four months, four deaths that we know of, and I'm guessing you have very little to go on."

"We're making progress," said Detective Day.

Hartigan sipped his drink. "I worked in a psychiatric ward for a year after my residency. In Minneapolis. Eye-opening. The really crazy ones, well, they're crazy. No doubt about it. But there were a few in there, when you looked into their eyes, you could see they were brilliant. Evil, yes. Dangerous, without a doubt. But you could see the wheels were turning and there was a frequency in that head that was tuned just a little higher than most people. It was very unsettling. If you have one of those, and I think you may have, I don't envy you."

Miller came back into the room.

"I'm sure we'll have more questions at a later time," he said. "But we'll try not to be a bother. I know how difficult this must be."

"Of course," said Danielle. "We will help anyway we can."

Miller smiled. "How was Europe?"

"Everything I expected it to be, and more," said Gallagher-Hartigan. "Can't wait to go back."

Miller nodded and turned to leave. Then he turned back again.

"By any chance," he said, "do either of you know Doctor Thomas Thomas?"

Richard Hartigan shook his head, but Danielle said, "Yes. Brilliant heart surgeon. I've known him ten or twelve years. Why?"

"Thank you for your time," said Miller. "They're finishing up and should be gone within the hour."

Detective Miller walked out of the house, followed by Kristen Day. Miller stood on the porch and looked out over the ambulance that was parked in front. Two attendants, waiting to be summoned in to take Elizabeth Clarke away, stood beside it smoking. In the fading light of the day, Erik Miller scanned the faces of the crowd gathered across the street. Later, he would study those faces in the photographs he had asked Jack Morgan to take, and he would talk with Scott Powers, a police officer out of uniform, who was now standing among the curious.

"It's not surprising that she knows Thomas," said Day as they walked down multiple steps to the street. "I'm surprised that he doesn't."

"I think we will find that she has been in the area a long time and that Doctor Hartigan may be a recent addition to Manchester," said Miller.

"Still, our Doctor Thomas Thomas keeps popping up in each murder."

"It's not him," said Miller. "Interesting what Hartigan said about looking into the eyes of madness and recognizing a higher intelligence. I've looked into the eyes of killers, and have never seen genius. I've seen cruelty. I've seen manipulative minds, working the angles, even while they gave the appearance of being bored. I've seen arrogance to the tenth degree. I've seen emptiness that is more than a little disturbing. I've even seen remorse for the crime, although not often. But I have never seen higher intelligence."

"You've been saying you thought the killer was intelligent, despite what you said in the bedroom," Day said as she opened the door of the car.

"Yeah. Well, I'm beginning to think I may have underestimated him."

The entire front of the residence had been taped off. On both sides of the tape, and across the street, the curious stood watching. As Miller walked to the driver's side of his Dodge, a voice called out to him.

"Detective Miller, has the killer struck again?"

Miller looked up to see a reporter from the newspaper, a man who he knew well from previous crime scenes. He was good at his job and he was a genuine pain in the ass. Standing beside him was a tall, thin woman, fashionably dressed, her long black hair framing an attractive face, a face that came into many New Hampshire homes at six and eleven each weekday evening from a television station in Boston.

"Detectives," she called out in that easily recognizable voice, "the people of Manchester have a right to know if they are safe in their homes. The people have a right to know more about these killings than the police are telling them."

Miller and Day ignored her and drove away.

"Four," said Miller. "We were warned that four would be the one where the crazies would come out of the woodwork and the public would become more vocal. I guess now we'll see."

IT WAS AFTER eight o'clock in the evening when they finally sat at Miller's desk unwrapping their burgers and fries. They had spent an uncomfortable few hours with Elizabeth's parents after leaving the Hartigan's house, informing them of her death and then bringing them to the morgue so they could identify the body. Mrs. Clarke appeared to be in a state of shock. Mr. Clarke, former military and veteran of Desert Storm, seemed ready to explode in a rage after identifying the body of his daughter. But his grief quickly overcame the rage and he broke down in tears after leaving the morgue. There were no words of comfort that the Detectives could share that would temper that grief. Before they parted, Mr. Clarke informed them that they would be taking Elizabeth back to Virginia to be buried in the family plot as soon as they were allowed, but they would return when her killer was captured.

Holding a fry in her hand, Day paused and looked at her partner. "Do you ever get used to it?" she asked. "Does it become easier?"

Miller swallowed the last of his burger, almost inhaling it he was so hungry.

"Does what become easier?"

"Telling someone their loved one is dead. Murdered. I can't imagine it becomes easier."

Miller shrugged. "Easier is not the word I would choose. It's never easy. And not for the reason you might think. It becomes more clinical. You become almost jaded. So many times it is the person you are telling who may be the killer, or the reason for the death, that you find yourself looking for any sign of that and not getting caught up in the grief they are displaying, or the emotions they are displaying, careful not to be fooled by what may be deceit. But in situations like we are dealing with now, it is still difficult telling someone their daughter, or wife, or loved one has been murdered.

"But what has changed, at least for me over the last few years, is the anxiety. Early on, when I first made detective, it was my job to find the killer. Piece together the clues. Put together a solid case that would bring the bastard to trial and hope the prosecutor didn't screw things up and the jury saw the truth and did their duty. That was the job. That was my mind set. That was it. Bowling league on Tuesday night, softball on Sunday mornings, maybe a weekend in Maine fishing and drinking with a few buddies. Back to work Monday morning. Back to the job."

Miller shifted in his seat. "But then you soon realize, rather quickly in fact, that any justice that is going to be dispensed, any relief that the grieving family may receive, rests entirely on your shoulders. Fuck things up, and the killer is never brought to trial, or he walks. Happens quite a lot. Not to me, yet, and hopefully never does, but one small mistake, and it could. Once that realization hits you, and after a few cases it does, the pressure builds. You've seen the faces of the loved ones when you've brought the killer to trial and the jury convicts and you always want to see that. You saw their anguish in the beginning, and now you want to see their tears again in the courtroom, but those are tears of relief. That doesn't happen if I don't do my job properly. There's the pressure. The pressure brings on the anxiety. Some people can treat this as just a job. I can't. Not anymore."

"Erik, that's not healthy. I get it, but you'll burn out. This is a job. Important, yes. Intense, yes. But you're not Superman."

"Let's see if you still feel the same way if we don't catch this guy soon," he said. "Let me know if you have no problem sleeping if the bodies keep piling up. For your sake, I hope if you do fall asleep, the faces you see in your dreams don't belong to Madeleine Seward and Elizabeth Clarke. I wish I could tell you that when I close my eyes at night, I don't see Maryanne Darrow, Helena Johnson, or Madeleine. I wish I could tell you that, but I can't."

Miller wrapped up what was left of his fries and put them in the metal trash receptacle next to his desk. He took several long sips of his drink through a straw and then put the cup on top of the fries. He leaned back in his chair and stared across the empty room. Day let the silence linger as she slowly worked on her dinner.

Finishing the last of the fries, Kristen neatly folded the paper wrapper and placed it in the bag and tossed it into the receptacle. "Where do you want to start tomorrow?"

Miller stirred like he was coming out of some day dream. "Well, we've already asked everyone in our files if they knew Elizabeth Clarke. No need to do that again. We canvas the Elm Street neighbors. See if anyone saw anything. Heard anything. Jack will have the photos ready that he took of the crowd. We check that with what we have of TV footage and see if any faces are the same. Check it with photos from the crowd at the museum and the cemetery." He looked at her. "Probably nothing will come of all that, but it needs to be done. We need to find Megan. Every fiber in my body is telling me that she is the key to all of this. We find Megan, we find our killer. She knows him. She knows who the killer is. She may not realize that she does, probably doesn't realize it, but I would bet my life that the killer is someone from Maryanne and Megan's past. I know it." He shook his head and looked away. "We have to find her."

12

KILLER STRIKES AGAIN! was the headline that stretched across Monday mornings front page in huge bold print. Below the headline, in smaller bold print, **4TH VICTIM FOUND! CITY ON EDGE.** And below that, dissected in half by the fold, a photograph taken of the scene in front of the Hartigan residence as Elizabeth Clarke's sheet covered body was being carried down the front steps on a stretcher. Two police cars, lights flashing, and an ambulance were in the foreground. Below the picture was the story, the words printed there telling less about the murdered victim and more about the growing unease of the residents of Manchester, complete with quotes from several neighbors fearful of what had happened in their neighborhood and what was happening in their city. Neither Doctor was quoted. The story continued on page five, including a photograph of Detectives Miller and Day looking over their car at something off to the side.

The two Detectives sat in their Chief's office, the morning paper resting on his cluttered desk. Outside the closed door of the office there was a bustle of activity, the weekend in the city having been more violent than usual. Chief Hendricks was in a foul mood.

"Four murders," Hendricks said, his eyes darting between the two Detectives, "and you're telling me there isn't one partial print, one fiber that shouldn't be there, one person who didn't see something, anything."

Neither Detective spoke, having told Hendricks exactly that only minutes before.

"Do we need help on this?" asked Hendricks. "Bring in the FBI?"

Miller shook his head.

"Not yet, Chief."

"What do you need?"

"There's a woman. Her name is Megan. I think she may be vital. I think she knows something even though she may not know she knows. We need to find her."

"Okay," said Hendricks. "Why don't we know where she is?"

"She's homeless," said Miller, then proceeded to tell his chief what he knew and what he suspected.

"Megan the Roach," said Hendricks with a shake of his head. "Just when you thought it couldn't get any weirder."

"I have a description of her. I've had a drawing made up. I want every cop in the city and surrounding towns to be on the lookout for her. She was homeless, probably still is. Probably still an addict. I've checked the shelters. They know her, but haven't seen her in months. They know to contact me if she shows up. We can't wait for that."

"I'll see it's done," said Hendricks. "I'll call the other Police Chiefs. They'll agree to have their officers on the lookout."

"I think this whole thing began because of Marianne. I don't think she was chosen because of her name, but because she knew the killer. I think killing her, for whatever grievance the killer believed justified him doing so, then manifested the sicko to continue on, leading into what we have now. I think the selection of victims because of their names came from Marianne Darrow having a name that resonated with the killer. Maybe he's a movie buff. Maybe he's just a *King Kong* fan and ended up doing what we did, looking up old horror movies and getting the names of actresses and the parts they played, so he could use them as victims. Who the hell knows? We need to find Megan the Roach."

Hendricks picked up a piece of paper from his desk and held it out to Kristen Day. She looked at it for several seconds, then leaned over and took it from him.

"What's this?" she asked.

"While Miller is co-ordinating the search for this Roach woman, I want you to follow up on this."

"Professor Wendell Weasley?" Day said, reading the name on the piece of paper.

"He's at Colby-Sawyer. Teaches a course on film making. Supposedly an expert on the early years of the industry. Silent movies and early talkies. He spoke with the Chief up there, who suggested he call me. Which he did just a half-hour ago. Won't hurt to talk with him. Maybe he can give us some insight that we novices in the film world might find useful. At this point, I'll take all the help we can get."

The two Detectives stood and walked to the door.

"We've already received seventeen calls this morning from people claiming to know who the killer is," said Hendricks. "I've received calls this morning from newspapers and television stations in Boston, New York and Chicago, and it's not even ten yet. I'm getting attention I don't want. You understand?" He gave them both a hard look before turning his attention to his monitor and hitting a key on the keyboard.

INSPECTOR DAY, DO you understand what it is you are dealing with?" asked Professor Wendell Weasley. "It appears you have a killer who is mimicking scenes from old horror movies. Not only that, but he is choosing his victims because of their names."

They sat at a table along the side wall in the spacious school cafeteria, far from the few students who were having a late afternoon snack. Each had a cup of coffee in front of them. Weasley's cup had a slice of apple pie beside it.

Kristen looked at the man who sat across from her, remembering that she had almost smiled too broadly when he had entered the cafeteria for their three o'clock meeting. His thin frame stood almost five and a half feet tall. He had light brown hair that was turning to gray, worn to a length that was more fashionable in the seventies. He sported a bushy mustache that cried out for trimming, and wore slacks and a suit coat that may have been worn by Robert Donat in *Goodbye, Mr. Chips!* complete with a neat bow tie. A man of eighty might have been able to carry off the look, but Professor Weasley looked to be at least twenty years younger than that and an elbow patched corduroy would have suited him better.

"I have only a few photos that have been in the newspaper, and reporting that has received very little information from the authorities, to go on, but, because of the names of the victims, it is obvious what the killer is doing."

"And what might that be, Professor?"

"Obviously, he is posing his victims in scenes from the old horror movies from the thirties. Of course I can't be one hundred percent sure because I haven't seen a photo of the first victim, but the body of that young woman at the museum, and the one at the cemetery, and now, according to the newspaper, a body found in a bed dressed as a bride, obviously *Frankenstein,* well, what else could it be? And then you have the names. Darrow, Seward, and the last unfortunate child, Elizabeth Clarke. What more evidence do you need? By the way, in case you don't know, Elizabeth does die in her bed, killed by the monster, in the book. Of course, in the movie, *Bride of,* she does survive."

Using a spoon, he took a large scoop of pie.

"The only problem I see with everything is, in the movies the women do not perish. It is the monster who dies. Of course, if the monster were to die now, we wouldn't have a serial killer would we?" Weasley chuckled at that. "I'm assuming you picked up on these clues. Am I correct in that assumption?"

Day leaned in a little, in a conspiratorial manner and raised her brown eye brows, her brown eyes peering into his.

"Can I trust you to keep this conversation private, Professor? Something just between the two of us?"

"Of course, Inspector Day. I am well aware of how sensitive information, leaked to the citizenry, can cause the police damage in the case they are building. Mum is the word." He placed an index finger over his lips and gave a slight nod. Kristen almost smiled.

Weasley leaned in, his eyes alight, both their upper bodies now over the table.

"You are correct," whispered Day.

The Professor nodded.

"Do the police have a suspect?" he whispered, and then quickly looked around to make sure no one was listening. When Kristen didn't answer, he quickly said, "Well, of course you couldn't tell me, could you? Four young women. This is a very evil person. I do hope you apprehend him before he strikes again."

Kristen leaned back and sipped her coffee.

"Professor, we are leaning towards your theory and have been for about a month now. We have a rather large list of names, and ideas of which books or movies may be used. If you were committing these murders, which monsters might we expect to be used next?"

"Me? Oh, I would never," said Weasley, leaning back. "I abhor violence."

Kristen said, "Yet you study and teach about movies that are incredibly violent for the times that they were created."

"Oh, no," said the Professor. "The 1930's was a very violent time in our history. Newspapers were full of gangland slayings. The movies made during that time really had the pulse of the country. Maybe more than at any time before or since. Violence made big movie stars out of Cagney, Robinson, Bogart, George Raft. Oh, many others. Even before all of that gangland violence, *Frankenstein* was a huge success. Made tons of money for Universal Studios. Saved the studio, actually. And then came *Dracula, The Mummy,* all the Sons of and sequels to that Hollywood could make. You have to understand, the country was in a terrible economic Depression. Money was scarce. Yet all these movies made money. The public wanted monsters. They wanted to be frightened out of their minds in the safety of a theater. They couldn't get enough of it."

Weasley took another bite of pie. "Think about it. Emotionally, it was the most frightening time in this country's history. If you had a job, you might find it gone tomorrow. You may have been one week away from being unable to feed your family. Entire savings were being lost in the blink of an eye. And Monster movies were packing theaters across the country. Really quite incredible when you think about it."

"You must cover all of that in your lectures," said Day.

"Of course. It's rather fascinating, don't you think?"

He finished off the pie, dabbed at his lips and mustache with a napkin, missing a small piece of crust nestled among the bristling hair above his upper lip, and took in a long breath.

"I was born in nineteen fifty-one," he said, "and was rather sickly as a child. While others were out playing, the days of my youth were usually spent on the sofa in front of our television, a black and white model until I was fourteen, I might add. In the early days of television, it was quite common for old movies to be on in the afternoon. Especially when new stations beyond the big three began broadcasting. It was all they could afford to offer, you see. I fell in love with those old movies. They were the only companions I had."

Weasley smiled. "You appear to be quite a healthy woman, Inspector. I imagine you had a rather active childhood. Running and playing. Lots of friends to occupy your time. Mostly, I was alone. Father was Vice-principal at the high school and mother taught third grade. They home schooled me at night until I entered high school. So, I had a great many hours in which to watch old movies during the day. It was either that or game shows. Can you imagine?" he said with a shake of his head, signaling his obvious distaste.

"I found that I enjoyed the movies from the thirties more than the ones from the forties. I didn't like the war movies, the ones made during and after World War Two. I wasn't particularly fond of the light comedy romance movies like Tracy and Hepburn made. Or the silly detective movies like The Thin Man or Charlie Chan. I wanted more substance. I wanted an edge to the story. Some excitement. Something that made me sit up on the sofa. The gangster movies from the thirties did that. Police cars chasing the bad men, speeding along city streets, screeching tires taking hairpin turns, sub machine guns spraying non-stop bullets. It was all so exciting. Tough guys, Cagney and Robinson, talking tough, acting tough, playing outside the rules. And even though you knew that they would get theirs in the end, you found yourself rooting for them."

Professor Weasley paused, smiled, and his eyes scanned the nearly empty cafeteria.

"Isn't it strange," he said, his gaze settling on Kristen. "that we would root for the bad guys? That they had our sympathy, these killers? That we would feel despair as Cagney was led to the electric chair? That we would weep as Edward G. slumped to the ground after being shot? That, in the end, they had our empathy?"

Kristen sat quietly while Professor Weasley silently sipped his coffee, his eyes staring down at the empty pie plate. When he finally looked up, he smiled again.

"And then, one day, *Frankenstein* was on. Well, has there ever been a more sympathetic creature?"

He shook his head sadly.

"Have you seen the movie, Inspector? Not the remakes. The original. With Karloff."

"I have," said Kristen.

"What did you think?"

Kristen smiled. "I tend to agree with you, Professor. So far, we believe we have had scenes from *Frankenstein, Dracula, The Mummy* and *King Kong,"* she said, steering him back to why she was there.

"King Kong," said Weasley. "Of course I surmised that because of the victim's name. That would have been the first killing? The one the press has no photographs of? Interesting that. Doesn't really fit the mold of human killers, does it? Quite interesting. Mmm. I wonder what it means?"

"I suppose it doesn't fit the mold," replied Day. "We believe we may see scenes from *The Wolf Man* and *The Hunchback of Notre Dame*. *The Invisible Man* is a possibility. Can you think of others we may not have thought of?"

"Well, let me think," said Weasley, the index finger of his right hand scratching at his mustache. "Have you considered *Jekyl and Hyde?* It is a marvelous movie starring Fredric March from 1931 and, of course, a splendid book by Robert Louis Stevenson. John Barrymore was magnificent in the 1921 silent. Spencer Tracy took a fling at it, also, but March is the standard bearer. *Nosferatu* is one of the more famous silent movies, a frightening looking vampire. It was Bela Lugosi who gave the vampire sex appeal. I think you are on the right track with *The Wolf Man* and *Hunchback.* They were within that time frame. *Wolf Man* just a few years beyond the thirties. I would go with those two and *Jekyl and Hyde.*"

Weasley put his right hand up, suddenly, like he was going to ask to be excused so he could go to the bathroom.

"Wait, wait," he said. "Before the 1941 *Wolf Man,* there was a British movie from 1935 called *The Werewolf of London* starring Henry Hull. Quite successful and really well done. You may want to check that out."

He smiled and nodded in satisfaction. Then he said: "Have you seen the Charles Laughton *Hunchback*?"

Kristen nodded and almost smiled as she watched the older man's mind bouncing from film to film.

"Wonderful performance, don't you think? But try to get your hands on the silent from 1923 with Lon Chaney. Incredible. Chaney was the best.

"There were many other horror movies from the thirties," continued Weasley, in his element now. "Hollywood couldn't make them fast enough. There were so many, in fact, and they were becoming ever more gruesome, that the censors had to step in. First, insisting that the movies receive an "H" to designate them accordingly, and then even becoming more rigid. Eventually, by the end of the decade, the genre crumbled under the weight of all the productions. There was a brief rebound with *Son of Frankenstein* and two years later *The Wolf Man,* but by then the movie going public was moving on from horror movies and gangster films to other things. The Depression was over and the world was at war. Karloff and Lugosi needed Abbott and Costello to keep them on the Silver Screen. Such a shame."

"You mentioned other movies?" asked Day.

"Oh, yes," said Weasley. "Quite a few, actually. The early part of the decade saw movies like *Doctor X* with Fay Wray, famous for *King Kong* and directed by Michael Curtiz, who, of course, did *Casablanca*. *Island of Lost Souls* with Laughton and Lugosi. *White Zombie* from 1932, also with Bela. *The Mask of Fu Manchu* with Karloff. *The Raven* with Karloff and Lugosi. Dozens of them, Inspector Day. My course covers the early horror talkies and the silents from the early days, but I could spend the entire semester just doing horror movies from the thirties and never cover them all."

The Professor smiled sympathetically. "I'm afraid there is a huge body of work that your killer can draw from. I don't envy you."

WHEN DAY WALKED into Homicide in the late afternoon after her drive back from seeing Professor Wendell Weasley, all the desks had detectives sitting at them. Matt Blanchette was the only one to look up and nod at her. Mark Allen, back from his brief sabbatical, kept his head lowered. Two others were busy finishing up written reports. Erik Miller was on the phone. Day sat at the chair beside his desk and waited for him to finish the call.

"So, how did it go with the college Prof?" asked Miller when he hung up.

"It was interesting," said Day, "but I don't think you're going to be happy." She then filled him in on her conversation with Professor Weasley.

"I've never heard of any of those movies," said Miller.

"Me either," said Day. "I'm going to go online now and see what I can find. Type in all movies from the thirties and then see which ones were horror movies and had maniac killers. Then I'll type in each of those and get a cast list and a character list and start a new name list."

"It'll be hundreds of names," said Miller.

Day shrugged.

"You think it could be a monster beyond the list we have?" asked Miller. "Beyond the more famous ones?"

Again Day shrugged.

"Jesus Christ," whispered Miller leaning back into his chair.

13

It was almost seven before Miller and Day decided to call it a day. They had added twenty more movies to their list based on what Professor Weasley had said, adding another seventy-five names to watch for on the Missing Person reports. They then checked old reports to see if any of those names had already popped up, which they had not. It was all overwhelming. Miller had suggested getting a beer before going home, and Day had agreed to go with him.

The bar on Union Street was nearly empty, the afternoon customers having gone home and the evening crowd not yet arrived. Miller held up two fingers when Eve looked over from behind the bar, and then moved to a corner table, Kristen following.

"I don't want to talk about the case," said Miller. "I don't want to think about that list of names until tomorrow."

"Fine with me," said Day. "What do you want to talk about?"

"I don't care. Anything but the case. Or nothing at all. I'm fine just sitting here in peace."

Eve came over with two bottles of beer and set them down.

"Eve, this is Detective Kristen Day," said Miller as he scooped up one of the bottles. "Day, this is Eve, a genuine pain in my ass."

Kristen smiled up at the attractive, young, black woman, searching her face to see if Miller's comment had upset her. She saw no sign that it had, and she had the immediate sense that there was affection between the two of them. Where could that have come from, she found herself wondering.

"Are you helping Erik catch the serial killer?" Eve asked.

Kristen noticed that Eve smiled when she asked the question, but that her dark eyes were coolly appraising her at the same time. Kristen's first thought was, Eve was jealous. Jealous of another woman sharing the company of Erik. But then she decided, no, that the young woman wasn't jealous at all. That Eve was appraising her like a mother might do to a woman her son brought over to diner for the first time, or a daughter might do to the woman her divorced father had suddenly taken up with.

'Ballsy little bitch, isn't she?' thought Kristen. She found, surprisingly, that she wasn't angry with Eve's judgmental eyes. In fact, she found it amusing that Miller had a little pit bull watching out for him, and he probably was unaware that he had.

"We are working the case together, yes," said Day, also smiling. "Personally, Eve, I think he is working much too hard on it. It's beginning to wear him down, I think."

Eve quickly nodded her head. "That's what I told him. I said, Erik, you are looking very tired. Don't let this guy get to you. Even Matt agreed with me. How do we get him to slow down, Kristen? I'm really worried about him."

"Hey, I'm sitting right here, you know," Miller said, exasperated. "Stop talking about me like I'm not." He looked up at Eve. "Go wipe down the bar, or something."

Eve frowned at him, then smiled at Kristen. "You and I should talk sometime," she said. "Make sure our boy here is taking care of himself."

"Eve!" Miller loudly said.

"Okay, okay," said Eve and winked at Kristen as she walked away. Half way to the bar, Eve turned around and said, "When you coming to hear me sing?"

"I'm not," said Miller. "Go away."

Eve smiled and then executed three perfect pirouettes that brought her behind the bar. Kristen noticed that her compact body moved with grace. She turned to speak, but Miller cut her off before she could.

"Long story," he said, "and I'm not in the mood."

"She adores you, you know."

"Yeah, she's the mother I never wished for. Enough about her."

"She's a singer? She any good?"

"She's singing Rap karaoke at some places in town. I've never heard her sing. She says she can. Enough about Eve. Some other time." He paused, then said, "She's a good kid."

Day took a sip of the beer. She was not a beer drinker, preferring red wine instead, but this was a bar where the customers drank beer. Or something stronger. But not wine.

"Alright, no talk about the case and no talk about the cute kid behind the bar," said Kristen. "What should we talk about?"

"Let's talk about you," said Miller.

"Me?" Day said. "I'm never comfortable talking about me."

"Fine. Then tell me some stories from your playing days in college. Some of the women you played with. Some games that got a little crazy. Make them funny. I could use a laugh. Hell, you played four years. There must have been a few crazy nights."

Kristen looked at him, and then looked over at Eve working behind the long bar. She was talking to an old man who had just sat down. Kristen noticed that every so often Eve looked over at their table. Day looked back at Miller, slouching in the chair, his legs stretched out in front of him. He had loosened his tie, the suit coat unbuttoned. She felt like saying, 'You comfortable,

Erik? Want me to entertain you with stories from fifteen years ago about college basketball? Something funny, because you've had a bad day? Something maybe a little crazy so you can have a little laugh? Sure, why not'.

Except she had none to share. At least none that were funny. All-Conference her freshman year, followed by a slow downward spiral that had her playing less than five minutes a game her senior year. The coach, hired before the start of her junior year, was an asshole, as was one of the assistants who had kept hitting on her. During Kristen's junior year, the team was led by a freshman center who was a colossal talent and a first-rate prima dona bitch. That was the beginning of less playing time for Kristen. Kristen's senior year, a freshman point guard ran the offense and it was rare when the ball ended up in Kristen's hands on offense during the seven minutes she was in the game. And those seven minutes of court time could easily disappear if complaints about any of that were voiced. Such fun. Lots of laughs.

Kristen Day had been in this situation before, several times, with colleagues who sought to know more about the person they worked with. The innocent questions about playing college ball that were only the opening salvo for what was to come; the more personal queries about past affairs and on-going relationships. Why not married, why no children, all a prelude so they could lament the failures in their own lives of failed marriages and relationships. Kindred spirits, were they not?

But Kristen had no desire to share past indignities with her partner. Nor did she care to hear his. So, in between sips from the bottle, she made up several tales and spun them across the table doing her best to make them humorous. A slight smile was frozen on Miller's face as Kristen recounted things that had never actually happened, but, looking into his eyes, Kristen could tell he wasn't really listening to what she was saying. His mind was somewhere else. And she knew where that was.

"I'LL COME DOWN," Detective Erik Miller said into the phone before hanging it up. He looked over at Kristen Day, who was looking over at him from her desk, held up an index finger to signal he would be back in a minute, and walked out of the room. A minute later he entered again, accompanied by a man.

Day looked at the man and furrowed her brow. He stood about six foot three, about three inches taller than Miller. His body was lean, but he had wide shoulders and his bare forearms appeared powerful. The face was thin, unwrinkled and clean shaven. His sandy colored hair was long and tied in a neat ponytail. He wore a solid black tee shirt that was tight across his chest and tucked into beige khakis. A black cashmere sweater was casually draped over his shoulders with the sleeves knotted around his throat, as if he were a singer of songs keeping his voice box warm. The black framed eye glasses perched on his nose were so large as to be almost comical, a disturbing contradiction to the panther like effect that his body projected. Miller caught her eye, nodded toward the interrogation room and steered the man towards it. Day followed quickly, closing the door behind her and taking a seat next to her partner and across the table from the other man. The man smiled up at her, a smile of amusement which Day found disturbing.

"This is my partner, Detective Day," said Miller. "This gentleman is Mr. Rene Cormier. He believes he may have some information that can help us with our investigation."

Day raised her eyebrows. "Really? And what might that be?"

"It's a theory, really," said Cormier, "but I think, from what I have gathered from what has been written in the newspapers, that it is an educated theory, and, perhaps, not one you may have entertained."

"And what, exactly, might that theory be?" asked Miller.

"I believe you may have a copycat killer on your hands, Detectives, and I may be able to help you catch him if you share some information that you have withheld from the public."

"A copycat?" said Miller, ignoring, for the time being, the request for more information, which would never happen. "I see. You think the recent murders of young women may be similar to killings that happened somewhere else, or in another time? Can you be more specific, Mr. Cormier?"

Cormier shook his head quickly twice. "Well, no, not actual killings." He smiled at Day again, while answering Miller. "Not real life killings. No. I believe this killer is mimicking murders, and scenes, from horror movies from the past. Movies and books, actually."

Miller shot Day a quick look. "Could you explain?" he asked Cormier, who had slipped off his glasses and was deliberately polishing them with a handkerchief produced from a pants pocket..

"Of course. It's rather obvious, really. Taken separately, each murder seems bizarre, but taken as a whole, well, there is a method to the madness."

Miller smiled. "Enlighten us if you would."

"So far, judging by the pictures I have seen and the reports I have read in the newspaper, the killer has been using his victims to create scenes from old horror movies. Or books. Actually, it was a scene from a book that made me realize what was going on. Up till then, I gave the murders very little thought."

"And which victim was that?" asked Miller, knowing the answer already.

"Obviously, the murder of Elizabeth Clarke," said Cormier, placing the glasses back on his face. As he did, Day noticed that he looked older than she had first guessed he was. From a distance he had looked like a man in his late thirties, but she saw now, up close, that he had had some surgery and he was, probably, closer to being in his mid-fifties.

"Why obviously?" asked Day.

"Because she was found lying in a bed dressed in a wedding gown. At least that is what has been reported in the newspapers. You didn't share that with the press, did you Detective? But there is a rumor going around, and if that is true, and I have no reason to doubt it, then the killer is copying a scene from the novel *Frankenstein* by Mary Shelley. In the movie, Dr. Frankenstein's intended does not perish at the hands of the monster, but in the book, she does. This is the act that sends the Doctor on his search for the monster, so he can kill him.

"That murder was the one that got me thinking. Then I looked more deeply into the killings from the last few months. The girl tied and dangling from a tree limb could easily be *King Kong*, if one was piecing a scenario together. The lady left in the cemetery, propped against a cross, well, by itself it may seem an attempt at a religious statement, but, when looked at in the context of the greater picture, *Dracula* certainly comes to mind. The young woman left in front of the museum, well, singularly it makes no sense, but, again, in the larger context, we could make a case for *The Mummy.* The problem with all of this, of course, is *King Kong*.

"Supposing your theory is correct, Mr. Cormier," said Miller, "why is Kong a problem?"

He looked at Miller and smiled condescendingly. "He doesn't belong in this. Has no place in this scenario. The monster movies, *Frankenstein, Dracula, The Mummy,* etc, were done by Universal Pictures in the early thirties. Great movies. In fact, it's well known that Universal was very near bankruptcy when they made *Frankenstein* and that the incredible success of the movie with the paying public probably saved the studio. But it was RKO who did *King Kong.* At least it was done in 1933, similar time frame as the classic monster movies, but it wasn't a

Universal film."

"You seem to know a lot about these movies, Mr. Cormier," said Miller. "You have a fascination with them?"

"Oh, it's a hobby of mind," said Cormier. "I'm a bit of a movie buff. Particularly horror. Over the years, I have watched the remakes of these movies done by the big stars of our times, and I became curious about the earlier versions. So I rented them and watched them and found them to be more interesting than the remakes. And all of them in black and white. Anyway, I found myself reading up on all the old movies, and it became an obsession. I have quite a collection, I must say, of paraphernalia from those movies. Quite extensive, actually. I'm very proud of it."

"A collection?" asked Day, leaning slightly towards the man.

"Oh, yes," said Cormier, beaming. "I have a first American edition of *Frankenstein: Or the Modern Prometheus,* as it was titled by Mary Shelley, from 1833. Published by Carey, Lea and Blanchard of Philadelphia. A two volume set in very nice condition."

He turned slightly in his seat to better face Day. "A stunning first edition of *Dracula* by Bram Stoker from 1897, the yellow boards amazingly still vibrant. It came from a very famous collection of a noted author, by the way. Oh, and recently, I acquired a first edition of *The Invisible Man,* the H.G. Wells classic, in pristine condition." Cormier's eyebrows raised, his eyes opened wide and he looked quite ecstatic. "Signed," he said, and added a knowing nod for punctuation.

"Quite the collection," said Miller, having no idea if they were valuable or not, but thought they might be. "Are first editions valuable?"

"In the condition mine are in, you could purchase a brand new Lexus."

"Interesting."

"With each book," said Cormier with a slight nod.

"Not just books, Detective, although they are the cream of the collection. I have a set of boots that Karloff wore in *Frankenstein*. The suit coat Lon Chaney, Jr. wore in *The Wolf Man.* Also, an outfit that Evelyn Ankers wore in the same movie. The frock Maureen O'Hara wore as Esmeralda." He shook his head and pursed his lips. "Recently, I believed I had the inside track in owning a dress that Fay Wray wore in *King Kong*, but a collector in Arizona outbid me. That was most disturbing. I'll regret not bidding higher for the rest of my life. Can you imagine owning that?

"I have a signed screenplay from *Frankenstein,* signed by Carl Laemmle who produced the film, and another from *Bride of Frankenstein* signed by James Whale who directed it. A signed picture of Elsa Lancaster in make-up on the set of that picture. I have a coat that Claude Rains wore in *The Invisible Man.* I have many other pieces from those early movies, but those are my pride and joys."

Cormier leaned forward and gave a devilish smile. "There's a rumor going around, among us collectors, that the person who owns the incredible outfit that Zita Johann wore in *The Mummy*, along with the outfit Karloff wore as he stood over her prone body, will soon be offered for bids. I can only imagine what they are going to cost, but whatever it ends up being, I have to own them."

"What is it you do for a living, Mr. Cormier?" asked Miller.

"Oh, I'm retired."

"Rather young to be retired."

Cormier smiled.

"I'm a very wealthy man, Detective. Very wealthy. Made a fortune in software. So I can indulge my passions as much as I want. Buy anything I want."

"So you're a computer genius?" asked Miller.

"Not hardly. I don't understand how the internet works at all. Only that it is amazing. With a few words typed in, I can be looking at people and places who have things that interest me. Quite remarkable, really. No, I made my fortune buying stock in companies where the people running the company knew about the internet and knew where it could take us."

"What did you do when you worked?" Miller asked.

"Not that it has anything to do with your investigation," said Cormier with a patient smile, "but I worked for the government. NASA to be exact. I was, what layman refer to as, a rocket scientist. A different kind of genius from a computer genius, but a genius just the same."

Cormier looked from Miller to Day and grinned. "I'm assuming you have picked up on the monster theme already, because you didn't seem surprised when I mentioned it. But," Rene Cormier paused and looked at each detective again, "did you pick up on the names of the victims? How similar they are to the characters in the movies or the women who played them?"

Seeing no reaction in the eyes of the two detectives, Cormier slouched back in his chair. "You did, didn't you? I must say, I'm impressed."

Miller stood. "I want to thank you for coming in to see us, Mr. Cormier. You've given us an interesting perspective on the killings."

Cormier stood, looked at both again, and nodded his head a few times. "Detective Miller, I don't believe I have given you anything you didn't already have. And yet, you still haven't caught the killer. This must be extremely frustrating for the both of you. Perhaps, if you take me into your confidence, I may be able to help you."

"It's an ongoing investigation," said Miller, "but, who knows, as it moves along we may call on you for your expertise."

Cormier walked slowly to the door, paused and turned around, disappointment obvious in his stance. "You can expect that *The Wolf Man* will get used. Also, *The Invisible Man* could be on the list."

"Any thoughts on *Godzilla*?" asked Miller.

"Oh, I seriously doubt that," replied Cormier. "Made in the fifties. A female character in the movie, yes, the scientists daughter, but the similarity ends there. Not a Universal movie, either. No, I would be shocked if that one is used." Cormier smiled, "Of course, if the killer uses all the others, then he may have to resort to the fire breather.

"I'm up in Center Harbor, and you have my number, Detectives, if you find yourselves with any questions about those old movies. Good luck."

Erik Miller sat back down after Cormier left and looked over at Kristen, who was smiling.

"Quite the character," she said.

"Did it occur to you, while he was telling us all this, that he might be the killer?" asked Miller.

"What? That guy? No. No way. He basically told us what Professor Weasley said to me. They might not be the only two out there with this fascination with old horror movies, either. I won't be surprised if another one shows up."

Miller wasn't listening to his partner. His eyes were narrowed and unable to focus on anything in the room.

"He comes in here and tells us what the killer is doing. Posing bodies. Even tells us he's picking his victims because of their names. Mocking us. You guys are so dumb, you don't even know what's going on, so here, let me help you."

"Erik, I don't think....."

"No, this is exactly what the killer would do. Taunt us. Just like every taunting note he has sent. Now he escalates it, taunting us in person. He just told us he's a genius. Rocket scientist. Smarter than every dumb cop. He hides behind the good Samaritan routine. I really want to help you guys. Let me help. Tell me some stuff that you think you know. Dumb bastards don't even have a clue."

Miller slammed a palm down on the metal table.

"Rene Cormier, if that's even his name, is probably laughing to himself all the way to his car. At our expense. The son-of-a-bitch could have been sitting right here."

Miller kicked out at the folding chair that Cormier had sat on, sending it skittering across the floor and bumping into the far wall.

"Erik...."

Miller suddenly stood and headed for the door.

"I want to go over the photos we took of the people who were standing around during the last three crime scenes. I'll bet a paycheck, Mr. Rene Cormier will be standing in that crowd. The son-of-a-bitch."

"Erik," Day called to him again as he opened the door.

"Son-of-a-bitch," she heard him say again as he left the room.

Day went to her desk and typed 'Rene Cormier' into the computer. A dozen hits came up. She scrolled past the first four and eventually came to a picture of the man who had only a few minutes before been in the Interrogation Room. Younger, but the same man. The short bio confirmed that he had, indeed, worked for NASA up until ten years before.

Days' cell chirped. She looked at the number and didn't recognize it.

"Detective Day," Kristen said as she placed the phone up to her ear, keeping the speaker off in the confines of the room.

"Detective Day, this is Doctor Thomas. Do you remember me?"

Kristen smiled and gave a slight shake of her head. 'Men. They were so damn predictable.' For effect, she hesitated before answering.

"Detective Day?"

"Dr. Thomas. Yes. Of course I do. Have you remembered something about Ms. Johnson?"

"No, I'm afraid I haven't. I really had no dealings with her except for the times we talked about her father's surgery. No, I'm calling about Dani Gallagher."

"Mrs. Gallagher-Hartigan?" asked Day, forcing herself to put a touch of surprise into the question. This was a call she had been expecting ever since the woman had told them that she knew Dr. Thomas.

"That's right, yes," said Thomas. "Of course, yes, she's married now. I just read that. Actually, I knew she was getting married last year when the announcement was made. I don't know her husband. Never met him. I understand that he is a doctor, also. "

"Why are you calling, Doctor?"

"Yes. Right," said Thomas. "I'm sure you're busy. I'm calling because I happened to have dated Dani eight or nine years ago. We dated for quite a while. Actually lived together for a month or two. I was thinking, you know, because I know her so well, that if you had some questions about her, well, you know, I might be able to answer them for you. We were quite close."

"She's not a suspect, Dr. Thomas," said Day. "They weren't even in the country when Elizabeth Clarke was abducted."

"Oh, no, I don't mean anything like that," said Thomas quickly. "But I know Dani can be a difficult person to talk with. To get information from. She can be quite self-centered, which is why we broke up. And just a bit scatter-brained."

"I find it surprising you would say that, having talked with her," said Day. "She seemed to me anything but scatter-brained."

"Perhaps she has changed," said the Doctor. "Thirty seems to do that to some people. Still, I could give you some insight if you think it might be helpful."

Kristen, playing Doctor Thomas, hesitated.

After several seconds, Thomas said, "Just meet for coffee downtown, is all I'm suggesting."

"You don't want to come to the station?" said Day, and smiled.

"I'd rather not," said Thomas. "I'd hate to be seen by anyone I might know entering or leaving a police station."

"Of course," said Day. She hesitated again. Then, "What's a convenient time?"

"Tonight. Seven thirty," said Thomas, his response quick and his tone more forceful, more sure of himself.

Again Kristen smiled to herself, smiled at the predictability of the man. Coffee had just become drinks.

"Where?" is all she said.

He told her where and said goodbye. Hanging up, Detective Day looked over at her partner's desk. Miller hadn't returned yet. She considered telling him about the call from Thomas, but decided against it. At least not yet.

14

I loved my grandfather. I loved him more than I loved anyone else. More than anything. And I believe that he loved me, too. More than anyone else did. I think about that as I drive along this back road with Mantovani playing softly on the cd player.

His daughter, my mother, was not mother material. She lacked a maternal instinct, I'm afraid. I believe she cared for me and, if asked, she would have said she loved me. And she probably would have believed it. But she didn't. I think, in those quiet moments late at night, sitting on the sofa in the dark of our living room, a cigarette burning down between fingers of one hand and a half empty glass of gin in the other, she resented me. Resented my being alive, wishing for the life she could have had had I not been born.

I believe my father loved me, but I believe he saw me as a burden. I remember watching, year after year, as life seemed to slowly wear him down, eroding away his spirit and making him seem old before his time. I think, in hindsight, I now see that it was the long hours of his job and the stabbing criticisms of his wife that aged him, and not me, but back then I placed the blame squarely on my doorstep. I think I may have done that quite a bit, placing blame on myself for things which were not my fault.

But I do think, even now, that had I not been born, my father would have quit his job, quit his wife and searched for a more agreeable existence. So, I guess, in fact, I was to blame.

I think my Grandmother loved me, at least until the accident, but she was not a demonstrative woman, and as I got older I saw that she was an angry woman, and not a very pleasant person. After Grandfather died, she became quite belligerent and that put even more of a strain on my parent's marriage. And, of course, her attitude towards me became one of indifference. I couldn't blame her for that. Not after what had happened. She died ten years after her husband, and in those ten years she had never uttered a single kind word to me. Again, in hindsight, I probably should have expected none. Still, it hurt.

But Grandfather loved me and I knew it as sure as I knew the sun would light the sky every morning. He loved me unconditionally, regardless of what mischief I may have been up to, or what catastrophe my mother accused me of creating. He recognized things in me that others failed to notice and loved me just the same. Who knows, but perhaps, in his younger days, in the earlier decades of the twentieth century, he may have been an aggressive lad among his peers, too, and caused his parents, my great-grandparents, who died long before I arrived, some grief. Maybe he recognized something in me that he knew well. Maybe that was why we read books, watched movies, built models of men who weren't quite normal. Men who caused some mischief in accepted society. Men who earned the designation of monster, undeserved in my opinion. Could he have been trying to show me that I wasn't all that bad? That I wasn't a bad human being, just, perhaps, that I had a darker side hiding in me that most others did not have? Was that why we watched movies and read books about these men? Was he trying to show me what evil was really like and that I was not evil? Not like them. Not like those men we watched and read about and then built models of. Perhaps.

In my young mind, I did not see these monsters as evil. I saw them as men who were misunderstood. Men who had been cruelly treated by society for circumstances that were beyond their control. Frankenstein had had no wish to be re-animated. The Count and Larry Talbot did not seek the bites that afflicted them. Quasimodo didn't ask for the deformity that led others to torture him. These men were to be pitied, not despised.

The ridicule I suffered in my young life was nothing like what these monsters faced, and I'm sure Grandfather wanted me to see that. But the taunting hurt me just the same. I think, in retrospect, I may have over-reacted to the bullying and the taunts. But I was young and didn't know how to ignore them or not be affected by them. And I became angry. I did things that were not nice. And after I did them, after the anger passed and I saw that what I had done was not how a person should act, a person who wanted to be good, I felt some guilt. Unable to talk with my preoccupied mother, or absent father, about these things I had done, I finally confessed my sins to my Grandfather. He listened patiently, nodding as I spoke, and, when I was done, he hugged me and said that he understood why I had done what I had and that it really wasn't that bad. And then he said, 'You want to see people doing bad things? I'll show you people doing really bad things. And then you'll see what you did is not so bad. But you should learn to control your temper'. That was how we began reading the books, watching the movies, building the models. It was the reason for it. But as time passed, and we finished Frankenstein and Dracula and Wolf Man, I came to realize, that for my Grandfather, the time we spent together was more than just for me. It was also for him.

Grandfather was right. The things that I did in anger back then were not so very bad. I never struck anyone. I wasn't cruel to animals or anything like that. I didn't kick puppies or drown cats.

At least not on purpose. I may have flattened bicycle tires of the kids who taunted me. I may have placed used bubble gum on the classroom seats of those who bullied me. Maybe, a few times during recess, I may have gone through their book bags and found their homework and ripped it up. But I was never physical with anyone. Certainly not before I had my growth spurt. Maybe a little after.

I think the frustration I feel now when my partners don't participate in what I hope to accomplish, probably stems from those days of taunting and bullying. Maybe I'm looking for something I had back then with my Grandfather, those times when we were together and I was at peace, and found solace from the constant taunts in the simple act of building something together. Maybe that is what I'm hoping to find now with the women I have chosen to help me. That peace that eludes me on a daily basis. Unfortunately, that has not happened. Not yet, anyway. But I keep hoping.

I no longer am taunted by anyone, no longer do I allow others to bully me. One only has to look at me to know that I would not tolerate anything like that and to do so could be hazardous to your health. But that doesn't mean I don't recognize the slights that I have had to deal with over the years. Those are real, and they sting and anger just as much as any bullying ever did. Bullying erodes a person's self worth, as does being passed over for career advancement in your profession, as does rejection in affairs of the heart.

I've read the newspaper accounts and listened to the talking heads on television reporting the crimes I've committed and I am well aware that what I am doing is not acceptable behavior in the society we now reside in. Taking the life of another, is wrong. Ending the life of an innocent woman, is wrong. I wish my efforts didn't have to end like they do. But, of course, they must. Taking someone against their will, regardless of how important it may be to do so, is a punishable offense. Conviction would bring prison time. Incarceration is out of the question. So I have no choice in the final act of our performance, or the finality of it. Still, it hurts me to read and hear reports that label me a monster. A sick killer. What the hell do they know?

I wish I had someone in my life now who would share my desire to connect with a happier time in my life, who would help me go through the process, from start to finish, so I would not have to seek partners in the effort. Unfortunately, I do not. Not anymore. Not since Maryanne.

Maryanne.

Maryanne Darrow.

We were together almost nine months. Two hundred and fifty-six days, to be exact. I loved her. I loved Maryanne. I loved that she was with me. I was adrift before she came into my life. I was angry. Angry with everyone and everything. And then, suddenly, I found Maryanne Darrow and life became bearable.

There were other women before her, but only two who I felt a serious connection with. Those feelings eventually waned over time, especially when one of them cheated on me and then taunted me with her affair. But I got even with that bitch. It took a while, but I did.

But Maryanne was different. Maryanne needed me. She was fragile. When I found her, she was broken. I fixed her. I nursed her. Nurtured her. Loved her. Little by little during the months we were together, I let her in, slowly peeling away the layers of the person I show to the world, allowing her to see me. The real me. And she did the same. The hard, angry exterior she used to shield her from the horrors of this world crumbled away bit by bit, until only the frightened child beneath was laid bare. And I hugged that child. Caressed her cheek. Whispered softly in her ear. Patiently allowed her to seek a peaceful sleep in my safe embrace. And for the first time in many, many years, I was happy. I was content. I was at peace.

And then that bitch Megan showed up, crawling up out of the cesspool where she has always lived her life, and reclaimed the soul of my love. Poisoned Maryanne again, as she had when they were young. Expertly wove the web that caught my happiness in its grasp and took her from me, leaving me shattered once more. Over four years have passed since then, but when I find Megan I'll kill her. And I will find her. Just like I found Maryanne.

People are creatures of habit. They tend to do the same things over and over again, sort of like a schedule that they follow, and they have a timetable that rules that schedule. Take a simple thing like the weekly grocery shopping. Everyone does it. It's a necessity. Some people go when they can. Some do it on the same day of the week, but the time varies. I like to study people, and in my studies I have found that some not only shop on the same day each week, but they do it at the same time. Kay is a perfect example.

Kay is a retired psychiatrist. Well, semi-retired. She still treats several patients weekly in an office in her home. Quite informal, I believe.

Kay also does a weekly stint of therapy for patients at the State Women's Correctional facility. She does this pro bono. This volunteer effort she does on the first, second and third Thursdays of every month, except December. In December she does every Thursday, I assume because it must be particularly stressful on the inmates to be away from family during the holidays. They probably should have thought about that before doing the crime.

On those Thursdays when Kay is at the facility, she shows up at exactly three forty-five in the afternoon, parking her classic red 1966 Mustang in the visitors lot. Nice car. Immaculate inside and out. She immediately enters the main building. At precisely ten minutes past nine, she walks back out of the facility and heads straight to her car. From the prison, she drives to a grocery store, parking her antique car further back in the parking lot. I assume she does this hoping to keep it safe from carelessly opened doors of cars that might park beside her were she closer to the entrance. She leaves the store five minutes before the official closing time of ten P.M. With only employee cars left in the parking lot, she walks to her Mustang carrying two bags of groceries. Always two bags. Two canvas bags that she has brought with her in a small effort to save the planet, I assume again, because plastic is a no-no. In those canvas bags are various fresh organic vegetables, a can of coffee, a small tub of butter that isn't really butter, almond milk, free range eggs, several varieties of health snack bars that she will munch on during her morning jog, a loaf of bread made from God knows how many different grains, organic pasta, a jar of organic sauce to go on top of it, several packages that contain no meat but will be the main course during dinners, and three bottles of white wine. Twice now, I have been behind her at the register while she unloaded her cart onto the moving belt, and that is exactly what Kay unloaded from her cart. Oh, but then the coup de grace. While one girl is scanning all the healthy items, another is opening up the cigarette display case and pulling out a carton of Winston's. The absurdity of that gives one pause.

From the parking lot, Kay drives twelve miles through back roads to her home and this is the fourth Thursday that I am behind her. Not one variation and everything almost to the minute. Yes, thankfully, some people are creatures of habit. Predictability. Sometimes, it's a good idea. Other times, it can be hazardous to your health. In fact, it can be downright lethal.

But not this night.

From a hundred yards behind the Mustang, I see the right blinker begin to signal the turn. As Kay takes the right onto her street, I continue driving by, giving a little wave as I pass her street and see her pulling into her driveway. Reaching out, I turn the volume up on the Mantovani CD. The strings make me smile.

Kay will soon have her part to play, and I think she will be a marvelous assistant. But not yet. Not with this next model coming up. Kay will be number six. Her name, actually, is perfect for that one. And while she really is too old, I am an equal opportunity employer, so I'm already looking forward to our time together.

I've already decided on number five, too. I know who she is. I've seen her. Studied her. She's perfect. In more ways than one. But, frankly, I don't hold out much hope for her as far as her embracing the task we will share. I think she will probably prove to be difficult. I'm expecting it. Fortunately, or unfortunately, depending on how one looks at it, our time together will be short because there will be no book to read. Really, I should choose someone else. There is a woman in Wilton with almost the exact same name as the actress who starred in the movie. She would have been a good choice. A great choice. But she's pregnant. And I'm not a baby killer. Those monsters deserve to die. The baby killers. I'd kill them myself, given the chance. With my bare hands. But who knows, maybe I'm wrong. Maybe the one I will take next will get into the process. It is what I hope for more than anything. As soon as I decide where I want to leave the body and how I want to make my statement, I'll secure her.

15

Hendricks stopped at a door that led to the entrance of the police station lobby. Detectives Erik Miller and Kristen Day stopped beside him.

"Miller, I want you behind me on my right, and Day, you on my left" said Hendricks. "I don't want either one of you to talk. I'll answer all the questions that the Mayor doesn't. This is her show, but when the questions get tough, she'll turn it over to me. We'll let the lions have a go at me for a few questions, and then we'll break it up. We clear?" The two detectives nodded. They were both fine letting their superiors occupy the hot seat.

Later, in Hendrick's office, Miller and Day sat in front of the oak desk and watched as the strain of the press conference slowly drained from their Chief's face.

"Jesus Christ," said Hendricks as he sipped from a cold bottle of Ginger Ale. "I expected we'd have a few more reporters than usual, but I wasn't expecting that mob."

Hendricks took another sip. "The Globe and the Times. And two Boston television reporters. Two others, the tall guy and the fat guy sitting together in the front, did they say they were with what agency? Reuters?"

"Reuters was the woman sitting behind them," said Day. "Those two guys were with Chicago papers."

"Chicago?" Hendricks said. "Jesus Christ. And did you see the

Mayor? First chance she got, after all the photos were taken of course, she handed it off to me, like Brady dumping the ball out to Welker with the blitz on. Shit. I felt like I was in the witness stand and Johnnie Cochran was grilling me."

"You did fine, Chief," said Miller.

"I did shit," said Hendricks. "Everyone asking questions I couldn't answer. Not that I didn't want to answer, but that I couldn't answer. Five months. Four bodies. And we have nothing."

Hendricks picked up a pencil and tapped the eraser end hard on his desk several times, then snapped it in two.

"The goddamned governor called me this morning," he said. "The governor. Never called me before. Wanted to know what the hell was going on down here. Why hadn't we caught the son-of-a-bitch. Said this was making the state look bad. Like we were a bunch of backward hacks. That the rest of the country was shaking their heads at us, just a bunch of incompetents who could never make it on a big city force. Then she says, 'What do you need to solve this? Do you need help from the State Police? We've got some pretty sharp guys.' "

Hendricks flung the two pieces of pencil into a corner. "Those bastards, for Christ sake!" he barked loudly.

He looked at his two detectives who sat still, saying nothing. Then his eyes moved around the room and he took in a deep breath.

"Was anything different?" he asked.

Detective Erik Miller said, "No. Other than Maryanne Darrow, the other three are all similar. Each have had traces of a drug called Propofol. We assume the killer is using it to sedate the victims. It works fast. Each has had a significant amount of Fentanyl Citrate in their systems. Four times the amount needed to be fatal. That is the cause of death. Except for Maryanne. Her neck was broken. All four have evidence of facial abuse. It appears most damage is caused by an open hand, although there is some damage that is more severe and is probably caused by a closed fist. It appears that damage is inflicted early in the abduction. Because the Propofol puts the victim out quickly, we don't believe the abuse is done during the taking of the victim. We believe the physical abuse comes later, maybe as a means to keep the victim quiet or to make the women cower. A way to control the screaming. Maybe a way to get them to do something. Darrow and Johnson had significantly more abuse to their bodies than Seward and Clark. No idea why."

"But none have been sexually abused," stated Hendricks. He knew all this. Everything that Miller was telling him had been told to him before. "What else could the guy want that he would have to beat them? Any ideas?" He looked from Miller to Day. Day shrugged. Miller frowned.

"We don't know," said Miller. "Maybe he just gets off slapping women around. Maybe he has major anger issues and can't control himself. Again, I think it's important to note that Maryanne had much more significant bruising to her body and less to her face. She was brutally beaten before she was killed. Again, with hands, not with objects. And I think the manner of the beating shows an uncontrollable rage. To me, I sense her abuse to be one of passion, while I think the others were beaten just to emphasize dominance."

"You agree with that assessment?" Hendricks asked Day.

"I do," she said. "It does appear the killing of Maryanne may have been more personal."

Hendricks nodded a few times. "What else?"

"Four murder sites and not one clue. Not one footprint, not one fingerprint. Four bodies, and not one fiber or hair on the victims that isn't theirs. Nothing under their fingernails, yet they must have resisted at least once. There is no similarity to the victims. Heights range from five-two to five-seven. Weights range from one hundred and ten to one hundred and forty-five. All are under thirty years of age. Hair color and facial features all different, so the killer isn't fixated on a particular type. All had different occupations. None knew each other. They are being selected because of their names, but why is the real question, isn't it? Because of old movies? Maybe. But I think there's more. He's sending us a message with each killing, and I don't mean his taunting notes. He wants us to see something. Something that bothers him. He's making a statement, but I'll be damned if I know what it is."

They sat quietly for a few seconds, Hendricks finishing the Ginger Ale.

"There are a few things we do know," Miller said. "He's strong. The strength needed to lift Madeleine Seward to the top of that crypt tells us that. Or even to carry Elizabeth Clarke up the stairs to the bedroom. Also, and I keep going back to this, he knew enough to have a broom with him to sweep the top of the crypt. Think about that. I know I do. One more thing about Maryanne Darrow; unlike the other three, her ankles showed no bruising from being tethered. So either she was abducted and killed right away, or she knew the killer. And somehow, some way, she displeased him and paid for that displeasure with her life. It was only a few years ago that she straightened out her life. Got a job. Got a steady boyfriend. Maybe she ran into someone from her past, her wild past, someone she had screwed over. Maybe killing her caused the psycho to flip out and now three more women are dead. I don't know. But I will say it again, what I do know is, if Maryanne and the killer were friends, or were intimate at one time, then I will bet the mortgage Megan knows the killer. My gut tells me she is still in Manchester. But where, I don't know."

THEY WERE SITTING at Miller's desk eating burgers and

fries and they had the spacious room to themselves.

"I had a drink with Doctor Thomas last night," Kristen Day said out of the blue after a lull in their conversation. She carefully watched Miller's face for a reaction, and admitted to herself that she was impressed when she saw none.

Miller licked the ketchup off a single fry before inserting it in his mouth.

"Do you think that was a good idea?" he asked, his tone even, his eyes not looking at her.

"He said he wanted to talk about Dr. Gallagher-Hartigan. Said he knew her and might be able to give us a better handle on her."

"Why would we need that?" asked Miller, chewing on another fry.

Day had to fight to keep from smiling, because, while Miller projected calm in voice and manner, she could tell he was seething.

"Thomas expressed to me...."

"Thomas?" said Miller, sitting upright and finally looking at her. "Thomas, as in first name Thomas, or Thomas, as in last name Thomas?"

Day frowned. "Dr. Thomas expressed to me that knowing Dr. Gallagher-Hartigan as well as he did, he said that she could sometimes be less than forthcoming with information. That she would only share what she thought to be important, and would never consider that she might not know just what was important."

"And this was something he could not tell you over the phone?" asked Miller. "Or stop by here to tell us?"

Kristen shrugged.

"He could be our killer?" said Miller.

"You keep saying it's not him."

Miller wrapped up what was left of his fries and tossed them in the metal wastebasket. "Yeah, and you should believe that because I'm right on top of this investigation, aren't I? Got it all figured out."

He leaned back into the chair and gazed around the empty room. "You planning on having anymore drinks with the married Dr. Thomas Thomas?"

As Detective Kristen Day cleaned up the rest of her lunch and deposited it in the wastebasket, she said, "What I do with my private life is none of your business, Miller. But, no, I will not be having drinks again with Dr. Thomas. I just thought, maybe, in a more intimate setting, he might slip up. Say something. I'm not as sure of his innocence as you are."

Miller stood, lifted his suit coat from the back of the chair and shrugged into it. "I'm going down to Lawrence. I'm going to dig around until I get more info on our Megan the Roach. Want to come?"

Day shook her head.

"I've been thinking about what Weasley and Cormier have told us. If the next victim comes from *The Wolf Man*, well, you've watched the movie, the setting could be almost anywhere that's secluded. But if it is *The Hunchback of Notre Dame,* I think we need to consider a Catholic Church as a setting. I'll take a look at St. Joe's and St. Anne's."

Miller nodded. "I'll meet you here later."

Day watched him walk through the doors.

DETECTIVE ERIK MILLER merged from 495 North onto route 93 North, returning from Lowell, Massachusetts. The search for more information on Megan the Roach that had begun a few hours earlier in Lawrence, had also taken him to Lowell. He didn't have her, but he did have a name. And a picture. And a faint memory.

A secretary in the main office of Lawrence High remembered Maryanne Darrow. She remembered her as a pretty sophomore who often volunteered to help her teachers and could be seen in the main office after school hours using the copy machine and running off copies of homework that a teacher would assign the following day. She remembered Maryanne as being quiet, pleasant, a little shy and very respectful. She also remembered being surprised when she heard that Maryanne was being rather difficult to her teachers during her senior year and that her grades were close to failing. The secretary knew nothing about a Megan who hung around with Maryanne, but she told Miller that one of the schools English teachers, a Mrs. Broadhurst, had been in Maryanne's home room when they were both seniors. Perhaps she would know who Megan was.

Mrs. Broadhurst, tall, heavy, with thick glasses and lots of hair, remembered Maryanne Darrow quite well. She also remembered Megan. Megan Riley. Megan was two years older than her and Maryanne. Megan, who lived two streets over from Emma Broadhurst, had dropped out of school beginning of her junior year and Mrs. Broadhurst was sure none of the teachers were upset about that. Megan was trouble.

'She was this tiny slip of a girl, with mousy brown hair, angry eyes and down-turned mouth. She hardly ever talked to anyone and if she did it was to complain about something. She was always angry about something. We all knew Maryanne was hanging with her after school and on weekends, and we were all surprised. Maryanne was so pretty. Then, after graduation, we started hearing the stories. The drugs. The parties. The orgies over in Lowell.'

Mrs. Broadhurst told Miller that she had heard the Riley's no longer lived in Lawrence, having moved away about five years before. She had no idea where they had moved to. She gave Miller the name of someone who knew both girls quite well at the time. Luis Costas. Costas worked for Parks and Recreation. Miller tracked him down. Costas told Miller what Miller already knew about the two women. He had no picture of Megan Riley. The last time he saw either one of them was a few months after graduation. He did, however, give Miller the name of a guy in Lowell who knew the girls and was partying with them back then. The guy now worked as a car mechanic and raced cars at Hudson Speedway, where Costas had run into him just last summer. His name was Donny. Donny Finnegan.

Miller found Donny Finnegan just before the mechanic was to leave work for the day. Yeah, he reluctantly said, he remembered the girls. Yeah, they had partied hard back in the day, he said, but the girls were of legal age he was quick to point out to the detective, so no crime in that. All in the past. He was married now. He had two kids.

While Donny spoke, Miller had been looking around his messy work area. Tacked to the wall above his tool box was a Polaroid of a group of people. Five guys in biker gear and two women. Young looking women. He could see one of them was a young Maryanne Darrow. Miller asked Donny who the other woman was in the picture. Donny said she was Megan. Didn't know, or care, what her last name was, he said, but she was always around. One of the guys, Donny couldn't remember who, had nicknamed her The Roach. Everyone laughed when he did, but the name fit her, said Donny. Finnegan was reluctant to allow Miller to take the photo, only relenting after the detective promised he would return it, and also promised this would be the end of all questions about those days. Donny was married now, he said to Miller again. He had two kids. And a good job.

Driving north on the interstate towards Manchester, Miller now had a picture of Megan that he could blow up and distribute to others so they could keep an eye open. Megan the Roach was no longer a mystery. Only her whereabouts was. But Miller knew, as soon as he had seen the photograph, that he had seen that face before, and just as he crossed over the New Hampshire/

Massachusetts state line, he remembered where that was.

IT WAS A group of people in their twenties that occupied the dozen small round tables that had been situated with forethought and empathy for the two waitresses who roamed the area inquiring on beverage selection. The clientele was loud and boisterous, as the young so often are when alcohol is in attendance. Kristen Day sat alone at a table near the far wall, furthest away from the tiny stage that occupied a corner of the room. On the stage, a couple were doing their best to sing a duet made popular by Kenny Rogers and Dolly Parton a few years before most of the people in the place had been born. It didn't matter. Except for one table near the stage, where two people sat listening, conversation at all the other tables continued on. Polite clapping followed the performance. The emcee then waved Eve up onto the stage.

Eve and the emcee huddled for several seconds, Eve speaking, the guy nodding. Then he keyed a few things into a computer and lifted the microphone.

"Let's all welcome back Eve L onto the stage. Tonight she'll be doing "Ladies First" from the Queen's first CD." And with that the beat began thumping from the speakers.

It was not surprising to Day that Eve looked so relaxed on the stage. She moved with purpose and energy and really played to the audience. She knew the lyrics, no prompter was needed. Day noticed that about half the tables were actually watching and listening to Eve. Day wasn't particularly impressed with the young woman's voice, but there was no denying the energy, or that the crowd was getting into it the more Eve danced around. There was more than polite applause at the end. The emcee promised that Eve L would be back after a few more karaoke performers sang their songs.

A smiling Eve slapped a few high fives as she walked back to a table that she shared with a young man who hugged her before she began to sit. Over his shoulder, Eve noticed Kristen. Eve whispered something to the guy and then came over to Kristen's table.

"You came," said Eve, a questioning look on her face.

"Sure," replied Kristen with a smile. "Wasn't easy finding where you might be singing, but I am a cop. And I made a few calls."

"What did you think?"

"Not really my taste in music. But the audience was really into it. And you looked so comfortable up there. I was impressed. How long have you been doing this?"

"Not long. About six months. I keep asking Erik to come, but you know him. Never going to happen."

"Yeah. I wouldn't hold my breath on that one."

Eve sat in the chair opposite Kristen. "I'm worried about him, Kristen."

"He's a big boy, Eve. He's seen a lot in his years on the force. He'll be alright."

"I've seen him on cases before. The intensity, the fire. Always in control. This one, he looks lost. Looks like he doesn't have a clue. Worse. Looks like he doesn't have a clue but thinks that he should. This one is different."

"Yes. It is different," said Kristen. "All the other murders he's investigated ended with the murder. Now solve it. But these murders are going to go on and on until we solve it. Big difference."

"You seem to be handling it better than him," said Eve.

Kristen shrugged. "He's lead, so the pressure is on him. I'm probably still caught up in the uniqueness of it all. Serials don't happen every day. I won't say I'm enjoying it, because that would sound awful, and, obviously the deaths are terrible, but I am enjoying the tension. It's a bit of a high."

Kristen smiled.

"You know that tingling feeling you get up there on the stage when you realize that you have connected with your audience? Well, it's a little like that. Like when I was playing ball and it was a conference game, clock ticking down on a tied score and the ball is in my hands." She shrugged again. "Hard to explain, but there is some excitement to all of this. So, tonight you have pink hair. Looks good."

Eve waved her hand. "Last time I was here it was green. Wigs. Even the blonde I use at the bar is a wig."

"I noticed," smiled Kristen.

"My hair is very short. Easy to maintain. Makes me feel like a revolutionary who will change the world, or a super cool CEO of a high tech company. But that isn't for the world to see. At least not yet. Maybe someday."

"Good for you. You have something to say, say it. Don't let anyone steal your voice."

As Eve began to stand, Kristen said, "Who's the guy?"

Eve smiled and looked over at her table where her date sat tapping his fingers on the table to a country song that was just beginning. "We've gone out a few times. He's very nice. Steady job, too. And he likes my singing."

"Sounds like a keeper," said Kristen.

"Really. Thanks for coming. You going to stay? You can join us."

"I'm good. One more of your songs and then I'm out of here. Work day tomorrow."

"Okay. I'll see you around. Thanks. This means a lot."

16

Megan Riley?"

"Yes," said Miller. "And this is her about seven years ago." He put his index finger above her face on the Polaroid that lay on the desk in front of Day. "The other girl is Maryanne. The guys are the biker club they partied with."

"And you say you've seen her before?" asked Day.

"Yeah. When I was a cop on the street. It took me a while to remember, it was no big deal at the time, but it hit me on the drive back. I've seen her before."

"Where?"

"It was five or six years ago. I was on patrol. I may not have this exactly as it happened. You know how it is. You patrolled at one time. Trying to recall situations that happened in the past, you end up joining separate events together, maybe out of sequence, but the dynamics stay fairly true."

"Sure," said Day. "What happened?"

"So I'm driving down Chestnut. It's mid-May, evening, and it's raining. I mean a real heavy rain. Wipers are going like crazy. Suddenly, in front of Victory, someone runs out between the parked cars, right in front of me, and falls in the street. I jam on the breaks. I hit the flashers and get out of the car. On the sidewalk at the edge of the park, in front of the monument, are four or five people in a group who looked like they may have been chasing the person lying on the street. They stop when they see me and then start running the other way. I can't pursue. Car is in the middle of the street blocking traffic. Visibility is horrible. The person lying in front of the cruiser is attempting to stand, but can't get to their feet. The person looks like a child dressed in this heavy coat. I go to help them up and see that it is a girl. I start to help her up and she begins flailing at me. Trying to get away from me. I say, hey, take it easy. I'm the police. I'm here to help you. She gets even more agitated, trying to escape my grasp. I can see she's zonked out. I get her to her feet and put her in the back of the cruiser. Then I drive over to the parking lot and park. All the while, she's kicking the back of my seat, wailing that I can't arrest her. She's done nothing wrong.

"I tell her I'm not arresting her, but if she doesn't calm down I'll cuff her. That gets her to calm down a little bit. I think I have a sixteen year old kid in the cruiser, but when I put on the light, I see that she is a grown woman. Early twenties, probably, but she looks much older. She's a mess. Heavy coat is soaked and ripped. Thin, bony face is dirty. Short brown hair is dripping and knotted. She looks like a drowned rat. Her eyes can't focus. They're darting all over. Looking at everything but me. Even through the thickness of the coat, I can see she probably weighs ninety pounds. I can also see she's high on something.

"When she finally calms down to where she's just twitching, I try to find out if she knew who was chasing her from the park and why. She certainly didn't look like she had anything of any value on her, so it wasn't to rob her. She says she doesn't know why they went after her, or who they were. She was just walking through the park minding her own business when they came after her. Yelling at her to get out of their park. So she ran."

"Did you go looking for them?" asked Day.

"I drove around the park, but it was empty. The rain wasn't

letting up and the poor woman was shivering in the back of the cruiser. I asked her where she lived. She wouldn't tell me. Just said I had to let her out there and she'd be alright. She hadn't done anything wrong and I couldn't arrest her. I told her I was trying to help her. She actually laughed when I said that. Eventually, she had me bring her to a shelter on Pine Street. I brought her inside. They told me she was staying there. Had been there about a week. They said they would take care of her. So, I left her there."

"And then what happened?" asked Day.

"Later that night, in the Emergency Room of the Elliot, a guy is brought in with knife wounds to his arm and leg. Nurse on duty calls us and an officer is sent to see what happened. Come to find out, the guy got into an argument with a woman over drugs and she stabbed him in a rage. It happened in Victory Park. I find out about it the following afternoon when I come in for my shift. The description of the woman the guy gave to the officer matched the woman I had helped the night before. So, I went back to the shelter immediately. But by then, the woman was gone. Never to return to that shelter as far as I know. The guy recovered from his wounds and I gave it no more thought. I mean, I kept an eye out on patrol for the woman, but she was a pretty low priority. Hassles among the homeless happen all the time, you know that. I never did tell anyone I had the assailant in my cruiser for an hour and then let her go. She had given me a name, but, of course, it was false."

Day nodded a few times. "How does this incident match up with Maryanne's time line?"

"I can go back and check dates," replied Miller. "See when we investigated the call from Elliot. See if there were any follow ups. I've been here four years, and I think that night happened during my last year on the streets. So, let's say it was five years ago. Three years ago, Maryanne began working for the DMV.

Had an apartment. Seemingly, a stable life. Met Houle two years ago. Engaged a year after that. I guess it's possible Maryanne and Megan were still together that night I picked Megan up. Still living on the streets. It's possible Maryanne was in the shelter when I brought Megan there. Who knows?"

"Sure. Now what?"

"I'll have this blown up and start showing it around the streets. If Megan is still around, we'll find her."

Miller leaned back. "But it now has me wondering. What does the killer mean when he says to go back to the beginning? That the clues are there. Does he mean the killing of Maryanne, which is what we have assumed? Or is the beginning somehow meant to mean Megan? Is that why the taunts? I never met Maryanne. So it must be Megan. Why would a one hour interaction with Megan, five years ago, cause the killer to zero in on me?"

He looked at Day. "He's made it personal and I have no idea why."

DURING THE AFTERNOON of the fourth day that Miller was out on the streets distributing flyers of Megan Riley, the precinct dispatcher called him back to the station. There was a six inch cubed sealed cardboard box waiting for him at the Sergeant's desk. When Miller entered the Detective's Room, he brought the box into Chief Hendrick's office. Kristen Day hung up the phone and followed her partner into the office.

"Shut the door," Hendricks said to her as he stared at the package on his desk. She did, then took a seat beside her partner.

There was a soft knock at the door, it opened and Matt Blanchette stood there. Hendricks motioned him in. Blanchette closed the door and leaned against it.

"We got a box, but no name?" asked the Chief.

"I've been checking the list twice a day," said Day. "Nothing has matched."

"Three weeks since the Clarke woman," said Hendricks. He looked at Miller. "Go ahead. Open it."

Miller hesitated several seconds, then stood, took the scissors offered by Hendricks and cut through the packing tape. The others watched as he lifted the flaps and peered inside. Miller reacted as if he had been slapped hard, taking an involuntary step backwards, falling into the chair. His face drained of color. Hendricks, shocked by the reaction of his Detective, leaned over the box to see what had caused such an untypical reaction, his mind prepared for all matter of heinous amputation. But all that was in the box, resting on a square piece of cotton gauze, was a thin silver chain with a two inch oval religious medal attached to it. He looked inquiringly at Miller, confused by his man's reaction, then lifted the medal out of the carton. The medal, like the chain, was silver. It depicted a haloed man in a long robe. In tiny bold letters across the bottom was printed PRAY FOR US. SAINT MATTHIAS was printed in similar letters across the top following the curve of the oval shape.

Suddenly, Miller bolted from the chair for the door, Matt Blanchette barely getting out of the way before Miller opened it and went running through the double doors of the Detective Room. Hendricks looked at Day, and then Blanchette, to see if they understood what had just happened. Day shrugged. Blanchette's face went hard, eyes narrowed. He looked up from the medal.

"He knows who that belongs to," said the old Detective. "He gave it to her."

DETECTIVE KRISTEN DAY was sitting at her desk when Erik Miller entered the Detective Room at seven that night. He moved slowly, his shoulders hunched. He sat heavily into his chair and stared across the room. Kristen gave it a few moments, then went and stood beside his desk. He turned towards her, looked surprised that she was there.

"We've been calling your cell all day," said Kristen. "Matt told us about the medal."

"She didn't show up for her shift yesterday or today," said Miller, again staring at nothing across the room. "Her mother said she didn't sleep at home the last few nights, but in the last month that wasn't unusual. Said she had a boyfriend. The mother gave me a name. I tracked him down at work. He's a postman. He hasn't seen her since Sunday night when they went to dinner and a movie. She left his place around eleven. She had decided not to spend the night. Her car is still parked down the street from his apartment. He didn't notice it there. He tried calling her last night, but got no answer."

Neither spoke for long seconds, the room completely still. Then the doors were pushed open and two detectives entered, one doing the talking and the other nodding. They acknowledged Miller and Day with a nod, then sat at a desk in the far corner of the room and continued their conversation in muted tones.

Miller looked at Day and waited. She took a breath.

"I double checked everything," she began. "There is no main character or main actress with the name of Eve Brown in any of the movies we have on our list. The only one even remotely close is Evelyn Ankers in *The Wolf Man*. Was Evelyn Eve's full name?"

"Eve is her name," said Miller, refusing to address her in the past tense. "Just Eve. I don't think the name matters here. He's gone off script. He's made it personal. Again."

Day said nothing, just went to her desk, picked up a folded piece of paper, and returned to Miller, laying the paper on his desk in front of him.

He looked at it for several seconds, then picked it up, unfolded it and read what was written there. It was the shortest note yet from the killer.

Your actions took from me someone I loved, Erik.
Now I've done the same to you.
Now you know how it feels.

Miller folded the paper back up and laid it in the center of his desk.

"Was there more?" he asked.

"In the center drawer."

Opening the middle drawer, Miller saw the folded piece of white bond paper. He took it out and read the poem left for him by the killer.

During Eve's midnight stroll the clouds parted
Revealing a full moon rising in the East.
When she paused to admire its splendor
It was then she encountered the Beast.

"I don't think there's any doubt that it's the Wolf Man," Day said. "You've watched the movie. It presents a difficult problem."

When she got no response from Miller, she continued.

"I've thought about it. Larry Talbot was found in the woods. There were Gypsies near by. An old Gypsy woman had warned Evelyn Ankers character, Gwen Conliffe, to be very careful, and to not be in the woods at night. The old woman knew that Talbot had been bitten. She could sense the evil that was now in him. And then that night when the monster appeared, it was the cane with the silver handle that beat him, finally stopping and killing the Wolf Man. When his body was found at the base of a tree, in the sparse forest, in the fog, Talbot had transformed again into a man."

When Erik turned towards her, she saw the pain in his eyes. "I'm sorry," said Day, "I know this hurts. But I am thinking we need to concentrate our efforts on watching the woods. That would be an impossible task given how many wooded areas we have in Manchester, but if we narrow it down to wooded areas where the homeless have set up encampments, we might get lucky. It's a long shot, I know, but the homeless are as close to Gypsies as we have today. In the mind of the killer, it may make sense to leave Eve somewhere near them. Also, we can expect Eve to be left near a trail that is used so that the she will be easily found."

Again there came no response from her partner. Not an utterance, not a nod of agreement.

"Eve went missing Sunday night. It's Thursday now. I don't think we have much time, Erik. What do you want to do?"

"I need to think," said Miller after a long few seconds. "Give me a minute to think."

Detective Erik Miller sat quietly, staring at a spot on his desk. Day said nothing as the minutes ticked by. Finally, Miller spoke.

"I gave Eve that medal after her father died. She was seventeen. I was concerned that her father's death might trigger a relapse. She had been clean for over a year. She had it together. It had been a struggle for her, but she was winning. But you know how it is sometimes with addicts. A small thing can set them back. This was no small thing. She was close to her dad. He was a good guy. Through all her problems, he stood by her. And his death was sudden. I spent a lot of time with her in the months following his death, but I wasn't in a good place either. It was right after my divorce. One day I saw a medal hanging around the neck of a guy I was talking with after breaking up a scuffle. I asked him about it, you know, trying to calm down the situation. He told me it was a Saint Matthais medal, the patron saint of addicts. He told me every time he thought about using again, he would hold that medal tightly in his hand until the need passed. He had been clean for six months and, he said, he knew he would remain clean for the rest of his life as long as he just held on to that medal when he needed to. The next day, I gave

Eve the Saint Matthais medal."

Miller took in a deep breath and let it out slowly. "Eve's had a hard life. She doesn't deserve this. The bastard has her, and it's my fault. My fault. What did I do? Or didn't do?" He looked at her. "Kristen, I have no idea. No idea."

Miller went back to staring at the same spot on the desk and the room became quiet for several minutes.

"I went to see her sing," said Day.

Miller looked at her.

"Friday night. At a club on Merrimack Street. She was good."

She could see the hurt in his eyes before he looked away.

"You could see she really enjoyed performing," Day said softly. "She was happy. She came over to my table and we talked for a few minutes. She was with a guy, but when she asked me to join them, I said no. I really had to be going, I said. They seemed comfortable together and I didn't want to intrude."

"I never went to hear her" said Miller barely above a whisper.

Kristen reached out and laid a hand on his arm.

"She said that. But she said it was okay. She knew it wasn't your kind of thing."

Miller stood.

"I've got to go," he said.

Day leaned back in the chair.

"Go where?"

"I don't know. But I can't just sit here."

"Tomorrow we check the woods around the camps?" asked Day.

"Yes," said Miller as he moved toward the doors.

"Decide how to set up surveillance?"

He made no response to that.

"Erik, we maybe have two days, tops."

He went through the doors without saying a word.

17

Artie DeMarais put the left blinker on and then patiently waited for the traffic to thin before pulling into the dirt parking area of Brown-Mitchell Park. He drove his 2005 Volvo to the far end of the deserted lot, shut the car off and sat quietly for several seconds, enjoying the silence. It was seven o'clock on a cool, crisp Friday morning, the sun rising in a cloudless May sky as Artie leaned back in the comfortable seat, closed his eyes and grinned. He knew this would be the best part of his day. In two hours, he would be standing behind a register at WalMart, doing his best to be a genial WalMart employee to customers who were not always genial to him. The job was stressful. Even the drive to the park had been stressful. People were always in such a rush.

Stepping from the car, Artie looked at the path that led into the heavily wooded area that ran all the way down to the river, and he smiled. The air, on a gentle breeze, smelled liked pine. Artie locked the car door, then walked to the back of the vehicle. He paused at the trunk, scanned the area once more, then inserted the trunk key, popping open the lid. Reaching in, Artie lifted the duffel bag from the trunk and gently closed the lid.

Entering the path into the trees, he stopped about twenty paces in. The air inside was ten degrees cooler than outside of the forest, and Artie DeMarias liked it that way. He placed the duffel on the ground, then placed both hands on the trunk of a tall pine tree and did five minutes of stretching exercises. When that was done, he opened the duffel and reached into it, rummaging among the contents until he found what he was looking for. He pulled out a bright yellow Frisbee Disc that had a death's head stamped in the center of it. Artie took a balanced stance, gazed down through the trees to a chained receptacle about fifty yards away, took a deep breath, and let the disc fly from his hand on a right to left arc that would hopefully clear the trees that were in his way.

There was a time, back in the seventies, during his college days, when Artie could toss a Frisbee almost the length of a football field, the disc rotating and floating so beautifully yard after yard. He and his friends could play for hours. Now, the disc still floated true and wonderfully toward the intended target, but the arm wasn't quite what it once was and the Frisbee came down to Earth and skidded forward, still twenty yards from the target. Still, Artie was pleased with the effort. He was set up perfectly for his second shot.

Picking up the duffel, Artie began walking to where the disc lay. He drew in several deep breaths, enjoying the pungent aroma of the forest and enjoying the quiet of the course. He was alone at that early hour and that was how he enjoyed playing. No distractions. He normally got in at least fourteen holes before he had to leave for work. Occasionally, if his shots were spot on, he could play all eighteen holes. Upon reaching his disc, he looked toward the chained container, reached into his duffel and selected another disc. Taking aim, he let it fly. The Frisbee curved in flight slightly, landed and skittered to within four feet of the target. Artie smiled.

As he reached down to retrieve the first disc, something caught his eye. At the base of a clump of birch trees on the edge of the clearing lay a dark mass that he had never noticed before. A lump that looked strangely human. Artie took several steps towards it and then froze when he saw it was a human body, a woman, curled up in the fetal position and naked. Artie DeMarias took a frightened step backwards, lost his balance, fell on his backside and quickly pushed himself backwards several more feet until his body banged against a thick oak. Long seconds passed before Artie composed himself enough to reach into his front pocket and pull out his cell phone. Flipping it open, he pressed 9-1-1 and waited.

THREE POLICE CRUISERS and Day's Jeep Cherokee were parked at the end of the lot when Detective Erik Miller slid to a stop behind them. Kristen heard the disturbance of gravel, looked up from the body of Eve Brown that she had been kneeling beside, and saw Miller hurrying towards her. She stood and met him half way.

"It's Eve," she said as she stood in his path. "You don't have to see her like this."

He looked at her like she was crazy, then stepped around her and went to the body. He was still standing there, motionless, when Forensics showed up minutes later. Day came and stood beside him.

"I'm sorry, Erik."

He didn't hear her. As he stared down at the battered face of the woman on the ground, he felt light-headed, felt as if he were someone else, standing somewhere else, as if he were a bystander coming upon a tragic scene and viewing it from afar. He allowed Day to maneuver him to a spot twenty feet away from the body as Forensics did their thing, and the photographer did his. Miller went to the body as it was placed on a stretcher and walked beside Eve as she was wheeled to an ambulance. He stood quietly while she was placed inside and watched as it drove away.

Reporters for the newspaper and television were standing at the entrance to the parking area and had begun shouting questions at him as soon as he had walked out from the trees. He barely heard their questions or noticed the crowd that had gathered.

Detective Day had requested more police presence at the sight, and now, with the body gone, the officers spread out and began a systematic search of the area. Several minutes after the ambulance had gone, Miller joined in on the search, but after a few minutes of that he walked over to his partner.

"I need to inform Martha Brown," Miller said. "I'll see you later."

"Do you want me to come with you, Erik?"

Miller shook his head and walked out from the shelter of the trees.

DETECTIVE KRISTEN DAY was sitting at her desk reading over reports she had received on the death of Eve Brown when Miller walked into the bullpen. He slowly walked to her and sat in the chair beside her desk.

After long seconds of silence, Miller said, "She kept asking me why. Why would anyone want to kill Eve? Why? She insisted on going to the morgue. I tried to save her from that, but she insisted." He shook his head, as if that would erase the memory.

"Why, she kept asking, and I didn't have the guts to tell her why. Didn't have the guts to tell her her daughter was dead because of me. Because of something I did. Or didn't do. I don't even know."

Day looked at him. There was nothing she could say that would ease his pain, lessen his suffering.

Miller looked at the paperwork on her desk.

"Anything?" he asked.

She nodded her head. "Traces of Propofol. Lethal amount of something called aconite. Looks like it is very toxic and was used to tip arrows when hunting wolves. A small amount can cause a great deal of suffering, but Eve would have died quickly with the amount in her system. The walking stick that was lying beside her had a heavy handle that had traces of silver in it. It created heavy damage to the facial bones, but Eve was probably already dead from the aconite, so she wouldn't have suffered."

Kristen paused. When there was no response to that, she continued.

"The cane may give us something to go on. There can't be that many stores that carry canes. My guess is it may have been purchased at an antique shop, so we can canvas all of them. That will take some time. There are tons of shops like that in this area, and even more further north near the lakes and countless shops in Maine. We'll need some help with that. But it does help that the handle is unique. Anyone selling it will remember it."

"Like the damn movie," said Miller.

"Yes."

"Anything else?"

"Matt is going over photos of the people who were gathered at the entrance, seeing if any match up with our other crime scenes. And I heard from Rene Cormier. He saw the report on the noon news. He asked if there was a cane or a heavy stick lying near the tree where the body was found. If there was, he said, then the murderer was copying *The Wolf Man* movie. Once again, telling us what we already knew."

"How would he know there was a body lying beside a tree?" Miller demanded, suddenly more attentive.

"That's what I asked him. Seems the news had a picture, taken with a long range lens, that showed us standing near something on the ground inside a forest. He said you couldn't tell what was there, only that it was something. He figured it was a body."

She saw that Miller's mind was working.

"It's not him, Erik. I checked him out. He is what he said he is. I checked some of the things he said he has, and they are worth quite a lot of money. Plus, he wasn't even in the state when Maryanne was found. He has a place in Florida. A high rise condo in Ft. Lauderdale. Neighbors swear he was there all of February."

"You've been busy."

"One of us has to keep going while you're chasing around looking for Megan."

"You think it's a waste of time looking for her?" Miller asked defensively. "Don't you think, after the notes the killer has sent, that Megan is crucial?"

Day ran a hand across her forehead. "No. No, I don't mean that. No, I agree we have to find Megan if we can, but there is just so much to do and so little to go on." She leaned forward and looked at him. "And I'm worried about you. Especially now. The department has people you can talk to. People who can help channel the grief."

"I don't need a shrink," said Miller. "I'm fine. My heads on straight. I know what I'm doing."

Day frowned. "Hendricks saw me before he left for the day. He asked if I thought the death of your friend would affect you, cause you to lose perspective. Knew you would blame yourself for Eve's death, and he asked if I thought you could still be effective in this investigation."

"Why the fuck would he say that?" Miller angrily said. "What did you tell him?"

"I said you would be fine. That there was no way you should be taken off this. No way."

Miller stood. "You're Goddamned right. No way I get off this. I'm going to catch this bastard. If it's the last thing I do, I'm going to get him. Son-of-a-bitch, take me off this case."

He began walking away.

Kristen said, "Cormier said there were still several movies we should be concerned with, but if he were a betting man, he would look to Hunchback being the next one."

Miller stopped halfway across the room and turned.

He said, "We get the package and one day later Eve is dead. We've always had two or three days before a victim is discovered after receiving the package. Why the change in time? Does it mean something? It's like he knows we are on to him and what he is doing, and he's getting more cautious."

Miller turned and started for the doors again.

"Where are you going?" asked Day.

"To find Megan Riley," he said as he walked out.

Kristen's cell phone chirped.

"This is Detective Day."

"Inspector Day, Wendell Weasley here. Have I caught you at a bad time?"

"I can talk," said Kristen, suppressing a grin.

"I have just now caught the news," said Weasley. "I am so sorry. You seem to have another victim."

"So it appears, Professor. Any thoughts?"

"You do know it appears to be Wolf Man," said Weasley, "though the name of the woman is not that of any character in the movie. So, perhaps I am wrong. Although there are no Eve Browns in any other horror movie either. The scene of the murder is definitely Wolf Man, however. So, an enigma wrapped in a mystery we seem to have.

"I'm going to have to give this a little more thought, Inspector. But with this killing, it seems the killer is definitely sticking to the classics. Therefore, were I you, I would expect to see either Hunchback or Invisible Man next, assuming of course, that you haven't apprehended the killer before then. I must run. I'll be in touch."

18

The fifth death led to an explosion of media coverage, with newspapers across the country covering the killings, and as the calendar flipped from May to June, Rene Cormier had somehow become a source that the media turned to when all their questions received no answers from the authorities. His input had started with a quote in the Union Leader and had escalated into an actual appearance on a CBS national news show. Cormier was also being credited with the name now attached to the killer: The Universal Killer. At first, newscasters explained why that name was coined, that the killings mirrored deaths in the old monster movies created by the Universal studio, but after a while they stopped explaining and just used the catch phrase, making it seem that of all the serial killers there have ever been, this serial killer topped them all.

'What a Goddamned circus', was a phrase Chief Hendricks uttered at least five times a day. His phone rang constantly with requests for interviews coming in from every newspaper and publication across the country. Podcasts were begging him for a quote, and if none were forthcoming they simply made some up. All manner of things were being reported by the online mouth pieces and very little of it was factual. Some of it they did get right, however, and when that happened Hendricks went on the warpath, threatening to fire any detective who was talking to the press. Hendricks himself, by a directive of the mayor, held a weekly press conference where he fielded questions and where he divulged very little. Not that he had much to divulge.

But as June neared an end, the story of The Universal Killer slipped from page one to page three to page ten. One month after the brutal murder of Eve Brown, and the media had moved on. But Detectives Erik Miller and Kristen Day had not.

Megan Riley, aka Megan the Roach, had not been found, and both detectives were quite certain she was not in their city. Her picture had been distributed to every police force in the Northeast without one hit. Either The Roach had fled the area for warmer climes, or she was dead. Of course, there was always the possibility that Megan had done what Maryanne Darrow had done, cleaned up her act and was off the streets.

Early on, there was hope that the distinctive cane that had so brutally been used on Eve Brown, would lead to something, but the detectives found that every antique shop from Hartford to Bar Harbor had a variety of canes in their inventory, along with every flea market and ads for canes in the Sunday Magazines. They worked it, but all for naught.

Day had several conversations with Professor Wendell Weasley concerning *The Hunchback of Notre Dame* and *The Invisible Man.* The Professor believed, if the murders were to continue, that those two movies would play their part. In his opinion, they were both just too rich for the kind of mayhem the killer was using. His first choice was the Hunchback. The pitiful brute and the beautiful Gypsy girl. Quasimodo and Esmeralda. The press would have a field day with that one. When Day had relayed that message to Miller, his response had been, "The asshole from Center Harbor has been spouting off about that movie for a month now. Imagine the attention he'll get if it happens? He can write a book and it'll be a best seller."

It was the last Thursday in June, almost six weeks since the death of Eve Brown, and Miller and Day sat in a diner on the border of Litchfield and Manchester eating lunch. Day had a salad, Miller a burger and fries. He picked at his food.

"This is the longest stretch between murders," said Miller. "Doesn't make sense. There was an increasingly less interval between murders, up until now. Classic. Almost all serials do it. The time frame between victims becomes less. But not this time. Does it mean something? Are we missing something? Could there be a body out there that we haven't found?"

"I don't think so, Erik. No missing person that matches one of our names. No box with a clue in it. No taunts."

"Then why?"

Day shrugged. "Maybe the killer went on vacation. Maybe they found God. Maybe company came for a visit. Maybe they got tired of the whole thing."

"I'm serious."

"I know you are. But you're asking questions that can't be answered. And worrying about things that you have no control over. Just be thankful there are no bodies."

"Without another body, we're at a dead end. Sick as it may seem, we need a body. Or at least a name. We need something."

They were both working other investigations, keeping busy until a name showed up on the missing persons report. A name that meant The Universal Killer was at it again. As they did every work day, they met for lunch to touch base on the investigation, and then went separately to the case they were working on. But the five women's deaths were the only conversation between the two of them during these lunches. Nothing else the other was working on interested them.

As the lead investigator in the killings, it was Detective Miller who received the calls from the families of the victims, demanding to know if there had been progress in the on-going investigation, always ending the calls with pleadings not to forget their loved ones death. After each call, Miller always found himself angry, and he realized he was angry not with the pleading of the loved one thinking he might ever forget their loss, but angry because he could give them no relief from their pain. He felt as if he were failing them. And, in fact, he knew he was.

In the parking lot of the diner, Miller and Day agreed to meet the following day for lunch at a diner on the Hooksett line. As it would turn out, that lunch would have to wait.

MILLER'S CELL VIBRATED in his suit coat pocket. Looking at the number calling in, he saw it was from Day. It was 12:17.

"Hey, I was just about to call you," he said. "I'm not going to make it."

"We have a name," said Day.

Miller stood about half way up a wooden stairway that led to a creaking second story back porch of a three decker, watching two paramedics lifting the lifeless body of a teenage boy onto a gurney.

"Miller, you there?" asked Day when she received no response.

"Yeah. What's the name?"

"Kay Lawrence."

Again, there came no response.

"*Creature From the Black Lagoon*," said Day.

"Jesus Christ," said Miller. "So much for the so called experts. Was that movie on our list? Never mind. I'll get back to the station as quick as I can." He pressed end. He didn't bother telling Day to find out as much as she could before he got there. He knew she would.

Miller gazed across the postage stamp sized back yard and noticed that each adjoining property had people standing and watching the same scene he was watching. What were they thinking, he wondered. What would they say to the reporters should one of them be asked about the victim? *He was such a nice boy. Never any trouble. Always would help if you needed any help. This is such a quiet neighborhood. They were such nice people.* Sure. That was why the father felt compelled to shoot the kid when his son was beating his mother in the kitchen of their second floor apartment. The kid had managed to flee through the back door onto the porch before toppling down the staircase and breaking his neck. The mother had been taken to Elliot to repair broken bones in her face. The father was sitting in a room at police headquarters waiting for Miller to question him. And someone with a name that was of interest to a psychotic killer had gone missing. Just another day in paradise.

THE CONVERSATION WITH the father was brief. In just a few minutes of a Friday morning that had begun just like every other morning, his entire world became shattered when his only son suddenly went crazy. The man, still in a daze, answered every question with single syllable answers, his head slowly shaking back and forth in reaction to what had happened and what he had done, like it must all be a dream and when would he wake up. Miller got all he was going to get from the man, and before leaving him suggested he use his one call to call a lawyer.

When Miller entered the bullpen, he saw Day sitting at her desk. She was on the phone. Miller nodded at her and then entered Hendricks' office. He brought the Chief up to date on the morning's fun, then Hendricks told him to keep him informed on the missing woman named Kay Lawrence. Miller said he would, then went and sat beside Day's desk waiting for her to end the call.

Hanging up the phone, Day said, "Kay Lawrence is a sixty-four year old retired psychiatrist from New Boston. Her car, a classic red 1966 Mustang, was found last night parked along Route 114 in Goffstown, about five miles from her home. There were groceries in the trunk, keys in the ignition, no one in the car. The police, after getting no answer to calls placed to her cell, went to her home. She wasn't there. There was nothing in the car, or around it, to suggest anything nefarious, but the Goffstown police know Ms. Lawrence and they were immediately concerned."

"They know her?"

"She does volunteer work at the Women's Correctional facility. In fact, she had been there only hours before. The groceries came from a supermarket on her way home. The area where the car was found is sparsely populated and heavily forested. There is a search going on in the area right now."

"Why bother?" said Miller. "She has a cell phone. If she could have, she would have called someone for help. Did she have Triple A?"

Day shrugged. "I'll check."

"Do we know if there was a mechanical issue with the car? Was it out of gas?"

"Police said when they popped the hood, they found a wire on the distributor cap had come loose."

"That doesn't happen by accident," said Miller. "I don't care how many pot holes you hit. It was loosened and then came unconnected while she drove. Then our boy shows up and asks if she is having car troubles. The Good Samaritan. And then, while he is pointing out to her the problem, a quick needle filled with Propofol in the neck. Does the grocery store have surveillance on the parking lot?"

"They do."

"You need to make any more calls?"

"Just Triple A."

"Okay. You do that. I'll fill in Hendricks and we'll go watch some footage of the lot."

Miller stood. "How come this movie wasn't on our radar?"

"I suppose it should have been," replied Day. "It was produced by Universal-International. But it was released in 1954. That is more *Godzilla* time frame than classic monster time frame. We have been concentrating on the thirties."

"Why did her name catch your attention when you spotted it on the report?"

Day shrugged. "We've been expecting something, haven't we? I've been Googling every new name on the list, just in case, knowing how futile that may be because the victim could have a combination of the name we would need. Still I was doing it. Kay Lawrence is the exact name of the character in Black Lagoon. We got lucky."

"Yeah, well, she didn't."

Day shrugged again.

"I've never seen the movie," said Miller. "You think that video store has a copy?"

"I'll check."

"And call your Professor guy. See what he knows about the movie."

"I'm waiting for his call back."

Miller nodded at her and walked into Hendricks' office.

MILLER AND DAY sat in the interrogation room, a can of Coca Cola in front of Miller and bottled water in front of Day. They sat watching Day's lap top that was showing a clip from the grocery store's surveillance from the previous evening.

"Why the hell did she park so far back in the lot?" asked Miller in frustration, as he watched the Mustang pull off the main road into the store's parking lot and slide into a spot along the far side. There were five other cars parked in that area, two of them backed in. The Mustang was four spaces from the nearest one, parked in an area where the lighting didn't quite reach.

Day looked at him and raised her eyebrows in response to his question.

"Because that's where the employees park," said Miller, answering his own question, "and no one else would park that far from the entrance to the store. Wouldn't have to worry about someone opening their car door and dinging her paint job." He leaned back. "Or walking along the side of it and keying the paint job. Only cops, priests and psychiatrists are that aware of the depth of human stupidity and meanness."

They watched Kay Lawrence walk the distance to the front of the store. The time on the video was 9:28. She passed six cars on her way in. At 9:34 and 9:37, two more cars entered the lot and parked as close to the entrance as they could get, their drivers hustling into the store. Three cars left the lot between 9:37 and 9:41.

At 9:43, a dark figure stepped from the treed boundary at the far end of the lot. Miller paused the recording. The figure was dressed in dark clothing from head to foot in what appeared to be black sweatpants and a black pullover with a hood that was entirely covering the head. Black gloves completed the ensemble. Miller tried zooming in, but in the poor lighting in that area the picture became too blurry, and he pulled back. They watched as the figure quickly popped open the hood of the Mustang and leaned in over the engine. Ten seconds later, the hood closed. The figure turned, keeping their back to the camera and stepped back towards the trees. At the treeline, the figure stopped, raised an arm, waved, then stepped into the trees.

"Son-of-a-bitch," Miller whispered, leaning forward towards the lap top. "He knew there was a camera. Knew we'd be watching. The bastard waved to us."

"There are cameras everywhere, Erik. No brilliance there."

Miller shook his head.

"Do you find it amazing that this woman, this Kay Lawrence, obviously an intelligent person, a doctor, educated, successful career, somehow reasons that her car's safety is more important than her own safety?"

Day shrugged. "Nice car. Probably worth a bundle."

"They're a dime a dozen," said Miller. "Never understood the appeal. Give me Mopar everytime."

Between 9:47 and 9:50, one by one the cars left in front of the store drove away. At 9:55, Kay Lawrence, carrying two cloth bags by their straps, walked out of the store and crossed the lot to her car. She opened the trunk and put the bags inside. They watched as she started the car, backed out of the spot, drove up to the road and took a right on her way home, a home she would never arrive at.

Miller and Day watched the recording four more times, each time pausing it when the killer stepped out of the trees, and pausing again at the wave. But they saw nothing more that would help them. Later, they would drive to the store and search the area near the woods to see if they could find where the killer may have parked a vehicle, but they would find nothing. No tire tracks of any kind. No cigarette butts. No footprints.

"So what do we know?" asked Chief Hendricks after being briefed by his detectives.

"In that lighting it is difficult to be exact," said Miller. "But we can determine that the killer is tall, by their height compared to the front end of the car. Well over six feet. Maybe six-five. That they are not obese. That they appear to be fit. That they knew the habits of the victim and knew where she would be parking her car in that lot. Knew her route home, probably."

"What was the name of that heart surgeon?" asked Hendricks.

"Doctor Thomas," said Day.

"Isn't he a tall guy?"

"Six-five," answered Miller. "We're going to see if he has an alibi for last night. Where he was around ten o'clock. But I don't think it's him."

"So you keep saying," said Hendricks. "But we seem to have an awful lot of doctors involved in this investigation. Him, the two over on Elm Street, and now this one. Plus the nurse. I don't like it.

"Alright. Go see if you come up with anything in the woods around the store. Maybe a camera somewhere away from the lot that the killer didn't figure on." Picking up a pencil and tapping it on the desk, Hendricks asked, "I've never seen this Creature movie. Heard about it, but never saw it. So where can we expect Ms. Lawrence to end up? Any thoughts?"

"I haven't seen it either," said Miller, "but I would expect water will be involved. I'm thinking somewhere along Massabesic. A trail along the water would make sense so the body is found. We're going to get a movie to watch. Maybe that will give us a better idea."

"Again," Hendricks said, "whatever resources you need. We have the weekend. That would mean overtime. No problem. Bring in all assets you think you need." He paused. "The lake covers a lot of area. Borders Auburn. I can check to see if we could use some of their personnel. I'm sure they'll be aboard. Let's catch this bastard."

Their time spent walking around the area of the store proved fruitless. They stopped at the hospital to speak with Doctor Thomas and was told he was at a seminar in Cleveland and had been there all week. He was expected back in Manchester that evening. They met with the cop who had found the abandoned Mustang. He offered nothing new except to tell them he had spoken with Doctor Lawrence's son in Denver to apprise him of the disappearance of his mother. The son was flying in as soon as he could get a connecting flight from Chicago. He had also met with the Doctor's married daughter who lived in Hollis. She immediately began calling friends of her mother. Finally, in the fading light of a Friday evening, the two detectives stood in the parking area on the edge of expansive Lake Massabesic, looking at the miles of shoreline that would need to be watched that encircled the over two thousand five hundred acres of the community's drinking water. Behind them, the road that led to Auburn and Derry dissected the lake, while three quarters of the shore area was heavy with trees.

"It's a lot of area to cover," said Kristen Day.

"It is," said Miller. "But we concentrate on areas that have paths. He wants us to find the body. He needs us to find the body. We'll use that need. Maybe we'll get lucky."

Miller took a long, slow look across the lake, the water rippling slightly, the few sail boats bobbing at anchor. He hoped Kay Lawrence had a few more days of life, that would give them a few more days to try and be where the killer would bring her. They had always had two or three days after receiving the package before a body turned up. That script ended when Eve was found the morning after the box arrived. The script, he also knew, had been altered with Eve, because her name really was not a part of any movie. An argument, he supposed, could be offered for Evelyn being the link, but he didn't buy it. Eve had been personal, meant only to strike at him. Now, with Kay Lawrence, he felt the killer was back on script and that they would have the two or three days after receiving the box.

"I think we have some time," he said to Day. "I'm going to spend the weekend walking around this area. There are over fifty miles of Fire Roads crisscrossing through here that are constantly used for hiking, biking and strolling, especially now with the nicer weather. But I believe the body will be found in the Manchester part of this place and, seeing that about seventy-five percent of the lake is in Auburn, I'll be able to cover it all."

"Want me to join you?"

"No. We can't put all our eggs in one basket. I need you to check out Pine Island Pond and Great Cohas Brook and Swamp. I'll ask Matt to take Nutts Pond and Stevens Pond. I'll send officers to Crystal Lake and a few other spots in town."

Miller frowned.

"If the killer decides to use the Merrimack, we're screwed. This is daunting enough. No way we cover the length of the river."

"It won't be the river," said Day. "I think we can count on it being a swampy area."

She looked around one more time and started back to the car.

"Come on," she said. "Let's go pick up the movie."

19

Her eyes flutter, close, and then flutter again. Slowly, they open. She looks up at me, then up at the floor joists, then back at me. Still a little bit groggy, she rises up on her elbows, then into a sitting position on the mattress, then leans back against the bare cement wall. She looks down at her shackled right ankle, then back up to me.

"You're the killer that's been on the news?" she asks, her voice remarkably calm.

I smile down at her from my stool. "Are you comfortable? Can I get you something to drink? I've had to sedate you for a while."

"You're not what I expected," she says.

"Life is full of things you don't expect," say I. "Wouldn't you agree?"

"Yes," she replies. "I have found that to be true."

She rubs her temples.

"I'm still a little dizzy. What did you give me?"

"Nothing that will linger." I smile again, pleased there are no theatrics like all the others. "Beginning tomorrow, we have some work to do, you and I."

"Is that right? What kind of work? I'm afraid I'm not as spry as I once was. Not sure how much work you'll get out of me."

"Oh, nothing physical," I say with a pursing of my lips and a shake of the head. "You just have to sit there. I'll do the work. You just have to listen and watch and participate. We'll be a team, you and I. It'll be fun."

"And you'll kill me when we're done having fun?"

My smile fades. "You're not going to be a problem, are you? Not like the others?"

She pushes herself up a little higher. I am more than pleasantly surprised at how calm she appears. All the others had been raving maniacs when they first woke up. Kay - that is her name, Kay Lawrence - is being remarkably calm. Actually, she is being more than that. I can see in her eyes that she is already coolly calculating her situation and working on devising a plan on how to free herself. Good luck with that, Kay.

"I've seen the posts on social media," Kay says. "You've beaten those poor women rather badly. Are you going to beat me, too?"

"I'd rather not, Kay. I'm not a monster. I got no pleasure from doing that to them."

"But you did beat them."

"They wouldn't listen. They wouldn't participate. What was I to do?"

"I understand," she says.

She understands. I almost laugh. I have read her bio on line. A sixty-four year old retired psychologist who now works part time for the State, working with patients in the prison system. She has probably seen and heard it all. This could be fun.

"Well, if all I have to do is listen and participate, I can do that. I will do that. When my children come to identify my body, I would like it if they didn't see my face all black, blue and swollen."

"Then we are going to get along just fine."

"Any chance I can have a cigarette?" asks Kay.

"I don't smoke. It's a filthy habit, Kay. My Grandfather smoked and it killed him. You really should stop."

"Might be a little late for that," she says. "Don't you think?"

She gets me to smile with that one.

"What kind do you smoke? Winston's right?"

Of course I know what kind she smokes. I watched her buy a carton at the supermarket. I made sure to buy a pack for her, just to make sure she would know I was committed to making our time together an enjoyable time.

"I happen to have a pack right here."

"Your grandfather? Were you close?"

"He's the reason you're here?"

"I don't understand. I thought you said he died."

"He did. You'll understand soon enough. And, yes, for a few years we were very close. He loved me very much. And I loved him."

I toss the pack of Winston's to her. Shifting a few items on the workbench where I sit, I come up with the stainless steel Zippo that had been my Grandfather's lighter, and I toss it to her. She lights one up. I motion that she should toss the lighter back, which she does. I watch her smoke, taking the poison deep into her lungs.

"Nice lighter," she says. "Haven't seen one of those in years."

"It was my Grandfather's."

" PRT. Those his initials etched into the front?"

"A present when he retired from the railroad," say I. "Thirty-two years and he gets a cigarette lighter."

She is a trim woman, a little over five feet tall. Her skin is still quite firm for her age. Her hair is a lovely silver gray, cut no-nonsense short and straight. Her nails are crimson red. Her eyes are pale blue and kind. I can imagine her patients finding compassion in those eyes.

"Why me?" she asks after a while, snubbing the cigarette out on the cement floor and tossing the remains into a five-gallon bucket that she will be using as a toilet.

I smile again. Reaching over, I lift the model box off the workbench and hold it in front of me so she can see it. She stares at it, uncomprehending.

"I don't understand," she says again.

"We're going to build this, you and I. Together. As a team. It'll be fun."

I see it then in her eyes, that she understands. She actually smiles.

"I was eight years old when my mother and father saw that movie," Kay says. "I remember they came home after seeing it and I was still awake, playing a board game with the baby-sitter, and my mother said, 'Kay, honey, we just saw a movie and the character in the movie had the same name as you. The very same name. Kay Lawrence. Imagine that?' You know, I think they saw the 3D version of it. They said it was too scary for me to see. As strange as it may seem, I've never seen the movie."

"You'll get to see it now," I say. "But not in 3D. Sorry."

She frowns. "Do you know, if I had kept my husband's name after the divorce, I wouldn't be here now. Dr. Kay Abbott would have held no interest for you, would it?"

She asks for the Zippo and lights another cigarette, returning the lighter with a deft flick of her well manicured hand.

"It took me six years of marriage to figure out he wasn't worth keeping around and another twenty to completely wipe him from my life after my daughter graduated college. If I had kept his name, and the constant reminder of him that it would have been, there would be another woman sitting here and I'd be at my Zumba class. Still, I'm not sure I didn't make the right choice going back to my maiden name."

She exhales a great plume of smoke in a rush and looks up at me.

"You married? Ever been?"

"No and no," I reply.

"How did you find me?"

"Internet. Find anything you want on the Internet. There are actually quite a few women with the last name Lawrence, but only two Kays within a hundred mile radius, believe it or not. You were closest. A little older than you should be, you know, for the story, but I had scouted you out and you are in terrific shape, so ..." and I shrug.

"Yeah. Pilates. A little jogging. Some Zumba. Figured I'd live to ninety even with the smoking. If I'd known what was coming my way, I'd have eaten more cake and ice cream. You don't have any, do ya?"

I stand. "I can appreciate what you are doing, Dr. Lawrence. I really can. More than you know. The charade you portray of being calm. I can understand that. My life is a charade. Every day. I show the world one face, but here, in my home, the other face emerges. Jekyl and Hyde, you might say. I can see that you must be very good at your job. Cool under pressure. Manipulating the conversation, looking for information that you can use to build a conclusion, in this case a way to keep me from killing you. Sparing your life. I admire what you are doing. I envy your control. I'd like to think I would react in the same way if the shoe were on the other foot. I'm not sure I would. I do have a bit of a temper. I think if I was in your situation, I would be in a rage. I'd be angry."

"What makes you think I'm not angry? What makes you think I'm not raging inside? I'm faced with the prospect of being killed by someone I don't even know for absolutely no good reason. But anger isn't going to save me, is it?"

"No, it is not, Dr. Lawrence. And as far as why? In the next few days, I will show you why."

"It won't be reason enough," she says. "You must know that."

"It will be to me."

SATURDAY EVENING. MANTOVANI begins playing softly as I pop the movie out of the VCR and place it in the protective colorful sleeve of the black and white movie.

"So, what did you think, Kay?" I ask, and then pop the final Oreo into my mouth.

"Seemed a little silly," she replies. "Not sure what all the hoopla was about. Maybe it's scarier in 3D. Maybe the fifties were a more innocent time."

She hasn't touched her food.

"You haven't touched your food," I say. "You need to keep your strength up."

"Not hungry. Wouldn't mind a smoke, though."

I toss her the pack and the lighter.

"You were gone all day," she says after exhaling. "At least I think it was day. I was craving one of these. What is it you do?"

I smile down at her. We've played this game for two nights now, and I'm not sure how I feel about it. With the others, their whining, their general lack of becoming involved in the process, their total lack of enthusiasm to what I hoped we could accomplish, often led me to lash out at them. And, while that would unfortunately leave my partner with some kind of facial bruising, and me with a small degree of guilt at the violence committed, the lashing out actually calmed me down after. Not sure why that is. Perhaps I should discuss that with Kay. After all, she is a certified shrink. But, no, I don't think I will. If she's any good, she'll bring it up after observing me for several days. I mean, that is what she is doing. Observing. Looking for something she can use to save her life.

I'm normally a rather aggressive individual, so being quick to anger has always been a part of my make-up. What can I say? We are all wired differently. But what I am doing now, this keeping women tethered in my basement, this is causing me a great deal of anxiety. I know it is, and I think that when I hit someone, that somehow releases that tension and that is why I feel a calming effect after doing it.

I almost giggle. This is totally me. Here, I have a licensed professional who would only be too happy to delve into my psyche, pro bono, too, and I am self-analyzing instead.

"So, tell me," I say, not interested in talking about my day, "what did you think about the creature? Did you find any sympathy for him?"

"Sympathy? Not really. He did try to take Kay off the boat several times. Eventually, he got her and took her to his cave. He killed at least five guys. Maybe six. I lost count. The Creature was not someone who generated any sympathy from the movie going audience, I wouldn't think."

"With some of the others, there was a book to read," I say, not wanting to debate sympathy just yet. "If you haven't been keeping up with the newspaper accounts of my previous partners, those would be *Dracula* and *Frankenstein.* Reading them before watching the movies, gave me an opportunity to discuss the differences between book and movie with my partner. Unfortunately, they missed even the most obvious errors."

"Do you know that you keep referring to these women as your partner?" Kay asks.

"Yes," I reply. "Of course. That's what we were. What else would you call two people who are joined together in an effort to create something? Partners. You and I are partners."

"Is that what you believe?"

I didn't like the way she said that. There was no anger in her voice. No look of disgust on her face. No violent shake of her head or sneer at my statement. It was said in a clinical tone, much like a doctor might say, 'You have the common cold. Take two aspirin and get some rest.'

"Yes, that is what I believe," I snap at her. "It's exactly what it is."

"Think about this," she says, again her voice calm. "The women you have had down here, held captive by a chain wrapped around their ankle, do you think that they think of themselves as your partner? That they are thinking about anything else besides getting away from here? Escaping? Or when they realize that they may die down here, do you think they care what it is you are reading, or watching, or creating? That is not how the human mind works. From the second they open their eyes on this mattress, escape and survival are the only things on their mind. You must realize that?"

Of course I realize that. I'm not stupid. I understand their confusion. I understand their terror. But shouldn't that pass? Like being a captured soldier. Once you realize the situation you find yourself in, doesn't it make sense to just make the best of it?

"The Dalai Lama says, 'Although you may not always be able to avoid difficult situations, you can modify the extent to which you can suffer by how you choose to respond to the situation.' I counter that my partners should have responded better. Should have understood the opportunity to join with another human being in a worthwhile journey. Should have helped me in my pain."

"Helped you?"

"Yes! Helped me. Helped me. They could have recognized my need, should have recognized my need."

I can feel myself becoming agitated. Is everyone so Goddamned blind? Even a professional?

"Look around you, Doctor. Do you not see it? The workbench. The television, VCR, stereo, the mattress. Are these the things I would need were I just a simple murderer? A mindless taker of human life? There is a reason for all of this. A reason why these women are not just slain in their beds, or on the street, left to shed their blood in the gutter. There is an opportunity here. Look around you, Doctor. You have an opportunity. A chance to do something worthwhile. A chance to connect with another human being and share something very special."

"And what is that?" Kay Lawrence asks.

I stare down at her and slowly count to ten.

"I am making a statement. We, will be making a statement. With the death of each partner, the manner of their death and the posing of the body, it is my hope that the public, through the news outlets, finally understands how ungodly we are to each other. We are a society devoid of compassion. Of empathy for those we see as different from us."

"So, you believe that killers should be shown sympathy for their actions?" Doctor Lawrence asks, but not in a judgmental way.

I smile down at her, but inside, I am in turmoil. If I can not make an educated person understand what I hope to accomplish, what hope is there that the average man will grasp the meaning.

"That's just it, Doctor. These men are not killers. They are fighting for their survival, caught in situations not of their own making. I don't believe Mary Shelley wrote *Frankenstein* to be a book about a killing monster. I believe she wrote it to make a statement about the human race. Doctor Frankenstein is God. He creates a man. All this man wants is to live in peace and to love and be loved. Isn't this what most of us want? It is certainly what I want. But not all men are like that. There are men who crave power, lust, riches, turmoil, and have no desire for love. These men prey on others. They prey on the weak. When they see someone different it worries them, and their first thought is to destroy that which they perceive as a threat to their order. They do not look for the beauty inside, or attempt to understand. Violence is their first response. Always. Throughout the history of the world, either through religious beliefs, desire for more riches, or simple fear of another, violence is the first response.

"Have you read *Frankenstein,* Doctor Lawrence?" I ask, after pausing for a few seconds.

"In college. A long time ago," says the good doctor. She's staring at me now. God only knows what she is thinking.

"And you've seen the movie?"

She nods. "Many years ago. A midnight Creature Feature along with *Bride of Frankenstein* and a three month old with an ear infection."

"Then you know that Shelley gave us the opportunity to be sympathetic to the monster, while Hollywood did not. But not just Frankenstein. All of them. The old films, I mean. Not the newer ones where these killers are just mindless psychos. But Dracula, Wolf Man, Quasimodo, these poor men who are haunted and hunted through no fault of their own. They are just like all of us who are different, aren't they, Kay? Would the world not be a better place if we all had more compassion and less hate for those who we deem different?"

Kay motions for another cigarette. I can see she is carefully forming the words she wants to say next, while using Grandpa's Zippo, being careful not to say something that might upset me. But no matter what she says, I won't become upset. Finally, I have someone, an educated someone, who I can discuss all of this with. I used to have these discussions with Maryanne. She rarely responded, but she did listen and she did agree.

"You quoted the Dalai Lama," Kay says, smiling. "I find that interesting."

That's disappointing. Taking the easy way out. Going in another direction with the conversation before, no doubt, doubling back and trying to catch me into revealing something I might not reveal otherwise. Goddamn shrinks. I want to tell her this isn't necessary. I'm prepared to talk about what I am doing and why. I want to tell someone.

But she's the doctor, so, instead, I say, "I find his words

comforting. When I find myself feeling anxious, I read some passages in his book and his words calm me."

I look away and listen to the music for a bit.

"When I was younger," I say, "I didn't know how to deal with anger. In those times, it wouldn't take much to set me off. Five years ago, I lost the love of my life. There was so much anger in me after that, I thought I was losing my mind. And then one day, I picked up the Dalai Lama's book. Someone had left it in my dentist's waiting room, and I was just leafing through it, waiting for my turn in the chair of torture. And what I read resonated so strongly in me. I left the office with the book. I keep it on my nightstand. I read it often, still finding comfort in it."

"When you say you lost the love of your life, you mean they died? That can be quite traumatic."

"She left me, Doctor. Rather abruptly. She died recently. I don't want to talk about her."

Standing, I pick up my plate "Are you done eating?"

Kay nods. "Are we going to build that model kit? Is that what we do next?"

"We start tomorrow," I say. "This should be fun. I've never built this one before."

"So this is what you've done with the other women. Read books, watched movies, built the models."

"Of course. That is what I've been doing."

"And after the model is built?" Doctor Kay Lawrence asks.

I pick up her plate. Standing over her, I smile. "Let's not worry about that right now."

20

Seven o'clock Sunday morning. Kristen Day entered the nearly empty bullpen carrying her laptop, a box of doughnuts and two large coffees from Dunkin's. Detective Erik Miller looked up from a folder on his desk, then stood. The two of them entered the interrogation room and sat next to each other on the same side of the table. They were both dressed casually in jeans and spring weight jackets. Miller's denim was blue, Day's black. From a pocket of her maroon colored jacket, Day pulled a circular disc in a protective paper sleeve. Popping open a tray in the laptop, she inserted the DVD. While she did this, Miller opened the slit in the top of the coffee container and reached into the box of doughnuts, extracting a honey dipped.

"How was your night?" he asked as he watched Day copy what he had just done.

"Quiet. How about you?" she asked after sipping some coffee and placing a powdered doughnut on a napkin.

"Zonked out about eleven. I must have walked twenty miles yesterday. Maybe more. I had no idea there were so many trails in those woods. Fire trails. They weave all over."

"Yeah. I covered a lot of ground, too."

"And?"

"Cohas is a possibility. I don't think Pine Island is. Back in the day, maybe, when it was an amusement area, but not now. Too congested. I had some time, so covered some of Mosquito Brook. I think that would be a great spot, but the body might never be found."

She noticed he wolfed the doughnut down and selected another. She had noticed the belt on his jeans had been close to the last hole, confirming what she had been thinking for the past month, that he hadn't had an appetite since the death of Eve and had lost weight. Maybe his appetite was coming back.

"I heard from Matt last night," said Miller. "He walked Stevens Pond and the water at Livingston. He didn't think they would be used. Not enough vegetation. His money is on Massabesic, although, he did admit, he has never seen the movie."

Miller nodded at the laptop. "You ready?" he asked.

Day pressed a button and the movie began playing on the small screen.

About half way through the movie, they saw Detective Mark Allen walk into the Detective Room. There had been a murder in a bar on Elm Street the previous evening, and it was his investigation. He saw Miller and Day watching a video, smirked, but didn't comment as he went to his desk.

After the movie ended, Miller, finishing off his third doughnut, said, "Might have been more interesting in color. Scenery would have been great. But we have ourselves a major problem."

Day nodded. "Agreed."

"A pond of water surrounded by vegetation," said Miller. "Where do we start?"

"There will have to be a trail nearby that is used frequently," Day said. "We know this. Anything you see yesterday that fits?"

"Oh, yeah. All over Massabesic. But the western side of the by-pass, I think, holds more promise. Yeah. All along Lake Shore Rd. Then out behind the ball fields there is a fire road that connects the By-pass with Lake Shore Rd. It's a lot of area, but it needs another look. I spent most of my time yesterday on the east side of the by-pass. Today, I'll do a thorough look all the way to the Cohas. What about you?"

"I'll check a few spots around the back end of Crystal Lake. And I want to take another look at Mosquito Brook again. This time, I have spray with me in the car. That was not fun yesterday with the damn bugs."

Miller finished up his cold coffee.

"This is like a needle in a haystack, Kristen. There has got to be a hundred spots that would work for him. We don't have the kind of manpower it's going to take."

"Maybe we'll get lucky," Day said.

"Sure. I have been thinking, almost everywhere the body will be left, the ground should be soft. We might get a print. Vegetation is thick. Bushes. Maybe we get a fiber. Unfortunately, our Kay Lawrence isn't like the actress in the movie. Julia Adams was a well built statuesque woman. Our Kay is petite. Probably a little over a hundred pounds. If he needs to, our guy will be able to carry her a long way from his vehicle to where he leaves her."

As he stood and began picking up after himself, Miller said, "But the movie only affirms what I said before."

"And what is that?" asked Day as she replaced the DVD into the protective sleeve.

"Our Kay Lawrence parks her car in a bad spot with no concern for her safety. The movies' Kay Lawrence jumps into a lagoon in the Amazon for a swim, with no concern for what inhabits that water. Could have been a fatal decision for her."

Miller looked at his partner.

"It's probably going to be a fatal one for our Kay Lawrence," he said.

Before leaving the room, they agreed to meet for a late lunch to discuss what they had discovered.

THEY MET FOR lunch at a diner on the border of Hooksett. It was late afternoon. They shared what they had discovered on their surveillance, each admitting that there were any number of places that would be suitable for what they feared the killer would be looking for. They agreed that it would be impossible to keep a constant watch on all the sites. They would need to keep it as a night vigil and select a number of sites that could reasonably be manned. They decided to wait for the expected box to be delivered before putting their assets into place. That gave them some time to narrow down where the assets should be placed. How much time they had, was not something they knew.

21

I lay the pieces out neatly on the workbench after snipping them from the plastic poles. They are lined up in such a way that Kay can see them from where she sits, sucking in smoke from a cigarette. It is her third one in the last twenty minutes. Good thing I had purchased another pack.

When I first come down the stairs, carrying our plates of dinner, there had been a potent stench of vomit and diarrhea. I was used to that. Fear and anxiety can affect the bowels adversely. I immediately had taken the bucket out to the back of the house and dumped it, washing the bucket down with a garden hose. Then I had sprayed the cellar with a very pleasant disinfectant that smelled like apples and cinnamon. Kay had apologized several times for what she had done. I had told her no apology was needed. And none was. It wasn't her fault she was tethered in my basement.

"Have you thought some more about the movie?" I ask as I fidget with the model's pieces.

"What do you mean?" she asks.

"In relation to what we discussed last night."

"I did," she says, almost wistfully. I am impressed by her continuing composure. Very impressed.

"And?"

"I can see what you mean. About how the people on the ship reacted to the creature."

I stop touching the plastic pieces and look at her. She gets it. Finally, someone else gets it.

"Yes. Exactly," I say. "No different than the town's people in *Frankenstein* or the crowd in Hunchback. Kill the creature is their first thought. Mark uses a spear gun. Shoots the creature in the back. His first reaction upon seeing it. All the men on board the ship, firing bullets into the water, trying to kill the creature. But why? Up until then, the creature hadn't done anything to them. Why are they trying to kill it?"

"Well, there was a dead man in the demolished tent at the camp site," says Kay.

"Yes," I agree. "But they couldn't be sure it was the creature who did that, could they? They are in the Amazon. Filled with predators. No. In every one of these movies, the first thought is to kill the monster. No empathy. No compassion. No attempt at understanding. Just kill."

"But you know that this is just a movie," she says to me, a slight smile to keep me from getting too wound up, as I tend to get when discussing the injustices. "The movie has to have the villain so that it can have the hero."

"We've talked about this before, Doctor. Movies mirror real life. Human beings immediately become defensive when faced with something they don't understand."

I take a bite from my peanut butter and jelly sandwich. Kay has not touched her food.

"Have you ever seen the movie *The Day the Earth Stood Still*? The visitor from another planet wasn't a creature. He looked like us. Other than that eight foot tall robot, Gort, he posed no threat. He was one man. And still he got shot. Why?"

"Because it was a movie," Kay says again.

My turn to smile slightly.

"No. And you know it. You, Doctor Lawrence, have all too often heard the dark side of the human psyche. You witness it every Thursday at the prison. You know all too well the capacity for violence that lies within us all. As do I. I am sick of it."

She picks up a section of her sandwich and takes a few nibbles from around the edges. Then a few sips from the carton of milk. I notice her water bottle is empty.

"I see your point," she says after a while. "But might there be a better way for you to make it? In your mind, you might be seeing this as a wake up call for the public. But in reality, I'm afraid, you are only reinforcing their belief that killing the monster is the only way to keep them safe. Don't you see? You are seen, by the reporters, and by the public, to be a killer. A monster who has taken the lives of five women. Were the police to report tomorrow that you had been found and killed, people would not mourn your passing. They would rejoice. You, in what you are doing, are only reaffirming that which you are trying to illuminate."

"Well," say I, "time will tell." I had thought about that very thing and knew she was correct. But, in reality, public perception of the monsters mattered little to me. It was the argument I liked to use sometimes, but it wasn't the end game. Far from it.

I begin touching the pieces of the model again, moving them ever so slightly. There are many pieces that make up the Creature, but there is also the rocky base, a large lizard, a stunted tree, dead with skinny limbs, and a long snake that shall cling to those limbs, along with a few other things.

"When I was young, and built models with my Grandfather, this was one of my jobs. Twisting all the pieces from the plastic poles and lining them up on the bench. I took great pleasure in that."

"You built models with your grandfather?" Doctor Lawrence asks.

My back is to her, so she can't see me smile. Lord, but she jumped on that rather quickly.

"Oh, yes. It is one of my favorite memories from a childhood that had very few. He had a workbench similar to this one. Just a little smaller. I needed more space for the television and VCR. When we watched the movies, we did it in his living room."

"So, what we are doing here, you did with your grandfather?"

I turn to face her, holding the lizard parts in my hand.

"Yes. He had a room set up that he called his study. It was a small room, but we read the book in there - well, he read the book, I listened - then we watched the movie in the living room and then we went back into the study to build the model. Over the course of a little over a year, when I was nine and ten, we built six models together. We were a team, Doctor. And I was an important part of that team. I knew how important it was to my Grandfather that I took an active roll in the process. That I was committed to the project from the beginning to the end. I knew that he was counting on me to help him, and I would have sooner died than disappoint him."

I place the lizard parts gently down on the bench.

"Can you understand now, Kay, why I want my partners -and I include you - to join me in what I am doing? How important it is to me to have someone who understands what it is we can accomplish? Do you get it?"

"You loved your grandfather?" Kay asks. I can see the wheels spinning behind those pale blue eyes.

"With all my heart," I reply. "And he loved me more than anyone else ever has."

"How old were you when he passed away?"

I lean back on my stool, chew an Oreo up and wash it down with some milk.

"Passed away makes it sound like he he slipped from this world peacefully in his sleep, Kay. It wasn't like that. I was ten when he died."

"I'm sorry. That would have been terrible for you. Had you been six, the bond between the two of you may have not been so strong. Sixteen, you could have processed it easier. Better. Ten, eleven, twelve, that is the worst time to lose a loved family member.

"When a loved one dies, and we don't have a chance to say good-bye, that can be difficult for us, too. We lose the chance to tell them how much we love them one last time. You say he didn't die peacefully. Was it an accident? If you knew he suffered, that could have been very traumatic for you."

I sit here looking at the good doctor, unsure now if she is playing me, looking for any 'in' that she can use to save her life, or if she is actually concerned with what happened and how it affected me. Also, I led us into this conversation, wanting her to ask questions, wanting us to discuss what happened, because I have never discussed this with a professional before, or anyone else for that matter. But now that we are in this discussion, I suddenly don't want to continue it. The pain is too great. I feel like I am suffocating.

But, I stand and begin slowly unbuttoning my shirt. Doctor Lawrence at first looks confused by my actions, and then she looks worried. But she stays silent. When the last button is undone, I take the shirt off and look deep into Kay's eyes. Then I turn so she can see my back, and the damage that is there.

After letting her get a good look, I put my shirt back on, button it, sit down again and finish the rest of my Oreo's and milk.

"Do you want to talk about it?" Doctor Lawrence asks after several minutes of silence.

I suddenly feel exhausted. So very, very tired.

"We can talk about it," she says again. "If you want. I think we should."

Do you really, Doctor? You think we should? And what good is that going to do me now? What relief can you possibly give me now, after all the years of pain that I have suffered? Jesus Christ, I am getting tired of this woman. Her false concerns. Her understanding. Her false empathy. Of course it is false. Her only concern is to get away from me. The only understanding she has is that she must play me in her attempts to get me to set her free. Her empathy is complete bullshit. It takes all of my willpower not to spin around on my stool and slap her lying mouth with the back of my hand.

I feel the tears welling up in my eyes. I hate this woman. My God, how I hate her right now. I wonder, if I tell her what happened, will she understand my suffering? Tell me I was just a child? I should carry no guilt? I have suffered enough? I must let it go? It wasn't my fault? Can she give me some relief? Can she help me? Can I believe her?

My Grandfather's bench had drawers where things were stored. I have no drawers in my bench. Instead, I have shelves above the bench. Two of them. The top shelf holds the models that have been built. The bottom shelf the tools needed to do the work, along with the VHS tapes of the movies, several Mantovani albums, and some cleaning supplies I need for my partners. I reach over and pick up a thin tube of model glue.

"Do you know what this is, Doctor Lawrence?" I ask, holding the glue up so she can see it. I still have not turned to face her.

"A tube of adhesive?" she says.

"Very good, Doctor. Yes, a tube of model glue adhesive. It is how we will connect all these pieces to make the picture that you see on the box. This really is wonderful stuff. Only one problem with it. And do you know what that is, Kay?"

I turn now to face her. She shakes her head.

"It is highly flammable. Highly. Probably shouldn't be available on the market. Certainly should not be allowed in the hands of a child."

I can see in her eyes that she has figured it out. That she knows what happened to me. But she doesn't know all of it. No, not all of it. And I am torn. The turmoil in me is almost more than I can bare. Half of me wants to slap that look of pity off her face, the other half wants me to fall on my knees in front of her, confess my sin and beg for forgiveness. Plead for relief from this guilt that I have carried for far too long.

Instead, I say, "We were working on Frankenstein. It was raining outside and I could hear the rain falling on the back porch. My Grandmother was in the living room watching her soaps. Mantovani playing on the Philco. My Grandfather sitting beside me, lighting up a Marlboro with his Zippo as he watched me putting two sections of the monsters torso together, making sure they would fit. He then reached into a drawer and took out a tube of glue. Much like the one I am holding now. It was a new tube, so he had to poke a hole into the opening. As would sometimes happen, some glue would be squeezed out, and that is what happened, a small puddle of it landing on the bench. We gave it no thought. It had happened before. We would clean it up later. Grandfather handed me the tube and I ran a thin bead along the sections of each torso piece, and then placed the tube down on the bench. A little more glue slipped from the tube when I did that, also puddling next to the other bit of glue that had escaped before.

"Just then, the last song on the album finished and Grandfather went to flip the record over as I stuck the two pieces together. For some reason, and I had never done it before, the Zippo had a sudden fascination for me. I had never touched it other than to hand it to my Grandfather. This time, maybe because I was feeling so happy that we had begun making the model, I placed the torso on the work bench and picked up the Zippo, flipped open the top and rolled the wheel with my thumb, as I had seen

Grandfather do a hundred times. An immediate flame appeared. I had some glue reside on my fingers, and I clearly remember watching in fascination as a flame appeared on my right thumb. In a heartbeat, the pain hit me. I dropped the lighter and started hitting at my hand with my other hand, quickly putting out the flame. But I had dropped the Zippo right on the two puddles of glue."

I look off across the cellar, over to where the oil tank sits. The scene I am playing in my mind, I have played a million times before. Doctor Kay Lawrence doesn't say a word. She patiently waits for me to continue.

"It was like everything was moving in slow motion. My shirt sleeve brushed the burning glue and ignited. As I pushed away from the bench, the flame jumped to the back of my shirt. I yelled out for my Grandfather. I began screaming. I could feel my skin being burnt as my shirt went up in flames. My Grandfather, seeing what was happening, I remember he began hugging me to him, I guess in an effort to douse the flames. Then he shoved me to the floor and, taking his garden work jacket off a hook, he smothered me with it and put out the fire in what was left of my shirt. I was in agony. Sobbing and screaming in pain. In his effort to douse my clothes, unfortunately, his clothes had caught on fire. I watched, screaming, as he tried to smother his flames with the coat, but he couldn't do it. He fell to the ground and began rolling, but the room was just so small he couldn't really roll. I remember the door opening and my Grandmother screaming when she saw us. She pulled me from the room, ripping the smoldering shirt from me, then ran for a blanket. Through my pain, I watched as she covered my Grandfather with it, finally extinguishing the flames, all the while screaming out his name, and calling on Jesus to help her. The ambulance came and took us both to the hospital. I survived. Grandfather did not."

Over twenty-five years later, and I am still an emotional wreck every time I think of that day. I turn from Kay and look up at the shelf that holds the models I have built these past six months. Mummy, Dracula, Frankenstein, Wolf Man, and, with Maryanne, King Kong. But that one we did almost five years ago. It saddens me, and angers me, that all of them could have been done with Maryanne. We could have shared them all. And would have, were it not for Megan Riley.

I look back at Kay. I can tell she wants a smoke, but she doesn't ask for one. Maybe she's feeling a little apprehensive about asking for the Zippo. I toss her the smokes and the lighter.

"Almost four years of skin grafts. In and out of hospitals. Learning very quickly to always wear a long sleeved shirt. In school, in gym class, at a pool party. In the heat of summer. At the beach. Always a long sleeved shirt. Kids can be cruel. And they have long memories. They only had to see my back one time, and the names never ended. Quite creative they were, too."

I point to the box of the model we will soon be making.

"This one was a particular favorite. As was Godzilla. Especially during my growth spurt. Yeah, Godzilla was a favorite one they used. Later, dating became a bit of a problem, as you might imagine."

I turn back to the pieces, select two, the two pieces that will make the Creature's left leg. Then I pick up the tube of glue and pull out a pin I have stuck in the opening, so that the glue will flow easily. Then I place everything back on the bench and turn slowly towards my helper, smile at her, and indicate she should return the smokes and the lighter. Once I have them, I turn back to my work.

"I think it is interesting that you kept your Grandfather's lighter. What else do you have that was his?"

I turn again to face her. "Nothing else," I say. "While I was in the hospital, Grandmother had everything that was in that room taken to the dump. All the models, the Philco, the records, everything except the recliner. Even had the walls painted over. Our first visit over there, must have been almost a year later, I went into the room. I had had no idea what she had done. I stood in the doorway almost in shock. I couldn't believe she had discarded our work. I was going to put the models in my room at home. I was crushed. I fell to my knees. I started to cry. And then I saw a glint from under the chair. Something was reflecting the light. It was the lighter. I never wanted to see the Zippo again, and yet that was all that was left for me from my Grandfather. I picked it up and put it in my pocket.

"Do you know what she did? My Grandfather had two rings that he wore besides his wedding band. She gave them to her sons. He had a Purple Heart from World War II. She gave that to one of my cousins. She gave all his clothes to Goodwill. She gave me nothing. You know, I have always believed that she regretted pulling me from that room and ripping off my burning shirt before dousing the flames on her husband. From the day of the fire, to the day she died, she never said a kind word to me. In fact, she hardly ever spoke to me again."

Kay is looking at me as she smokes, her face showing so much sympathy for me that I am caught off guard. Does she truly feel my pain? Does she understand? I would like to believe she does.

"While I glue the pieces together, we can discuss the movie in more detail," I say, changing the subject. "Maybe try to depict a scene with the pieces we have. Your job, Doctor Lawrence, will be to select the colors we should paint it. I know the movie was in black and white, but use your imagination. Tomorrow night we will paint it."

Smoke from her exhale drifts by me. I really hate the smell of smoke. None of the others smoked. Maryanne smoked, but I cared for her so much, I forgave her that vice.

"We should take more time in this process," says the Doctor.

"It would give us more time to talk about you. I think we can make progress. I think we can ease some of that pain you are burdened with."

I have already told this woman, this complete stranger, more about me than I have ever told anyone else, except Maryanne. I told Maryanne almost everything in the two hundred and fifty-six days she was with me. I turn to look at the good Doctor.

Doctor Kay Lawrence is kneeling on the mattress, only a few feet from where I sit. Her eyes are clear, small wisps of smoke rise in front of them. I look into those eyes and I see sympathy for me. The sympathy I wish others would have for my monsters, I see in her eyes. For me. For the monster that she believes I am. And I see it then. She doesn't understand at all. The bitch has been playing me. And I almost fell for it.

"I really do believe I can help you," she says and she smiles.

Of course you would say that, Doctor. Let's spend a week, a month, a year, healing me. Maybe not.

I smile the most friendly smile I am capable of. Two can play this game.

LATE SUNDAY NIGHT. The fourth night that Kay has been with me, and I have no complaints. She has been the best partner so far, just as I knew she would be. We had finished gluing the last of the pieces, and it was she who had suggested placing the snake a little more forward on the dead tree limb than I thought it should go. I had to admit, doing it her way lent a more sinister look to the reptile.

We have had a long discussion about how dark a green the Creature should be, but in the end we agreed the darker the better. I am now painting the third and final coat of that green. When I am done, we will be done.

Throughout the hours, as we worked, Doctor Lawrence tried delving more into my past. I shared a little, here and there, but I just couldn't get past the feeling that every question, every comment, was calculated. This was her not so subtle attempt to get me into believing the best thing for me was to allow her to leave here. That this did not have to end like all the others. I played along. I never agreed that I thought she was right. To do so would have signaled to her that I was not sincere in that agreement. I had to appear as if I was slowly coming around to the idea of letting her live. I had to give her hope. Which I did. And then I sat back and enjoyed the drama.

At one point, as we finished up our peanut butter and jelly sandwich, she said to me, "I have an idea that you may want to consider."

"And what is that?" I had asked, picking up the small dark brown paint container that I would use on the tree.

"I know, from our conversations," she had said, "that you understand that killing people is not acceptable in our society. You know that."

"Of course I do."

"Don't say it like that," she quickly said. "You might be surprised to learn that not everyone does. There are people who have no problem taking the life of another. They have no moral conflict about that at all. Kill a human, kill an ant. It's all the same to them.

"But," she had continued in a very clinical tone, "that is not you. Yes, you kill, but in your mind you are justified to kill because you have something that you want the world to recognize. The end justifies the means. I have a great deal of experience working with patients who have done some horrific things for the same reason. They did what they did because they felt compelled to. It was something they had to do to justify their own existence."

I made sure to nod my head a few times, as if I were seriously considering what she was saying. And then I had asked her,

"Wasn't it Jung who said, 'Sometimes you have to do something unforgivable just to be able to go on living.'"

Oh, the look that was on poor Kay's face! Priceless.

"You've read Carl Jung?" she asked incredulously.

"And Freud," I had answered. "More impressed with Jung than Freud."

What I could have said was, I thought they were both charlatans. Give me the Dalai Lama's words every time when looking for clarity.

She recovered quickly.

She said, "Jung also said, 'The healthy man does not torture others. Generally, it is the tortured who turn into torturers.'"

"So, you believe I may be a tortured soul?"

She had brightened at that.

"Yes, of course. And there is a reason for that. Jung also told us the reason. 'The foundation of all mental illness is the unwillingness to experience legitimate suffering.'"

"I read that, too. But I have suffered, Doctor Lawrence. I have experienced tremendous suffering in the death of my Grandfather and in the duplicity of the love of my life."

"Yes, but you haven't grieved," she had told me. "A period of healthy grieving that allows the person to come to terms with their suffering, is how we get past that terrible loss and move on with our life in a healthy, normal way."

"I see. And what is it you think I should consider?" I had asked, hopefully conveying just a touch of wonderment at her analysis.

"I have helped patients who have suffered, come to terms with their loss," she had said quite seriously. "I have helped them see that there is a path forward in their lives that can lead to a more peaceful mind. That they can once again feel some degree of happiness and contentment."

"And you think you could do that for me?"

"I have done it for others."

Obviously she could do it for me, was left unsaid.

"Here is something to consider," continued the good Doctor. "If you give yourself up to the authorities, you will be tried as a murderer. No question. Can't get away from that. However, a plea of insanity would be justified in your situation. I am confident of that."

"You would testify to that?"

"I would," she had quickly replied. "And I am sure other psychiatrists would concur."

Of course they would.

"But I don't believe I am insane, Doctor."

"Of course you don't," she had said so softly. "Yet what you are doing is the perfect definition of insanity. I don't believe you would be sent to prison for what you have done. I believe a psychiatric facility is where you would go. And there you would receive the help that you need. I see no reason why you can not be treated successfully. You just need help."

And of course, after my rehabilitation, I would be set free. That, too, is understood. Do I really give the impression that I am that big a fool?

And now, after a day of interesting conversation and shared effort, we have finished our work. The model of the *Creature From the Black Lagoon* is complete. I lift it up and show it to my partner, turning it ever so slowly so that she can see all sides of it. The lizard, posed along the back, I feel, really adds to the scene. The Creature, arms reaching out, like all the other models, is terrifying. I am very pleased with our effort. I place the model on the higher shelf, beside the Wolf Man. Six down. Two to go.

I smile at Kay. "We should celebrate," I say. "I have chocolate cake with frosting. We should have a piece. Would you like coffee or tea, Kay?"

I can see there is so much apprehension in Kay's face. It seems she has shrunken in size as the day progressed. There were moments where she appeared hopeful while we spoke, and other moments where she had abandoned all hope. And now, with the model completed, she is unsure of her fate and unsure of herself. But with the suggestion of cake, a spark of hope enters those pale blue eyes.

"Cake sounds delightful," she replies, her tone light, giving no hint of frayed nerves. "And I think tea would be just as delightful. And we can talk some more?"

I smile again. "Of course."

In my kitchen, I cut two generous slices of store bought cake - I don't bake - while the kettle is heating up. I search through the counter drawers and come up with two plastic forks. When the water begins to boil, I shut off the burner and pour the steaming water over the tea bags. My cup has a scene of the Sagamore Bridge and Welcome to Cape Cod written on it. Kay's cup has a bright red lobster painted on it. Everything goes on a tray.

As I come carefully down the cellar stairs, Kay is kneeling on the mattress near the end of her tether, finishing up the cigarette I gave her before going up. She is watching me very carefully. I wonder if she hopes I will trip and break my neck in the fall? Probably not. Much too rational a human being. My death would solve one problem for her, but create another.

"Kay, I can't begin to tell you how pleased I am with how the project went," I say, stepping onto the cement floor. "I knew, I just knew, that you would be the perfect partner, and you didn't disappoint."

I put my plate and cup on the bench, then the tray on the floor. With my right foot, I push the tray closer to Kay until it is in arms reach.

"I did try to do as you asked," she says, looking at the cake, but not picking up the plate and fork.

"Careful with the tea," I warn her. "It's quite hot."

I take a large piece of cake into my mouth and savor it, theatrically making noises of delight. When I look at her, she has not picked up her plate. With good reason, I imagine, she is wary. I frown at her and give a slight shake of my head. Bending over, I take her plate and leave mine in its' place. Then I take a large bite from the piece I had given her. Whether not wanting to offend me, or actually desiring the dessert, Kay lifts the plate and begins eating the cake. When she is finished, she picks up the cup of tea, blows on it for a few seconds, then sips at it.

"There is no need to rush into a decision," she says as she sips at the hot liquid. "I understand how apprehensive you would be to what I suggested. We can take our time with this. Talk about it. The idea of surrendering must be quite frightening to you. But if you surrender, a judge and a jury would see that as a positive sign. That you had seen that you were not acting rationally and that you realized you must get help before harming anyone else."

"I have considered what you have said, Doctor. It certainly has merit."

Isn't this lovely. The two of us, sitting together on a quiet Sunday night, sipping tea and conversing. Both of us speaking earnestly. Both of us lying through our teeth.

"I think, if we spend more time, talk it all through, that you will see it really is the best way forward," Kay says. "If they catch you, the insanity defense goes out the window and you spend the rest of your life in prison. If you voluntarily surrender, there is a very good chance you could be released from a psychiatric facility in two or three years."

She places the empty cup on the tray and I toss her the Winston's and the Zippo. She lights up and inhales deeply.

"In fact," she says, "I can see your case being one that would draw a great deal of interest from the psychiatric community. I can see articles being written. Discussed. Even in legal circles. What constitutes means to an end in a disturbed mind, brought on by pressures from society and bullying? Obviously, all the attention to your case will give you what you desire most; attention to why you did what you did. You do see that, right?"

And now she has played what she believes is her trump card.

"I see only one problem with your suggestion, Doctor," I say, and I smile down at her.

"Yes, I know," she says, frowning a bit. "Loss of freedom is a frightening prospect. But it would only be for a short time. Don't forget, your trial would be sensational. It would be covered by all the news outlets. What you are attempting to show the world would be out there for all to see."

"No, Doctor. I'm afraid you don't understand."

Kay looks up at me with a confused look. As the cigarette slips from her fingers, I slide off my stool and sit on the mattress next to her, picking up the butt and tossing it away from us. Her look of confusion lasts but a few seconds, replaced by one of incredible sadness. As she slowly teeters sideways, she looks at me and a tear slips from her left eye. I reach out to catch her, gently cradling her head and bringing it to rest in my lap. She looks up at me, her lips forming words that her voice cannot speak. I smile down at her.

"I want to thank you, Kay. You kept your promise to help, and I kept mine."

I brush her cheek with my fingers. Her skin is soft. And, as I had promised, free of bruising. I hold her and gently rock her until she ceases to breathe, and for many minutes we sit like that.

Thinking back over the last few days and nights with Kay, I was happy to have had someone to confide in, but, I must confess, disappointed that she was insincere in her wanting to help me. A psychiatric hospital? Really? Fat chance that that would ever happen. Besides, those places are for crazy people.

I run my fingers slowly through her short silver-gray hair,

caressing her head and face that are still warm to the touch, until my thumb comes to rest over her left eye, the one where a tear had escaped. It is then I think of Detective Erik Miller.

"He's the reason you are here, Kay," I whisper into her ear. "Should you meet him in the afterlife, tell him that. Soon, you'll have your chance. Very soon."

Time to prepare Kay for her posing. Nothing too elaborate this time. A one piece white swim suit is all that is needed.

But first, something for Erik.

22

Detective Erik Miller was sitting at his desk, head bent over a map of the city, making X marks on it where he wanted surveillance coverage, when Kristen Day entered the bullpen. It was 6:30 Monday morning. He looked up to see her holding a six inch cubed cardboard box, exactly like five others from the previous six months. She stopped at his desk.

"It was on the hood of my Jeep this morning," she said.

Miller looked at the box for several seconds, then nodded at her. She placed the box in the center of his desk as he folded the map up and put it off to the side.

"Do you want to wait for Hendricks?" she asked.

He shook his head. "Every minute counts."

As he reached into the middle drawer for scissors to cut the packing tape, Hendricks walked through the doors. He nodded at his two detectives, then saw the box on the desk. He nodded toward his office and the three of them went there, Miller carrying the box.

"Who brought it in?" asked the Chief as he slipped from his suit coat.

"It was left on the hood of my car at home," replied Day.

"So he knows where you live," stated Hendricks. "You better be careful."

"My middle name, Chief."

"No time to be cavalier, Day. He's out to hurt Miller. He got Eve. He might come for you. I think we need to think about having a cruiser parked near your place."

"I can take care of myself, Chief."

"We'll talk about it," said Hendricks. Then he looked at Miller who still held the box. "What's that written on top?"

"Just my name," Miller said.

"Well, go ahead and open it. Let's see what he has to say this time."

Miller placed the box on the desk and cut through the clear tape, folding the flaps back to reveal a white folded sheet of copy paper. He lifted that out and laid it on the desk. Below that was white gauze. He gently lifted the gauze and found himself staring at a pale blue eye that was staring back at him, the bloody nerves still attached. Miller swore softly.

Hendricks peeked inside, saw the eye, uttered a disgusted curse and slumped back into his chair. Kristen leaned forward, saw the eye, said nothing. Miller looked at her and she nodded.

"Kay Lawrence had pale blue eyes," she said.

"What's the note say?" asked the Chief.

Miller handed the paper to Day. She looked at him, then at Hendricks, then she frowned and read:

In murky depths the creature lives and breathes,
Residing below a calm inviting surface, unseen.
But in the protected darkness, anger seethes,
And death awaits the rising of the green.

Day looked at the two men. Neither commented. After several seconds, Miller said, "Is there more?"

Day continued reading. *I wanted Kay to have a chance to get a good look at you, Erik. Now, when she sees you in Hell, she'll recognize the man who cut short her life. THE UNIVERSAL KILLER. I like that. Now that we all know what is going on, it is*

perfect, don't you think, Erik? Have you been reading the newspapers, watching the telly? We're quite infamous, you and I, Erik. Me for my impressive deeds, you for your ineptitude. Which Universal monster will The Universal Killer copy next? Don't turn that dial. Wow! That's something you don't hear anymore. But really, old friend, who's next?
UK

"He signed it UK?" Hendricks asked harshly.

Day held the paper up so he could see.

"The son-of-a-bitch!" Hendricks said, his face reddening.

"What's the plan?" asked Hendricks after a few seconds, regaining his composure.

"I've designated areas around the water spots of the city where we should set up surveillance," Miller said, "based on what we know. The body will probably be left near water, but where it will be noticed in a relatively short time line. That would mean, walking and jogging paths. Biking paths. Populated streets along ponds and lakes. Hopefully, not the river.

"We can expect the body to be left somewhere at night. Now, taking into consideration the large amount of places that could be, and the man-power that we have, it looks like each spot can only be manned by one officer. Not ideal, I know, but unavoidable. And it has to begin tonight. With Eve, we found her the morning after receiving the box."

"You have a list of who is available?" asked Hendricks.

"I do. As soon as I bring the box down to Forensics, Day and I will place an officer's name at the sites we need to cover and get on the phone to give them their assignments. Tonight, we'll hit each site to check on them. Bring them a coffee. Do it again tomorrow night if we have to. And the night after. I'm going to request that our night patrols do more patrolling around the lake and Cohas area than they usually do. Watch for anything suspicious."

"You've got Auburn involved?" asked Hendricks.

"And Londonderry and Chester," said Miller. "They're giving us some personnel."

Miller frowned. "All of this assumes we know what the killer is going to do. Of course, we don't. But I don't know what else we can do."

Hendricks looked at Day.

"You have anything to add?"

She shook her head.

"I'm going to see about having a black and white covering your place," he said.

"Don't need it, Chief," Day said. "I can take care of myself. Besides, Goffstown can't afford that kind of coverage."

"Then I'll send one of ours."

Day frowned. "We'll talk about it later. I'm sure I'm safe until after Kay Lawrence is found."

Hendricks grunted and waved them from the office.

Miller opened the map he had been working on that morning and laid it on Days desk. Then he gave her a list of names with phone numbers.

"Put a name at each place I marked an X," he began. "When I get back, we'll start calling. Keep the other towns officers as close to their borders as possible. If you see a spot I missed, or you think the X could be moved in a place you checked out, do it. But this list is all we have. And we're already stretched thin."

Miller stood beside her desk, Day looking up at him, waiting for him to say something else or to head down to Forensics.

"What?" she said when he did neither.

"He is taking some pride in having himself labeled," said Miller. "The notoriety. It changes them, you know. They begin to get careless. Looking to make a bigger splash, and they slip up."

"Let's hope that happens here," said Day. She looked down at the map, then back up at Miller who still hadn't moved.

"I don't need anyone watching out for me," she said.

"I didn't say anything," said Miller.

"But it's what you're thinking. I can take care of myself."

"He's a big guy. And he's smart."

"No, I'm smart," said Day. "And I've kicked the shit out of big guys before."

"Tabled until a later date," said Miller with a smile.

"Never to be discussed again," said Kristen Day with finality. Then, "Don't you have somewhere to bring that box?"

BETWEEN FOUR AND six o'clock they met with each police officer at the area designated for their surveillance, giving them instructions on how they wanted this to go down. Twenty-one cops in all, ten of whom were covering the vast Massabesic area and the multiple fire lanes. Miller and Day met up at a Dunkin's not far from the Massabesic traffic circle when they were done.

"Any problems?" asked Miller as he handed Day an iced coffee through the Jeep's window.

"No. They all know what to expect. They all have bug spray. They all had a thermos and sandwiches. Looks like it will be a clear night and a quarter moon, so that's good. Don't know what else we can do."

"I wish we had more men. We need more men. We haven't got it all covered."

"We have a huge area covered, Erik. We are as prepared as we could possibly be. Too many out there, and the killer would be scared off. There isn't a trap, if the trap is obvious."

"I'm heading home to get some sleep," said Miller. "I'm going to be back out here around midnight. My gut tells me the trail behind the ball fields is where he'll try and leave the body. Boudreau is covering, but it's a long trail."

"There's a spot off the highway where I can see most of the swampy area leading to the Cohas," said Day. "As good a spot as any."

Miller nodded at her, went to his car and drove off. Day sat quietly in the Cherokee sipping coffee and watching the traffic driving by. She had a long night ahead of her and she was hungry. She put the Jeep in gear and headed home.

AS THE DAY began to dawn, Miller and Day showed up at headquarters at the same time and went up to the bullpen, each carrying a coffee. Five minutes later, Hendricks walked through the doors. He had told them to call him if anything had happened the night before, but his sleep had gone uninterrupted.

"You do the same thing tonight," said Hendricks.

"Providing he didn't elude us," replied Miller. "We've got five officers coming in at seven and we're all going to walk the areas, make sure he didn't beat us last night."

Hendricks nodded and went into his office.

"You okay?" asked Miller, smiling at his partner as he looked down at her legs and the mud splattered boots and pants.

"Long night," replied Day.

She was dressed in a gray, long sleeved hooded pullover, black nylon pants that hugged her long legs, and black boots that came halfway up her calves. Her hair was pulled away from her face and clipped in the back. Despite the long night, Miller thought in this outfit, instead of the standard pant suit that his partner wore to work every day, Day looked quite attractive. Athletic and fit. Her face glowed, and she had the healthy look about her of an outdoor enthusiast. She looked younger.

She noticed him checking her out.

"Three o'clock this morning," she said, feeling the need to explain, "from where I was parked, I thought I saw a faint light in the marsh. Drove down there and walked around for a while. Didn't see or hear anything besides the animals. Never saw the light again."

To reciprocate, she looked him over, too. He was dressed in a long sleeved dark gray cotton shirt that had the Patriots logo on the front, black jeans and hiking boots. His boots also had mud on them. She thought he looked like a farmer who hadn't slept in days, out in the elements struggling to save his crops from some disaster, and losing.

"You don't look so good yourself," she said.

Miller nodded and smiled. "I never said you didn't look good, Day. I walked most of the area during the night. Saw nothing. Heard nothing. I couldn't get over how quiet it is out there. If someone was moving around, I would have heard them."

"Maybe the killer heard you moving around," said Day, smiling. "Ever think of that?"

"I can be a cat when I need to be, wise ass," said Miller, also with a smile.

The room began filling up with men on duty and each one looked at Miller as they walked past the desk. To each look, Miller gave a slight shake of his head. When Matt Blanchette entered, he came over to them.

"Looks like you two had a long night," he said. "Anything I can do?"

Miller nodded. "We have a crew coming in soon and we'll be walking the area. You want to help? Anything on your plate this morning?"

"Nothing that can't wait," said Blanchette. "Due in court at ten, so you have me for a few hours."

At seven, Miller and Day brought the five officers into the interrogation room where Miller had hung a map of the wetland areas. Counting Blanchette, there were eight of them. Miller created four sets of two man groups and gave each an area to cover. He teamed with Blanchette."

"Any questions?" asked Miller.

There were none.

"It's a big area," he said, "but concentrate on trails that are used. Don't wander off on side trails, or too far from the edge of trails. The killer wants the body to be found."

THEO POULOS GAVE a slight tug on the leash, prodding his beagle to move on from what the dog was sniffing at. It was seven thirty and the day was already becoming very warm. The mosquitoes were heavy and Theo kept swatting at them with his left hand and pulling on the leash with his right.

"Come on, Ringo, do your business and let's get back home," he said to the dog. Ringo was in no rush to go back home, however. Ringo enjoyed his morning walk, and knew, if he relieved himself too soon, the walk would end. It was Ringo who discovered the body of Kay Lawrence.

"What are you barking at, Ringo?" asked Theo Poulos. "Just do your business and leave the squirrels alone."

Theo tugged on the leash, but Ringo refused to budge and kept barking. He walked towards the dog. As he had been forced to do many times before, he was prepared to pick Ringo up and forcibly move him further up the road. As he bent to scoop up the dog, he saw the white fabric in the tall grass and scrub beside the road. And then he saw the bare flesh of a leg. While Ringo continued barking, Theo stepped into the grass and looked down at the woman who lay there on her stomach, dressed only in a white one piece bathing suit. Theo touched her shoulder. It was cold to the touch. He felt for a pulse at her neck and found none.

Standing, he reached for his cell phone in the back pocket of his cargo shorts.

"Quiet, Ringo," Theo said harshly. The dog, not used to such a sharp tone, immediately stopped barking. Just as Theo began punching in 9-1-1, he saw the police car driving down the street. He waved to them as he stepped to the side of Lake Shore Road.

MILLER AND BLANCHETTE had just reached the beginning of a fire lane on the east side of the by-pass when Miller's cell rang. He listened, frowned, and said, "On our way."

"She's been found," he said to Detective Blanchette. "Lake Shore Road. Son-of-a-bitch."

They walked back to Miller's car. It was less than a half mile to the body as the crow flies.

When they turned onto Lake Shore, Miller saw the flashing lights in the distance near where the road bends to the west. Driving up to the site, he saw two of the policemen he had sent out that morning to check along the west banks of the Massabesic. Another police car arrived from the south and set a road block across Lake Shore. As Miller and Blanchette exited their car, Miller saw Day's Jeep speeding up from the south, coming from the expanse of the Cohas wet lands.

Miller was bent over the body as Day came up to him.

"It's Kay Lawrence," he said. "Left eye gone. She wasn't just tossed from a car. Look how she's laid out. Lying on her stomach. Head resting on her right arm. Legs straight out. She could be sleeping. Other than some bruising around the eye and the left ankle, there isn't a mark on her. At least not what can be seen. Maybe the bathing suit is covering up the abuse."

"Maybe she wasn't beaten," said Day.

"Maybe," said Miller. "But why not? All the others have been. What changed? And where the hell do you find a bathing suit that women wore in the fifties?"

Miller stood. "Matt and I will have a look around. See the guy across the street with the dog? He found the body."

Kristen nodded and walked over to Theo. There were already a dozen people standing near him, as the houses across from the wetlands emptied out to see what was going on.

The earth became soggy not far from where Kay lay, and through the thick vegetation Miller could see the water's edge.

He and Matt searched for footprints, or any fibers that the bushes may have caught, but found nothing. Standing near the edge of the marsh, Miller looked back towards the road.

"We had a man about a hundred feet south of here," he said, pointing to a split level house across the road at the far end of the bend. "How could he not see someone leaving a body here? How the hell is that possible?"

Blanchette shrugged. "Maybe he fell asleep. Warm night. Long night. Was he one of ours?"

"Johnny Parent."

"Good kid," said Blanchette. "Wife just had a baby. I can tell you from experience, no one gets much sleep with a newborn in the house. You'll know more after you talk with him."

As they stood there looking back at the activity near the road, Forensics showed up, followed by the coroner, and seconds later, Jack Morgan. Miller noticed that Scott Powell was already standing in the growing crowd across Lake Shore Rd. Six bodies, he thought, and they had nothing. Last night they had a chance to catch the killer and what? Someone fell asleep? He looked at Blanchette.

"You can't make this shit up, Matt. Who the hell would believe it?"

DETECTIVES KRISTEN DAY and Erik Miller sat at Day's desk in an empty bullpen, exhausted at the end of a long night and day, both going on less than four hours sleep in the last forty-eight. What they knew was that no one in any of the homes on Lake Shore Road had noticed anything suspicious the previous night. No one had any outside surveillance around their homes. No one had heard anything. Patrolman John Parent sadly admitted he may have nodded off for a few minutes sometime after two A.M., but only for a few minutes if he had. Yes, he would have had a clear view from his vantage area of the spot where Kay Lawrence was discovered, but it would have been by looking through his side view mirror, because his car was parked off the other side of the road facing in the other direction. There was a greater expanse of wetland in front of him and that was where he had concentrated most of his attention through the night. He apologized more than once for failing them.

When Matt Blanchette had returned from his court appearance, he had gone over photos of the crowd that had grown to over thirty people. He found no face in that crowd that matched any face in their other photos of other crime scenes, except for the face of the Union Leader reporter.

Kristen had taken two calls from Wendell Weasley, but he really had nothing new to add. They had had no chance to catch the six o'clock news, but if they had they would have seen Rene Cormier telling the world that obviously The Universal Killer was using another Universal film in their spree. This time it was *Creature From the Black Lagoon.* The bathing suit on the victim proved that. And just for extra added theatrics, Cormier held up a speargun that he claimed was the actual prop that actor Richard Denning had used in the film, telling the television audience that he had purchased it years ago at a sale at Universal Studios of their film property. When asked which movie the killer might use next, Cormier, without hesitation, responded that he thought *The Hunchback of Notre Dame* would be high up on any list he could think of. It was just a matter of time.

Miller read over the autopsy report again. Traces of Propofol, large quantity of Fentanyl Citrate. More than enough to kill. Undigested chocolate cake. That was new.

"Chocolate cake, with chocolate frosting," said Miller. "What do you think? His birthday? Hers? Small, intimate party? Candles and balloons?"

"Not hers," said Day. "She was born in October."

"No bruising," continued Miller, "other than the eye and the ankle. Not a mark. Why? Why beat the other five victims, but not this one?"

"Maybe," Day said, "because she was older. Maybe she didn't resist. Maybe, because she was a psychiatrist, she realized that remaining calm might give her a chance to live."

"So, you think he beats them to control them, not just because he enjoys beating women."

"It's a theory we've been kicking around, Erik. I think this cements it. Kay wasn't beaten."

Miller nodded a few times. "The daughter was devastated. But did you notice, the son seemed to handle it in an almost detached way."

"He's a psychiatrist, too. Probably, in a few days, this will all hit him. Maybe after the funeral. We all grieve differently, Erik."

They sat silently for a few minutes.

"You know," Miller said, "I've been thinking about something and I want to check it out."

"And what is that?"

"What if there is more than one killer?"

"A copycat?" asked Day, frowning. "That's a long shot. With the taunting notes that the public doesn't know about? No, I don't see it."

"Not a copycat. Two people working together."

"For what reason?"

"Hear me out."

"Which two people?"

"Listen," said Miller, raising a hand to quiet his partner. "Think about this."

"You're going to try and lump Thomas and Cormier together. Aren't you? Somehow or other, rationalize it."

He lifted his eyebrows at her, his lips forming a slight smile.

"Which Thomas is it this time? Doctor Thomas or Thomas?"

Kristen wasn't smiling. "Don't get cute. Where is this coming from?"

"Are you going to hear me out?"

"It's late," said Kristen, frowning. "I'm tired. But go ahead. I'm listening."

"We need to see if there is a connection between the two of them," said Miller.

"What makes you think there is?"

"Long shot, I know, but Cormier retired at a very early age. Right? What was he, forty-two? That's young to retire, even with a portfolio worth millions. What if he had health problems?"

"You mean like a bad heart?" said Day, again frowning.

"Sure. Why not? Worked for NASA. High stress. Maybe led to a bad ticker. You have some problems with the pump, and you live up here, where do you go?" Miller raised his eyebrows again. "Exactly. Seacoast, Lake Region, doesn't matter, you are coming to CMC."

"Okay," said Day. "Assuming all that, but I'll tell you now, Rene Cormier doesn't look like a man with a bad heart or one who has ever had a bad heart, why would they suddenly become partners in this wild murder spree. I mean, that's like that old joke. 'Guy picks up a hitchhiker. Hitchhiker, after a few miles, says to the driver, aren't you worried I might be a serial killer? Driver says, nah, what are the odds there would be two in the same car?' Cormier and Thomas are both wealthy men. What's the reason?"

"How about this?" said Miller, pointing his finger at his partner. "We know Thomas knew the second victim. She was the daughter of a patient of his. He dated the third victim, Madeleine Seward. Possibility he supplied drugs to Maryanne Darrow, which started this whole thing."

"Wait a second," said Day, waving her hand through the air. "We have no evidence of that. None. That was you trying to think of a reason he would have known Maryanne."

Miller nodded. "I know. I'm just brainstorming. He dated Doctor Gallagher. Maybe he was jealous that she married. Decided to leave her a present in her bed. Now we have another doctor. Kay Lawrence. They may have known each other."

"We have found no evidence of that," said Day. "And we looked for it. Besides, he was out of state when Kay Lawrence went missing. In Cleveland."

"Yes, I know. But Cormier wasn't. And Cormier was in Florida when Maryanne Darrow was killed. But Thomas was here."

"So, that's why you need the two of them working together," said Day, shaking her head. "Again, Erik, for what reason?"

"Not for the reason that serial killers kill," said Miller, "but for the reasons everyone else does."

"In this instance, what exactly is that?"

"Let's say, for arguments sake, years ago, Doctor Thomas and Maryanne Darrow partied together. Again, for arguments sake, he's giving her drugs for sexual favors, which we know Maryanne was very comfortable doing when she was younger. She cleans herself up, becomes engaged, plans for a wedding, needs money. Threatens her former supplier that she will rat him out to the medical board if he doesn't come up with some cash. Then one night, sitting at a bar with an acquaintance, either a friend or a former patient, after a few drinks the doctor shares this problem he is having with a former girlfriend. He knows the guy he is with is as intelligent as he is. He's a rocket scientist, after all. Made a bundle in the market. Maybe he can come up with a way to get the doctor out of his predicament. The wheels in the brain of the rocket genius begin to turn. Maybe there's a way for him to profit from this."

"Why.....?" Kristen began to say, but Miller cuts her off.

"Why does a rich man need money? Maybe he's not so rich anymore. Don't forget, the stock market got hammered a few years ago. Property values tanked. Two thousand eight saw fortunes lost overnight. Maybe Cormier suffered losses that placed him in a bind. He's retired. Living off his investments. What if those investments were no longer valuable?"

"You're supposing an awful lot of stuff here," said Kristen. "So, what? You think he offered to kill Maryanne for money? He was in Florida."

"No," replied Miller, "that's not it. But Cormier cooks up this scheme. One death, the death of Maryanne Darrow, and with enough digging into her past, maybe the doctor's name comes up."

"So for a second victim, they pick another woman who could be tied to the doctor?" said Day with a shake of her head. "And then a third and a fourth. And that makes sense?"

"If you think about it, yes. The third victim, Madeleine Seward, is linked to Thomas because they dated. Elizabeth Clarke, as far as we know, had no link to Thomas, but her body is left in the home of Doctor Gallagher-Hartigan, a woman Thomas was intimate with ten years ago. Maybe that is done for a reason. Doctor Thomas becomes the common link in three of the first four deaths. We can't ignore that. If we assume the reason to kill Eve was to get to me, as the note strongly suggests, then he had a reason to kill her even though there is no tie to him. But then Kay Lawrence disappears and is killed while the good doctor is conveniently six hundred miles away and surrounded by esteemed men of medicine who will swear to that in a court of law. Because of that, that alibi, the serial killer cannot be Doctor Thomas Thomas. If there is only one killer, he has the alibi he needs."

"But I don't understand," said Day with several shakes of her head. "Why is Cormier a part of this?What's he get out of it?"

"Again, let's assume his finances have taken a hit. What does he own that is valuable? That's right. Movie memorabilia. Monster movie memorabilia. First edition books that he has bragged to us are quite valuable. Props that are valuable and one of a kind. The idea comes to him as soon as Thomas says Maryanne Darrow's name. Cormier would immediately think of King Kong. He sees it all, right away. A serial killer on the loose, mimicking old monster movies, and for an added kick, victims whose names are similar to those of the women in the movies. In fact, the names are vital. We might not pick up on the scenes, but the names are a dead give away, no pun intended. Three, four victims, it becomes a national story. He inserts himself into the narrative. The scholar trying to aid the officers in their investigation. An off the cuff remark to a newspaper or television reporter, and suddenly Cormier is the definitive voice on what is happening in the kill zone of Manchester, New Hampshire. He takes on national attention. He is now a celebrity. People know his name. They see him on television, so he must be someone knowledgeable. All of it goes viral, and instantly the world knows his name, sees his face. He coins the phrase 'The Universal Killer'. Can a book deal be far behind? And what of his collection? How much are Frankenstein's boots worth now? How much for the dress that Fay Wray wore in King Kong? The interest in all of his stuff would be incredible and they increase in value ten fold. Maybe a hundred."

"But what about the taunting notes to you?"

"Megan Riley," said Erik Miller. "Maybe, because of Megan, Maryanne got the idea to blackmail Doctor Thomas. Or maybe it was Megan who was blackmailing Thomas, Thomas found Maryanne, killed her, but couldn't find Megan. Or maybe he did, and Megan is dead, too. And he blames me for it all, because I didn't arrest Megan and put her in jail that rainy night I helped her."

Kristen Day stood and stretched. "I think you are way off base, partner."

"Maybe. But tomorrow we begin looking for any connection

between the two. We might not be able to get medical records on Cormier, but we can talk to people he worked with and see if they know anything. We find out things about his finances. See if there may be bills past due. I want to check those sites where memorabilia gets bought and sold. Contact some of the people who use the sites. See if some new things are being offered at a much higher value than they may have been six months ago."

Miller suddenly stood. "I'm starving. You want to grab something to eat?"

Day shook her head. "The only thing I want to grab is some shut-eye."

"We have a busy day tomorrow," said Miller as he headed toward the doors. "Get some sleep."

And he was gone.

Kristen sat back down and frowned. Her cell began to chirp.

"This is Day."

"Inspector Day, Wendell Weasley here. Sorry to bother you again. Have I caught you at a bad time?"

"No, Professor, you have not."

"I have thought of something, silly that I haven't thought of this before, stupid actually, and I think we need to speak. Can you come up here tomorrow?"

"I can, but you can't tell me now?"

"I would rather not. I think I need to see you in person to make sure I properly convey the impact of what I have to tell you. So, you can come tomorrow?"

"What time is convenient?"

"Does three work for you, Inspector Day?"

"Three will be fine," Day said. "Where?"

"The main building. Out front. Perhaps, we could walk while we talk. Would that be alright?"

"Of course," replied Day.

"One more thing," said Weasley, the tone of his voice changing dramatically, "be very careful this evening. Very careful, indeed. Until tomorrow, goodbye my dear Inspector Day."

Day looked at her phone when the call ended and furrowed her brow. Between Weasley and Miller, she wasn't sure which one of them would be the reason she probably wouldn't be able to get a restful sleep.

23

MILLER WORKED THE phone all morning, while his partner searched for sites on the Web that could help them. Between the two of them, they managed to find and talk with several people who had worked in the same department as Rene Cormier at NASA in the early to mid-nineties. According to them, at the time, Cormier was fit as a fiddle. One of them remembered that Cormier jogged every morning before going to work. One man recalled that Cormier would often attend small parties that associates always seemed to be having, would regale the group with marvelous stories of his travels, and never drank to excess. When Miller asked if he thought Cormier might have exhibited signs of undue stress, the man actually laughed and said that Rene Cormier may have been the most relaxed man he had ever been around during his time at the Space Agency.

Day obviously could not access the financial accounts of Cormier, but she accessed upcoming court cases for bankruptcy, or suits for non-payment, and none showed Rene Cormier as the person being sued. There was no lien on his waterfront property that tax records showed had a taxable value of two point five million dollars. He drove a 2010 Mercedes that was leased. He was single, divorced in 2002, and had no children.

Day provided Miller with several sites she had found that were interested in movie memorabilia, and the names and phone numbers of people he should talk with. Most were on the West Coast, so Miller had waited until noon to call them. He spoke with four different men, from four different sites, two in California, one in Arizona and one in Portland, Oregon. All four spoke enthusiastically of their collections and none showed any inhibition about discussing what was currently out there for bid, or what rumors they were hearing.

Yes, they all agreed, because of the press coverage of the murders by The Universal Killer, certain items from those early monster movies had increased in value, the asking price now as much as ten times what had been asked before. And, not surprisingly, there were a lot more items available. They all told Miller the same thing, that this was not surprising. It was known in the business that when a movie star died, any item that they had used in one of their movies, if it was available, took a price jump. It was to be expected. But the killings in Manchester took everything to a whole different level. The bidding on these items, that would normally progress at a quiet, but expected pace, were now anything but. One dealer likened the frenzy to Dutch tulips in the sixteenth century. It was a crazy market. And when the killings stopped, if they stopped, he warned that the market for these items would dry up and these investors would get burned. He, himself, was not getting caught up in the mania, he said. And then, in the next breath, he said, almost to himself, that one of the actual claw hands from the suit in Black Lagoon was now available and wouldn't it be great to own that.

Miller's last call was to a gentleman in Portland who owned quite a bit of memorabilia. Yes, he knew of Rene Cormier, although he had never met him. They had, however, bid against each other in the past on several items. He found Cormier to be an aggressive bidder on some items and not so aggressive on others.

At one o'clock, Miller hung up the phone, leaned back in his chair, and rubbed his eyes. The desk sergeant came through the doors, walked over to him and handed him a lined page of paper with a dozen phone numbers on it.

"These are just the calls I got this morning," he said before turning around and going back through the doors.

Day came over and looked at the sheet Miller was holding.

"I'll take half of them, if you want," she said. These were the phone numbers that always came in after a murder, of people who said they had information on the killer.

Shaking his head, Miller said, "I have this. You should get some lunch and then head off to your meeting with the professor. Any idea what he wants?"

She shook her head. "No. You don't want to get lunch?"

"Not hungry. But I was right about the value of these props. Everyone I spoke with this morning said the bidding on anything available now is going out of sight. You find out anything on Cormier?"

"Doesn't look like money is a problem. But you never know. Did you know, on the news last night, he held up the original speargun from the movie. Or at least he said it was."

"What an a-hole. Women are dying and he's smiling into the cameras. I'm beginning to hope it is him."

KRISTEN PARKED NEAR the front of the center building along the curved drive of the college, and saw Professor Weasley standing patiently near the entrance doors under letters that spelled COLGATE. He waved to her as she exited the Jeep, smiling as he came down the stairs. He then gently steered her along the wide, tarred path that led to the street. They exchanged pleasantries and small talk as they leisurely strolled along the main street through the town. The day was clear and warm and

Kristen was enjoying being out in it and away from her desk and the phone.

"Would you care for tea and a piece of pie, Inspector?" asked Weasley as they approached a small restaurant. "They have the best lemon meringue pie I have ever had."

Once seated at an outside table with a view of the street, and their order given to the waiter, Kristen said, "This is very nice, Professor, but why have you asked me to drive all the way up here? Not that I'm complaining, but I am on the clock."

Slightly embarrassed, Weasley lifted his cloth napkin from the table, unfolded it, folded it again, then unfolded it one more time before placing it on his lap.

"I am sorry to say," he began, "that I may have placed you in great danger."

"Me?" said Kristen, taken aback by his announcement. "How could you have possibly placed me in danger?"

"Quite simply, I'm afraid, by neglecting to mention a movie that places you in peril, my dear Inspector Day. How I could have been so blind is beyond me."

She smiled at him. "Why don't you tell me what the movie is, and why you believe I may be in danger."

Just then the tea and pie were placed in front of them. The young waiter smiled at Kristen, and left them. Weasley pushed the cup and plate off to the side, folded his elbows on the table, leaned forward and lowered his voice.

"Have you heard of *The Phantom of the Opera*?"

Kristen stared at the older man with the bushy mustache for several seconds, then took a sip of the tea.

"Of course, Professor. Who hasn't? Several years ago, a friend and I saw the stage production in Boston. It was magnificent. It seemed to me more of a love story than a horror."

"Yes," said Weasley, "I suppose one could see it as such. But that is not what the author, Gaston Leroux, intended when he wrote it. And it was not how Hollywood filmed it, either. The romance is ill-fated, but the suspected ghost of the Paris Opera House is real, as is the terror he inflicts. Have you seen the Lon Chaney movie?"

Kristen took a bite of pie and dabbed at her lips with a napkin after swallowing.

"No," she said. "I have seen a picture of him as the Phantom, as I'm sure everyone has. His face disfigured."

"You know," said Weasley, "that Chaney created that look with very little make-up. Quite incredible, really. Women fainted when he became unmasked. Gasps and shrieks filled the theater. The silent was a huge success. Made in 1925, it made more than three times its cost. Produced at Universal by Carl Laemmle, who also did *Frankenstein* and some others in the thirties."

"So, we have another movie to add to our list. Is that what you are saying? You could have told me that over the phone, Professor."

Weasley took a bite of pie. "There was a 1943 version of the Phantom starring Claude Rains. It was very loosely based on the book. But the silent was faithful to the novel. I don't know why I didn't think of it sooner."

"Well, perhaps because it was a silent and made in the twenties. The killings seem to be concentrating on the thirties, other than this recent one."

"Perhaps. But it could have been a most unfortunate blunder for you, and one I would have never forgiven myself for."

Kristen finished the pie and pushed the plate to the side.

"Why do you believe I may be in danger, Professor? I don't understand."

"Well, isn't it obvious, my dear Inspector? Your name."

"My name?"

"Kristen Day. The singer in Phantom, the beautiful woman who the Phantom is in love with, who he is willing to kill for to make her a success, her name, if you remember from the play, as it is in the novel, is Christine Daae."

Weasley stared across the table into Day's eyes.

"Kristen Day. Christine Daae. The names are too similar. You must see that."

"I suppose they are," said Kristen. "Yes, I suppose they are."

"So, you must see that you may be in danger. All precautions must be taken, my dear friend. We are dealing with a madman here. A crazed human being. He could strike at any time. In any place. I believe you must alert your superiors to the danger you are in. They must supply you with some degree of protection. Perhaps a police presence at your home while you sleep."

Kristen smiled across the small space between them. "I appreciate your concern. But I am quite capable of protecting myself, Professor." She sipped some tea. "We do have the movie on our list. The 1943 version. We actually watched it several months ago. If I remember correctly, the girl's name was Christine DuBois, not Daae, played by Susanna.....Susanna...."

"Foster," said Weasley. "Yes, Susanna Foster. The movie was not faithful to the book. I found it rather silly, myself. Claude Rains played the Phantom. And they gave him this silly name. Enrique Claudin. Why they would change the name from Erik, I have no idea. If they wanted to distance themselves from the original, then they should have come up with a different title. But, amazingly, it is the only Universal monster movie to capture an Academy Award. Cinematography, I believe."

Professor Weasley leaned back in his seat, dabbing at his mustache with the napkin.

"I have no doubt you can protect yourself, Inspector Day, but I do hope you understand that you may be targeted by this maniac. The Phantom supposedly dies in a fire at the Opera House in the end. An horrific ending. This is no love story. It is madness. Please, be very careful."

IT WAS FIVE o'clock by the time Day got back to the station house. Entering the bullpen, she saw Miller still at his desk.

"What was so pressing that your learned friend needed you to drive up there?" he asked as Day sat in the chair beside his desk.

Day decided not to mention his concern with the Lon Chaney Phantom. Miller and Hendricks already wanted her to have a police presence around her, and she wanted no part of that.

"He believes we could be seeing a scene from one of two movies in the next killing. *Hunchback* or *The Invisible Man.* He also feels that now, with the killer leaving the thirties with this last murder, that *Godzilla* may enter into it. Although he did doubt it, he said all possibilities must be looked at. He feels Hunchback will definitely be one of them, and he believes it will be next, because he feels it lends itself to this drama better than any others. While finding someone named Esmeralda to be the victim will probably be impossible, he said we should probably concentrate on the actress who played her in the silent movie with Lon Chaney. She was an actress named Patsy Ruth Miller There are a few Miller's around." She smiled when she said that.

Frowning, Miller said, "We watched the Charles Laughton Hunchback. With Maureen O'Hara. So, there was a silent one also?"

"There was. According to the professor, 1923, and the highest grossing silent movie that Universal ever had. He at first spoke about the Laughton movie, back before we had the Universal link, but that was produced by RKO. If the Universal Killer is staying with Universal movies, then it would have to be the Lon Chaney movie, is what he said."

"Is it like the Laughton movie?"

"I imagine so. The story is the story. How much could they change it? Must still have towers and bells."

"Check to see if the video store has the movie," said Miller. "Maybe something on YouTube."

"YouTube?" said Day with a smile. "Since when do you know about YouTube?"

Miller frowned at her again. "Anything else?"

"He also said, if the killer stuck to the script, *Dr. Jekyl and Mr. Hyde* is out. The versions that were filmed were done by Paramount. He did impress upon me, that some of the sequels to these movies already used, could be candidates. Different cast, different cast of characters. I showed him the list we have compiled of names and combinations, and he was impressed.

"What about you? What were you up to while I was gone?"

"I took a ride over to the hospital to speak with our favorite doctor. Asked him a few questions. Asked him about Fentanyl and the effects it may have on the heart. He was eager to speak about that. Then I casually mentioned Rene Cormier. I saw no recognition in his eyes. No sense that he was instantly wary. Either our Thomas Thomas is a good actor, or he doesn't know Cormier."

"I told you it was a long shot," said Day.

Miller stood and stretched.

"I need a beer," he said. "Care to join me?"

Kristen shook her head.

"Cormier has been talking about Hunchback for two months now," said Miller as he slipped into his suit coat. "Now your professor says the same thing. Have you checked all the towers that have bells?"

Day nodded. "All of them. The best one may be City Hall, but it will probably be a church."

"So we need to be on the lookout for a missing woman with some combination not of Maureen O'Hara, as we thought, but of Patsy Ruth Miller in the name. I think we should put the towers under surveillance beginning now. Not wait for a missing person."

"You want cameras set up on all locations?"

"Yeah. I think we should. We'll talk to Hendricks in the morning."

"And if it's *The Invisible Man*?" asked Day.

Miller shrugged. "Then the next one will be Hunchback. Or the one after that."

"Erik," said Day as he walked towards the door. He turned to look at her. "Any sisters in your family?"

He stared at her for long seconds. "Just a brother. He's in California."

"Ex-wife," said Day. "Is she still around?"

"Last name now is Cote. Husband is Chief of Police in a small town in Indiana."

"You think you should call her?"

"Her? Not if I don't have to. But I'll call him. He'll know what to do."

Miller turned and pushed hard on the doors on his way out.

MILLER AND DAY worked the case of The Universal Killer through most of July until there was no more they could do, and then spent the rest of the summer on the never ending supply of aggression that plague all large cities in times of uncomfortable warmth. The coverage of The Universal Killer crimes left the daily papers, finding an occasional reminder in the last few pages of the news section of the Sunday papers. Calls stopped coming in from across the country. Other than from the daughter of Kay Lawrence, the calls from the loved ones of the victims about any news in the investigation, had slowed. By the beginning of September, Day and Miller were knee deep in their own investigations, speaking briefly each morning over coffee in the bullpen, their meetings for lunch now a thing of the past. Day noticed that Miller's suits hung loosely on his frame, and she also noticed that occasionally it appeared as if he had slept in the suit. His eyes were puffy. Some mornings he hadn't shaved.

In August, it was rumored that Matt Blanchette was retiring from the department to take a security job with his nephew's company. Shortly after Labor Day the rumor was confirmed. October twenty-eighth would be his last day. Also, the day after Labor Day, Detective Mark Allen was again placed on administrative leave. No reason was given.

In the middle of September, almost three months after the murder of Kay Lawrence, Chief Hendricks summoned the two detectives into his office. He asked questions, most of them had no answers. He asked if either had a feel for why the killings had ended, or had at least paused. His two detectives could only shake their heads.

Three days after that meeting, the Desk Sergeant entered Homicide carrying a six inch cubed cardboard box. DETECTIVE ERIK MILLER EYES ONLY was written on the sealed top in bold black magic marker. Miller was out on an investigation, so the box ended up on Hendricks' desk. Hendricks called Miller's cell and told him to get back to the station ASAP. And then he called Day.

"You've been keeping up with the Missing Person list, right?" Hendricks asked as the three of them settled into chairs behind the closed office door.

Day nodded. "Every day. Beginning of the shift, end of the shift. No name even remotely close."

"Open it," said Hendricks to Miller, handing him scissors.

Miller carefully sliced through the clear packing tape and folded back the flaps, prepared for whatever heinous mutilation might be inside. The box was empty, except for two pieces of folded white eight and a half inch by eleven inch unlined copy paper, and a tiny brass heart shaped locket on a thin gold chain that lay on a square piece of yellow felt on the bottom of the box. He lifted the items out.

"This is all there is," he said to the other two.

Unfolding the first sheet of paper, he read aloud:

Fifty shocks I suffered for love,
My only escape to the darkness above,
Where sanctuary and peace I find
And kings and God treat me kind.

Miller looked at Day and she shrugged.

"Chalk one up for Cormier and your professor," he said.

"Hunchback of Notre Dame?" asked Hendricks.

Miller nodded, then opened the second sheet.

He read aloud: *Have you missed me, Erik? It's been a while. I have to confess, I thought about stopping. I did. I really did. But you and I, we have unfinished business. By now, you must know what that is. How can I stop until we settle what you have done to me? How can I rest until the debt you owe me is paid? I have tried, God knows I have tried, to stop making others suffer for what you did to me. But I cannot. The emptiness in me never goes away. It never leaves me. I can find no peace anywhere. I am alone. And I am alone because of you. My life is empty, because of you. My nights are haunted, because of you. Until our final reckoning, Erik, The Universal Killer will be exacting revenge for what you did.*

UK

P.S. The Gypsies will weep for her, Satan will welcome her.

Miller folded the paper back up and put it in his suit coat pocket. Hendricks picked up the locket and looked at it closely, front and back. There were no inscriptions. He popped it open. Inside were two tiny photos. On the left, a black and white of a female child that appeared to be under three years old. On the right, a color photo of a smiling baby dressed in blue sleepwear.

"Looks like our victim has children," he said, handing the locket to Miller. "Check your reports. See who has children. Have we been checking on the cameras we have set up at all the towers?"

"I check them every other day," said Kristen. "They are working fine."

"What's this thing about Gypsies weeping?" the Chief asked. "Any of that make sense?"

"Esmeralda was a Gypsy girl," said Day. "She befriends Quasimodo. The actress name we have for her is Patsy Ruth Miller."

"And no name on the Missing Persons remotely close to it?"

"None."

"Okay. When did you last check the cameras?"

"Yesterday," said Day.

"Go check now. And check in the towers."

He looked at Miller who sat quietly in his chair staring at a spot on the carpet. "I want a police presence at each tower. Twenty-four seven starting right now."

It seemed Miller didn't hear.

"Miller, did you hear me?" Hendricks asked.

"I'll make the calls," said Miller as he stood and went out of the office.

Hendricks looked at Day.

"He's under a lot of strain," she said. "You can see it. We all can see it. I think half of him was hoping we would never get another box, and the other half was desperately wanting another box. This whole thing is eating him up. He's been going downhill since Eve."

"You're the one who argued he shouldn't be taken off the investigation, Day. You changing your mind now?"

"No. Not yet. Let's see what happens now that we have something. I think he'll pull himself together."

"I hope you're right. Go on. Get to work. Keep me posted."

MILLER MADE THE calls he had to make. Officers had been

chosen for this operation soon after the discovery of Kay Lawrence, in the chance that the next victim would be mimicking a scene from Hunchback. When the time came to put the plan in action, each officer had been assigned surveillance of a tower, working twelve hour shifts and hidden from view. Miller was telling them now that surveillance would begin immediately. They were not to leave their post until their relief showed up. And God help them if they fell asleep.

With the calls done, Miller and Day split up the churches and towers that they had previously selected. Day got the churches on the east and south side of the Merrimack River, while Miller, after checking out the tower at City Hall, would cross over the Queen City Bridge to the west side of the river and the churches there.

While this area of New Hampshire, only fifty miles north of Boston, began seeing settlements in the early 1700's, there were few of those early settlers who were of the Catholic faith. A hundred years later, that slowly began to change. Britain took control of Canada from the French in the 1763 Treaty of Paris. This led to almost one million French Canadians immigrating into the United States over the next hundred years. The Catholic population of Manchester swelled as many of those immigrants from Canada were drawn to the Queen City by the need to fill jobs at the mills that stretched for a mile on both sides of the Merrimack River. In the last quarter of the 19th century, the landscape of the city boasted several Catholic churches with towering spires. The church that dominates the West side, built in 1881, was one of the earlier ones..

As Detective Erik Miller drove over the Queen City Bridge, he saw the church in the distance, sitting atop a hill, its' steeple and bell tower rising high above the hospital that was just off to the side, and the renovated mill buildings that stretched below it at the banks of the river. He had been in the church many years before while renovations had been going on, as an usher at a fellow officers' wedding. Miller was not a religious person. But he remembered feeling an overwhelming sense of peace while sitting there in a pew, even during the excitement of watching a wedding ritual being performed. Several times over the next year, as his marriage was disintegrating, he found himself sitting in the back of the church during a Sunday Mass, listening to the priest and trying desperately to find that peace again. But he never did.

Miller pulled into a parking space in a lot on the side of the church. At the side entrance door stood a caretaker patiently waiting. He had been alerted that the police were on their way and they would need access to the tower and the bells that it held. Exiting the car, Miller nodded at the man, then walked to a spot forty feet away. He looked up, searching for the camera that he and Day had set up almost three months before. The camera wasn't there. Searching the ground, he found the device shattered and lying useless at the base of a bush. Miller went to the front of the church, to the wide stoned area that led to the steps and the main entrances to the building. Looking up into the branches, he saw that that camera was also gone. He found the shattered remains in the vegetation that runs along the border with the sidewalk. Flipping open his cell, he called his partner.

"Where are you?"

Day was just pulling up in front of a church.

"Saint Augustine's. Been to St. Joe's. Where are you?"

"Ste. Marie. The cameras have been destroyed." He disconnected as Day was saying she was on her way, took in a deep breath, and went to meet the caretaker. Just then, a car pulled into the lot and Officer Brian Simpson, in uniform, exited and met Miller at the side door. Miller told him to make sure no one entered the church, other than Day who was on her way, and then he asked the caretaker to take him to the tower entrance.

The bell tower rises majestically in the front of the cathedral, and atop it a spire cuts boldly into the sky, crowned with a cross. The tower is home to four magnificent bells that were dedicated in 1906, all different sizes and weights. The smallest of the bells is named Sancta Maria. It weighs 1,795 pounds. It sounds the G note. The largest of the bells, known as The Great Bell and named Sancte Petrus Quirinus in honor of its donor, weighs an incredible 7,150 pounds. It was over this bell that the woman was draped.

He heard footsteps on the stairs.

"Miller?" came the call from his partner.

"Up here. Come up alone."

Day came up to stand beside him.

"Have you called it in?"

"Not yet. I just came up. My French isn't so good. What's inscribed on the bell?"

"*Je suis la voix de celui crie le desert. Bienheyreux ceux qui ont oreilles pour entendre,*" said Day peering past him at the inscription. "I am the voice that cries out in the desert. Blessed are those who have ears to listen."

"Damn," said Miller.

Miller walked to the other side of the bell, noticing that the dust along the platform had been swept, just like the top of the crypt had been in the third murder. With this new angle he could see the woman's face, and he grimaced. It was horribly bruised. The body was completely naked. It, too, was bruised. The back, the legs, the thin upper arms gave proof that she had endured a terrible beating. She was little more than skin and bones, her thighs not much larger than a grown man's biceps. She would have been easy to carry, thought Miller. He also thought, looking at the discoloration of the skin, that she had suffered more than the others. Why? What had she done to deserve that? Who was she to have been selected?

"Shit," Miller exclaimed suddenly as he looked closely at the thin, bruised face.

"What?"

"I think we found Megan."

MILLER, DAY AND Hendricks stood by Hendricks' car as the body was brought out of the church. The Parish priest stopped the gurney, bent over it, and said a prayer. Then stepped away.

"I don't like it," said Chief Hendricks. "The cameras were twenty feet off the ground. Hidden. How does the bastard find them? How does he even know to look for them? How does he find a woman every cop in the city has been looking to find for the past five months? He's always one step ahead of us. There is never a clue. No fingerprints. No shoe prints. No fibers, hairs. Always knows where the cameras are. And now he's placed another victim two hundred yards from where one of our suspects works, like he knows Doctor Thomas is a suspect."

Hendricks looked at Miller. "What if he's one of us?"

"One of who?" asked Miller.

"I've been thinking about this for a while," said Hendricks. "What if he's a cop."

Miller and Day stared at their superior.

"Think about it," said Hendricks. "He knows how to keep a crime scene clean. He knows how to beat our surveillance every time. He knows when he has time to pose a body and when he has to move sooner. This is a perfect example. She's placed in the tower even before we get the box. He knows Day checks the cameras every other day. He takes them out after she checks them, then brings the body here that night. Knows how to get inside the building. Knows about our surveillance of the wetlands. Knows we have an inkling about Doctor Thomas. Hears things around the precinct. Knows things, even though we are trying to keep a lid on it. Think about it."

Hendricks looked around at the activity in the lot. There was a sizable crowd of at least forty people watching the police activity. He spotted Officer Scott Powers standing among them.

"Check the CCT footage we have before the cameras went down," he said. "Go all the way back to the first day they were installed. Look for someone who is here a lot."

"There's an eight o'clock mass every weekday morning, Chief," said Day. "Chances are, many of those people will be here quite a lot."

"I know that," said Hendricks. "But our guy won't be a regular, just someone who had to be here enough to get a look inside the church and get a look for the cameras, but be here enough so he doesn't stand out as someone who was only here for those reasons. Plus, he's got to be a big guy, right? Then when you have someone, or someones, of interest, see if that face matches any cop. Go into the database. Check Manchester and every other town from Keene to Portsmouth, Salem to Laconia. All of it. There has to be something."

Hendricks slapped the hood of his car hard, then slipped into it and drove away.

"What do you think?" Miller asked Day.

Kristen shrugged. "He could be right."

"But in all of this, I've been targeted, too. That would mean some cop has a grudge against me. I can't imagine why anyone would have a problem with me. Fifteen years on the force, I've never had a major blowout with anyone. Differences sure. Petty shit. But nothing major that would cause anyone to have a vendetta."

"That you know of."

"What's that supposed to mean?"

"Maybe you pissed someone off, Erik. To you it was a small thing, but to them it was more."

"Pissed them off enough that he had to go on a killing spree?"

Day shrugged.

"This began with Maryanne Darrow," she said. "The notes tell us that. Somehow, you got brought into it. Probably, had you not been the Detective on the scene for Maryanne, you would have no part in any of this. Let's check the CCT."

"First, we need to check out the homeless centers and the camps," Miller said.

"Again? Why?"

"The killers note," said Miller. "Gypsies. The closest people we have to Gypsies are the homeless. Simpson is knocking on doors around here, asking if anyone saw or heard anything last night. He'll take care of that. We hit the camps. I still have the posters of Megan in my car. Let's see if anyone will talk to us now when they hear she is dead."

Miller got behind the wheel. "Leave your Jeep. The women may be more inclined to confide in you."

As he pulled out of the lot, he said, "What's with the locket he sent us? Was that supposed to be something Megan wore. Her baby picture with her brother? The locket didn't look that old. We'll stop by the station. I want to bring that with us."

24

THEY BEGAN WITH the shelters along Pine Street and Union Street, but had no luck. One woman remembered Megan, but hadn't seen her in several years. She was surprised to learn that Megan had still been in the area. She didn't recall Megan wearing a locket.

Over the summer, a homeless camp had sprung up under the Queen City Bridge. Miller and Day spent the afternoon moving among the tents and tarps, showing Megan's photo, asking if anyone had seen her. If they noticed a hesitation, or a nervous twitch, they said that Megan had had an accident and all they were trying to do was get some information. Megan was not in trouble. They showed the locket to impress that point. Still, no one volunteered any information.

The following morning, the two detectives spoke briefly with Officers Simpson and Powers. Both had canvassed the area around the church and they reported that no one had seen anything. Powers had recognized no one as he had walked among the gathered crowd at the church the day before. Matt Blanchette had scoured the photos of the crowd and reported the same thing. Only the Union Leader reporter was the constant face from previous photos.

A picture of the covered body being wheeled from the church entrance filled the top fold of the morning paper, with the story below the fold. Chief Hendricks was quoted, refusing to give the name of the victim until next of kin were notified, saying only that it was a female approximately twenty-eight years of age and that her death was being investigated as a homicide. He was non-committal when asked if this was the seventh victim that could be tied to The Universal Killer.

Page three carried the rest of the report, along with a close-up photo of Hendricks, Miller and Day standing by the Chief's car. The report finished with several sentences in quotes from Rene Cormier. "I would need to know a little more about the crime scene to know for sure, but a Catholic Church setting certainly points to *The Hunchback of Notre Dame.* As I have been predicting, this Universal movie lends itself spectacularly to this madman's rampage. *The Invisible Man* may well be the next movie selected if the police don't capture this psycho."

By mid-morning, Miller and Day were at another homeless camp that had sprung up recently along the banks of the river, not far from where the body of Maryanne Darrow had been left hanging in February. The results were the same as the day before. By eleven, they were in the Valley Street Cemetery preparing to check on another camp.

Miller parked his car about fifty yards in from the main gate and the two detectives walked among the headstones, ducking under a low hanging tree as they walked towards a large crypt. Upon reaching the crypt, they paused and looked down into a sunken area of the old graveyard. At the bottom of a well worn path, another homeless camp had been set up.

The day was hot and uncomfortably humid, and Miller was sweating by the time he had walked to the bottom of the path and into the camp. There were more sites here than in the other two sites combined. Leery eyes from those who were awake and out from their tents and tarps watched as the two detectives entered the campsite.

Miller stopped in the middle of the sprawl, Day beside him. He held a poster of Megan above his head and spun slowly around so anyone who was looking could see it.

"Her name is Megan Riley," said Miller loudly. "Some of you know her. We know this. We are not searching for her. She has had an accident and we want to help her. We need your help so we can do that."

He held the locket up and let it twirl on the end of the chain. There came no response, other than more people coming out from the places where they lived and slept to see what the commotion was about.

Miller spun the photo around again so all could see, walking slowly in a circle, making eye contact with as many people as he could. Most looked away.

"We are not searching for Megan," Miller said. "We know where she is. We want to help her. We need you to help us so we can do that."

"What kind of help can you give someone in the morgue?" asked a voice behind Miller.

Miller turned to see a young man sitting on the ground leaning against a tree. He held a bottle of Poland Springs water. He had a straggly beard, was shirtless, his hair was long and thick. When Miller looked at him, the man held up that morning's newspaper.

"How do you know it's Megan?" Miller asked.

"Why else would you be here?" asked the man. "I don't see that you brought us doughnuts out of the kindness of your heart. It would be nice if you were here to protect us from the punk gangs that torment us. Or if you were returning things that were stolen. But you're not here for those reasons, are you?"

Miller walked over to the man and stood above him. Day stood behind Miller. She kept her eyes on the rest of the camp.

From experience, she knew trouble could come from anywhere and it could come fast. A badge was no protection here.

"You knew Megan?" Miller asked the man.

"I know a lot of people," he said and sipped from his bottle.

"What's your name? I'm Detective Miller."

"I know who you are. Nice picture in the paper." He looked at Day. "Photo doesn't do you justice, Detective."

Miller gave a tight smile. "Listen, it's pretty early in the day. It's hot. We aren't looking for any trouble. You understand? Yeah, Megan is dead. Someone killed her. We want to find out who that was. We could use some help. Did you know her?"

The guy stood, nimbly coming to his feet. He was shorter than Miller, but standing on the root system of the tree, their eyes were at the same level.

"When the hell did the police ever want to do something for us?" he snarled. "Go fuck yourself."

Day's arm flashed past Miller, her hand slamming into the bare chest of the man and ramming him against the tree.

"Who the hell do you....." she began to say, but Miller quickly pushed her arm away and stepped in front of the guy to keep Day away from him. Miller noticed the man's eyes were wide with fright. He also heard the murmurings behind him from the residents of the camp.

"Like I said, it's pretty early in the day, and it's hot." Miller took one of his cards from his suit coat pocket and slipped it into a front pocket of the man's jeans. "Call me if you decide Megan deserves justice."

As Miller turned, he caught Day's eye and gave a slight shake of his head, then began to walk away. For a second Day stood looking down at the man, then followed Miller. An older man, with an unkempt beard and thin strands of hair on the top of his head, rose from a milk crate he was sitting on in front of a tent and walked up to Miller.

"There was no need of that," he said to Miller while he was looking at Day. "The boy might be young, but he already knows the score. No need to rough him up."

"Did you know Megan?" asked Miller, not interested in debating the conduct of officers and punks.

The old man looked at him for several long seconds, then said, "She has spent some time here, off and on. She kept to herself. Wasn't interested in conversation. At least not with an old dog like me." He pointed to a tiny yellow tent near the far end of the encampment. "That was her place." Then he went inside the tent he had been sitting in front of.

While most of the people disappeared into their spaces, some others watched as Miller and Day entered Megan Riley's home. There wasn't much. Several soiled and torn blankets that she had used as a mattress. Items of clothing, both for warmer weather and cold were neatly folded atop a plastic milk crate. A few plates, cups, silverware. Six paperback books of different genres. Some crackers and cookies not yet open. And a framed 5x7 picture of two children that matched the pictures in the locket. Miller took that before exiting the tent. The detectives had barely ascended the path that led to the crypt before Megan's tent was descended upon by those seeking its treasures.

"That wasn't necessary," said Miller as he entered the car.

Kristen shrugged. "We're trying to help. There is no need to give us shit. We're the good guys. You know, maybe the old man wouldn't have shared anything if I hadn't been forceful. Maybe he sees himself as the wise old man of the settlement. You know. Sitting Bull. Give the White Man what he wants and maybe he leaves us alone."

Miller thought about arguing the point, but wisely kept his mouth shut and drove away.

After lunch, they spent the rest of the afternoon going over CCT footage taken from the two cameras at Ste. Marie. It was going to be a long process, and they had only gotten to the end of July before Miller said he had had enough. He was going for a beer, did Day want to join him? Day shook her head, and she noticed that he seemed peeved about that. A quick 'see you tomorrow' and he was gone.

She checked the missing persons list and then headed home after stopping for groceries and Chinese take-out. It was almost ten and she was reading when her cell rang. She recognized the number on the screen.

"Doctor Thomas," she said. "I thought I might hear from you."

"Quite a little bit of activity in the church up the street the last few days, Kristen. Is it courtesy of the one they call The Universal Killer?"

She noticed he sounded different. His voice was deeper. He spoke slower. Probably high.

"Ongoing investigation," she said. "How was your trip to Cleveland?"

"That was months ago," he said, and then he actually giggled. "Have you been checking up on me, Detective? Anything you want to know, you just have to ask. I'm an open book. Or if you wanted to get together and talk, I'm here now."

"Why are you calling, Doctor?"

"I thought we could get together for another drink. I thought it would be good for you. Help get your mind off this case for a little bit. I can only imagine how stressful it must be."

"I'll pass," said Kristen.

"Are you sure? I've been known to be quite successful in relieving stress in women."

"I'm sure you have. Go on home to your wife and kid, Doctor. Don't call again." She ended the call.

A minute later the phone chirped again. She angrily snatched it up, prepared to be more forceful, when she saw the call was from Wendell Weasley.

"Good evening, Professor. I assume you have seen the news."

"Yes. Last evening. I'm sorry for the lateness of the call. Faculty meetings."

"No problem. Well, you were correct. It was Hunchback."

"Yes. Really a pity. And the woman was so young. I suppose a lot like Esmeralda, who was not much older than a child."

"Any thoughts, Professor?"

"Anything I could offer we have spoken of before. That is not the reason for the call, my dear Inspector. Have you taken to heart what we discussed when you came here last week? Do you now have protection around you while you sleep? Are your superiors aware of the imminent danger you find yourself in?"

"Yes, Professor Weasley, all precautions are being taken. There is no need for you to worry about me. I'm fine." She smiled to herself with the lie.

"Good," said Weasley. "Then I shall sleep more soundly. Good luck in your investigation, and do be careful. Good night, my friend."

Kristen placed the phone down and picked up the book. She had read it before. It was a favorite of hers.

BY FRIDAY, FOUR days after finding Megan Riley, Miller and Day had gone through the entire CCT, had selected three men who fit the criteria they were looking for, and had eliminated all three from being anyone known to be a police officer in southern New Hampshire through face recognition software. Miller had spoken with a priest at the church, showed him pictures of the three men. The priest knew all three. Two were orderlies at the hospital, the other a custodian at the high school down the street. They did not live in the parish, but would come some mornings to the 8:00 o'clock mass when the need to be close to their God couldn't wait until Sunday. Miller had then spoken with each man and had eliminated all three as suspects.

While Miller was doing this, Day was trying to track down the parents of Megan Riley, plus an older brother of hers that birth records in Lawrence indicated she had. Her investigation led her to make a phone call late Thursday afternoon to a cell number tied to an area code in South Carolina. Duncan Riley, Megan's father, answered the call. When Day had informed him that his daughter had died, there was a brief pause, and then he said that his daughter, Megan, was dead to him ten years ago. He then ended the call.

Kristen contacted Duncan Riley Jr. early Friday morning. The area code on the cell was 617, Massachusetts, but Riley now lived in Buffalo, New York, working for an insurance company. He said he was sad to learn of Megan's death, but he wasn't surprised. The only surprise, he said, was that she had lived this long. It was such a short life span, he said, in which to have made so many bad mistakes. No, he also said, he would not be coming back to claim the body. But maybe his older step-sister would. He gave Day her contact information. Day called her.

Melissa Ford lived in the outskirts of Austin, Texas. She had had no contact with Megan in six years, because the only times Megan had called her was to ask for money. Melissa had changed her phone number, married, moved away, and written her step-sister off as a lost cause. She was sorry Megan was dead, but, in her mind, she had buried Megan years ago.

The toxicology report showed no Propofol or Fentanyl in Megan's system. She was dehydrated, but death had come from physical trauma. Like Maryanne, she had been beaten to death and the force of the beating indicated a deep rage.

IN EARLY OCTOBER, three weeks after the discovery of Megan Riley, Chief Hendricks called Miller into his office and told him to close the door and to sit down. Hendricks looked at his best detective and didn't like what he saw.

Getting right to the point, Hendricks said, "You have unused vacation on the books. Beginning tomorrow, no, beginning right now, you are on a two week vacation."

Miller leaned forward, "Wait a minute, ..."

"Save it," interrupted Hendricks. "This isn't a suggestion, or up for discussion. You look like hell and you need a break. Go somewhere. Get out of the city. Lay on a beach. Find a nice place to relax. Just do not be here. I see you anywhere near here in the next two weeks, you'll be on suspension. Understand?"

"And if we end up with another body?"

"Then I'll call you in. I'm not taking you off the case, although it is my inclination to do that. Day has talked me out of doing that, but the way you are now, well, you need a break. I won't pretend that I've ever gone through what you're going through, Miller, but I can recognize burn-out when I see it. Two weeks. Don't come back here sooner unless I call you. Now get out of here."

Miller was raging inside. He wanted to protest this order. Argue it. Demand that the Chief rescind. Instead, he stood and walked out of the office and out of the bullpen. Day, puzzled by his exit, went to Hendricks' door.

"I was just about to call you in, Day. Close the door and sit."

He looked at her. Her hair was pulled back and neat. Her eyes were clear. The attractive face showed no strain. Her outfit, dark purple this day, was neat, clean and pressed. She didn't appear to have gained or lost a pound since joining the investigation seven months earlier. She was handling the pressure better than her partner.

"I've sent Detective Miller on a two week forced vacation. Forced, because he didn't want to go. But he's burnt out, Kristen. You can see that. We all can see that."

Day remained quiet.

"What about you? You need some time off? Maybe a week?

You have time on the books."

"One of us should be here in case something happens," said Day. "Maybe when Miller comes back."

Hendricks nodded. "He's not to come in here. He calls you, tell him he's on vacation. Tell him what I told him. He needs a break. The world won't end. I find out he's still running around out there, I'll suspend him. I'm serious here, Day. He looks like shit. Can't have him working cases in the state of mind he's in now. Bound to screw up something at a scene. You know it. You understand? He calls you, you back me up on this."

Day nodded. "Hundred percent, Chief."

Hendricks rubbed his eyes. "You see Cormier on the news last night?"

"No."

"Talking about movies that The Universal Killer might use next. Kept going on about *The Invisible Man.* Watch out for apartments that are above bars, he warned the viewers. And the talking head is egging him on. The guy is loving his fifteen minutes, I'll tell you. What do you think? You think he's right?"

"As good a guess as any," replied Kristen. She hadn't, and wouldn't, mention Phantom.

"You're checking missing persons?"

"Twice a day, Chief."

"You in court this morning on that thing over on Montgomery Street."

"In an hour. Probably be there the rest of the day."

"Okay." He waved her off, but stopped her at the door.

"I'm serious, Day. No interaction with Miller about work. Don't mess with me on this."

Day nodded again and went out.

25

MILLER SAT IN a folding chair on the balcony of his apartment building and watched the activity in the parking area below his second floor digs. In was 10:30 on a workday morning. The activity in the parking area centered around a squirrel who scurried around searching for whatever it was that made squirrels scurry. There was a nip in the air that Miller found comforting. While his mind, at first, had railed against the forced banishment imposed upon him, by the fourth day he had come to peace with it. Once that happened, it was like a curtain being pulled back on a window allowing light to enter. The night before, for the first time in months, he had slept through the night, followed by a substantial breakfast, shower and shave. A third cup of coffee within reach on a folding tray, waited patiently for him to reach for it.

He had called Day three times that first day of exile. She finally told him, after the third call, to knock it off. Hendricks was right, she told him. He needed some time off. Use the time wisely and rest up, she had said. That didn't keep him from calling her three more times on the second day. By the time he punched her number in for the second time on the third day, even he knew he was being a pain in the ass. He canceled the call and hadn't called since. If something happened, she'd call him.

He had left his apartment only once in the last four days and that was to do some food shopping. Instead of a thirty pack, he had purchased a six pack. He watched no newscasts, read no papers. He looked forward to a weekend of college and pro football on the television. And yet, as he sat on his deck, his eyes closed, enjoying the peace and quiet of a world where all his neighbors had left for work, he knew it was all an illusion. Six days off, two weeks, four months, it didn't matter. Eventually, victim number eight would be found and it would all begin again. This was just the calm before the next storm.

5:45 SATURDAY, THE college game had just ended and Miller was preparing a Porterhouse for grilling on his small gas grill on the balcony, when his cell rang. Looking at the number, he didn't recognize it.

"Miller," he said as he walked to the sliders.

"Inspector Miller?" the male voice asked.

"Yeah. Who am I talking to?"

"Inspector, my name is Wendell Weasley. Perhaps Inspector Day has mentioned me to you?"

"Professor," said Miller and he immediately smiled. The man sounded exactly as Day had described him. "Yes, she has mentioned you. I didn't know she gave you my number."

"Yes, at our first meeting, Kristen gave me both of your cards."

Miller smiled again at the use of Day's first name by Weasley.

"What can I do for you, Professor Weasley?"

"Yes. I called your police station yesterday morning after my calls to Inspector Day went unanswered. Could you give her a message that I need her to call me?"

"She wasn't answering her cell?" asked Miller.

"No."

"Didn't they patch you through to her desk?"

"I was told she was not in the building. They would provide no other information to me."

"Why don't you tell me what this is about, and I'll try to reach her and pass it on."

"I've been calling her since Thursday," said Weasley and Miller recognized the concern in his voice. "Has there been another murder? Have you two been busy?"

"Professor," said Miller, "give me your message and I'll see that Detective Day receives it."

Miller lowered the flame on the grill and placed the meat on the rack.

"Have you spoken with her today?" asked Weasley.

"No, Professor, I have not. Today is Saturday. Detective Day doesn't work on Saturdays. But I will call her for you if you just tell me what it is you need from her."

"Need?" said Weasley. "Inspector, I don't need anything from her. I am concerned for her safety. That is all."

As the steak began to sizzle, Miller looked out across the parking lot and felt the slightest tingle in his stomach.

"Why would you be concerned for Detective Day's safety, Professor? What are you getting at?"

"Well, it's obvious, isn't it? She's told you that she might be in danger. That she might be on the killer's list. This threat is very real, I assure you. And now she isn't answering her phone. Were you together yesterday?"

"Explain yourself, Professor. Why is she in danger? What list are you talking about?"

"Oh, dear, she didn't tell you."

Miller was beginning to lose his patience as the tingle grew stronger.

"Tell me what?" he demanded.

"*The Phantom of the Opera,*" said Wendell Weasley.

"Okay," said Miller, his mind quickly remembering the film. "It's been on our list. I watched it several months ago. Claude Rains. An actress named Foster, uh, Susan Foster. Explain what you mean, Professor."

"Susanna Foster, " corrected Weasley, "but you have the wrong film. Universal's Phantom was the silent movie with Lon Chaney. His co-star was Mary Philbin. She played the role of Christine Daae. Do you see now my concern, Inspector Miller. Christine Daae. Kristen Day. The similarity in the names is why I am concerned. I warned her about this when she came here recently. I warned her that she should have protection around her. She assured me she informed her superiors and that precautions were in place."

Weasley took a long breath. "Are you telling me now, that she did not mention the danger to you?"

The calm of the past week melted away, and Miller felt the approaching dread.

"I'll have to call you back," Miller abruptly said into the phone and disconnected. He immediately hit Day's number. After several rings, it went to voice mail. He called again. Same result. Maybe, he thought, she wasn't near her phone. Maybe she was sending him a message by not picking up, that he was on vacation and that meant no interaction with her to discuss the case. Or maybe, he worried, she couldn't answer.

He called Matt Blanchette and caught him at home.

"Did you talk to Kristen yesterday?" Miller asked as soon as Blanchette answered.

"You feeling a little better after a week off? You up in Maine?"

"Matt, did you talk to Kristen yesterday?" Miller asked again, ignoring the small talk.

"No. She's been out since Thursday. Flu or something. Why?"

"She called in sick?"

"Half the room thinks she's shacked up with you," Blanchette said with a laugh.

"Did she call in?" demanded Miller.

"Sent a text to Hendricks Thursday morning. Said she'd rest up and be in on Monday. Everything alright?"

"I'm sure it is. Just can't seem to reach her."

"Well, buddy, just like you, maybe she needed a break, too. And that included a break from you. It hasn't been easy being around you the last few months you know. Another week off and you'll be your old self again. Why don't you just let her get some rest over the weekend and bother her on Monday?"

"Sure," said Miller absently. "Have a good weekend." He disconnected.

While the Porterhouse continued cooking too much on the one side, Erik Miller stared out across the parking lot to the trees on the edge of the lot and made a decision. He shut off the grill, slipped on a pair of sneakers, grabbed his car keys and phone, and headed for the door.

HE HAD NEVER been to Day's house, didn't even know how to get there, but the GPS got him to the address. The ranch styled house was situated on a large, heavily treed expanse off a narrow country road in Goffstown. The Jeep was parked in the unpaved driveway. It was the only vehicle there. Dusk had overtaken daylight. There were no lights on in the house that Miller could see from his vantage point twenty-five yards away from the edge of the driveway. He had a dilemma and wasn't quite sure what to do.

On the one hand, if Day wasn't answering her phone because she wasn't feeling well and didn't want to be bothered, she would not be happy with him being there, checking up on her. On the other hand, if she was entertaining a guest for the weekend, she would really not be happy to have him intrude. Of course it was possible that she was ill and sleeping and that was the reason for no lights on. And it was also possible that she had been picked up and was out with someone, or with friends, and she wasn't even home. All of that was possible. But as Miller sat there in his idling car, all of the possibilities meant nothing to him. The only possibility that meant something, was the one that Kristen was in there with The Universal Killer and she was in trouble. Or she had been taken and the clock was ticking. If she wasn't, he would gladly suffer her wrath at him for checking up on her. He drove into the driveway without headlights and parked behind the Jeep.

Stepping quietly from the vehicle, he took his weapon that was tucked in behind his back, flipped off the safety and returned it to the waistband of his slacks. Then he quietly approached the house in darkness. Circling around back, Miller noticed a faint light coming from a back window. He peeked through the window into the kitchen area, saw a lit candle in a glass jar on the otherwise empty kitchen table. He listened, but heard nothing. Going to the back entrance, he pressed an ear to the door, held his breath, and listened. Nothing. He tried the door knob. It turned easily in his hand and the door silently opened with very little pressure. Stepping into the kitchen, he again listened. Other than the refrigerator that had just kicked on, there was silence.

Miller stood in the kitchen for several seconds before deciding he would call out for her, but then he saw her phone on the kitchen counter, the charger plugged in. So, he determined, Kristen was home. But was she alone? He decided. Screw it. If she wasn't alone, and she got pissed at him, so be it. But he wasn't about to walk in on her in her bedroom if she wasn't alone. And he wasn't about to leave until he knew she was okay. He decided he would call out her name.

"You take another step, I'll blow your fucking head off." The voice came from behind him, from the hallway that led to the bedrooms. It was Day's voice.

"Put your hands where I can see them," she said, "and get on the floor."

"It's me, Kristen."

"Miller? What the hell are you doing here?" The hall light came on behind her as Day flicked the switch.

"You weren't answering your phone," Miller said weakly, realizing it was a flimsy excuse for walking uninvited into her home.

"Jesus Christ, Erik. Really?" She lowered her weapon and placed it on the counter. "Sometimes people just need a break, you know. Why didn't you just knock on my door? You had to come creeping around to the back?"

He looked sheepishly at her standing at the other end of the kitchen. She had on a white negligee that was knee length. The light behind her showed through the thin material and gave testament that that was all she was wearing. When she saw where his eyes were looking, she said, "Sit down. I'll be right back."

He was sitting at the kitchen table when she returned. She had put on a knee length emerald green cotton bathrobe that had long sleeves. Taking a seat opposite him, she said, "You want to tell me what the hell is going on?"

He told her about the call from Wendell Weasley, that the professor was concerned that she wasn't answering her phone. He told her about calling Matt Blanchette and finding out that she had been out sick for two days.

Looking at her then, in the quiet of the house, the incandescent light of the kitchen softer than the fluorescent of the bullpen, he noticed the lines around her eyes, and it punched him in the gut that he selfishly hadn't realized that Kristen was suffering just as much as he was. That she, too, felt the effects of his inability to stop the murders. The distress he felt at that moment overwhelmed him and he had to look away.

"Why didn't you answer your phone?" he asked softly, taking a calming breath and regaining his composure. "You had us worried."

"Us?"

He looked at her again, and smiled. "Me and the professor."

She shrugged. "I forgot to charge it, and then when I did I put it on vibrate so I could get some sleep. I was going to check messages when I got up."

"You have a cold, or just exhaustion?" he asked. He noticed she had brushed out her hair when she had gone into the bedroom for the robe.

"It's nothing," she said. "A twenty-four hour thing. I'm fine. But I am hungry. Have you had dinner?"

"Left a big steak half cooked on the grill when I rushed over here," he said. "You want to go get something? My treat. Least I can do for barging in like this."

She smiled at him then. "You're in luck. Made a delicious beef stew in the crock pot yesterday and there is plenty left. I'll just heat it up."

Kristen began to rise, but then sat back down and looked at him.

"Speaking of barging in, why the hell were you sneaking in my backdoor? Why not just ring the front doorbell?"

"Why was your backdoor unlocked?" asked Miller.

"Don't change the subject."

"I wasn't sure you were alone."

"Not alone? What? Did you think I was with my lover? Together in the dark? And you thought it was a good idea to walk in on us?"

Miller looked away, then back at her and smiled. "You have a lover?"

She smiled at that.

Then he got serious.

"I didn't know if the killer had you in here. No lights on. Car in the driveway. I wasn't taking chances of alerting him by ringing the doorbell or knocking."

"The killer?"

"Weasley told me about Phantom. About the similarity in the names. Why the hell didn't you tell us, Kristen? That wasn't smart. I panicked. What can I say. I'm sorry. I knew you'd be pissed about me being here, but I couldn't not come. You know that. I'm being targeted. It cost Eve her life. You could be next."

"So you were worried about me?" Kristen asked, her voice teasing.

"Don't do that. There is nothing funny about this."

"You're right. I'm sorry. But I can take care of myself. You don't have to worry about me. I'm at the top of my game."

She got up and went to the refrigerator, took out a large glass bowl and placed it on the counter.

"You want a beer?" she asked.

"Sure."

She easily unscrewed the cap and handed him the bottle, then turned back to the counter. When she reached up into one of the cabinets for plates, he admired the tautness of her calves. He noticed that the belt on the robe, tied tightly, accentuated a waist that was much smaller than the hips. The sight of her standing in front of him, holding a gun and back lit, flashed into his head, and he allowed that sight to linger there, in his mind, for a few seconds. With the professional way that she dressed at work, the shapeless pantsuits that covered her from neck to foot, her shape was one of a rectangle. But now, he had seen that it wasn't. 'Mid-thirties,' he thought, 'and she still has the body of an athlete, while I'm going soft.'

Kristen Day had now been in Homicide for one year, and Miller's partner for seven months, and Miller had never thought of her as anything but a fellow officer. In the warm kitchen of her home, on a quiet Saturday evening, as she ladled beef stew into two bowls, that had suddenly changed. With his eyes still closed, he kept that vision of her silhouetted body in his mind for a few more seconds, then forced it away. He took a breath. When he opened his eyes she was looking at him.

"You okay?" Day asked.

He smiled. "Yeah. I was just thinking of something, is all. Something pleasant."

He stood.

"Where's the bathroom?" he asked.

"Down the hall. Don't mind the mess. And don't peek in the medicine cabinet. None of your business."

When he returned to the kitchen there was a steaming plate of beef stew next to his beer and Kristen was standing in front of the microwave waiting for her plate to be ready.

"Dig in while it's hot," she said, as she placed a loaf of bread on the table.

The microwave dinged and she sat opposite him, and as they ate Miller told her that he was thinking of heading up to Bar Harbor on Monday or Tuesday. That he had been up there several times and had always enjoyed himself. Always out of season. The peace, the quiet, the food. Kristen listened, smiled when he complimented her on how good the stew tasted, smiled again when he asked if there was more. She got him another beer while he waited for the microwave to heat up seconds.

Neither spoke of The Universal Killer.

26

MILLER WOKE AND shook his head several times to clear the image he had of sitting under a large shade tree and peering out over the waters of Bar Harbor. It was such a vivid image in his dream that he actually felt as if he were there. He lifted his arms in a stretch, rolled onto his back, and it was then he realized he was in total darkness. Usually, the lights from the parking lot seeped into his room through the windows of his apartment, so he was never in total darkness even in the dead of night. His head still felt heavy, and through the fog he realized he didn't remember driving home. He then had the uncomfortable feeling that he had stayed at Kristen's, and the even more uncomfortable feeling that if he had, he was in her bed. As pleasant as that thought was, it made him uncomfortable because of what that would mean in their relationship at work, and even more uncomfortable because, if he was in her bed, he had no memory of any intimacy they may have shared. He reached out to see if she was there beside him. His hand felt nothing. Funny, he thought, that relief can feel so disappointing. He needed to take a leak. He took in a deep breath, but when he attempted to swing his legs off the mattress, only one leg moved. It was only then that he realized that he was naked and that his left ankle had some kind of a strap attached to it.

"What the hell?" he whispered into the dark as he struggled to sit up. Reaching down to his ankle, he felt the chain and tugged on it hard. It had no give. He concentrated on the night before. What was the last thing he remembered? They were eating. They were talking. He had a beer. Maybe two. Maybe a third. And then nothing. Was he now dreaming?

Suddenly, there was light. He heard a door opening and footsteps coming down stairs. He looked down at the tether on his ankle and the chain that was bolted to the cement wall ten feet away, the soiled mattress that he lay on. Turning quickly, he saw the green robe descending the stairs. He rose up on his haunches, prepared to defend himself as best he could.

She stopped on the bottom step and looked at him, at the rage that was overcoming the stupor as the drug slowly wore off. She saw the anger in his eyes. And the fear. 'Good', she thought, 'you should be afraid. You should be very afraid, Erik. It's time to pay for the pain you've caused.'

Day moved to the stool in front of the workbench and sat, staring down at him. Suddenly, Miller came up in a lurch, his arms outstretched, reaching for her leg. He cursed, his face a mask of rage, and fell hard as the chain stopped him, his legs on the mattress, his torso on the cold cement floor still four feet from Kristen. He quickly pushed himself back up on his knees into a defensive position.

He stared at her, his face red from exertion and anger. She stared back at him coolly, as if looking through the glass enclosure in a zoo at an agitated lion, her lips slightly curled. The victor looking down upon the defeated. Slowly, Miller brought his breathing under control, felt his head clearing. He quickly took in his surroundings. The cellar stairs. The oil tank on the far end of the cellar. The washer, dryer twenty feet away. The wood workbench behind Kristen. The flat screen and VCR on the bench. The shelf that held the painted models of the monsters. Seven models for the seven victims of The Universal Killer.

They stared at each other for a full minute, until Miller took in a deep breath and asked, "Why?"

Kristen Day lowered her eyes and looked at her hands that were calmly folded in her lap. Then she looked back up, defiance in those eyes.

"I never intended all of this," she said, "but sometimes, sometimes, a person can just be pushed too far. Treated too badly. Taken advantage of too many times. And sometimes, when that happens, revenge is their only recourse."

"Why Eve? Why any of them? Those women never did anything to you."

"It's not about them!" Day said harshly. "Don't make it about them, Erik. I'm the one who has been wronged. All my life. Me. My partners were needed so I could show the world that society cannot treat people with so much disrespect. That we are all human beings, no matter how different or grotesque you may find us, and we deserve to be happy. We deserve to be treated with respect. We deserve to be treated fairly."

She sneered down at him. "You don't believe me. I can see it in your face. What the hell could I possibly have to complain about? College basketball player. Attractive. Smart. No way I could be unhappy about anything, huh? So, I must be crazy. You think I'm crazy. I can see it in your eyes. Just a psychotic killer. The great Erik Miller, the Golden Boy of Homicide at MPH, doesn't get it. Can't say I'm surprised. After working with you for seven months, the only thing that surprises me about you is that you can tie your shoe laces. Seven victims, and you never had a clue. It took Hendricks to tell you the killer might be a cop and it took him nine months to make that suggestion."

"You're right. I do think you're crazy," said Miller. "I think you're a psycho. What else would you call someone who murdered seven people? A sick psycho."

"What does that say about your deductive powers? I've studied some of the cases you've worked on in the last four years, Erik. Shoddy performance at best. You got lucky with the judge's murder, you know it's true, and you've been riding that luck ever since. For seven months you've been working side by side with The Universal Killer, and you had no clue."

"You're bat shit crazy," spat Miller. He was hoping to anger her. Get her so angry that she would lash out at him. Use that temper that he had witnessed and heard about. To provoke her into trying to hit him. To come within arms reach where he could grab her.

But Day wasn't listening.

"And you know what really pissed me off, Erik? Do you know, when the Brass took you off the streets and gave you that Detective's badge, there were two finalists for the job. Can you guess who the other person was, Erik? Can you? Yeah, it was me."

Kristen stood and moved towards the steps, then turned and came back and sat down again.

"I deserved it more than you did," she said. "Instead, you got it. You got off the dirty streets. Got to dress up in nice suits. Got your name in the newspapers. And what did I get? Vice. Four years of Vice. Every day wallowing with the lowest scum on Earth. Back alleys. Filthy rooms. Crack head whores and pimps with knives, with lawyers who had them back on the street fifteen minutes after a bust. Every night, feeling like no matter how long I stayed under a hot shower, the filth wouldn't wash off. Four years! And why? Because you're a man and I'm a woman. Do you see the injustice in that, Erik?"

"You're sick, Day. Very sick."

Kristen smiled then and raised her eyebrows.

"Yeah, maybe," she whispered. "The last few months I've been thinking the same thing. But I was too far down this road to stop. Besides, there was still the debt you owed me that had to be paid."

"Because I got the job and you didn't?" said Miller. "Bullshit!"

Kristen spun on the stool, leaned on the bench, her back towards him.

"Usually," her voice calm, "when I have a new partner, we read the book of the model we are going to build, if there is a book to read, and then we watch the movie." She turned to face him again. Smiled. "Have you figured out which book and movie we will be doing, Erik?"

"What are you talking about?" he asked. "Movie? Book?"

She shook her head at his confusion.

"Let me explain," she said as if speaking to a six year old. "With each new partner that I choose...."

"Partner?" Miller snapped. "You wrote about partners in the notes you wrote. These women weren't your partners. They were victims. They were innocent victims. Don't try to make them anything other than that. You killed innocent women."

Day frowned. "May I continue?"

He stared at her.

"With each partner, I would read to them the book of the model that we were to build." She pointed to the shelf with the models. "Did you notice them, Erik? They're beautiful, aren't they? After, we would watch the movie and discuss any differences between book and movie. And then, with their help, I would build the model."

"And then you would kill them. You crazy, sick son-of-a-bitch."

She smiled again. "Daughter of a bitch, actually. There is no need to be vulgar, Erik, but, yes, then it was time to get them ready for the world to see them and for my statement."

"Your statement?"

"Well, to call attention to the monster in question by using a scene from the movie. By doing that, it was only going to be a matter of time before the great Detective, Erik Miller, would realize what was going on. The newspaper reporter figured it out before you did, Golden Boy. I wanted the tie in to the monster. It was important."

Day reached up to take the King Kong model down, and as she did her robe rode high up revealing a toned naked thigh.

"You've now watched all the movies, Erik, except for the one you and I shall watch tomorrow night. What is the one thing that the audience can count on? The movie going audience. What do they demand?"

When Miller didn't answer, she said, "The monster has to die. Right? In the movies, the woman lives and the monster dies. In the books, that's not always true. Anyways, I thought it only proper that the women die and the monster lives. For most of my life, I have felt that the monsters got a raw deal from Hollywood. The authors were much kinder to their creations. All I have done is try to be faithful to the written words."

"Bullshit," Miller spat out again.

Day shrugged from her seat. "I didn't expect you to understand. You're a man. Man's first reaction to what they don't understand is to shoot first and ask questions after. Empathy is a woman's trait. A mother's reaction." Day frowned at that. "Well, some mothers. Not all."

Day seemed lost in thought. Miller studied her sitting there on the stool, her shoulders hunched, her legs parted. He could see she was naked underneath the robe and he felt that she wanted him to see that she was. Her right hand absently brushed at the fabric of the robe along her right thigh.

"Kristen," he said, his voice controlled, almost tender, "tell me about Maryanne."

As if coming out of a trance, she gave her head a slight shake and then focused on him. In her eyes he saw anger.

"You don't get to talk about Maryanne, Erik. Not after what you did. You don't get to say her name."

"What did I do, Kristen? Tell me what I did, because I don't know. One of the notes said this was all my fault. What did I do? How is it my fault? Tell me. I think I deserve to know."

She sneered at him. "You deserve nothing, except the death you're going to have. Do you have any idea how often I have sat across from you in some diner eating our lunch, and the whole time we sat there I had to fight the temptation to lunge across the table and plunge the knife I was holding deep into your neck? The only thing that stopped me was the plan I had for how you should die."

"Fine. Tell me why. I don't remember ever meeting Maryanne. Tell me why!" Miller demanded.

Kristen came off the stool and took a step forward. "Because of you, she left me," Kristen said angrily. "If you had done your job, we would still be together, all those women would be alive. None of this would have happened. If you had just done your Goddamned job!"

"Megan?"

"Yes, Megan!" yelled Day. "That skank whore. You should have arrested her that rainy night. You should have investigated why she was running from those druggies. You should have found out that she had stabbed a guy. She should have been in jail. And then she never would have been able to take my beautiful Maryanne away from me."

Kristen took another step closer to Miller and he prepared himself for another lunge if she took one more step. But she did not. Instead, she turned and walked to the stairs.

"Tell me what Megan did," Miller said quickly, attempting to keep her angry and talking.

"Go fuck yourself, Miller," Kristen said as she began climbing the steps.

"No, tell me," Miller yelled as the lights went out.

MILLER HAD NO idea how many hours had passed when the lights came on again and Kristen came down the stairs carrying two plates. She was dressed in tight black stretch pants and a long sleeved white blouse buttoned to the neck. One of the plates she lay on the floor and pushed it towards him with her foot, until it would be within his reach at the end of the tether.

"What time is it?" he asked, looking at a peanut butter and jelly sandwich and four Oreo cookies that were on the plate, along with an eight ounce container of milk and a handful of potato chips.

She frowned, then the frown became a cruel smile and her eyes became larger.

"I would never have found Megan The Roach if it weren't for you," she said. "I'd been searching for years for good old Megan. I mean, I owed her. Never could find her. I had no idea what she looked like until you brought that photo up from Lowell. Then you began circulating her picture all over town and, bingo, I find out where she is. So I suppose I have you to thank for that."

Miller made no response, although he was curious how she had found Megan when he couldn't.

"Poor, Erik," Day said, after swallowing a bite from her sandwich. "He's confused again. Remember how anxious everyone was getting this summer, waiting for The Universal Killer to strike again? By the way, I like that name. Anyways, three months and no box. No body. I thought you were coming unhinged. I was enjoying that. But it wasn't planned. The long stretch wasn't planned. I was going to grab a homeless woman for my Gypsy Esmeralda. Where do you find someone named Esmeralda today? You don't. I thought about using O'Hara, for

Maureen O'Hara, the actress who played Esmeralda, but I thought using a homeless as the Gypsy was a better idea. Any homeless woman would do, just as long as they were young. The younger the better. Hell, we have some sixteen year old kids on our streets. I thought I'd use one of them.

"Then one day, it was late July, remember I was working that crime scene on Canal Street, and as I was coming out of the building I see a face I recognize in the crowd across the street. An old stoolie of mine from my Vice days. He waves to me, then he walks down to the corner and stands there, waiting for me. So I go over to see him. He pulls a flyer for Megan out of his pocket. He asks if the cops are still interested in finding her. He knows where she is. Twenty bucks later, I know where she is. Or at least where he says she is. Homeless camp in Valley Street Cemetery.

"Now, I can't just waltz in there looking for her. Not for what I have planned for Megan The Roach when I get my hands on her. So, instead, every night at dusk I'm in the cemetery waiting. Waiting for the night that Megan will be walking back to the camp alone. Five weeks it took before I see her, weaving through the headstones sipping on an ice coffee. I recognize the scrawny little bitch right away from the picture you provided. And she's alone. I'm on her before she even realizes it. And then she's mine."

"Did you have to beat her that badly, Kristen? No one deserves a beating like that."

"She did. She deserved worse. What would you do to someone who completely destroyed your life?"

"And how did she do that? When did you two cross paths?"

"You never have pieced it all together, have you, Miller?" Day said, shaking her head in disdain. "With all the notes, and all the clues, you still don't get it. Maryanne and I were together. We loved each other. Until Megan turned Maryanne against me."

And then Detective Eric Miller thought he did get it. He thought he understood it all.

Kristen could tell that Miller now thought he understood, but she knew he really had no clue of what had happened, and she was going to get some satisfaction in telling him. Eventually. She reached over to the end of the bottom shelf and took a book from it. Settling on the stool again, she opened the book.

"I don't want you to read, Day, I want to talk. You and Maryanne? When? How?"

Kristen Day closed the book and sighed.

"There is a way that things must be done," she said. "I have to read the book. We have to watch the movie. I have to glue the pieces of the model together. This is the way it has always been done. This is the way it must be done. If I don't do this, I could lose my mind. Can you understand that, Erik?"

"I think that ship has sailed, Kristen," he said, still trying to get a rise from her.

"Please, Erik," she said, her voice pleading. "It's important."

For a brief second, Miller saw her tough veneer crumble, revealing a frightened woman sitting before him. This was a part of Day he had never witnessed before. He pressed.

"No!" he said. "Put the book down. Tell me about Maryanne Darrow. Nine months of this, I think I deserve to know. You want to talk about almost losing your mind? How do you think I've felt all these months? In fact, you know how I've felt. Enjoying every minute of my pain, weren't you? Tell me. Now. What the hell is this really all about?"

"I should just kill you now," she hissed at him, recovering quickly from her moment of weakness. "Kill you and be done with it."

She threw the book onto the bench and stomped up the stairs, shutting off the lights and slamming the door. Miller listened for any noise from above him. At first there was none. But then he heard her swearing, and he heard things crashing onto the floor and loudly breaking or rolling around.

He knew he was playing a dangerous game with a psychotic, short-tempered woman who owned a gun and was proficient in using it, but his options were limited. He had to push her buttons. Had to drive her to make a mistake. Anger her to the point of distraction, without driving her so far that she killed him in a fit of rage.

All this time, he thought as he reached for the sandwich, he knew Maryanne Darrow was the reason for the killings, and that Megan Riley was the key to solving the crime. The physical beatings that both had endured, much worse than the others, gave testament that they were victims in a crime of passion, and not to keep them under control. But that the beatings had been administered by a woman, and not a man, had never crossed his mind. Everything had pointed to a tall, physically strong person being the killer. Why wouldn't he have thought it was a man? Everyone else did.

How to play it when she next came down? he wondered. How to stay alive until he could figure a way out, was all he could think of.

KRISTEN CAME DOWN several hours later. Miller saw that she had regained her composure. She made no attempt to pick up the book, just stood at the base of the stairs staring at him. He stood, also, naked and defiant. She tossed a bottled water on the mattress, noticing he had eaten everything on his plate. After several minutes, she spoke.

"I used your phone to send Matt a text," she said. "You'll be enjoying a few days, maybe a week, up in Maine. The rest is doing you a world of good. I sent a text to my phone, too. Same message. But you did tell me to call you if The Universal Killer struck again. Needless to say, I won't have to make that call."

"And how are you planning on posing my body, Kristen? What's the grand scheme?"

"Well, if you knew anything at all, Erik, and it is painfully clear that you don't, you would know that you will die in a horrific fire, just like your namesake is supposed to do in the book you don't want me to read."

She smiled.

"That's right, partner. Can you believe it? In case you haven't figured it out yet, we will be doing *The Phantom of the Opera.* This has actually been planned since that day back in January when you showed up at the River Walk and began the investigation into the death of Maryanne. I can remember sitting at my desk in the bullpen when you walked in and the room found out where you had just been and what you had just seen. In that instant, I began to put all of this together. Just imagine. If Matt or Allen or one of the others had been the first on the scene, maybe none of this would have happened.

Day gave her head a few shakes as her eyes traveled up and down his body.

"You should really join a fitness club, Miller. It's so easy to let yourself go. Listen, I'm going to try and get some sleep. It's late and I have work in the morning. Tomorrow night we'll try again. I'll bring you some breakfast before I go. While you're lying here in the dark, think about the coincidences that have brought us to this point. I know I have. I think about them a lot. There are too many for this not to be preordained. I know, crazy, huh? But think about it and we'll discuss that tomorrow night. And maybe start the book. It really is a good story. You'll enjoy it."

Kristen went up the steps. Miller let her go without saying a word.

27

DETECTIVE KRISTEN DAY was sitting at her desk when Matt Blanchette entered the bullpen.

"Got a text from our boy last night," he said, walking up to her. "Said he's going to Maine. Did he ever get a hold of you over the weekend? He told me he called but he couldn't reach you."

"Yeah, he did. I got a text last night, too. Good to see him getting away and relaxing. I was worrying about him."

"We all were," said Blanchette.

"Hey," Day said, smiling, "just a few more weeks. You getting excited?"

Blanchette shrugged. "Not really. I think I'm going to miss this. Security at the Fidelity complex is going to be so boring I'll probably go out of my mind. But the wife will be happy." He smiled. "And you know what they say, 'Happy wife, boring life.'"

Hendricks entered the room as Matt went to his desk.

"Anything on the missing persons over the weekend?" Hendricks asked Day.

Kristen shook her head.

"Miller driving you crazy?"

She shook her head again.

"Got a text," she said. "He's off to Maine for the week."

Hendricks nodded. "Good. Real Good. What do you have today?"

Kristen tapped a file she had open on her desk. It was the first investigation she had worked on when becoming a Detective, and it was just now going to trial.

"Court at ten," she said. "And probably tomorrow, too. Thursday, court again on one I worked on in Vice."

Hendricks grunted as he moved towards his office, but made no comment.

Too anyone looking over, it would appear Detective Kristen Day was deep into the reading of what was in the file, but she was not. She remembered the investigation. She didn't need a refresher. Instead, Kristen's mind was on the prize she had secured in her cellar, and how ridiculously easy it had been to get him there.

'Men are so easy to manipulate,' she thought, smiling to herself.

How to get Erik Miller shackled in her cellar was the problem she had contemplated for months. She knew there was an easy way to do it. Just invite him over for dinner. Partners having a nice evening together. A few beers, Red Sox on the television. But where was the challenge in that? She had thought about flirting with him, a few casual remarks that could be taken as an invitation, a few buttons not buttoned, a breast grazing an arm as she passed by. But she wasn't sure he would bite. Partners off limits in an intimate relationship seemed to be a rule Erik Miller might not bend. But, she now realized, she may have been wrong about that. Saturday night she had seen how he looked at her with the hall light shining through her sheer negligee, and she was now fairly certain that he would have only resisted just so long. He was a man, and men wanted her. It had always been that way. Ever since high school. It was a hell of a thing, she thought, and so damn funny, that they desired her and she wanted no part of them.

So, the easy way of getting her prey into the cellar had held no appeal, but, with some considerable thought and planning, and more than a little luck, she had set in motion a series of events that would bring him to her. The plan had begun with dear Professor Wendell Weasley.

At her first meeting with Weasley, way back in the Spring, she had given him her card and wrote Miller's cell number on it. She had realized during their conversation in the cafeteria, that the old Professor would probably become someone who would feel the need to stay in touch with her as the victims added up. She had done nothing over the long months to dissuade him from his interest in the case, and had, in fact, allowed him to believe she found his interest in the case, and in her safety, to be a comforting thing. She had expected that at some point he would mention *The Phantom of the Opera* and make the connection between her name and the young soprano in the book. But as the months went by, and the list of movies and victims grew longer, he never did. Then he called and said it was urgent that he see her. On that drive up to the college, Kristen had decided she would bring it up. Plant the seed. It was needed for her plan to get Miller out to her house. But it was Weasley who did bring it up. It was Weasley who, in his concern for her, begged her to be very careful. She, he said, was in great danger. All she then had to do was not answer his calls. His concern for her would do the rest.

Kristen was confident that after a day or two of being unable to reach her, the Professor would panic. She could imagine him tearing his office apart looking for the card with Miller's cell number on it, finding it and then calling Miller with his concerns that he could not reach Inspector Day. That she may be in terrible trouble. That she could be the next victim of The Universal Killer, and that she might already be. And he would tell Miller why he thought that. Then Miller would call her. And she would not answer his calls either. He would then speed to her house to check on her, his concern for her safety magnified by the loss of Eve, only to become the fly trapped in the web.

And it had all happened exactly as Kristen Day had planned it, aided by a little luck. She hadn't foreseen Miller being forced into taking two weeks vacation. Had he actually gone away that may have presented a problem, but when he didn't, that presented an opportunity. She could do what she wanted to do with him now and not worry about the problems that would arise when he didn't show up for work. It was perfect, really. And his tragic death? Kristen marveled at how much easier it had all become.

Day closed the file and leaned back in her chair, watching the activity around her. Matt Blanchette looked up and smiled at her. She smiled back. Luck had certainly played a part in all of the mayhem of The Universal Killer, Day knew. But she also knew that it was her careful planning that had moved the pieces around the board with such skill. And now, the killings would end with Miller, burned to a crisp in her bed. How the tongues would wag then. After the shock, of course.

Five years before, surfing sites on the internet, mostly EBAY, she had found and purchased eight models during the time Maryanne had lived with her, with the intent that she and Maryanne would build them together, like she and her Grandfather had done twenty-five years before. They would take their time. Years probably. From the classic novels, chapters would be read while in bed before falling asleep in each other's arms. Movies in black and white would be watched curled up together on the sofa, the beautiful Maryanne snuggled in her embrace, a bowl of popcorn shared between them. The models would be carefully glued together and painted at the kitchen table, while they drank coffee, or wine, and shared a snack, and spoke of how they had spent the day. That was how they had built King Kong. That would be how they would share the building of each monster. It would be wonderful, just like it had been with her Grandfather when she was a child. There was no rush. They had all the time in the world. And then Maryanne vanished. For years the sealed boxes were stored away in a closet waiting for the time Maryanne would return.

Her Grandfather had had eight boxes, she remembered, and she had helped him build seven of them before the fire took him from her. Now, with her different partners, they had helped her build seven of them. With Miller, she would build number eight. And once again, as it was when she was ten, fire would consume her partner. The only difference this time, she would not grieve the death.

But as Kristen sat there, looking out over the Homicide room that she had always wanted to be a part of, she had one more important decision to make in the case of The Universal Killer. Would she survive the blaze a second time, or would she join her partner this time and be consumed in the flames, as she had so often wished had happened twenty-five years before. Their charred remains to be discovered in a lover's embrace by first responders, satisfying the pigs who believed Miller and Day were secret lovers.

Either way, the killings would end with Miller.

Kristen got up and went to pour a cup of coffee. Blanchette walked over to where she stood.

"Did I hear you say you have court today?" he asked.

"Could be all week, unless they plea bargain," she replied. "That's fine. I can use the break."

"You know," said Blanchette with a shake of his head, "even after I get out of here, I have some cases that will go to trial and I'll need to be in court. I don't mind court. Never have. I like seeing justice metered out. Of course when the bastards get off, well, that feeling of anger never leaves you. You ever lose one?"

Kristen shrugged. "A couple during my time in Vice. Good defense lawyer, lousy prosecutor. Or witnesses who didn't show. But I know what you mean about the anger."

"You know, I've been thinking," said Blanchette. "Does it bother you that the killer found Megan Riley when we couldn't? We scoured the city, came up empty, and he finds her. How the hell does that happen?"

"The homeless were protecting her, Matt. She would probably be alive today if they weren't. And you know what? The people in those tents and tarps probably don't see the irony in that."

AFTER A DAY spent in court, Kristen pulled into her driveway and parked. She sat behind the wheel looking at her house and the property that it was surrounded by. She owned it all free and clear. There was no mortgage. The life insurance policy on her father had paid off the mortgage years ago. After her mother died, she sent a check to her brother to cover his share.

The house was a three bedroom ranch that sat a hundred feet off a road that had not yet seen an interest by builders in developing. But the town was growing, and she knew it was just a matter of time. There was a patchy lawn in front of the house that she mowed on weekends from May to October, and a potpourri of plants that ran the length of the foundation that had been planted with no thought or reason and which she spent little time caring for. Behind the house there was an expanse of tufted grass above the septic and leach field. Beyond that, the rest of her property was a forest of white birch, oak and pine. On the driveway side of the house, two large propane gas cylinders stood beside the house. Propane was how she now heated, having changed from oil heat almost ten years before. Propane was how she was planning on blowing up the house and causing the fire. Only question that remained, would she be in the house when it happened?

From the time her father had purchased the house in 1989, and dragged his wife and children from a hectic life in a suburb of Boston up to the boredom of a small town north of Manchester, Kristen had hated the house. She got the smallest of the three bedrooms when they moved in, a room almost half the size of the one she had in their house in Malden. Instead of a five minute walk to school, she had a thirty minute school bus ride. Instead of her group of friends, small as that may have been, here she had no one her age who lived even remotely close. Instead of her mother having friends to visit and stores to shop in within walking distance of Malden Square, up here all her mother had was the phone, a bottle of vodka, and Kristen to torment. The one saving grace, her father had set up a basketball hoop at the end of the driveway. Kristen had spent hours everyday shooting baskets by herself.

Kristen hated the house. Always had. And now, as she walked towards the back door, passing by the propane tanks, she smiled. If she decided to not be a casualty in the blast that those two tanks would create, she would take the insurance money, purchase a condo, and never mow or prune again. And she would have a modern kitchen and a bigger bedroom. If she decided to live.

Entering through the back door, Kristen listened closely. All was quiet. She quickly made up two plates of peanut butter and jelly sandwiches, Oreo cookies, chips and milk, and grabbed a blanket from the hall closet. October was usually the time the cellar took on a chill. She opened the heavy cellar door, snapped on the lights and descended the stairs. Miller was sitting on the mattress, his naked back leaning against the wall. Kristen lay a plate on the floor where he would be able to reach it and tossed the blanket at his feet. Then she sat at the workbench and started eating, with her back towards her captive. Miller sat very still and watched her. And waited.

Kristen plopped the last Oreo into her mouth, washing it down with the rest of her milk. Then she turned on the stool to look at Miller.

"Everyone asked how you were doing," Day said, "like I'm supposed to know. I think most of them think you and I have something going on, Erik."

She smiled. "I think, after seeing how you looked at me the other night, that you wish that we had."

Miller said nothing, just stared at her.

Kristen stared back, and wondered if it was possible to hate him more than she did at that moment.

She turned, found the book she had tossed the night before, then said, "Why don't you eat while I read, Erik."

"Tell me about Maryanne," Miller said, his voice a bit raspy from the dryness in his throat.

Kristen looked at him. "Drink some milk. I'll get you another bottle of water."

"Tell me about Maryanne," Miller said again.

Staring at him, she realized she had been wrong a minute before. She could hate him more.

"The quicker we get through the process, the quicker you can be put out of this misery," Kristen said, her voice not betraying the anger that was building in her at his refusal to allow her to begin reading.

Opening the book, Kristen read, "The Opera ghost really existed. He was not....."

"Tell me about Maryanne," Miller said, his voice louder and stronger.

She looked up quickly, scowled, then back to the book. "He was not, as was long believed...."

"Maryanne, Day. Tell me about Maryanne." Miller rose to his feet and walked to the end of the tether. "How an I involved with

Maryanne? Tell me."

He saw the hate in her eyes. That was good. He knew her anger was his only chance at leaving the cellar alive.

Day stared at him and counted very slowly to ten. And then silently on to twenty. Finally, she closed the book and laid it on the bench. He's going to die because of it, why shouldn't he know? she reasoned. Why shouldn't he know the pain he has caused me? Why shouldn't he know why he's the reason seven women have died? He should have to carry that guilt to hell.

"It was my first year in Vice. First few months. You were upstairs in Homicide, all dressed up pretty, and just beginning the investigation into the murder of the Judge and his wife. Meanwhile, I'm getting acquainted with the names and faces of every whore, pimp and addict on the streets of Manchester. One night, Cam Boyce and I are walking around the theater district on Hanover and Amherst, you know, the mayor wanting to keep the sullied away from the good citizens who have come to our city to enjoy a night of entertainment. As we passed by an alley, we heard a voice yell out, 'Careful with those teeth you stupid bitch!', followed by a sharp slap and a groan. Boyce yelled, 'hey', and we ran into the alley. In the dim light from a halogen high up on the building, we see a guy standing beside a dumpster, leaning against a brick wall, his pants down around his knees. A small figure suddenly rose up in front of the guy. Scrawny little thing. Looked like a kid. It bolted the other way, toward an opening out to Amherst Street. Real quick, too. The guy was struggling to get his pants up, so he wasn't going anywhere. Boyce headed for him, while I started to give chase to the elf who's almost made it out of the alley. All of a sudden, another figure popped up from in front of the guy and begins to run. I saw that it was a young woman. Taller than the runner, but just as thin. She took about three steps and fell flat on her face. She tried to scramble up, but I'm on her before she can."

Day paused and looked down at hands that were folded in her lap. Miller patiently waited as he picked up the blanket and wrapped it around himself.

"The woman on the ground didn't resist. She was so zonked out, there was no fight in her. When I flipped her over, I could see she had scraped her forehead on the ground and there was a nasty welt that was just beginning under one eye where I guessed the guy had hit her. I brought her to her feet and steered her towards a cement slab in front of a door, where we sat down. Meanwhile, the guy's being belligerent to Boyce while he's pulling his pants up, saying he had done nothing wrong. He sounds drunk. Boyce had blocked off any idea the guy might have had of running towards Hanover and I had the other direction covered. Boyce was waiting for the guy to pull up his pants before putting the cuffs on."

Miller wants to ask if this girl is Maryanne, but doesn't want to interrupt. After a deep breath, Kristen resumes her narrative.

"So, I'm sitting there with this girl, sitting on a cement slab on a chilly night, and normally, in that situation, I would have been disgusted with the whole thing. A couple of two-bit crackheads giving a five dollar blow job in a dirty alley, all so they could buy another fix. I'd been in Vice just a couple of months and it seemed like this is what I had to deal with every night. Suddenly, I just wanted to slap this poor girl as hard as I could and yell at her to wake the fuck up. But just then she turned to look at me, and when I looked into those eyes, those huge brown eyes, I felt my heart break. They were the saddest eyes I had ever seen. They were eyes that you could look into and see to the very depth of the person's soul, and there was nothing but sadness all the way into that abyss.

"The women on the streets, well, you know, Erik, in their eyes you see hate. Defiance. Fear. Nothing. But in that young woman's eyes, that night, all I saw was an incredible sadness, and I don't know what came over me."

Day looked up from her hands. "I never imagined I had a maternal bone in my body, but I think that was what I was feeling. I mean, it took my breath away. I was trembling. Boyce got the cuffs on the guy and called for a cruiser to come and take him, and then asked if I was ready. I told him I needed a minute. I remember him saying, what for. I ignored him. I asked the girl her name. She whispered Maryanne. Those brown eyes suddenly teared up, as if saying her name caused her pain. And then I said, and I swear to God I don't know why I said it, I want to help you. I didn't think it. The words just came out of my mouth. She smiled at that. It was a smile that broke my heart. It was a smile that said, 'you know how many others have said that to me, but didn't mean it.'

"Boyce again asked what I'm doing. Again, I ignored him. I tell Maryanne that I will help her. I tell her to meet me in front of the old Union Leader building at midnight. I want to talk to her. I'll buy her something to eat and we'll talk. I make her promise to be there. She says she will. Then I tell her to walk away. When Boyce saw her get up and start walking towards the exit, he asked me what the hell I was doing. The cruiser pulled up in front of the alley on Hanover as Maryanne walked out to Amherst. I watched her until she turned the corner, then I walked over to where Boyce was standing with the guy.

"'You want to explain that to me', Boyce said. But instead of answering him, I punched the drunk right in the solar plexus. He doubled over, lost his diner, and gasped for air for the next five minutes. If the other cops hadn't been entering the alley, I would have kicked the guy right in the teeth. Boyce was yelling something at me as I walked back onto Hanover.

"After my shift, I drove to Amherst Street and the Union Leader building. I didn't really expect Maryanne to be there. In fact, I was kicking myself for letting her go. It was a stupid thing to do. She was a junkie whore and she should have been arrested. Sure enough, she wasn't in front of the building. But I decided to park and give her fifteen minutes. After a few minutes, she stepped from the shadows. I lowered the passenger side window and we stared at each other for several seconds, then she opened the door and got in the car. She looked straight ahead and never said a word and continued looking straight ahead as I drove her here. She never once asked where I was taking her. She offered no resistance when I took her arm and walked her inside. And the whole time I'm thinking, what the hell am I doing."

Kristen sat very still, staring at her hands folded in her lap. Miller picked up the milk container and drank it down, then stood at the end of the tether staring at her. He could see she was in some emotional distress and he didn't want to give her time to regain her composure.

"So then what happened?" he demanded. "How do I become involved in all of this? Is your beef with me because I got Homicide and you got Vice? Is that it? If you had gotten Homicide, you never would have met Maryanne? So, it's my fault that you did? Is that how you see it? Because I got what you wanted, you got involved with her and that makes it my fault when it didn't go the way you wanted? You're going to blame me for your screw-up? You bring an addict into your home, and when she screws you over, you're looking to lay the blame for it on someone else. In hindsight, Day, you can't see that you were a patsy?"

Kristen scowled at him. "You think you're so goddamned smart, Miller, don't you? You know nothing." She sneered at him. "Do you have any idea how I posed Kay Lawrence on the side of the road with Officer Parent sitting in a car a hundred feet away?"

Miller said nothing.

"Of course you don't. Never occurred to you. Never thought to look beyond the obvious. Parent says he may have nodded off for a few minutes. Your feeble brain believes it to be bad luck that the killer picked those exact few minutes to show up with the body. Jut like with Seward in the cemetery. Bad luck. See if this makes more sense? After you opened the box, you take off to do something, leaving me to call our crew and set them up in the designated spots. So I put Parent on Lake Shore Road. I know his wife just had a baby. He's probably a little tired already. Lack of sleep and all. Lake Shore Road is where I want to leave Kay. At midnight, I check on Parent. He's doing fine. I bring him a coffee with cream and sugar and a little something extra. He thanks me. I drive by again at two. He's out cold."

Miller let the taunt hang in the air for several seconds, then he very quietly said, "Tell me about Maryanne. Why did you have to kill her?"

Day came off the stool and stood within a foot of where Miller could reach her.

"Kill her?" Day shouted in anger. "I saved her. I...saved...her!"

"And then you killed her."

"Fuck you! I can't expect you to understand. Your wife leaves you and you become a monk. Crawl into your little cocoon and don't allow anyone in."

"My wife may have left me," Miller said, standing at the end of his tether, "but I didn't want to kill her because of it."

Day sneered, "Then you didn't love her enough, Miller."

"Tell me what happened with Maryanne."

"Shut up about her."

"Tell me about Maryanne. I have a right to know."

"You have a right to die!"

"Tell me! What did I do?"

Kristen had balled her hands into fists and her eyes blazed, but she didn't lash out. Instead, she slumped back onto the stool.

"You're a son-of-a-bitch," she whispered.

"I did nothing, Kristen. Whatever happened between you and Maryanne is all on you. You brought her here. What did she do? Did she steal from you like she did with the men from Lowell? Take something of value. So valuable, that when you met up with her again, after, what, four years, you killed her for it."

"You don't understand."

"No. I don't. So tell me. I want to understand. What did Maryanne do that was so terrible that she had to die for it? And how am I tied into it?"

"It doesn't matter now."

"It does to me."

A minute of their lives ticked by in silence. Kristen sighed.

"When I got her into the kitchen, I could finally see her in enough light to really see her. She was a mess. She was dressed in soiled denim jeans and a white tee shirt under a beige sweater that was way too big for her. Her face was so thin. Dried blood from the fall was still on her forehead, and the welt under her eye had turned a deep purple. Her hair was a mess. I put some food in front of her, but she only picked at it. I didn't think it would be a good idea to ask her a lot of questions right then, so we spoke little. I told her who I was. Asked where she was staying. Real simple questions without digging too much. I asked if she would like to take a bath. I remember, she actually smiled when I asked. While she ate, I ran a bath for her."

Kristen was looking down at her hands again. Miller sank to a sitting position on the mattress. He was aware that only a few minutes before he had almost caused her to get close enough to him to take a swing at him. He needed to try and get her that angry again.

"Maryanne came into the bathroom just as the water was reaching the level needed. Without any hesitation, she stripped off her clothes, neatly folding them and putting them on the hamper. Her legs and arms were so thin. I don't think she weighed ninety pounds. She had a nasty bruise on her right thigh, a bigger one at the base of her back, a smaller one under her right breast. She stepped into the tub and slid down into the water, her eyes closed. She let me wash her hair and her back, and I left her there to take as much time as she wanted."

Kristen looked up.

"I was going to take her clothes and wash them, but I thought that whatever drug she was on, if she was on something, and I thought she was, she probably had a supply in her pants pocket. If she stayed with me, there would come a time to get her off the drugs. If she didn't stay, then why destroy what she had. She'd only get more. That was not the time. That was a Friday night. By the beginning of the next week, that time had come.

"That first weekend, she slept late each day, almost to noon. She ate sparingly at first, but by Sunday night her appetite had returned. At night we watched television, but during the day she watched me working around the house, watched me doing my exercises, watched me cook, asked me a lot of questions about when I was a kid, where I grew up. Asked me a lot of questions about being a cop. If I had a boyfriend, parents, siblings. How come I didn't have a dog. But by Monday morning, I could see she was becoming agitated. I figured whatever drugs she had brought with her were now gone. It was time we had a serious talk."

Kristen Day looked sadly at Miller sitting across from her.

"I don't want to talk about this anymore, Erik."

"Yes, you do, Kristen. Yes, you do. You should have talked with someone a long time ago about this, and you know it. So you'll talk about it now."

She sneered at him. "You seem to forget which one of us is the prisoner."

"From where I sit," said Miller, "it looks like we both are.

Tell me about Maryanne."

After several long seconds where Kristen's eyes had darted around the cellar, and color had risen on her cheeks, she took in a deep breath and said, "I sat her down at my kitchen table. She was fidgeting, but I told her we had to talk. I told her I knew she was on drugs. I asked her what she was taking. She shrugged. Whatever she could score. Then she asked if I had any. I told her I did not. I remember, I wanted to reach out and take her hands in mine. I wanted to whisper to her not to worry. That everything would be okay. But I didn't.

"Instead, I said to her, that if she really wanted to, I would help her get off the drugs. But only if she really wanted to. I would help her and be with her every step of the way. She could stay with me. I would take care of her. She would be safe. But she had to be free from the drugs. I wasn't going to have an addict living in my house.

"She started to cry. She told me she was scared. I said of course you are. But what do you want? I told her I had to leave for work at three. Either she could stay here, or I could drive her back to where I had picked her up. But if she stayed, we would need to take precautions."

"Precautions?" Miller asked.

"I handcuffed her to the legs of the oil tank before I left. I put a rug down for her to lie or sit on, gave her water and a sandwich, and a radio. She understood the need of it. She was calm when I left, but a raving maniac when I returned nine hours later. I freed her and brought her upstairs, all the while she was calling me every name in the book. I pointed at the front door and calmly said you can leave if you want. Door's open. She went to the door. But you can't ever come back, I said. You leave, you can never come back. She had her hand on the doorknob and stood there for what seemed an eternity. I stood in the kitchen watching, my heart almost beating out of my chest.

Suddenly, she sobbed this terrible painful wail that wracked her thin body, and she sank to her knees crying and shaking. I went to her then, and knelt beside her. She turned and hugged herself to me fiercely, the strength in those thin arms surprising me with their need. She cried and shook and held onto me for dear life. After a while the tears stopped, but her grip on me did not loosen. And then, in this voice that sounded like it came from a child, she said, 'Please hold me. Don't let me go.'"

Kristen became quiet. She sat, staring at the model of King Kong, not saying anything.

"Then what?" Miller asked after several minutes.

Turning her gaze from the model to her captive, Day looked at him in silence for several seconds, then she stood and walked towards the stairs.

"What happened then, Day?" demanded Miller. He walked to the end of the tether. "Where are you going? Tell me about Maryanne. What happened?"

He had hoped to agitate Day into becoming physical, but instead she turned to face him, one foot on the first stair.

"You're a son-of-a-bitch, Erik," she said. There was no anger, just sadness. "A real son-of-a-bitch."

She went up the stairs and closed the door behind her. Miller listened to see if she was throwing another fit in anger, but he heard nothing from upstairs. He sat down and began eating the food she had brought.

He was now sure that he had never met, or arrested Maryanne. Day's problem with him, he reasoned then, must be something that happened between Day and Maryanne that Megan was a part of. Whatever it was, it may not have happened had he brought Megan in to the station that rainy night. How could anyone blame him for that, he wondered. How could he possibly be blamed for that? He had only done what Day had done with Maryanne. He had taken pity on a child of the streets.

28

KRISTEN DID NOT go back into the cellar after leaving Miller standing there demanding she tell him more. Instead, after leaving the basement, she sat on the sofa, hugged a throw pillow to her body, and stared out through the large picture window in the living room at the woods across the road from her property, remembering the many times she had sat there, staring out through that window while lightly stroking Maryanne's long brown hair. Maryanne would lie on the sofa, her head in Day's lap, her hand gently resting on her protector's thigh. They would sit like that for hours, sometimes never saying one word to each other, and Day could never remember a time when she was more relaxed, or more content.

She sat on the sofa as daylight became dusk, dusk became night and she woke the following morning with the first light of day, still sitting up on the couch, still holding the pillow. Her long legs cramped as she straightened out and stretched. After working out the cramps, she showered, dressed and opened the cellar door. When she walked down the stairs, she saw Miller curled up under the blanket along the wall. The cellar reeked of his body odor and his bodily waste. He had placed the five gallon bucket as far from him as he could. Day lifted the bucket, brought it out to the yard, dumped it and washed it out. When she brought it back in, Miller was sitting up, leaning against the wall. They stared at each other for several minutes, then Kristen placed two bottles of water in the bucket and set the bucket down where Miller could reach it. She then went to the bench and picked up the book that had been written by Gaston Leroux. Taking the book, she started back up the stairs. Halfway up, she stopped and turned.

"William Kemba Jackson," Day said. She stood looking at Miller impassively, then went up the stairs, shut off the light and closed the door, leaving Miller in darkness once again.

Miller crawled over to where Day had left the bucket, reached in and took the bottles out, then urinated into the bucket. Sitting in the darkness once again, he drank down half a bottle of water and searched his mind for any reference to a William Kemba Jackson. He didn't have far to search.

Jackson had been a low level drug dealer whose life had come to an abrupt end when he was stabbed to death in his first floor apartment on Wilson St. Miller had been the first Detective on the scene when it got called in. The police had arrived at Jackson's door after an anonymous phone call. They found Jackson slumped over on a vinyl covered couch in the front room, an eight inch hunting knife lethally embedded deep in his chest. An autopsy would later confirm that the knife had made six other journeys into the soft tissue of Jackson's obese body.

The police had also found, sitting beside the dead man and snoring loudly, one Manny Alonzo. When Detective Miller had arrived on the scene, he found Manny in cuffs sitting in the kitchen, looking like he had no idea where he was or why he was there. He swore he couldn't remember anything. Why was there blood on his clothes? he was asked. Manny didn't know. Was that his hunting knife in Jackson's chest? Yeah, Manny said, but he didn't put it there. He liked Kemba. Kemba sold good shit and would cut Manny some slack if Manny was light. He would never kill Kemba. They were friends. Then how did the knife end up in the dealers body? Poor Manny had no idea. Or so he said.

Miller now remembered that Manny, while being questioned at the station, said that while he and Kemba were sitting on the couch enjoying some really good stuff, he had taken out the knife that he had just acquired and showed it to Kemba. He said that Kemba had agreed it was a fine looking knife. And then there was a knock on the door. Manny remembered Kemba went to answer the knock, but admitted that everything right about then was beginning to get a little hazy. He heard loud voices. He saw two people entering the apartment. It looked like a tall guy and a little kid, but things were kind of spinning and he was heading off to dreamland, so he couldn't be sure. Manny, at his trial, testified that he remembered two people coming into the apartment, that there was an argument between them and Kemba, but then he passed out. Next thing he knew, he was sitting at the kitchen table in handcuffs, asking what the hell was going on. Manny got thirty to life.

Miller, sipping water on the soiled mattress in the dark, wondered what the hell Kemba Jackson and Manny Alonzo had to do with Maryanne Darrow.

DAY HAD SPENT another boring day in court waiting to be called on to testify. The defendant had refused the deal that the DA had offered the day before, but after two more witnesses had testified in the morning, the defending attorney had asked for a meeting at the bar. The judge then called a recess. At two-thirty, the judge informed the courtroom that a plea deal had been accepted and they were all free to go. Day then drove to the station, reported in to Hendricks, and then drove home, after stopping to buy bread, grape jelly and a bag of Oreos. After a a long, hot shower, she put on the soft, cotton robe over her naked body, made up two plates of peanut butter and jelly sandwiches, Oreos and milk, and switched the light on in the cellar. Miller was sitting up in the same place she had left him that morning. She placed a plate where he could reach it, then sat on the stool.

She nibbled at her sandwich, waiting for him to say something. When he didn't, she reached up to the higher shelf where she kept the vhs cassettes, her robe once again riding high up on naked thighs. She took her time finding the movie she wanted.

"I don't want to watch a movie," said Miller from where he sat.

"I really don't care what you want, Erik. I'm putting the movie on. Close your eyes. Go to sleep. Talk to yourself if you want. Sing out loud. I don't care. It's a silent movie and I'm watching it."

"What does Jackson have to do with Maryanne?" Miller asked, coming to his feet and walking towards her, the chain dragging behind.

"After the movie," said Kristen as she slid the cassette into the player.

"No! Now," demanded Miller.

She turned angrily, the robe parting slightly as she did, partially revealing quite a bit of naked skin beneath the fabric. "After the movie I said, or never. Take your pick, Miller. I can watch it upstairs, and you will never know about Billy Kemba Jackson. What's it going to be?"

Miller stared at her, and then slowly sank to a sitting position as his eyes lingered on the opened robe and the fullness of her breasts under it. He was sure that was what she wanted him to do, for whatever reason, so he did. Kristen leaving the cellar did him no good at all. He needed her to stay there with him. Needed her to remain so he could try to push buttons that would set her off. If that meant letting her put the movie on, so be it.

If it meant looking like he was being distracted by the flashes of bare skin, well, he could do that, too.

WHEN MY GRANDFATHER read the book to me, and he had to say Christine Daae's name, he always said Kristen, or Kristen Day instead," said Kristen as she replaced the VHS cassette into its protective cover. "That was his little joke. He made such a big deal out of our names being similar, and because he did, I felt very special. By the end of the book, I could see me escaping from the Paris Opera House as the flames engulfed it."

"Your grandfather read the book to you?" asked Miller. He had spent as much time watching Kristen watching the movie as he had watching the movie. He had the feeling, watching her, that during the movie, Day had completely forgotten where she was and who was with her, so enthralled did she seem watching the film.

"He read all the books to me, watched all the movies with me, and we built seven models together. He loved me very much. And I loved him. It was wonderful what we shared."

"Is he still alive?" asked Miller, looking for something that he could use to reach her emotionally.

Day sat very still, looking down at him from the safety of the stool.

"If I had read the book to you," she said, "you would have seen several differences between the book and the movie. I'm not even going to point them out to you, Miller. Waste of my time. But isn't it interesting that the girl's name is so close to mine, and the Phantom, the man who is going to show her how to be great, his name is Erik. Just like you. Crazy, huh, that we should end up working together, and being together when you meet your end, just like when Erik supposedly met his in the book."

Kristen smiled cruelly. "Tell me, when Hendricks told you he was going to have me work with you, did he, knowing that you preferred working alone, did he say what a great opportunity it would be for the new girl to have the chance to work with, and learn from, the great Detective Erik Miller? I can just see him saying that to you. Me, the eager student, desperate to learn, and you, the golden boy, showing me how it's done. What bullshit."

Miller took a long sip of water from a bottle.

"Considering how lost you seemed in your first two investigations," he said, "it was obvious you needed some guidance."

He saw her eyes flash, but she didn't rise to the bait. Instead, she said, "So, you and Hendricks thought the guy whose investigation got Manny Alonzo thirty to life for the stabbing death of Billy Jackson, was the guy who could mentor me? Wow, were you two sadly mistaken."

Miller stared at her. Day smiled back as she picked up her empty plate and milk carton and walked to the steps.

"Manny Alonzo never stabbed anyone," she said. "He was out cold on the couch. Megan the Roach stabbed Billy Kemba Jackson."

Kristen walked up the stairs and closed the cellar door, leaving Detective Erik Miller yelling after her and calling her a liar.

IT WAS ALMOST midnight when Kristen descended the cellar steps once more. Miller was sitting in the middle of the mattress, his arms hugging drawn up knees, the blanket draped over him. Kristen, still in the green robe, sat on the stool and looked at him. She tossed another bottle of water at his feet.

"Maryanne stayed here two hundred and fifty-six days," Day said, her voice and demeanor calm. "In the beginning, like I said, I wanted to help her. She shook the addiction. It wasn't easy, but she did. I found myself falling in love with her. She was so fragile, so vulnerable, in those first two months. She needed me.

And I needed someone to need me. I was lost at the time, too. My last relationship with someone of any duration had been over a year before. I was desperate for the touch of another human being. I ached for it. But as great as my need was, I made no overtures towards her. I feared doing so would cause her to leave. Maryanne slept in the room next to mine. Boundaries weren't imposed, just understood."

Kristen fell silent for several seconds, then she shrugged. "By the fourth month, she was gaining weight, no longer skin and bones. She was doing some of the cooking and cleaning. Keeping busy. I had planted a small garden and she delighted in weeding and watering it. She was tanned, her hair lightening up, muscles toning from being outside. She talked more." Kristen smiled. "She had a way of talking, when she was really into it, of appearing almost breathless. Her eyes lit up. She was very animated with her hands. Her laugh, oh, God, her laugh, was so infectious you couldn't help but laugh with her."

Kristen looked down at her hands folded in her lap.

"It was during that time, those warm days of early summer, when I would see her out back, gardening or just sun bathing, and she would take my breath away, she was so beautiful. One day we were just sitting out there, talking, being lazy, and I must have been looking at her in a way that she sensed my desire for her. I saw it immediately in her eyes. That she knew. I remember turning away. I was so frightened that she would think me horrible. That night, I hardly slept. The next day, while at work, I worried that when I returned home, she would not be here. That she would be so repulsed by what she now knew of me, that she would flee. But when I got here, it was almost midnight, she had cooked a very nice meal and we sat in the kitchen, eating and talking about our lives when we were kids. When we finished eating, I thanked her for the meal, and went in for a shower. When I came out of the bathroom, the lights were off and I quietly crawled into bed, saying a silent prayer that she had not left.

"I remember taking in a deep breath and slowly letting it out, releasing the last of the tension I had been feeling all night at work that Maryanne would not be here. And then I felt a movement beside me and I froze. Suddenly, soft lips were gently kissing my naked shoulder, moving slowly up to my neck and then finding my own lips. I was so stunned, I couldn't move. When Maryanne kissed my lips, her naked body came in full contact with mine, and it was then I reached out for her, pulling her tight against me, feeling the softness and warmth of her. I remember a cry escaped me, so great was my need. I felt her tense, because she didn't understand why I would cry. But then I began kissing her, smothering her face, neck and breasts with such passion that she relaxed. Immediately, she realized how much I needed and wanted her. It was then she took control. In college, I had had an older lover who took me to heights that girls my age had no idea could be reached. Maryanne, younger than me, took me to those heights again. And when we were done, it was Maryanne who now held me while tears of relief dampened my cheeks."

Kristen became quiet. Miller watched her, vaguely aware that she had slurred a few words and may have had some wine while sitting upstairs alone. Whatever she said next, if she said anything at all, he would use it to try and anger her. He sat quietly.

"From that night, until the day she left, we shared a bed together every night. Those five months, they were the happiest days of my life. Before Maryanne, I had had lovers who I thought I loved, women like Helena Johnson, but with Maryanne I finally understood real love."

"I could tell how much you loved her," Miller said harshly, "when I viewed her naked body at the morgue. The deep purple bruising all over her body told me that someone loved her deeply."

Day came off the stool and took a quick step towards him, her eyes angrily flashing. Miller braced himself for an attack. She may have been taller and had martial arts training, but he had forty pounds on her and three days of pent up rage. His plan, if he could get his hands on her, was to choke her to death with the chain that tethered him to the wall. And then wait until someone came to check on her when she didn't show up for work.

But Kristen stopped her advance after two steps and sneered at him.

"When she first came here, she needed me. But after that first night in my bed, the dynamic changed. I needed her. I didn't see it then. But after she left, and I was alone, I saw it clearly. I was empty. I also saw something else very clearly after she left. Maryanne never loved me. She used me. Used my love. Said things to me she didn't mean. Led me to believe things that weren't true. Manipulated me so she could have a roof over her head and food in her belly and warmth on a cold night. It didn't take me long after she left to realize she had never stopped being what she was; a whore. Trading her body for what she needed to survive."

Kristen sat down again and Miller relaxed, angry that he couldn't provoke her further.

"Yes, I hit her," Kristen sneered.

"But not her face," said Miller. "All the others had facial damage. But not Maryanne."

"I couldn't hit her face. Not that face. Not the face that I saw every night in my dreams. I just couldn't."

"You had no problem beating the rest of her, though, did you, Kristen? No one deserves that kind of beating."

"She did!" spat Day. "She deserved it."

"Snapping her neck like she was an animal."

"Shut up!"

"After four years?" said Miller "That's not anger or revenge. That's sick."

"Four years, ten years, a hundred years. What difference does it make? She lied to me. She played me for a fool and did it in the cruelest way."

"Maryanne didn't deserve to die. You are sick, Day. Very sick."

Kristen was red with anger and her head shook violently, but she did not step closer to him.

"Sick? No, I'm not sick, Miller. I'm empty. I've been empty for so long that nothing matters anymore. So many nights I've sat in my living room, staring into the dark outside, gun in hand, desperate to feel something, some emotion, even if it was only sadness at the thought of putting the gun up to my head and pulling the trigger. Even then, I felt nothing. It's not that she tricked me, Erik. I could get past the lies and deceit. Those are things I've dealt with most of my life. I just haven't been able to get past this feeling of being empty. I desire nothing. I dream of nothing. I care for nothing and no one. Not since Maryanne."

Kristen slumped back onto the stool and picked up the model of King Kong again.

"We built this about a month before she abandoned me. She made a big deal out of it while we were doing it, like it was an amazing thing we were doing together. But it was a lie. After she left, not knowing why she left, desperate to know what I had done, or not done, that caused her to leave, I searched for her. I hit every homeless center, every tent city. Contacted every stoolie I had and pressured them to find her. Every prostitute, pimp and druggie I busted, I demanded to know if they knew Maryanne Darrow. No one knew where she was. After a year of that, I gave up. It was obvious to me that she had fled the area. Knowing she was gone wasn't enough, though. I needed to know why."

A slight smile creased Day's face.

"Four years pass. I finally make Homicide. Vice is a thing of the past. And then I see the wedding announcement in the Sunday newspaper. Mr and Mrs. Peter Houle proudly announce the wedding of their son Arthur to Miss Maryanne Darrow. Date, place and time. Just a few lines in the newspaper. Could it be my Maryanne Darrow? I find out where Arthur Houle works. I follow him from work to his apartment in Nashua. I'm there every night. Watching. Waiting. Third night, Maryanne shows up. My Maryanne. I was going to confront her right then and there. Ask her why she left me. Ask what I had done. It was freezing cold that night and the cold must have gotten into my soul. I watched her walk into the apartment building and then I drove off. She wasn't my Maryanne anymore. I came back here, brewed a hot cup of tea, sat at my kitchen table, decided I needed more from her than just answers, and this," Day swept her hands in an arc, "is what I came up with. I would make her suffer like she had made me suffer. I had handcuffed her down here before to save her, I would do it again and maybe, this time, save me."

"I can understand revenge, Day. I don't condone it, but I understand it. But why kill Helena Johnson? Once you did that, you went from killer to psycho. You must realize that."

Kristen scoffed. "Don't grieve her death, Erik. Helena was a first-class bitch. I was young when I met her. Young, impressionable and naive. I thought she loved me, and I loved her. There were so many red flags with her that I didn't recognize at the time. She said we couldn't live together because her father, a man well known in the city, didn't know of her life style. If we went out to dinner on the weekend, it was at a restaurant in Boston, or somewhere else in Massachusetts. We vacationed together only twice, both times out of the country. She rarely stayed here overnight, and she lived with her parents, so, obviously, I never stayed there. Actually, I never met her parents. We were together for almost two years before I found out I was not her only lover. Helena was cheating on me, I think right from the start, although I might have been the one she was cheating on someone else with. I was never quite sure about that. When I had her here, last March, she wouldn't admit to that, but I think that was how it went down. There was a woman, an older woman, who she had been in a relationship with that had lasted years. Helena, when I met her, said that that relationship was over. That I was the only one she loved. She was a lying bitch. She got what she deserved."

Kristen smiled.

"And then I decided to pose her at the museum, and this whole thing about posing women in scenes from movies, and using names from the movies, just came to me out of the blue. And, of course, end game was getting you down here. And you know what? Having them here, doing things from a happier time in my life, gave me a purpose for going on. It's unfortunate that the women had to die, but for the first time in a very long time, I felt alive."

"Unfortunate that they had to die?" Miller yelled out. "They didn't have to die. You killed them. For absolutely no good reason, those poor women are dead. You are the sick bitch, Kristen. Not Helena Johnson. You."

Kristen shrugged. "We'll agree to disagree on that."

She smiled then, and spoke to him as if he were sitting across from her at a diner instead of chained to a wall in her cellar. "You'll get a kick out of this, Erik. One night, at a Y2K party in one of Helena's fathers restaurants, guess who was there? Never mind, I'll tell you. Doctor Thomas Thomas. Crazy, huh? When he came in, Helena was standing beside me at the bar, of course we were being discreet because her dad was there, and when Thomas walked in Helena pointed to him and said, 'there's

Tommy, the doctor who saved daddy's life'. And guess who was on his arm? You'll never guess. Doctor Gallagher. Small world, huh?"

Kristen became quiet as the smile faded.

"Did you ever find out why Maryanne left you?" asked Miller, moving a little closer to where Day sat. He was going to try and anger her. "Did you beat it out of her? Or did you just hit her over and over again, and not care anymore why she left?"

Day's eyes flashed in anger. "Whether I found out or not, she deserved what she got." Day sneered cruelly as she slid from the stool and stood in front of Miller. "But I did find out why she left, and that's what brought you into our little drama, Detective Miller. The reason why you're here. The reason why your ineptitude caused all of this."

"Bullshit," spat Miller angrily, as Day moved towards the steps.

"Bullshit? No. Had you been a better cop, a better detective, none of this would have happened."

Day began walking up the steps.

"What did Maryanne tell you?" Miller demanded. "What did I do?"

"Tomorrow night we build the model, Erik. The next night you get to choose colors. It'll be fun."

"What did Maryanne say, Kristen? What did she say?"

Miller was still yelling long after the door to upstairs had closed.

Sliding to his knees on the mattress, alone again in the dark, Miller was frustrated. His attempts at getting Day to lash out at him had failed, and because they had he feared he would die in her cellar. If he couldn't get his hands on her, he would surely die. When she came down again, he decided, pulling the blanket tighter around him in the chill of the basement, he would not participate in any model building. That would anger her, he was sure. He would pester her, demand to know more about what Maryanne had confessed during the beating she had suffered. Demand to know what Megan Riley had said during her beating. Demand to know his part in all this madness. If his demands drove her to kill him before she wanted to, so be it. Either way, he was a dead man if he couldn't get her within his reach.

29

DETECTIVE KRISTEN DAY had spent all of Thursday in court waiting to testify in a case that she had been involved with when she was still with Vice. It was late afternoon when she entered the bullpen, reported to Hendricks, reviewed the missing persons list, as she did every day just to keep up pretenses, and then nodded on her way out to Matt Blanchette, who was busy getting his files in order before his retirement date. Leaving police headquarters, Day got in her black Jeep and headed for home, where Erik Miller would be waiting.

They had built the model of the Phantom the night before. Actually, Kristen had built it while Miller demanded answers to questions that she ignored. She knew he was trying to anger her and she thwarted the attempt. But she had decided while in court that morning, that she would tell him all he wanted to know while she painted the model. Kristen felt he should know what he had done. He should know all of the harm he had caused. And then Erik could take that blame to his death when he perished in the fire that would consume everything. Everything except Kristen Day. She had decided, that very day while sitting in court, that she would not end her life. Not yet, anyway.

That morning in a sparsely populated courtroom, she had

realized that she now felt a sense of peace inside of her that had been missing for over four years. That for the first time in years, she had a desire to live. To go on. When she had thought about it some more, sitting alone in the rear of the courtroom, she believed she knew why she now wanted to live. With the deaths of Maryanne Darrow, Megan Riley, and soon Erik Miller, she realized she would be turning the final pages of the drama. That that chapter of her life could now be closed and she could finally move on to the next chapter. Uncertain what that may be though she was, still, she would be ready for it. The Universal Killer would kill no more.

As Day pulled out of the parking lot, Tony Pierce and Angel Carbone, standing across the busy street, watched.

"Tony, let's just go," Angel said. She was hugging Tony Pierce, her face resting on his chest, her eyes watching the black vehicle disappearing in the distance.

Tony gently rubbed her back, the polyester jacket she wore cool to the touch. Angel was such a worrier, he thought, and he was glad that she was. Because when she worried, and he did something that eased that worry, he looked like a big man to her. Her hero. Her protector. Tony liked being 'The Guy'.

"It's okay, Angel," he said. "She's gone. Come on."

He took her hand and crossed the street. At the door to the police station, Angel stopped.

"This isn't a good idea, Tony. Why do we have to get involved?"

Tony Pierce smiled at Angel Carbone, the back of his hand gently rubbed her cheek.

"I think we owe Megan, Angel. She was a friend. We should do this."

In reality, Tony didn't believe they owed Megan anything. But the big cop bitch had slammed him into a tree and she was going to pay for doing that. Just who the hell did she think she was?

"I don't think she would have done the same for us," said Angel, with pleading eyes and several shakes of her worried head.

"No," said Tony, "she would have. She was a fighter, Angel. She told us what she did for her friend. She would have done the same for us if we were in trouble. I know she would have."

He took her hands in his.

"Look, we'll just tell this Miller guy what you saw, and then we're done with it. That's all. Just tell him what you saw, Angel, and then we leave. Okay?"

Angel was shaking her head, but she said, "Okay," and entered the station when Tony opened the door for her.

"Detective Blanchette," said the Desk Sergeant into the phone, "I got a couple down here who want to talk with Detective Miller. Says it's real important. You have time to talk with them?"

"What's it about?" asked Blanchette.

"Something about Megan Riley, they say. Her death. They have information, they say."

Matt Blanchette looked into Hendricks office. The Chief was on the phone.

"Send them up," he said.

Blanchette looked at Tony and Angel as they came through the doors. He introduced himself, then had them sit at his desk. Tony was about his height, mid-twenties probably, with the beginnings of a full beard. He wore a winter coat over dirty jeans. Angel was thin, about five foot five, with straight orange hair that was cut short and black makeup that circled frightened eyes, like a raccoon caught in the glare of headlights. She wore heavy black boots and black denim jeans.

"What do you know about Megan Riley?" Blanchette asked, getting right to the point.

Tony Pierce looked around the mainly empty room.

"Where's Miller?" he asked.

"Detective Miller is on an assignment at this time. But I'm working on Megan Riley's murder, also, so you can tell me what you think you know."

"Tony, we should go," whispered Angel.

Tony took another slow look around the room and patted Angel's hand. "It's okay," he said.

"Megan was a friend of ours," said Tony. "We been hanging out the past few months, know what I mean?"

"Where was that?" asked Blanchette.

"Our settlement over on Valley Street," said Tony. "Angel and I been there about a year, and Megan set up about four months ago. She was chill. Kept to herself. But eventually, we got friendly. For an older woman, she was okay. Not a lot of crazy, like most of the older ones. Screamin' shit all night long in their tents, know what I mean? She was quiet. Angel here is good with stuff like hair and nails and she did some stuff for Megan. You know, her hair and stuff."

"Sure," said Blanchette, almost smiling at the thought that Megan, at twenty-eight years old, was thought to be an old woman by Tony. "When was the last time you saw Megan?"

"Well, we'd see her everyday," said Tony. "Her tent was only a few spots away from ours."

"When did you notice her missing?"

"About a week before her picture was in the newspaper showing she was dead," Tony said. "But we didn't think she was missing all that time."

"Why not?"

Tony looked at Angel who was fidgeting with her chair.

"Tell him, Angel," Tony said.

"I think we should go," whispered Angel again.

Blanchette smiled. "It's okay, Angel. Just tell me what you know. You've done nothing wrong."

Angel fidgeted some more and wouldn't look at Blanchette. She was looking at Tony, who was smiling and nodding, when she said, "It was just getting dark when I came up the hill to the big crypt and saw Megan being led out to the street by this woman."

"You said it was dark," interrupted Blanchette. "How could you tell it was a woman Megan was with?"

Angel glanced at Blanchette, then looked past him to a photo on the wall. "There is a street light at the entrance," she said. "It was on. But I know the difference between a woman's walk and a guys. It was a woman. She was a lot bigger than Megan, but I could tell she was a woman. And when she got to her car, I got a good enough look at her face in the light to know it definitely was a woman."

"Okay," said the detective. "Did Megan get in the car?"

Angel nodded.

"Did she get in, or was she forced into the car?"

"It looked like Megan was helped into the car. Like she was shaky on her legs. The woman had her by the arm as they were walking. Almost like she was steadying her or something. Know what I mean?"

"Sure," said Blanchette. "So you couldn't tell if Megan was going into the car of her own free will or if she was being forced?"

Angel looked at Tony, then gave a slight shake of her head.

"And that was the last time either of you saw Megan Riley?"

"Yeah," said Tony.

"Any idea what kind of car Megan got into?" Blanchette asked.

"It wasn't a regular car," said Angel. "It was high off the ground. Boxy. Black. Not like a regular car or SUV."

"Okay," said Blanchette. "Well, I want to thank you for coming forward. What took you so long? Megan went missing almost a month ago. If you had come in right away, it would have been better."

"We didn't know she was kidnapped until her picture showed up in the newspaper," said Tony. "We thought she might be with a friend. She had some people she knew looking for her kids. We thought maybe one of them found them and were taking her to them."

"Kids," said Blanchette. "What kids?"

"Megan had two kids," said Tony, pleased that he had information that, obviously, the police did not. "A two year old girl and a one year old boy. She wore a locket that had their pictures in it. Cute kids, huh, Angel?"

Angel nodded.

"And then," Tony continued, "Miller shows up at the camp with the locket."

"And where are the kids now?" asked the detective.

"Megan didn't know. From what she told us, she has lived on the street for years, ever since she was seventeen, but five years ago a friend of hers, a very good friend she said, convinced her that there was a better way to live. Megan used to do drugs. Her friend got her to stop. The friend got Megan into a rehab and then into meetings."

"That was where she met Bobby," said Angel, smiling.

"Bobby?" asked Blanchette.

"Don't know his last name," said Tony.

"He's the dad of Julia and James," said Angel.

"Megan's kids?" asked Matt.

Angel nodded.

"And Megan didn't know where they were?"

"No," said Angel, comfortable now in speaking and looking at the detective. "Megan told us Bobby took them away when Megan started doing drugs again. Told her he wasn't going to have his kids raised by a mother who was an addict. Said that's how he was raised and look how it had messed him up."

"So, one day he left the apartment where they were living," said Tony. "Took Julia and James and never returned. That was last year."

"And where did this happen?"

"Portland," said Tony. "Megan thought Bobby might have come to Manchester because he has family in the area, so she came back here, but she never found him."

"Anything else?" Matt asked.

Tony looked at Angel. Angel looked back at the photo on the wall.

"What?" asked Blanchette.

"Tell him, Angel."

Blanchette looked at the nervous girl. "It's okay," he said.

When Angel said nothing, Tony spoke up.

"Angel thinks she saw the woman again who took Megan that night."

"You think you could recognize this woman," asked Blanchette, looking at Angel, "even though you only saw her face from a long distance away and only under a streetlamp?"

Angel gave a nervous shrug.

"Angel knew it was her as soon as she saw her again," said Tony. "She told me. Angel is sure it was her."

"Okay," said Blanchette. "So you saw her again. Where and when did you see her?"

"She was with Detective Miller that day he came into our camp," said Tony. "She got rough with me, and Angel was watching from our tent. She got a real good look at her."

"What do you mean she got rough with you?"

"I said something to Miller," said Tony with a smirk. "Nothing too bad. Next thing I know, she's got her hand on my chest pushing me right into a tree. I thought she was going to crush my ribs."

"She was with Detective Miller?" asked Blanchette harshly. "What the hell are you saying here?"

"Tony we should go," Angel said as she stood up.

"Sit down!" Matt Blanchette demanded. He stared hard at both of them, wondering what the hell they were playing at.

"You know how much trouble you can get into when you lie to a police officer investigating a homicide? Do you have any idea?"

He looked from Tony to Angel who had sat down again. Angel was pale and she trembled.

"We ain't lying," said Tony defiantly. "Why the hell would we lie?"

"Because you got roughed up a little bit by a woman in front of your woman. Did it take you a couple of weeks to come up with this story? You're playing a dangerous game here, son."

"No game. It was her Angel saw. She told me as soon as the cops left. Said that was the woman she saw with Megan that night. And then Megan shows up dead a week later. We knew the cops were searching for Megan. We saw the handouts you guys passed around the city. And then you find her and Megan shows up dead a week later. We don't know what the hell is going on, but Angel and me we're trying to do the right thing here. Angel said we shouldn't do it. Said just forget it. But I say, no, we need to do this for Megan."

Blanchette stared at the two of them. They were implicating Detective Kristen Day in a crime and his first impulse was to not believe what they were accusing her of. Still, he wanted Hendricks to hear this.

"Stay right here," said Blanchette. "I'll be right back."

Detective Blanchette gave them a hard stare to make sure they knew he was serious, then he went to the Chief's door, knocked on it and entered. He told Hendricks what Angel and Tony had told him.

"What bullshit is this?" asked Hendricks.

Blanchette shrugged.

"The girl is petrified, the guy is adamant," said Blanchette. "I called him on it and he never wavered. Swears it went down just like they say it did."

"Well, it's nonsense. The girl said it was dark. She didn't see what she is saying she saw. Bring them in here. I want to talk to them."

Blanchette stepped out into the bullpen. He swore softly..

"They're gone."

Hendricks picked up his phone and dialed the Desk. He was told that the two had left the building a few seconds earlier. The Desk Sergeant looked out through the glass of the doors, but saw no sight of Angel or Tony.

Putting the phone down, Hendricks said, "Call Miller. See if he knows anything about this. Then call Day. See if she actually had tracked down Megan Riley and didn't report it."

Detective Matt Blanchette tried Miller's number and got nothing. He then called Day's cell and was told to leave a message. He told Hendricks the result of his efforts.

"Look," said the Chief, "I don't like it. These two kids might go to the newspaper. Or over to WMUR. I'm not going to be caught with my pants down by some reporter. Get over to Day's place if you can't reach her by phone. I don't want to wait until morning. See what the hell she knows about this. If she found Megan and kept it from us, I'll bust her a new asshole. She'll be back on the streets walking a beat. We could have given that poor girl protection. Maybe, she could have led us to the killer, like Miller has been saying. Jesus Christ, I can't believe this."

"The kids might be lying, Chief."

Hendricks took in a deep breath and released it slowly. "Yeah. Probably. Talk to her and see what she says. Call me after you talk to her."

Blanchette found out where Day lived. He would drive over to Miller's place first and see if he was back from Maine, and then drive out to Goffstown. He continued calling her phone while he drove.

30

Day was nibbling at her sandwich and holding the finished model up, slowly spinning it around. Miller knelt on the edge of the mattress, two feet from the end of the tether and eight feet from where Day sat on the stool. His plate of food remained untouched.

"Obviously," said Kristen, "his suit will be black and the dress shirt white. We can add a little color on the rubble around his feet. But what do you think, Erik, about the cape? Shall we do it black? Or maybe red like the one he wore during the masked ball?"

When Miller made no reply, she said, "We'll do it black. Black would be best. Of course you don't know the cape was red during the ball because you wouldn't let me read you the book. But it was. I love the way he's standing. Don't you? Holding the mask way up high. He really was a monster, you know? The Phantom, as you now know, Erik, now that I have told you what Leroux had written, was a genuine bad man long before he entered the opera house. Of all the monsters, he was the only one genuinely bad. Society didn't create him. He deserved to die."

She looked at Miller then. "Just as you do, Erik."

Erik Miller scowled at her. When she had first come down the steps, in her green robe, carrying their dinner on two paper plates, he had ranted at her trying to anger her, but it hadn't worked. He was channeling his energy for the next attempt.

Kristen placed the model on the bench and selected a small plastic cup of black paint and an artists brush with short bristles. Dipping the brush into the paint, she began on the Phantom's cape.

"It was a Thursday morning," Kristen said in a calm voice, as she applied the paint in firm, short strokes. "The two hundred and fifty-sixth day that Maryanne had been here. I was on the day shift. She was still in bed when I was ready to leave. I stood in the bedroom doorway looking down at her. She was so beautiful."

Day turned towards him. "You have no idea. She could take your breath away, she was so stunning. The pictures you had of her didn't do her justice. And what you saw at the morgue, obviously you couldn't tell. But take my word. She was beautiful."

Day turned back to the model.

"Her hair had grown longer. She was tanned. She was filled out and healthy looking, and lying there that morning with the sheet only covering the lower half of her naked body, I thought myself the luckiest woman in the world. I remember, when she had looked up at me and smiled, it took all of my will power not to call in sick and crawl back into bed with her. At that moment, my heart actually ached at the thought that I would be away from her for the next ten hours. On the way home after work, I stopped and bought a bag of Hershey's Kisses. Maryanne loved Hershey's Kisses. When I got here, she was gone."

Kristen paused, the paint brush hovered above the plastic cup. She let out a soft sigh, then dipped the brush into the paint.

"When I had her here in January, after almost four years of being away from me, I asked her why she had left, Erik. What had I done?"

She looked at him.

"You know what she said? She said I hadn't done anything to make her leave. That she liked being here. That she had loved me and was happy to be with me. You know, all the shit a captive would say to their captor if they thought it would help set them free. The lying little whore. She had fooled me once, she would not fool me again.

"She told me that that day she left, she had been watching the news at noon when the story came on that a man named William Kemba Jackson had been stabbed to death in an apparent drug deal gone bad. The alleged killer, Manny Alonzo, was in police custody. But Maryanne knew that Manny hadn't killed Jackson. Maryanne knew Manny from her time on the streets. Maryanne told me Manny didn't have the balls to kill anyone. But Maryanne knew someone who did. And that someone was Megan."

"Bullshit!" spat Miller.

"Bullshit?" said Day. "No. This is what happened, and it's all on you. That night you picked up Megan Riley from the wet street and put her in your cruiser, she was running from a group of people because she had stabbed a guy in Victory Park. That guy was William Kemba Jackson. But while the wounds required some stitching at the hospital, they were not life threatening. But that night, Megan, along with Maryanne, left Manchester. The city was no longer a safe place for them to be. They spent months on the streets of Boston waiting for things to cool down up here. Then they came back."

"Was there a reason Megan stabbed Jackson?" asked Miller.

"You mean other than she was a psycho bitch?" said Day. "Yeah. A very good reason. Something I probably would have done myself if Maryanne had told me what Kemba had done."

"And what was that?"

"The day before you picked up Megan, Maryanne had gone to Kemba for drugs. She had money. Kemba told her she could keep her money. He wanted to fuck her instead. Even trade. Maryanne said no. She had money. Megan told me Jackson really repulsed Maryanne. Trading sex for drugs was something Maryanne Darrow had been doing for years, but she refused to do it with Jackson. Kemba got angry, grabbed Maryanne, raped her, and was rough doing it. Plus, he took her money and threw the drugs onto her when he was done, leaving her lying on the dirty ground of a backstreet alley. When Megan found out, she went looking for Jackson with the small knife she used for protection. That was the night you picked her up.

"Six months go by. You're now in Homicide. I'm in Vice. Maryanne and Megan come back to Manchester and are right back doing the shit they have always been doing. Soon after, in an alley off Hanover, Maryanne, bleeding from a scrape on her forehead and a worsening bruise under her eye, is sitting with a cop who said she wants to help her. The poor girl, believing Megan will eventually get them both killed, decided to let the cop help her. And when that happened, Megan had no idea where Maryanne was. For the first time in years, Megan and Maryanne are separated.

"From what Maryanne told me when I had her here, Megan went crazy looking for her. She was worried that we had arrested Maryanne. Megan was the girl who went running from the alley that night and when Maryanne didn't show up later at the place they were staying, she thought the cops had brought her in. Because Maryanne was afraid of Jackson, Maryanne had argued that they should not have come back to Manchester. But Megan had promised to look out for her. Megan was feeling guilty that she hadn't. Feeling guilty that she had run from the alley leaving her bestie to fend for herself. Then, when Megan found out we hadn't arrested Maryanne, she hit the streets of Boston, Lowell, Lawrence and Portland, looking for her friend. - her only friend - thinking Maryanne had freaked and had gotten out of town.. When she couldn't find Maryanne on the streets of the other cities, Megan began to think that maybe Jackson had found Maryanne and had killed her in retaliation for the stabbing in the park. Megan, in a rage with those thoughts, came back to Manchester and found out where Jackson was living. Along with this guy she had been shacked up with since coming back to the city, she confronted Jackson in his apartment. Jackson got physical with the guy and while they were fighting Megan saw the knife on the couch where Alonzo was passed out. She grabbed the knife and stabbed Jackson. The boyfriend wiped the handle of her prints, and they left Kemba there to bleed out."

"You got all that from Megan?"

"Mostly from Maryanne, as explained to her by Megan. Megan didn't give shit up easy. That scrawny little bitch could take a punch, I'll tell you. She impressed me. More than Maryanne. Maryanne whimpered the whole time I had her down here. 'I'm sorry. I didn't want to leave. I really did love you. I'll come back. We can be together again.' All that crap. Like I would ever believe her again. Not Megan. She laughed at me through the pain. Even at the end, when she knew I was going to kill her, she was spitting at me when I came at her. I respected that, even though I hated her.

"And do you know why I hated her, Erik? Do you know why? Not because she had led Maryanne into a life of drugs and prostitution, although that was reason enough, but because, when it came right down to it, when Maryanne had to choose between me or Megan, she had chosen Megan. I loved her, and she chose Megan. I took care of her, saved her, and she chose Megan.

"And if you had been a better detective, Erik. If you had investigated further when Manny had told you there was someone else in the apartment. If you had asked around the neighborhood, collected some real facts, maybe the noon news would have reported that Megan Riley had been arrested for the murder of William Jackson. And then there would have been no reason for Maryanne Darrow to come looking for her old friend so she could help her get out of town."

Day placed the brush down and admired her handiwork.

"If it wasn't for you, Erik, Maryanne would still be here, all those women would be alive, and you wouldn't be chained to a wall waiting to die."

Miller suddenly smiled as he looked up at her.

"What are you smiling at, Detective Miller?" Day asked, a puzzling look on her face. "Do you find your death amusing?"

"Not at all. But I was just looking at the model, and thinking how much alike the two of you are."

"Really? In what way?"

"Think about it, Day. You show the world one face, but underneath that mask that you wear lies the monster that you really are. The monster that the world does not see, but is there all the same. Disfigured and ugly. That's you, Day. Disfigured and ugly beneath the mask, just like the Phantom."

Her eyes narrowed. "You think I'm a monster?"

"Of course you are."

"You think I'm ugly?"

"As all monsters are."

"In all monsters there is beauty," Day said as she slipped off the stool, "if only you possess the understanding to see it."

She loosened the tie at her waist and the robe opened, revealing naked skin. She stood looking down at him for several seconds, her face a passive mask. Then she shrugged her shoulders several times until the fabric of the robe was off them, and then the green robe slid slowly from her body to the cement floor, and she stood naked in front of him.

With raised eyebrows, and a teasing smile, she finally asked, "Do you still find me ugly, Erik?"

And then she turned so he could see the scarred back, the damaged skin, the horrible disfigurement.

"What about now?" she asked.

She turned to face him once again and their eyes met and held each other for a long time.

"I've had many lovers that became a one night affair when my deformity was more than they could stomach," Kristen said, making no attempt at picking up the robe. "But my scars had no affect on Maryanne. Actually, I think they made her love me even more. Because, while her scars were deep inside her, and causing her pain, I think she understood that my scars were much worse, because I could not hide them."

Kristen Day stood quietly with eyes closed. Miller calculated that if she would only take two steps closer, he would be able to grab at her ankle, pull her off her feet.

"The first few times we made love, I cringed when her hands hugged me, her fingers caressing my back, gently tracing the ridges and lines of the scars, like a blind person reading Braille. It was such an intimate, alien feeling. None of the others ever did that. Helena went out of her way not to have to hug me. If she did hold me, her hands were on my ass. Even my own mother stopped hugging me after the fire. But with Maryanne, she was so gentle, I found myself craving her touch. The feel of her hands on my back was every bit as erotic as anywhere else she would touch me. I desired that touch, needed it, longed for it, and Maryanne knew it. She knew she was in control. That in those moments of intimacy, I was her slave. I was at her mercy. But you know what, Erik? Despite knowing she had me at her mercy when we were in bed, Maryanne never once took advantage. I always felt that to her, my needs were more important than hers."

Kristen opened her eyes and there were tears in them.

"Is it possible she really did love me, Erik?" she whispered

Miller was about to angrily denounce any such thought in the hope of forcing an angry reaction, when they both heard the sound of a doorbell.

Kristen froze. Miller, not sure he had actually heard what he thought he had, knew as soon as he looked at Day that it must have been the doorbell. Stunned for a second, he scampered as far as he could toward the stairs and began yelling.

"Help!" he cried out. "Call the police. Call the police. Call them now."

At the sound of his voice, Kristen Day recovered quickly. She picked the robe off the floor and desperately searched for the pockets in the folds of cloth. As she did, she moved towards her captive. She knew the doors of the house were thick, but Miller had a loud voice. Two steps from him, her hand found the pocket. One step away, she secured the syringe in her hand and then barreled into Miller taking him to the ground. He let out a painful grunt as his ankle twisted at the end of the tether and he hit the cold cement ground hard on his stomach with all of Day's weight on top of him.

Day used the robe as a shield between her and Miller, covering his face with it to blind and muffle him. The bulk of the garment made it difficult for him to use his arms, and his right leg was useless because of the tether. The robe muffled his screams for help, and Day quickly straddled his upper body, pressing an elbow into his back. Miller tried squirming, but, again, the tension of the chain that held him captive also kept his lower body from freely moving on the floor.

Kristen, her face a mask of rage, cursed at him as she picked a spot on the robe where she thought his head might be, and pounded on it with her free hand. Miller, realizing that the robe kept him from reaching up behind him to grab her, placed both palms on the cement and pushed his body up in a standard push-up maneuver. Kristen was lifted off the ground with him. Her strong thighs squeezed his body in an attempt to hold on, as a rodeo rider would a horse or a bull, but the robe that had shielded her was now a liability. Skin on skin, she could have held him tight, but the robe prevented that. Her body began to slide off him, and only by getting a foot on the ground did she keep herself from being thrown on her side.

Feeling her weight off of him, Miller attempted to roll onto his back, one arm trying to remove the robe from him so he could see her and use his hands. As the robe bunched up around his shoulders, away from his head, he managed to roll onto his right side, the chain holding his right leg out straight and useless. From the corner of his eye, he saw Day's fist coming down at him and she caught him on the right temple, a grazing shot but still it dazed him. His face was then smothered by her right breast when she slipped throwing the punch and her full weight fell on him again. Recovering quickly from the punch, he realized she had had the air knocked out of her when she had landed on his upturned shoulder. He seized the advantage. His left hand reached for her face, seeking her eyes. His right arm, partially pinned under him, only allowed his right hand enough space to reach for the breast that wasn't in his face. He grabbed a hold of the soft tissue and pulled and twisted as hard as he could. Kristen, fighting to regain her breathing, moaned loudly from the pain and began wildly flailing at any part of his body she could hit. An elbow came down on his head, and Miller released his grip on the breast and tried covering up the punches that rained down on him.

Day managed to get her feet flat on the floor as she continued to pummel him, all the while spitting obscenities. With a deft motion, she swept the robe off him and Miller went flat on his back, both arms now available to try and protect his face. She was standing, straddling him, bent over and raining punches down on him that were having their affect. In a reaction that required no thought, he brought his left leg up as hard as he could from that position, the shin making hard contact with bone at her center. Although her buttocks took the brunt of the kick, still, Kristen howled in pain. She stood erect then, ceasing the assault on his head, and tried delivering an angry kick to his groin in retaliation. Blinded by her pain, the kick was off just a little, with Miller's thigh taking the brunt of the force. But there was enough momentum left that made contact and he cried out loudly, feeling the bile rising in him. Kristen gave another poor attempt at his groin, then dropped down on him, straddling his chest. She desperately searched for the syringe and spotted it a short distance away from where his head was. Leaning over to retrieve it, her breasts once again over Miller's head, he weakly reached up to grab one, but she slapped his hand away.

"I think you liked grabbing my tits more than I did, Erik, so we won't be doing that again," she hissed at him as her long arm reached for the syringe. He reached up for her face, but their was little strength left in him, and she slapped his arm away again.

"Time for our partnership to be dissolved, Erik. Say hello to Eve for me when you see her in Hell."

Kristen slipped the guard from the needle and sneered down at him. At last, she thought, it's finally over.

Miller saw the syringe and took a swipe at it, hitting her hand and causing it to slip from her grasp. It fell to his chest and Day grabbed at it before it could roll off of him, her left knee lifting off the cold floor as she did

"You bastard," she screamed. In that second, Miller reached down for every bit of strength he had left. His right arm, free again, reached up, circled her waist, and he rolled his body. Day felt herself toppling over and she placed a free hand out to keep herself from ending up under Miller. With her now off of him, he placed both hands on her left thigh and pushed himself away from her. For the first time since the battle had begun, Miller was not at the end of the tether or under her. He managed to get to his knees and reached down for her ankle at the same time. He knew if she had the opportunity to crawl away, he was a dead man.

He pulled on the ankle, bringing her closer to him. Day then lashed out with her other leg, her foot slamming into his shoulder. The force of the kick propelled him backwards, slamming him into the cement wall. He lost his grip on her ankle. Kristen then had the opportunity to get to her feet and move to a safe distance from him, but, instead, in a rage, she lunged at him. Guttural sounds erupted from her as her fingers tried clawing out his eyes. Miller lifted a hand to shield himself and she bit hard into the soft space between his thumb and index finger. He swore and punched at her face with his other hand. The punch had no effect on her. Her nails were scratching skin from his face and her knee was searching for his groin. And then, in Kristen's uncontrollable rage, she made her fatal mistake.

Kristen shifted her body, bringing it higher up, so she could grab his head, with the intention of slamming it into the wall. When she did that, her weight came off his legs. With her hands on either side of Miller's head, Miller suddenly twisted and lifted. Kristen ended up awkwardly on the floor, her shoulder pressed hard against the wall. Miller's knee drove into her mid-section. Once again, Kristen found herself gasping for air.

There was blood running into Erik's eyes from her scratches. He could feel himself near fainting from the exertion of the fight, coupled with the lack of food and drink from the last five days. He threw several feeble punches, but could tell they were not hurting her. He knew when she regained her breath, she would have him. Through the blood, he saw the chain that tethered him to the wall. As Kristen began to take in deep breaths, Miller grabbed the chain and quickly wrapped it around her neck, falling backwards so that her backside ended up on top of him. He wrapped his legs around her midsection, held on to the chain with every ounce of strength he had left, and slowly pulled it tighter. Kristen clawed at his hands and she jerked her body trying to break free, but she had no way to gain leverage.

"What the hell!" cried out Matt Blanchette from the middle of the cellar steps.

Blanchette quickly moved to where the two detectives sprawled naked on the ground, shocked by what he was witnessing.

"Erik! What the hell?" Blanchette yelled. "Let her go. You're killing her."

Miller had his eyes closed, and was concentrating so hard on keeping tension on the chain and staying conscious that he didn't hear the pleas of Blanchette. Day's legs were kicking wildly into the air, her hands clawing frantically at the chain and the hands that were pulling it tighter around her neck. Blanchette noticed Day's face was turning red. Matt dropped to his knees beside the two of them and began prying Miller's hands away from the chain. "Erik, let go!" he demanded.

Miller opened his eyes and saw his friend. "No, no, no!" he screamed as he felt his fingers being forced open. "She's the killer, Matt. She's The Universal Killer. No. Don't stop me."

But it was too late. With the loosening of the chain, Day managed to unwrap it from her throat and she then used her hands to force Miller's legs apart and she flopped over onto her knees and hands. Day struggled to take air in and she was wobbly on her knees.

Miller was wiping blood from his eyes and when he could

finally see, he saw Detective Blanchette standing near the bench, his gun drawn and pointed at the two of them.

"Matt, she's the killer," Miller said. "Don't take your eyes off of her."

Leaning back on her haunches, Day took in great gulps of air, her chest rising and falling quickly.

"Don't listen to him, Matt," she rasped, a maniacal grin on her face, eyes wild. "I don't know what the hell happened. We were just having some fun, Erik likes it a little rough, and all of a sudden he went crazy. He's never done this before. He just went crazy."

"She's lying, Matt," said Miller, breathing heavy. "Look behind you. The models of all the monsters are on the shelves. Look at me, Matt. Look at my leg. I'm chained to her wall. I've been down here five days. She's The Universal Killer. She killed all those women, Matt. She's a psycho and she's dangerous. If she moves, shoot her."

Blanchette took a step forward and saw that the chain was indeed bolted to the wall, and then took a quick look behind him at the shelf that held the models..

"What the hell?" Blanchette whispered as he finally grasped what was happening. But in that instant, with the gun no longer pointed directly at her, Kristen's long body came up off the floor and leaped at Blanchette. Blanchette saw a blur approaching and fired a shot, but the bullet ended up embedded in the floor joists as Day buried a shoulder into his midsection and drove him into the workbench. The gun fell to the ground as the two of them landed heavily on the cement floor. Immediately, Kristen's strong hands searched for his neck.

Miller stumbled to his feet as best he could. He saw the gun lying next to the workbench, but he was still tethered and it was out of his reach. He dove for Day's feet, but they were inches from his grasp. Coming back onto his feet, he saw that Kristen had Matt under her and she had managed to get her hands on his throat. Matt was wriggling under her, one hand pulling at her hair, the other pummeling her scarred back. Neither was doing damage. Day was shrieking unintelligible sounds as she finally gained the leverage she would need to begin squeezing.

In the insanity of the moment a clear thought came to Miller, and he searched the floor around him. He saw what he was looking for lying near the cotton robe. Hurrying, he picked up the syringe and moved back to where the two detectives were struggling on the ground. Matt was fighting for his life and his struggling had moved Day to where Miller could now reach her. Desperate, Miller dove again towards her body that was sprawled over Blanchette, and he moaned loudly from the shock to his ankle. His left hand stretched for Day's ankle, grabbed a hold, and he pulled on it, but he was only able to move her just a few inches. But it was enough. His other hand, the one that held the syringe, could now reach Kristen's thigh. The needle easily entered and Miller's thumb pushed the plunger all the way down.

Kristen Day didn't feel the needle, so intent was she to choke the life from Matt Blanchette. Matt was trying to pry her hands from his throat, as he felt the life being drained from him, and he feared he would soon pass out. But then her fingers loosened their grip a bit. Then a little more. Then he was able to pull them from his throat with no resistance and he looked at Kristen. Her mouth was open, but sound no longer came from it. Her wild eyes were looking at him, now confused and afraid. When Matt felt her hands lose all aggression, he pushed backwards with his heels trying to get out from under her. And then he stopped pushing as he saw that her eyes no longer held life and her chest no longer brought in air. Looking over her shoulder, he saw Erik Miller lying on the ground, eyes closed and cheek resting on the woman's smooth, white calf, his hand on her thigh, the needle still in her.

EPILOGUE

Detective Erik Miller, wrapped in a blanket, sat on the cement floor beside the oil tank and watched the Goffstown Police doing their job. A paramedic had tended to his wounds and he had already downed two bottles of water. He thought he had dislocated his ankle with that last dive towards Day, but it was just badly damaged. It would heal in a week or two.

Matt Blanchette, his back bruised from being slammed into the workbench, and his throat still red from the fingers of Kristen Day, stood a few feet away with Chief Hendricks. They spoke to each other in hushed tones, Hendricks often shaking his head as if he couldn't believe what he was hearing. Kristen Day still lay where she had died, but they were getting ready to take her away.

Miller considered himself very fortunate. He was alive because two homeless kids had decided to do the right thing. He was alive, because his friend, Matt Blanchette, had come out to the house and, when the doorbell wasn't answered, had wandered out to the back of the house. It was there he had spotted Miller's car parked inside the forest at the end of the cleared land, and it was then he had decided he needed to get into the house. He was alive, because in those final moments of the chaos, his mind did what it often did in moments of great stress, it had a second of clarity and he thought of the syringe.

But seven women had died in the last nine months, six of them while it was his investigation, four of them after he knew what the killer was doing, and three of them when clarity was nowhere to be found. In the weeks, months, maybe years ahead, he knew he would look back over the last nine months, and he knew he would blame himself for those last three deaths. His rational mind said he shouldn't, but he knew he would never look back on the killings with any rational thought.

He had already answered all the questions the Goffstown Police had asked. He had answered questions that Hendricks demanded answers to. There would be more questions when he got back to the station and a long discussion with Internal Affairs was in his future. But first, he would spend as much time as was needed to call the loved ones of the victims to let them know The Universal Killer was dead and would be killing no more. Also, first thing in the morning, he would set in motion the release of Manny Alonzo.

After all the questions were answered, Miller planned on taking some time off. He had never been one of those people who thought getting right back on after falling off was the smartest thing to do. Sometimes, he believed, reflection and self analysis was needed. Detective Erik Miller felt this was one of those times. He needed time to think, and he would take all the time he needed before going back to work. If he went back.

As the lifeless body of Kristen Day was carried up the steps, Miller took a final look around the cellar, eventually taking in all the models posed on the top shelf of the work bench. All the monsters lined up. All of them with arms reaching out for their next victim. So many of them, he thought. So many of them.

He suddenly thought of one of the lines from one of the

poems that The Universal Killer had written. It was the first line of the first poem. *This world is full of monsters who yearn.* Detective Erik Miller would never dispute the truth of that statement. There were monsters everywhere. Sometimes, right beside you.

THE END

ABOUT THE AUTHOR

Robert "Nappy" Napolitano was born and raised in Everett, Mass. a long time ago and has grown up and grown old fifty miles north in New Hampshire. Over the years, he has published several local newspapers and hosted several local access television shows for the community. His love of movies led to his owning a video rental store. Nappy had the opportunity to coach over 90 sports teams over the years in baseball, football and basketball, everything from T-ball to Varsity, with wonderful players who have given him a lifetime of memories. He has two sons and five grandchildren who have made it all worthwhile. Nappy spends his time playing softball, gardening, traveling and writing, although not always in that order.

Printed in Dunstable, United Kingdom

81093579R00218